FALLOUT

ALSO BY MARK ETHRIDGE

Grievances (2006)

FALLOUT

a novel by

MARK ETHRIDGE

NEWSOUTH BOOKS
Montgomery

ACKNOWLEDGMENTS

With deep appreciation to Dr. Michael Kaufman and Dr. Debra Wright for enduring my endless questions about medicine and physicians. Any malpractice committed in the writing about medical issues is my own. Special thanks to two wonderful editors, Jeff Kellogg, and Emily Ethridge, on whom I have depended heavily for their insights into language, plots and people.

NewSouth Books
105 S. Court Street
Montgomery, AL 36104

Library of Congress Cataloging-in-Publication Data available upon request

ISBN-13: 978-1-60306-161-2 • ISBN-10: 1-60306-161-4 (paperback)
ISBN-13: 978-1-60306-162-9 • ISBN-10: 1-60306-162-2 (ebook)

Printed in the United States of America

To Kay, Mark, and Emily

PROLOGUE

J. P. Holt's shiv-shaped, candy-apple red Tracker—loaded with an Elite 5X fish-finder, live bait wells and powered by a 115-horse Yamaha that reached hot holes in a hurry—tugged against its anchor line, neatly cleaving the Ohio's current.

Holt's buddy, a human fish finder named Woody Conroy, perched on a swivel seat tying a three-way bottom rig to an oversized rod and reel meant for saltwater fishing. The Ohio was home to dozens of fish species from pike and sturgeon to seven types of bass. But he and Holt were going for the big boys—

Blue Catfish. They could easily top one hundred pounds.

Holt had really been looking forward to this. Work had been brutal. He wouldn't have another chance to get on the river over the next two weeks, not with Old Fashioned River Days coming up. He consulted the 5X's screen. His calculation about where to drop anchor had been dead on. The drift had left the Tracker directly above one of the deep holes where the Blue Cats sought refuge from the fast-moving waters.

His phone chirped. He squinted at the screen. *Reds win.* He popped a beer. *I should be happy,* he mused. *It don't get no better than this.* Isn't that how the scene goes?

But happy was not how he felt. "Happy" wouldn't make the top ten.

Holt drank while Conroy fished. After thirty minutes and no action, they hoisted anchor. Holt bee-lined the Tracker to his second-favorite spot.

"Try dead bait this time," Holt advised. "The stinkier, the better." Blue Cats were known for their keen sense of smell.

Conroy baited his hooks with dead minnows and a chunk of putrid chicken. He lowered his line until the sinker hit bottom and waited.

Not very long.

"Fish on!" Conroy's rod bent into a quivering 'u.' The Tracker rocked.

Holt grabbed the wheel to keep from spilling out of his chair.

"Lunker!" Conroy yelled.

Holt was surprised when something big breached the surface. Conroy had a habit of declaring every bite a "lunker"—until the fish was boated. But this time he was right. The thing was at least five feet long.

Conroy pulled up and reeled in. The monster went deep.

Holt swiped a gaff but hit nothing but water. He tossed the gaff, grabbed Conroy's line and drew it in hand-over hand. Conroy reeled slack.

Holt began to get a bad feeling. Maybe the fish was just worn out, but it wasn't fighting. In some ways, it didn't even feel like a fish. The thing was acting like a dead weight.

When it broke the surface five feet from the boat, they both knew.

"Timber trout," Conroy said disgustedly.

"A damn log," Holt said. "A log for Woody." He reached over the gunwale to unsnag the lure. He fell back like he'd been hit in the chest with a rocket.

Conroy peered over the edge. The log wore jeans and stunk to high heaven.

Holt stifled nausea and looked again.

It was easy to see why he had mistaken it for a log. Chunks of flesh dangled from the dark brown torso like sloughed-off bark. Boney fingers poked from bloated hands and arms, like twigs from branches. Holt couldn't be sure, but he thought it was a man. Conroy's fishing line was deeply embedded in the pulpy neck.

The body rolled over in slow motion. The lower half of its face was gone, giving prominence to a solid set of teeth that made the corpse appear to be grinning. The remaining face, including the nostrils, floated languidly in the water, attached only at the left ear.

To Holt, the skin of the face looked like a slab of white cheese. He shuddered. He knew the image would join the others—the shotgun-in-the-mouth suicide, the car wreck decapitation, that burned thing/man from the plant—that swirled unbidden in his head like bats in his own belfry, at least until obliterated by alcohol. They were all horrible. But this was beyond a doubt the most disgusting thing he had ever seen.

Holt considered hauling the body into the boat but thought better of it. Holding the fishing line, he started the engine and set off slowly, intending to drag the dead man to shore.

The rotting flesh released the jig midway. The body returned to the current, yawing as it sunk.

Holt and Conroy watched until it seemed unlikely to resurface.

"Looks like he'd been in there a while," Conroy volunteered.

Holt nodded, but he wasn't sure. He'd seen any number of drowning victims—people like old man McCoy who'd simply filled his pockets with rocks and walked into the river when his feed and seed had gone bust. Those corpses were bleached, always bloated, misshapen.

Old Cheese Face was different. Different. And awful.

"You gonna drag the river?" Conroy asked when they had tied up.

"Not with the overtime budget going to River Days. I'll put it out on the wire, but for now, Old Cheese Face is going to have to keep on rolling. Probably won't stop until he gets to Possum Island."

Holt picked up the sack with the lunch they had brought but had left uneaten—cheese sandwiches. He doubted he would ever eat cheese again.

....

Chapter One

The sky darkened and the wind built. Cyclones of dead leaves danced through the parking lot of the *Winston News*. Thunder shook the squat prefab building and rain roared against the metal roof. Editor and Publisher Josh Gibbs, thirty-eight, took scant notice of the storm, even though his powers of observation were seldom off high alert. Tie at half-mast, shirt-sleeves rolled up to mid-forearm, Josh hunched over a low metal table proofing the *News*'s upcoming edition. He read each story and headline a third time. Then, just to be sure, he read the headlines again, this time aloud.

Since Josh's wife's death, the *News* had become more than a job. It had become a refuge where he could exert a degree of control over stories and schedules in a world out of control, a place where he could count on the press to run every Thursday at 3 p.m., a place where he always knew what he was doing, and where the newspaper's relentless demands meant pain was forgotten, temporarily, in the mad crush.

At big city newspapers, the editor and publisher wrote no stories, sold no ads, did no editing. A few might dash off an occasional—or even regular—Sunday column. But in terms of contributing to content, that was about it. If the editor or the publisher absented himself for a week or two, the newspaper would still publish every day—possibly with even greater efficiency. Subscribers would never notice.

Not so at a small town weekly. As owner, editor and publisher of the *Winston News*, not only did Josh oversee advertising sales, printing, production and circulation, he covered meetings, wrote stories, edited the sometimes barely literate copy of the rural correspondents and handled the inevitable complaints about waterlogged papers. If Josh didn't show up, there wouldn't *be* a paper.

Josh had lived the big city, daily newspaper life once and found it to his liking. He specialized in stories that exposed official corruption or advocated for the powerless against the bureaucracy. Atlanta had been a target-rich environment. He'd attracted some notice. And he'd connected with a young woman there, the daughter of the owner and publisher of the weekly newspaper in a small West Virginia town.

He was a reporter. Sharon Hardesty sold advertising. He was impressed that she respected journalism. She was amazed he understood the business side. They'd breeched the church-state divide between their departments with secret lunches and cocktails after work, had fallen in love and gotten married. After two years of monthly heartbreak and frustration, they rejoiced with the miracle workers at the

Emory University Medical Center and welcomed Katie into their happy family.

At the paper, Josh had been promoted to the investigative reporting staff—on track for a Pulitzer, he was sure. Until the scandal. Was that the right word? Sharon's word, "incident," was too non-descriptive. The paper had labeled it a "mistake" but he still wasn't prepared to accept it as such. Scandal was right. Whatever else was said about what happened, "scandal" fit.

In the middle of it all, Sharon's father died and left her the *News*. Still stung by what had happened and his subsequent demotion to the night cops beat, Josh suggested that they move with baby Katie to Winston. He'd take over production of the paper.

Quitting had not been easy. He still kept two buttons stuck to a cork board behind his credenza that the Atlanta staff had given him at a beery, sometimes teary, send-off. The buttons commemorated two of his favorite newsroom sayings. One read, "Rake Muck." The other, "Question Authority." But when he left for Winston, Josh understood he was forsaking forever investigative reporting, the hope for a Pulitzer Prize and the chance for journalistic redemption. Just as well. He'd had about all the crusading he could stand.

An enormous task confronted him at the *News*. Technology and innovation had been put on hold during the late publisher's declining years and Josh found himself deeper into computer issues than he ever hoped to be. On the other hand, the work meant there was little time to look back—except, inevitably, when Pulitzers were announced in April and he suffered until the news cycle moved on.

Socially, the adjustment was easier than he and Sharon had expected. Fueled by new jobs, Winston had started to grow after a century of stagnation. The high school that Katie would soon attend was brand new. Big brick homes owned by executives now perched on the first low ridge that swelled from the flat land. They made friends. The shopping center on the edge of town brought new businesses that proved to be new sources of advertising revenue for the paper.

They'd run the *News* together until Sharon got too sick. For the last three years, the job had been his alone.

With Sharon, the workload had been manageable. They'd even been able to carve out two weeks of vacation—the week in the summer after the special issue that focused on the town's Old Fashioned River Days festival and at Christmas when the editions were combined into a special year-end review.

Without Sharon, the workload was crushing. Except for Sunday, which he reserved exclusively for Katie, there was a deadline every day. Monday, correspondents' copy and editorials; Tuesday, news copy, ad placement and page design; Wednesday, story placement and headline writing; Thursday, proofing, printing and delivery; Friday, ad sales; Saturday, catch up on the business side—the payables and receivables, and the big question: which advertisers he could afford to carry another week before they paid and which he could not. It was an important question. Advertising was not a product like a car or a television that could be repossessed if the buyer failed to pay. On the other hand, it was tough to turn down business as long as there was hope for remuneration.

The pace was perfect for life after Sharon. It was predictable. He was good at the work. It consumed almost every conscious moment of his life that wasn't devoted to his daughter, filling some of the emptiness, distracting him from his suffering until bedtime stabbed him in the heart again.

He looked at the two silver-framed photos on his desk. His beloved Sharon, poolside, smile brighter than the sun, hair pulled into a ponytail, when she was healthy. Katie in her red and black soccer uniform, one foot perched on a ball. When you're a father raising a thirteen-year-old daughter by yourself, Josh reflected, it helps to have at least one place where you know what you are doing.

Despite that, he had decided it was time to move on. Weeklies like the *News* hadn't yet suffered the circulation and advertising declines of daily newspapers, but who knew how long that would last? Although he wasn't ready to inform his staff, he'd reached a handshake agreement to sell the *News* and its commercial printing operation, hoping to close the deal during the summer and relocate to Atlanta in time for Katie to start high school in the fall. He'd asked some of his former colleagues to alert him if they heard about a good deal on a house. He figured the proceeds from the sale of the *News* would tide him over until he found a job. He was thinking of something in public relations, although appearing before his former colleagues as a supplicant seeking favorable press for a client was going to be awkward.

Josh noticed with relief that the skies were starting to clear. Calls from readers who'd received wet papers were the worst. First, when they occurred, there were usually a lot of them. Second, he couldn't do much to fix the problem. Perhaps this week, he'd dodge the wet paper bullet.

Josh headed for the pressroom. He was pleased to see workers already replacing the conference room's threadbare carpeting, a long-neglected project he'd authorized so as not to leave a poor impression when representatives of the prospective new owners arrived for due diligence.

He entered the pressroom and tapped on the shoulder of Jimmy Mayes, a part-Indian whose jet-black ponytail and beaded leather hair tie made him unmistakable from behind.

"How's it going?" Josh signed.

Because the ability to speak and hear was of no advantage in the roar of a newspaper pressroom, and fluency in sign language was essential, press crews often included non-hearing, non-speaking operators. The *Winston News* was no exception. Mayes gave him two thumbs up. Josh felt the huge Goss Community offset press crank to life. He glanced at the tall oak cabinet with the hand-wound factory floor clock that had belonged to Sharon's father. Right on time.

He grabbed one of the first copies off the press and was waiting in front of Winston Middle School at 3:15 p.m. when its massive green front doors sprung open and a flood of blue-jeaned, backpack-laden kids cascaded down the granite steps into an ever-widening pool at the bottom.

Josh had no problem spotting Katie. Her jeans, blouse, backpack, blonde pony-tail pulled through a baseball cap—all those were within the current fashion norms that teens mysteriously established, communicated and regularly altered. But Katie stood out, literally. At age thirteen, she was five feet, ten inches—almost a head taller than most of the girls and all of the boys. His heart warmed at the sight of her.

He watched her scan the cars in the middle school pickup line until she spotted the Volvo. She sprinted to it, left arm flailing to balance the heavy pack on her right shoulder.

"Hi, Dad," she said as she plopped into the passenger seat and slung her backpack onto the rear floorboard.

He gave her a kiss on the cheek. Katie squirmed away giggling. "Dad, you're embarrassing me!"

Josh laughed. "That's what dads do. Now, let's go see Dr. Wright and find out what's up with your leg."

....

CHAPTER TWO

Allison Wright began making mental notes for the patient file. *Well-nourished, Caucasian male, appearing to be stated age.* She pulled on a fresh set of sterile gloves.

"Okay," she said, "take off your shirt."

Ricky Scruggs, twenty-five, hunched his shoulders to tighten the pectoral muscles under his tight, black t-shirt and admired himself in the examining room mirror. "I will if you will."

Allison cocked her left eyebrow and fixed Scruggs with her stare.

"Just kidding," he said quickly.

Allison considered giving him a lecture on sexism before concluding it would be wasted on a patient who'd begun by asking if he'd get to see a "real" doctor—presumably male. She raised the shirt over Scruggs's chest and gently lifted the ring piercing his left nipple. Scruggs yelped. She probed the inflamed, scabbed skin. Reddening. Ulceration. Necrosis of the dermis. "You might have come in when it first got infected," she admonished. "Take it out."

Scruggs maneuvered the ring from his nipple. Pus and blood oozed from the puncture holes. Allison spread a paper towel on a box on a counter next to the examination table. Scruggs placed the ring on it.

Allison cleaned the wound and examined the inflamed area with a magnifying glass. She judged it to be eight centimeters, about twice the size of a fifty-cent piece.

On any given day, her clinic—a yellow converted Victorian home three blocks from the river—saw a catalogue of the ills that had befallen mankind within a twenty-mile radius of Winston, West Virginia. Snake bites, cut feet, broken arms and ear infections, assorted injuries to workers at the plant, predictable diseases of the aged and dying. When someone in the area needed medical attention, they showed up at the Winston Medical Clinic. Allison enjoyed the variety. Every day was a new problem, a new challenge. And despite having to deal with occasional boors like Ricky Scruggs, every day provided a chance to help people who were hurting and who appreciated her help. It made her feel competent, useful—needed.

"How long have you had this piercing?"

"Couple days."

"You did it yourself?"

"Wasn't hard."

Allison cleaned and dressed the wound, scribbled a prescription for flucloxacillin and gave Scruggs half a dozen small tubes of mupirocin, the generic form of Bactroban.

"Take the pills twice a day and use the ointment until the samples are gone. If it doesn't clear up in a week, call me." She decided what she'd write in the case notes in the patient file. Infection—surely caused by a do-it-yourself job with an unsanitary instrument.

Scruggs pulled on his shirt. "What about the ring?" he asked.

"Leave the ring out while you heal. The hole will close but if you feel you must, the piercing can be redone. This time, use a licensed professional."

Scruggs put the nipple ring in his pocket and left without a thank you.

Allison sighed. If Scruggs was like a frustrating number of patients, particularly males, he would ignore her orders. The nipple ring would be reinserted as soon as the infection abated.

Her last appointment of the day was with Katie Gibbs.

"My God!" she exclaimed when Katie walked into the examination room. "You've become a clone of your mother!" Allison forgave herself for the reaction. It really was like looking at a ghost.

With the exception of what Allison called her "lost years," Sharon Gibbs had been Allison's closest friend from grade school until her death, sharing secrets, ambitions and causes. Winston had no *Race for the Cure* until Allison and Sharon started one. The irony was lost on neither of them when Sharon developed breast cancer. When the end was near, Allison had been there to provide palliative care—and afterwards worked with Josh to create a hospice county program in Sharon's honor.

"Hi, Allie." Katie blushed.

Allison couldn't believe how quickly the girl had grown—at least eight inches in the last year. She was definitely at the awkward stage—still a child in many ways but quickly becoming a woman, as evidenced by the baby fat turning to curves.

"What's happenin' with the Kate-ster?" Allison gave her a fist bump.

"My left leg hurts. Dad wanted me to get it checked out." She took a folded piece of paper from her pocket. "Also, I need you to sign this health permission form for soccer camp."

Allison took the form. "Camp Kanawha. I met my first boyfriend there because I had the perfect strategy for Sadie Hawkins Day."

"I know. Run fast." They laughed.

Allison measured Katie's height and weight. "All good," she pronounced. Katie sat on the examination table. Allison pulled a stool close.

Allison understood the principal diagnostic tool for any primary care physician wasn't a lab test or a machine but asking the right questions in such a way as to produce useful, honest answers. So as she examined Katie's eyes, nose, ears and throat, Allison pumped the teenager for information.

"How'd the soccer team do?"

"Decent. Fourteen and four."

"School's good?"

"It's nice being the highest grade in middle school. I can't believe how young the fifth graders are."

"Already on the way to being old and gray," Allison chuckled. "Like me."

"No way! You're a cougar. Half the boys in my class have a crush on you."

"Cougar, huh?" Allison smiled.

"Definitely."

"How are the grades?"

"All A's."

"How's your dad?"

"Okay, I guess. He misses Mom a lot."

"How about you?"

"I miss her. Lots of times I wish I could talk to her. I talk to Dad but it's not the same and it's awkward with some stuff."

"Like boys?"

"Yeah and other, you know, girl things. Sometimes boys can be so dorky."

Alison laughed. "You have a boyfriend?" It wasn't a social question. Having a boyfriend meant a whole array of potential health issues a physician needed to watch out for, from pregnancy to abuse.

Katie eyed her seriously. Allison saw in the girl a wariness—and weariness—beyond her years, a wisdom born of sorrow. Losing a parent at such a formative age, she knew, did things to a kid. Death was the great betrayer. Childhood's end. Trust always became an issue.

Allison wanted to enfold this girl, this lovely daughter of her deceased friend, in her arms and shield her from life's many hurts and assure her that everything would be okay. But that in itself would be a betrayal of sorts and a lie. No one could protect anyone else from anything. Allison was positive of that. In the end, she knew, each of us runs life's gauntlet alone.

"This is just between us girls," Allison added quickly.

"I have friends that are boys."

Allison smiled. Despite the coy answer, she was getting more from Katie than she did from most teens, especially boys who generally responded to her inquiries with grunts. She plunged ahead.

"Has your father had the 'birds and bees' talk with you yet?"

"No. He tried but . . ." She crossed her arms over her chest and said, "Anyway, we learned that in school." Allison knew she had pushed things about as far as she could. But there was one more question she needed to ask.

"What about sex . . . ?"

Katie flushed tomato red. "What? Me? Of course not!"

"I'm glad to hear that. That's a good decision for your health and for many other reasons. But if you are ever considering it, you should talk to me. Will you do that?"

Again, the wary eyes. "Okay. But why?"

"So I can try to talk you out of it, of course." Allison gave her a crooked grin. "And, if I can't, to make sure you're prepared." She steered the conversation back to simpler topics. "Any asthma or breathing problems?"

Kate shook her head.

"Fevers? Night sweats? Trouble going to the bathroom?" Another head shake. "Aches, pains?"

"My leg."

"Tell me about it."

Katie pointed to her left leg directly below her knee. "It started about a month ago. It hurts if I press it."

"Does it ever hurt on its own?"

"Sometimes."

"Has it gotten worse?"

"I'm not sure. But Dad said we should see you because it hasn't gotten better."

Allison applied moderate pressure with her thumb. Katie winced. "Tender." Allison observed.

"It's not bad. I've been able to play through it."

Allison massaged the joint. She felt nothing amiss structurally. She noticed a bruise. "Did you get kicked here?"

"Of course," Katie laughed. "And everywhere else."

Allison had Katie dangle her legs over the edge of the table and thwacked her left knee with a rubber-headed hammer. Katie's leg shot forward. She repeated the test on the right leg with the same result. "Reflexes normal," Allison said. "Could you have injured it any other way?"

"Maybe. It started hurting a few days after I jumped out of a tree."

Allison compared Katie's right leg to her left. She found no apparent differences. "What were you doing in a tree?"

"Getting a soccer ball that got stuck up there."

"How high did you jump from?"

"Not very high."

"Higher than you are tall?"

"Yeah."

"But you don't remember your leg hurting when you landed."

"No."

Allison considered the possibilities. Katie's mobility wasn't compromised, so she felt she could rule out a tear of the meniscus as well as damage to either of the collateral ligaments—good news since both injuries often required surgery and could be career-ending. A torn or strained muscle was similarly unlikely. That left two obvious culprits: bleeding between the leg bone and the periosteum—a deep bone bruise in layman's terms, likely the result of being kicked above the shin guard—or a stress fracture, perhaps from so much soccer, perhaps from jumping from the tree. Unlike a regular fracture, the precipitating event for a particular stress fracture could rarely be determined.

Bone bruises were painful but generally required no treatment. Stress fractures were another matter, usually requiring at least a month of limited activity. A stress fracture would mean no soccer.

Allison leaned toward the bone bruise diagnosis. The pain from a stress fracture was likely to be more constant than the occasional symptoms Katie had reported. That she had noticed the pain after jumping from the tree was likely coincidental, although the jolt could have aggravated the bruise. But she couldn't be sure.

"Probably a bone bruise," she told Katie. "Once you stop getting kicked in the shins every day, I suspect this will take care of itself. But I'm going to take an x-ray, just as a precaution."

"I can still go to camp though, right?"

"I'll clear you for camp, pending the x-ray. You're not going to damage it if it's a bone bruise. If it starts to hurt more, just stay off it for a while. Ice every day. And don't jump out of trees."

"But I like to climb trees."

"Then try climbing *down* the tree after you've climbed up it."

Katie gave her a grin and slid off the table.

"Not so fast," Allison consulted Katie's file. "You're due for a tetanus shot." Katie made a face. "I can't sign the camp form without it." Katie sighed. Allison administered the booster and took the leg x-ray. When they were done, she escorted Katie to the waiting room where Josh stood reading the bulletin board.

Allison had hardly seen him since Sharon's death. Sharon had been their link and the link had been broken. The limited contact was probably merciful, she decided. Sharon would have been the topic of conversation. The wound was still too raw for both of them. The loss of a young woman, a dear friend, of her own age was real enough for her. She couldn't imagine what it was like for Josh. Still, she found herself happy to see him. He looked stronger than the grief-ravaged husband he had been at the end and he positively lit up at the sight of his daughter.

"Katie looks fine," she reassured Josh. "I gave her a tetanus booster and took a precautionary x-ray of her leg but I don't expect to find a problem." Allison made a point of looking directly at Josh *and* at his daughter, acknowledging the girl's status as a full participant in the conversation about her own well-being.

"That's good news," Josh said. "How about the permission slip?"

Allison knew her own father—an unwavering stickler for doing things by the book—would never have signed the camp form without the results of Katie's x-ray. But she had adopted a more flexible approach that started with: Do what's best for the patient. "Sure," she said. "It'll save you a trip." She signed the form and handed it to Katie. "If I see anything on the x-ray, I'll let you know."

When they were gone Allison removed her lab coat, collapsed into the black high-backed leather chair behind her desk, and slipped off her shoes. She was starting to unwind when Coretha Hall, her nurse assistant, entered and plopped an armload of files on her desk. Allison stared at them. "Tell me again why I wanted to be a doctor?" she sighed.

Coretha laughed. "Your father used to sit right there and say the same thing. He just *hated* the paperwork."

Allison flipped her hair over the back of the desk chair. "What did you tell the old man?"

"I'd say, 'Dr. Wright, you were young and naïve. You must not have known what you were getting into.'"

"I suppose I can't use that excuse."

"No," Coretha agreed. "For as long as you dilly-dallied around, I'd say you can't."

Coretha was, Allison decided, equal parts compassion, humor and no-nonsense. Perfect for a nurse. In that way, she reminded Allison of her mother. It made sense since both women had served the same demanding man—her father—for much of their lives.

Coretha's dark skin contrasted with her white cotton nurse's uniform. Oversized bright red glasses hung from a cord around her neck. She lifted them to the end of her nose and looked at her watch. "Quitting time," she announced.

"You go ahead." Allison waved at the files on her desk representing the day's cases. "I've got paperwork." She grabbed the file of Ricky Scruggs. "People don't understand piercing is surgery," she said. "You can't use equipment that hasn't been sterilized."

"That what caused his problem?"

"Odds are. He did it himself."

Coretha shuddered. "You wouldn't catch me doing that. Is that what happened to the woman with the earlobes?"

Allison replayed her mental tape until it got to the prior week and the small, mousy woman with scraggly hair, her earlobes hot with infection that spread in flaming spikes across her jaw and down her neck. She hadn't thought of her when Scruggs showed up and she decided there was no reason she should have.

"The woman had her ears pierced years ago, not recently. Interesting coincidence but unrelated." Allison opened Scruggs's folder.

"C'mon," Coretha implored. "Let's lock up and get out of here. At least one night, you need to go home. If I'd known it was going to keep you here tonight, I'd have kept the paperwork on my desk. Anyway, it will still be there tomorrow."

"Exactly."

Coretha put down her purse. "You need a life, honey. Family. A husband. You can't hit the snooze button on your biological clock forever."

Allison made a face. At age thirty-seven, the issue was a sore spot. If anyone other than Coretha had brought it up . . .

"Just because you couldn't make it work the first time . . ."

Allison returned to the file and focused on the first page. "See you tomorrow."

Coretha stared at her a moment then gathered her purse and left.

A few minutes later, unable to concentrate, Allison picked up her keys, passed through the reception area with its tired collection of faded vinyl chairs, Formica coffee tables and tattered copies of *Ladies' Home Journal* and *Field & Stream*, locked the beveled glass door with the sign that still read WINSTON MEDICAL CLINIC, HORACE WRIGHT,

M.D. and headed for home. Hippocrates met her at the door, rubbing against her leg and purring. At least the cat was glad to see her.

She popped a low-cal frozen casserole into the microwave, ate a quick dinner and crawled into bed. She started to reach for the stack of medical journals at her bedside but reconsidered and snapped off the light. She reviewed the events of the day. She decided she would recheck the file of the woman with the earlobe infections. Seconds later, she was asleep.

....

CHAPTER THREE

Harry Dorn saluted, waved and strode off the ballroom stage of the Greenbrier Hotel with his audience in the middle of a standing ovation. Always leave them wanting more, he had learned early on.

As often as he had given the Liberty Agenda speech, it never failed to inspire almost everyone in the audience—including him. Tonight had been no exception. He'd been at the top of his game, and it couldn't have come at a better time. He'd done a table count during the Pledge of Allegiance. There must have been six hundred people in the audience. And the introduction! "Ladies and Gentlemen, the next senator from West Virginia and the future president of the United States!" Way overdone, but still . . .

The applause continued as he slipped out a side door. Before the speech, he'd been tired, dying to get out of his monkey suit and out to his weekend retreat on the river at Possum Island. But the speech had energized him. He was on a roll, eager for the next item on the agenda.

He ducked into the men's room and went immediately to the mirror. He arranged his remaining hair in the manner the consultant had suggested, straightened his black bow tie—he had switched to hand-tied at the consultant's suggestion—and prepared for the parade of men and women who had paid extra to have their photographs taken with him, pictures they would proudly display on den walls and office credenzas all over America.

Who could have imagined? What had the *USA Today* profile called him? A paunchy, balding congressman with a funny name from a backward state with few electoral votes? True, in large part, he conceded. But so what? Ike had been bald. He wouldn't be the first "Harry." Bill Clinton's Arkansas didn't offer any more electoral votes than did his West Virginia. And hadn't the West Virginia primary given Jack Kennedy just the win he needed in 1960?

He didn't mind the photo ops, the endless grip-and-grins. They allowed each donor to feel personally connected, yet they required almost no effort on his part. The aide who handled the introductions indicated through a code whether the congressman and the donor had previously met. "Of course, I know who you are," he would say to those he was meeting for the first time, inflating them with the illusion of official notice. "It's *so* good to see you again," he would say to the others, as if the previous meeting had been one of the memorable moments of his life.

He left the men's room and walked briskly to the private function area, shaking a few hands along the way. He took his place between the aide who introduced the donors and the aide in charge of ensuring they didn't tarry after the photo. Through the thin partitions, he could hear the clattering of dishes, the buzz of the staff as they cleared the adjoining room. A line of well-dressed people waited.

The end of the line did not arrive until after 11 p.m. By then, Dorn's right hand ached. He'd been blinded by the camera's flash so often that it took five minutes for his pupils to dilate enough for him to see. He passed the lobby bar—happily noting that Dan Clendenin, his chief political strategist, was procuring a paper cup of ice and scotch from a waitress in an intriguing Tinkerbell-like outfit—and collapsed into the back seat of a black Lincoln Town Car that waited beneath the hotel portico. A moment later, Clendenin slid in beside him. Dorn accepted the paper cup once the door closed. "Possum Island," he said, as much to comfort himself as to direct the driver. The congressman and Clendenin sipped and sat without speaking for thirty miles as the Lincoln swooshed over the interstate through the deep crevices of the West Virginia valleys, made darker than the night by the steep hills that loomed on either side.

Clendenin broke the silence. "I talked with the Carbon Forward people. This global warming stuff's really got their attention. You impressed them tonight. They want to help."

Dorn yawned. "They've helped us since they were the Fossil Fuels Council. They can't afford to have more tree-huggers elected."

Clendenin swirled his drink. "*Really* help us. Not just piddly individual contributions to your campaign. We're talking underwriting bloggers, Political Action Committees and 527 groups. It's powerful stuff."

Dorn couldn't argue. The Fossil Fuels Council had shown it had plenty of money to spend when it changed its name to the more progressive-sounding Carbon Forward and adopted the upbeat slogan, "Carbon—The Building Block of Life."

He retrieved that morning's USA Today from his briefcase and turned to the politics page. "Harry Dorn," the headline read. "Bigger Than The Boardroom." The sub headline added, "Not Just in Corporate America Has W.Va.'s Harry Dorn Become a Hero." Dorn, the story noted, was favored to become the next senator from his state and was already being mentioned as a possible presidential candidate following his Senate term, although possibly as soon as the next election. The story revealed that the head of the party in New Hampshire had issued a personal invitation for an escorted visit—a fact Dorn himself had only learned that morning when he'd first read the story in the breakfast alcove of his Georgetown brownstone.

He marveled at the turn of events.

As a boy, he had taken his state's high unemployment and poverty and low education levels as a given. As an adult, he had come to believe that these problems could be remedied and that he could help do it. Once elected to Congress, Dorn had brought literally thousands of jobs to his district through defense contracts and tax breaks for new industry. There was no question he had worked hard and that he had a real passion to serve.

He had also quickly become adept at playing political hardball—a requirement in West Virginia where votes were bought for a couple of slugs of moonshine and where terms in the governor's office were often followed by longer terms in federal prison.

But a lot of it, he had to admit, had to do with just showing up. You get elected to Congress. Then you get re-elected. And then you get a seat on an important energy committee because you represent a coal state and on a defense committee because you followed the party leaders and can always be counted on to support the military because, by God, that's where half the boys and girls in your impoverished state land when they graduate from high school or drop out. Jobs and contracts for your district follow, along with no shortage of lobbyists with checkbooks waiting in your anteroom.

He accepted the need to raise money. Despite all the recent efforts at reform, it was still the price of the game if you wanted to have an impact and especially if you had ambitions. He understood that it was endless.

Asking for the money was the easy part. The hard part was repaying the favor once elected because nothing in this business was ever given away for free. They *always* wanted something. A mitigation of a fine. A delay in the implementation of a new pollution standard. Maybe something like a custom-made, one-time tax credit for some company or somebody. "So what do I have to do?" he asked Clendenin.

"Carbon Forward has no doubt about your politics. They know you've been good for industry, good for America. Hell, good for the free world. They want to see you senator, then president. They're believers in the Liberty Agenda because they understand the Creator intended for natural resources to be used and that government is getting in the way of that."

"Not to mention getting in the way of their profits," Dorn interrupted.

"And they're right!" Clendenin continued. "We pay a bundle for gasoline while some of the world's great gas and coal reserves lie unexplored and unexploited, for God's sake. Harry, their only question is whether you can win. These people don't like throwing their money down a rat hole. We have to show you ahead in the polls, ahead in the money-raising, a lead pipe cinch to become senator. We have to show them that lots of others are behind you."

Dorn finished his scotch. "We *can*. We're going to shock them in the primary."

"By then, it's too late. We need to lock up the money now before the other candidates come calling. We need a TV ad and we need to get it out there now."

"We don't have money to spend on TV advertising this far in front of the primary."

"We won't have to pay to run it, just to film it. The Swift Boat people paid to air their Kerry attack ad once or twice. The media ran it over and over for free. Think YouTube. We make the ad now and we leak it. Better yet, we invite some national media to watch it being made and they leak it for us. We get two hits that way—now and when it airs for real. Plus, we get national attention, not just here in West Virginia." Clendenin leaned back in his seat and closed his eyes. "Something dramatic and visual. Prosperity and patriotic crowds. Misty-eyed parents and their perfect two-point-five children bursting with hope, with belief in Harry Dorn and his agenda. We need a setting that really connects you to the Liberty Agenda, proof of what the Liberty Agenda can mean."

Dorn had been sucking on an ice cube and spat it back into the paper cup. He had intended to remind his advisor about some talking point but found now that he couldn't remember what it was. Clendenin's vision had swept this—and all other thoughts—from his mind. Replaced them with cheering, adoring crowds.

The scotch began to have the desired effect. He slipped off his shoes and loosened his seatbelt. In moments he had fallen into that world between sleep and consciousness—still aware of the hum of the tires on the concrete, the press of his head against the window. He saw himself standing at a lectern before a vast sea of howling supporters, their faces ecstatic with adulation, eyes glowing with orgiastic fervor, with strength, pride and solidarity of purpose.

The Lincoln hit a bump. Dorn felt as if he were falling and jerked to full consciousness. "The TV ad," he said. "I know just where to shoot it."

....

CHAPTER FOUR

When Dr. Horace Wright ran The Winston Medical Clinic, he'd close at 1 p.m., walk three blocks to his house, enjoy a solitary lunch, catnap for twenty minutes and return to work refreshed.

His daughter's pattern was different. Occasionally, Allison would schedule a hair appointment, stop by the bank or—heaven forbid—eat a lunch she hadn't made. More often, she simply hung the "Closed" sign on the door and immersed herself in a cheap romance novel for the full hour and a half while sipping Diet Coke and nibbling on a sandwich she'd brought from home. Sometimes Coretha ordered from the deli and they read together in silence. For both father and daughter, the pleasure was a buffer against the chaos of the day. Allison guarded the time jealously.

Today, Coretha was using the lunch hour to be fitted for the costume she would wear in the town's Old Fashioned River Days historical pageant. Allison was eating a tuna sandwich and at a point in *Passions of the Prairie* where she was disinclined to be interrupted. She became aware of knocking on the clinic door. Its tentativeness was unusual enough that it piqued her curiosity.

With her black eyes and a shiny purple bruise that ran from her left cheek to her temple, the young woman reminded Allison of a raccoon.

She shifted the beam of her flashlight to the woman's mouth. "Open." Candi Cloninger's teeth were intact but her spittle was tinged with blood. Allison quickly located the source—the piercing for Cloninger's tongue stud. The blow must have reopened the wound.

"Tell me again what happened."

"I tripped and hit my face on the kitchen counter."

"A counter with knuckles?" She didn't try to hide her skepticism.

A long pause. "Darryl. He's a trucker."

"I suppose the tongue stud was his idea."

Cloninger looked hurt. Allison hated herself for sounding judgmental. The woman needed support, not another reason to feel bad. She lifted Cloninger's chin. "Nothing you might have done is worth being hit for. If he hit you, you need to leave before it happens again."

The woman rolled her eyes. "And go where?"

Allison knew there was no good answer. Winston didn't even have a domestic abuse hotline, much less a shelter. She x-rayed Cloninger's skull, gave her some anti-diarrheal samples when Cloninger mentioned her boyfriend Darryl was suffering intestinal problems—even abusers were entitled to medical treatment—and asked her to wait while the x-rays developed.

She remembered that she'd intended to pull the file of the woman with the earlobe infection but before she could, the clinic's day spun out of control. Sally McCollum's kidney stones acted up, Charlie Sizemore lacerated his arm when he tripped over a scythe and, at age one hundred and one, Lester Mullinax suffered cardiac arrest and died at home in bed. Allison made arrangements for Sally to get Vicodin, for Charlie to get stitched up in her examining room, and for Lester to get to the funeral home. She was still cleaning up when Coretha reminded her she'd asked Cloninger to wait.

Allison picked up a stack of x-rays. "These hers?" Coretha nodded.

Allison slipped one into the wall-mounted light tray and frowned. She quickly unclipped the film and substituted another. The film showed the outline of Cloninger's skull. Good news: no evidence of fracture.

But the second film registered the same anomaly she had seen in the first—a blurry black void roughly the size of a tennis ball in Cloninger's mouth, obscuring her teeth and part of her jaw. It was as if there was a large hole in Cloninger's head, allowing x-rays to pass right through and expose the film.

Allison snapped all Cloninger's films onto the light tray. All showed the same void. "Something's off with the film. Get her back in here."

Coretha returned a few moments later. "She's gone."

Allison scolded herself for probing too deeply into Cloninger's personal life. She'd obviously made the woman uncomfortable. "I hope the whole box isn't bad. Check other films we took today."

Coretha returned a few moments later with x-rays of Wade Pedroza's broken arm. "No problem," she pronounced.

"What about yesterday?"

Coretha pulled the only films taken that day—of Katie Gibbs, who had complained about pain in her left leg. She slid the three views into the light box. "Looks fine to me."

The films also looked defect-free to Allison but something caught her attention that hadn't a day earlier. She held a magnifying glass over a section of the film showing Katie's left tibia, right below the patella. She moved the film to a different position and studied more. She pored over the two other films inch by inch with the glass.

"What do you see?" Coretha asked.

"Maybe something, maybe nothing. Right now, I need you to call Josh Gibbs. See if he's free for a cup of coffee after work."

....

Chapter Five

Chief J. P Holt navigated his aging cruiser through Winston with growing dismay. American flags hung from the front porches of at least half the homes. Red, white and blue bunting decorated many of the rest. On one corner, the Sternwheeler Inn was festooned with both.

How could it be festival time again already?

Claiming a heritage that dated to George Washington, Winston had once been a bustling Ohio River community—a host to paddle wheelers and coal barges and home to boat captains and a riverfront hotel where guests legendarily fished from the mezzanine during the Great Flood of 1937.

These days, Holt patrolled a town of eight thousand people consisting of a twelve-block Main Street of three-story buildings, several leafy in-town neighborhoods, a shopping center, a small industrial park of corrugated steel buildings north of town by the Interstate, and a large new subdivision of split-level homes perched on the low hills just to the east.

Instead of river traffic, the economy depended on farmers who worked the bottomlands outside of town, Social Security checks, one large employer, and Old Fashioned River Days, a start-of-summer festival originally conceived as a weekend sales promotion which had evolved into a ten-day celebration of Winston's past, attracting tourists from several states who stayed in quaint waterfront Victorian guest houses, took river rides on replica paddle wheel steamers, attended a nightly historical drama in Winston's riverfront park and oohed and ahhhed at the fireworks after. There was even a carnival.

Everyone loved River Days and eagerly anticipated it for the entire year. Everyone, it seemed, except him.

He eased down Landing Street. Yard signs promoting an Old Fashioned River Days 10K run had sprouted overnight in neat front yards. A run? When had the organizers added that? What a pain. Of course, his over-worked men would be expected to provide traffic control. Naturally, no one had consulted him in advance.

He hadn't always felt this way. He had just hit the big five-o. That meant his first festival must have been—what? Forty years ago? The wonder he had felt when his father took him for the first time! The crowds! The clamor! The outsiders! Amid his boyhood memories, nothing topped the carnival rides, the shooting gallery, the delights of cotton candy, the thrill of successfully peeking through a tent flap at the girls who entertained at The Green Door.

The thrill was gone by the time he became chief. With festival crowds came petty crime. Events like 10K runs provoked howls from the citizenry about snarled traffic. Even the girls at The Green Door became an annual ordeal because of complaints from the clergy who knew full well the operation violated no local ordinances but demanded that he shut it anyway. He understood the preachers needed their congregations to think they tried. But every year, they wasted his time.

He passed the mayor's house. He couldn't count how many times he'd listened to him spout off about the festival's importance to the local economy. All that was true, but had anybody ever considered the impact on his tiny department? The festival produced lots of extra dollars for local businesses and lots of extra tax revenue for the state. But did any of that make its way back to law enforcement? Was there even an acknowledgement of the increased workload, of the fact that the population of the town suddenly increased by many times? Some decent money for overtime? Maybe even a bonus for his men? For him?

No. He and his department were expected to suck it up. They were taken for granted. Heck, it hadn't even fazed his old fishing buddy Woody Conroy when he'd pointedly noted there was no money to drag the river for Old Cheese Face. Then again, what could you expect? Conroy was a merchant, current head of the Chamber of Commerce. Maybe this year he'd send 'em a message, explain that his workload meant he no longer had time to be the chief *and* portray a trapper in the pageant.

He pulled over by the entrance to the Winston Memorial Gardens cemetery and poured a cup of coffee from his Thermos. He was still hung over. He hadn't gotten to bed until after 2 a.m. His beloved Cincinnati Reds were on the coast. The game with the Giants had gone into extra innings. At least the Reds had won. More important, the line had been Red -135/Giants +105, meaning his $100 bet had produced $135 in net winnings. Before Viggy's cut, of course.

He took a sip of coffee. Old Cheese Face. He saw the floating flap of flesh and smelled the decay. He spit the coffee back into his cup and fought not to be ill.

A Volvo approached from the other direction. There was only one Volvo in town. It belonged to the newspaper editor, Josh Gibbs.

Holt waved. The editor continued on by, his eyes never leaving the center of the road. I might as well be invisible, Holt thought.

Josh's head was filled with fears and possibilities. He imagined the worst. Katie was pregnant. No, that couldn't be, she hadn't even had her first period. Or had she?

He imagined the more probable. Katie had made a face and called him a worrywart but maybe he'd been right about a stress fracture. He hoped the doctor wasn't going to tell him she couldn't attend soccer camp but he was prepared for that. Despite an innately optimistic spirit, Josh had learned from experience that news from doctors was seldom good.

A hole opened in his chest. He loved his daughter so much and still there was so much about her he didn't know. It was only going to get more difficult as she grew into an adult. She needed a mother—something he could never be. Already, he felt he had failed her.

He parked on Main Street and walked the half-block to the coffee shop. It took a moment for his eyes to adjust and then he spotted Allison. She sat away from the other patrons, long legs crossed beneath a wrought iron table, making her black skirt appear very short. Shoulder-length light blonde hair framed her face. Josh searched her expression for some hint of whether the news was better or worse than what he had imagined.

....

CHAPTER SIX

Allison silently cursed medical schools for failing to teach how to deliver bad news.

Medicine could describe the function of almost every organ in the human body and instruct doctors what to do about problems. But courses on how to interact with fellow human beings instead of biological systems weren't part of the curriculum. State medical boards didn't test communications skills. It was something she had had to learn on her own.

Many physicians lacked the basic understanding that such communication was important. Allison noticed a correlation with certain specialties. Brain surgeons often saw individuals simply as the product of a series of electrical impulses. Anesthesiologists seemed to prefer dealing with patients who were unconscious. Radiologists generally were more comfortable with pictures, not people. Ob-Gyns and general practitioners tended to be the best at patient communication, although it wasn't always just about the specialty. She remembered one GP who'd fainted when faced with having to inform a patient he was HIV-positive. And communication wasn't her father's strong point, either at the clinic or at home.

Trial and error had taught Allison to have difficult conversations away from her medical office. Everything about it, from the big desk, to the mysterious medical equipment, to her white lab coat, fostered the impression that the doctor was a god delivering a pronouncement of doom to a weak and helpless mortal. Coffee shops, on the other hand, were places where everyone was equal and where friends gathered to share information and solve problems. She'd found nothing in the privacy portions of the Health Insurance Portability and Accountability Act that proscribed private medical discussions in such places—as long as they weren't overheard.

Ruling out the Koffee Kafe, which she was sure barely squeaked by its yearly health inspection, and the Cluck N' Cup, which closed at 3 p.m., she had picked the Java Joynt for her conversation with Josh, confident that so late on a Friday she wouldn't run into her ex, Vince Bludhorn. The overbearing, hardball-playing in-house lawyer and general fixer for the Recovery Metals recycling plant was such a regular patron that the establishment had named coffee with a double-shot of espresso "the Counselor" after him.

She had also observed that whatever attitude she personally adopted during bad news conversations tended to be the attitude that the recipient adopted. If she was scared, the patient was likely to be scared. If she was calm, the patient often would be calm. Today, her emotions were bouncing all over the place. She was worried about what Josh and Katie might be facing. She felt guilty, as if she had let Sharon down. She was sick at the unfairness of it all.

Arriving early, she had chosen an herbal tea to steady her nerves and claimed a quiet table toward the back. As Josh bypassed the barista and bee-lined for her table, she tried for an expression that conveyed: concerned, but not worried.

Unsuccessfully, judging by his face.

Josh scraped a chair across the tile floor and sat. "What's the headline?"

"I'd like to get some more tests run on Katie. There's a feature on her x-ray that may relate to the pain in her leg. It may be nothing but it could possibly be serious."

He stiffened. Anything termed "possibly serious" in Sharon's case had invariably turned out to be so. He took a deep breath. "How serious?" he asked calmly, thinking that if he limited his panic he could somehow limit the threat.

Allison knew Josh wouldn't stand for anything but the truth, straight and unvarnished. Even as Sharon faded he had badgered her caregivers to tell him the unknowable: How many weeks? How many days? She took a breath. She couldn't believe Josh had to hear the word again. "Worst case, I'm somewhat worried about the possibility of cancer."

Josh deflated into his chair. His eyes closed. His head weaved unsteadily.

"There's no need for panic. This is a concern, not a diagnosis. It could be nothing. I want someone else to take a look. Coretha's setting you up for Monday at the hospital in Columbus. There's a great children's wing."

Josh looked stunned.

"Cancer's not a death sentence." She regretted the words as soon as they left her mouth. It certainly had been a death sentence for Sharon.

"What kind?" Josh asked numbly.

"A bone cancer, *if* it is cancer. Osteogenic sarcoma."

"What stage?"

"If it is cancer, we caught it early." Josh looked dead. She placed her hand on top of his. "I know how you must feel," she sympathized. "This can't be happening again." Neither moved for a minute. She could see him start to regain his bearings. He withdrew a reporter's notebook from his pocket and uncapped a pen.

"What makes you think Katie has cancer?" He asked it like he would a question at a press conference, responding as a journalist, creating emotional separation from bad news.

"*Might* have cancer. She attributed her leg pain to jumping out of a tree. I x-rayed for a stress fracture. There was none. I was looking at the x-rays again this afternoon and I noticed an anomaly I hadn't seen before. It could be a bone bruise. It could be congenital. It could be a bad x-ray. It could be something else. I'm not a pediatrician, I'm not an orthopod and I'm not a radiologist. That's why I want someone else to take a look. I do this sort of referral frequently. Often, it's nothing."

Josh folded up the notebook. He lived by the mantra of his first great city editor, Walker Burns, who taught him to assume nothing. *If your mother says she loves you, check it out*, is how Walker had phrased it. "I want to see the x-rays," Josh said.

"You won't be able to tell anything."

"Maybe not. But I need to see."

Coretha joined them in the examining room at the clinic. Allison slid the three views of Katie's left leg into the tray and doused the overhead light.

"As you can see, the tibia and fibula show no sign of fracture, even a stress fracture. But look up here, at the bottom of the femur. Right above the knee cap." Allison touched a spot on the x-ray with a pen. "That's what I'd like an expert to look at."

Josh squinted at the x-ray. "Look at what?"

Allison moved to a second x-ray. "It might be easier to spot here." She circled an area above the knee. "This could be a mass about twenty-five centimeters diameter. See the irregular cloudy area, a denser white than the bone that seems to intrude into the surrounding tissue."

"No. I think you're seeing things."

"Possibly," Allison conceded.

"We had a problem with some x-rays," Coretha volunteered.

"What do you mean, 'problems with the x-rays'?" Josh said sharply.

Allison shot Coretha a look of disapproval. "Some films of a patient's jaw came out strangely this week. We don't know why it happened."

"Your machine is broken," Josh said calmly. "There's nothing wrong with Katie."

Josh was clearly in denial but Allison desperately wanted for him to be right. "I hope so," she said. "But we had several sets of x-rays taken at about the same time that didn't have any problem, including Katie's, as far as we can tell." She looked to Coretha for confirmation but found she had slipped out of the room.

"So some x-rays are screwed up and some aren't. I'm betting this whole thing is a mistake. What are the odds?" Josh demanded. He was feeling slightly better.

Allison flicked on the lights. "We don't know. That's why you're going to take her to Columbus."

Josh pressed close to the x-rays. "So what am I supposed to tell Katie?"

Allison took him by the shoulders and turned him so she could look him in the eye. "Tell her the truth. Tell her the doctor wants to find out what's causing the pain in her leg and that more tests are needed. That's all we know."

Allison summoned Coretha when Josh had gone. "Josh is having to live with this all weekend. Creating uncertainty in his mind about the quality of the x-rays didn't help."

Coretha looked downcast. "Sorry. I didn't even think about that."

"Well, if there is an x-ray problem, we need to find out."

"I'll call the company and get them to send out a tech. With any luck, they can be here Monday."

....

CHAPTER SEVEN

Josh parked in the driveway of his neat, two-story brick house, its window boxes now lacking flowers for a third summer. He realized he had no recollection of the drive from the coffee shop. He felt weak, outside himself, physically ill, as if a cold stone were lodged in his gut.

Once again, he was trapped in the cruel limbo between knowing and not knowing but having to imagine the worst. The next seventy-two hours would be a torture awaiting test results and consultations with specialists.

He slammed the steering wheel in frustration. What was he going to tell Katie? What *could* he tell her? He needed to say something but he wasn't going to make her worry. Cancer certainly would not be mentioned, especially since there was a good chance that this whole mess was the result of a problem with an x-ray machine, not with Katie's leg.

He took a deep breath and went inside. Katie was on the computer.

"Hi, Dad," she said without looking up from a women's soccer website. Josh gave his daughter a kiss on the top of the head and began the routine of making dinner. It wasn't easy. Every thought he had evaporated before he could finish thinking it. He had to read the instructions on the blue and yellow box of pasta three times before he managed to put four quarts of water on to boil.

Josh broke the news while Katie was clearing the table and he was at the sink doing dishes. "We need to go to Columbus Monday."

Katie shoveled a final bite of macaroni into her mouth and handed him the plate. "What for?"

"Dr. Wright wants a doctor there to take a look at your leg. She's not really a leg expert and we want to make sure you're in good shape for soccer camp."

"Do I have to miss school? It's almost the last day and Monday's a field trip to the plant."

Josh turned off the water and dried his hands. "Yeah. Sorry."

"Well, I already went to the plant with the Girl Scouts. Can I go to Emily's tonight?"

"Are her parents home?"

"Yes."

"What are you going to do?"

"Watch a video."

"Promise?"

"Daddy!"

"Be home by ten-thirty."

"It's Friday night!"

"Okay. Eleven."

He struggled with his fear for the rest of the weekend. He went to the office Saturday intending to review the payables and receivables but ended up scouring the Internet for information on osteogenic sarcoma. Later, having convinced himself that there was a good chance he was worrying for nothing, he buried himself in making a list of what Katie would need for camp.

Only once did he slip. He looked in on her Saturday night before he went to bed. She was so engrossed in the computer she didn't notice. He stayed to listen to the gentle sound of her breathing, marveling at how much she was growing to look like Sharon and disbelieving that something so perfect and pure could harbor something so offensive and deadly. The same thought he had had about Sharon's breast.

After a while, she became aware of his presence. "Hi, Dad. Are you okay?" she asked.

A lump formed in his throat. So like Katie to worry about others. For a moment he was speechless. "I was just . . . I wanted to say good night."

CHAPTER EIGHT

With no breakfast to eat Monday morning, it was only a few minutes until they were headed to the bridge to Ohio thirty miles away.

A mist rose from the bottomland as they snaked north. Josh snapped on the Volvo's yellow fog lights but was forced to slow. He read the clock on the dashboard and calculated. He had driven the route so damn many times with Sharon that he knew to the minute how long each segment should take, with variances calculated for every weather condition, every day of the week, every time of day. His math suggested that as long as the fog cleared by the time they crossed the river, they'd be okay. No, he thought. Not okay. On time.

So many times. All so futile. He looked at Katie sleeping in the seat beside him, covered in her mother's throw. Maybe this time it would be different.

The Volvo neared an old steel bridge that reminded him of something built from an Erector set. On the West Virginia side was the familiar faded sign that still pointed the way to Betheltown, a long-abandoned community condemned to make way for the recycling plant. The quick-rising sun burned off the fog as they crossed the bridge into Ohio.

The western Appalachian foothills flattened quickly into rolling fields of young corn, endlessly repeating. Signs touting newly sprouted gas stations, fast-food restaurants and a cluster of chain hotels hovered just over the tree line. A parade of high-tension towers marched across the hilltops in the rearview mirror.

Josh set the cruise control for sixty-four miles an hour. Ohio cops didn't mess with you if you were going less than sixty-five. He pinched his cheeks to stay awake. He yearned to turn on the radio but didn't, not wanting to wake Katie. His eyes burned. His chin sank toward his chest on several occasions, but when he pulled the Volvo into the parking deck at the hospital, adrenalin kicked in.

Katie clutched his hand as they rode the elevator to the hospital's entrance. "Daddy, I'm not going to miss camp, am I?"

Josh didn't answer.

A security guard nodded as if he recognized Josh. Josh nodded back. Sad, he thought, when the hospital is where they know you best.

The building's automatic doors opened and the bite of ammonia assaulted him, halting him in his tracks. Over the months of Sharon's so-called treatments, the smell had been an ever-present reminder of the sickness growing inside her. It was the smell of hopelessness, of murdered dreams and despair. Today, it brought him to his senses like a blow to the face. Anger rose in him like a burning, caustic tide. He felt a fierce protectiveness toward Katie, a primal sense of possession. She was *his* daughter—his last tangible link to the woman he had shared his life with for more than fifteen years. All his hopes, wishes, everything he held dear were embodied in this thirteen-year-old girl. It was his duty, his sacred honor, to keep her from harm.

Like you did for Sharon. It came to him unbidden and he chased it back to the darkness where irrationality reigned and fear was a constant companion. After Sharon, he had hoped never to see this place again. But here he was and as much as he wanted to believe that everything would be okay, months of conditioning had left their mark. The old wounds were opening, oozing dread.

At least he was about to get some facts. He had been living in a world devoid of them. That had enabled him to avoid thinking about diagnoses, treatment options, even whether Katie could still go to camp. Having no facts had made optimism easier.

But having no facts was a professional contradiction. As a journalist, he lived for facts. He felt uncomfortable without them. With enough information, he believed, most problems could be solved. Given facts, one could at least take considered action, exert some measure of control. Despite their potential for horror, facts were where it all had to start.

Hours later, he still didn't have any. The bureaucracy of insurance forms had taken forever, long enough for Katie to finish *The Red Pony* and many publications on the end tables in the main lobby. Then, infuriatingly, all the receptionists, office manager and other hospital personnel meandered off for a coffee break when he had a sick daughter and wanted answers. Josh fumed as one receptionist and the office manager stopped on an outside patio to smoke before they returned to work.

Katie left in search of more to read. Josh strolled to the unmanned reception desk in hopes of spotting a schedule, a sign-in sheet, anything that might give him a hint about when they might be seen. Nothing. Lured by a table with a stack of slick magazines, he wandered into an empty waiting area in administration. Disappointed when all the magazines turned out to be trade publications devoted to arcane aspects of hospital management, he killed time by practicing a skill at which he had once been legendarily proficient—reading things that were upside down. In his heyday, they had been memos and letters and papers on the desks of the New South business leaders and politicians and their secretaries across from him—documents that sometimes led to exciting scoops that no one could understand how he'd gotten. Today it was purely an exercise, a chance to see if he still "had it," the memos, apparently awaiting approval, as meaningless to him as the articles in *Hospital Manager Today*—one about how a cutback in Medicaid reimbursements meant the Hospital Authority would have to start charging employees for parking; a six-month-old directive about switching to UPS for isotope deliveries to the departments of Radiation Oncology and Nuclear Medicine; a new memo about blood sterilizer inventory; and a badly-in-need-of-editing letter from the hospital's legal department to the admitting desks about rights and responsibilities in dealing with undocumented, Spanish-speaking patients with no insurance. Josh could have summarized it in two sentences: *Don't* ask for proof of citizenship. *Do* get cash or a credit card up front.

He drifted back to the waiting room where Katie was looking bored and miserable. Josh was past fuming. He was exhausted, frustrated and ready to fight anything interfering with help for his daughter.

At last, a nurse called them and led them down a hallway decorated with bright stencils of circus animals and child-sized furniture. "I don't think a kid room is gonna work for you," the nurse said over her shoulder. "Let's use this one." She ushered them into an examination room and closed the door.

Seconds later, an impossibly young man with short dark hair breezed in carrying an oversize file. He wore a blue oxford shirt with the sleeves rolled up, a black plastic runner's watch, khaki pants, and boat shoes. He ignored Josh, went straight to where Katie sat and knelt so that his face was level with hers and said, "Hi, Katie. I'm Doctor Pepper."

Katie grinned. Pepper thumbed the blue stitching on his white lab coat. "Seriously. Peter Pepper, M.D. Doctor Pepper—just like the soft drink they named after me."

Josh smiled. The guy was good with kids.

Pepper continued, "Katie, we're going to do some tests today to find out what's going on with that leg. Your dad and I are going to talk for a few minutes then I'll be right back. Okay?"

Katie nodded.

"Fingers crossed," Josh whispered and instantly regretted it. How many times had he whispered the same thing to Sharon? Always whispered, for to voice such things aloud was to invite the notice of arbitrary and capricious forces. It was a fact that hospitals, beacons of scientific and technological progress, resurrected faith in the most primal fears and superstitions. 'Fingers crossed' had shown itself to be powerless. "Good luck," he amended.

Pepper led Josh to a brown-carpeted room where they sat at a small conference table. Josh noticed a book open face-down on a side table. *It's Time To Go: Preparing for the Death of Your Child.* Josh scooted his chair closer to the doctor.

"Mr. Gibbs," Pepper said, "I'm sorry for the circumstances that have brought Katie here but I want you to know that I am optimistic."

"Good," Josh answered cautiously. He felt himself relax.

Pepper slipped on a pair of glasses and aged ten years. "When did Katie first start complaining of leg pain?"

"Six week ago. I figured it was just something from soccer."

Pepper withdrew an x-ray film from a folder and snapped it onto a light box on the wall. "Yes, there it is." Josh looked but had no idea what he was supposed to see and Pepper didn't bother to explain. Pepper shoved the x-ray back in the file, fished out another film and slid it on to the box. "See that?" Pepper pointed to just below the knee.

Josh couldn't control his irritation. "Dr. Pepper, I didn't see anything when I looked at these in Winston and I don't see anything now. I am not here for an anatomy lesson. I am here to get some facts about what is wrong with my daughter."

Pepper raised his hand. "I'm sorry." His face softened. "I'm not sure what Dr. Wright told you, but that isn't at issue. My specialty is pediatric oncology. The orthopedic surgeons and I have looked at the x-rays and we agree. Your daughter has osteogenic sarcoma. It's one of the most common bone cancers among children . . ."

....

CHAPTER NINE

The words fell on Josh like body blows and for a moment everything—the doctor, the room, time—stopped. Presently, he became aware of his thudding heart, his quickened breathing and the boy doctor saying, " . . . it usually occurs in the long bones, just as it has in Katie's leg."

Josh released his death grip on his chair arms. "I'm sorry . . . can you repeat that?"

"I said osteogenic sarcoma in children generally presents in the long bones. Katie's case is classic."

"How can you be so sure that's what she has? Dr. Wright wasn't sure."

"Dr. Wright was correct not to speculate before Katie was seen by a specialist. And there is always the chance that a biopsy will tell us our suspicions are in error. Believe me, no one wants to be wrong more than me."

"I think you most certainly are wrong." Josh interrupted. He wasn't going to sit idly by and accept what he was told. He was going to fight, starting with the diagnosis.

"I have looked at a lot of x-rays and CT scans of this disease and I must tell you, I do not expect that outcome."

"If you're sure, then why are we doing a biopsy?"

"The primary purpose of the biopsy is to stage the disease—to see how much of the bone is affected and to determine if the cancer has spread to the other tissues." Pepper spoke slowly and evenly. "The process is called metastasis."

Josh felt old wounds reopening, the sickness and poison oozing forth. "I'm all too familiar with the term, doctor. Now, tell me—"

"The biopsy results dictate the details of treatment—what kind of chemotherapy and the nature of the surgery."

"It has to be chemo? Radiation won't take care of it?"

"We'll know after we run some tests but typically I'd expect thirteen weeks of chemotherapy, followed by surgery to remove the affected bone and tissue, followed by thirteen more weeks of chemotherapy."

"That's half a year."

"Could be less. Could be more. But that's a good number to keep in your head. After that, there'll be rehab, of course."

"Why 'of course'?" Josh challenged.

Pepper looked at him like it was something he already ought to know. "For a long time the standard treatment for this disease has been chemotherapy and amputation. Removing the entire extremity offers the best chance of excising all the cancerous tissue. More recently, we've developed techniques using bone grafts or artificial implants that allow us to save the leg in those cases where we can safely do so. In either case, Katie will require significant rehabilitation."

"But she's a soccer player," Josh protested, as if that would change things.

"I wouldn't think of that as a realistic expectation going forward."

Josh chafed that Pepper said it with such finality, offering no hope, as though this was an everyday setback, not the end of a way of life.

"Doctor, you brought me in here and told me you were optimistic about Katie. Now you're telling me she definitely has cancer, that you may have to cut off her leg, that we're looking at a half year of chemotherapy—"

"That's just—"

"A helluva lot of time in the goddam hospital, not to mention rehabilitation." Josh felt the heat wash through him. "So what in almighty hell are you optimistic about?"

Pepper set his jaw. "Mr. Gibbs, this is a first-class hospital. I have confidence in my training and ability. What I am optimistic about is that the orthopedic surgeons and I can save the life of your daughter. That is the priority here. My plan is to admit Katie this afternoon, have one of the orthopedic guys perform a needle biopsy to confirm the cancer and do a couple of scans. If it has spread, we start treatment right away. Those cancer cells are bad actors and once they start to metastasize, they're a ticking time bomb. If the rest of the body is clear, within a week or so the surgeon will perform an open biopsy so we'll know if we have a chance to save the leg. If there's no chance, he amputates. If there is, she'll get her first round of chemotherapy. Then, we'll be fighting this thing."

Thoughts tumbled into Josh's brain in no helpful order and spiraled away before he could get hold of them. To think forty-eight hours ago his chief worry had been that Katie might miss camp!

These doctors—so unshakably confident of their diagnoses and their hospital and their training and their abilities—made his blood boil. In the end, all their promises and protocols, their degrees and high-tech gadgetry amounted to nothing more than voodoo witchcraft. Sharon had died. And now this pint-size Dr. Pepper was taking him down the same old path, pushing him. And they weren't even sure Katie had cancer. Nothing had been proven. "You won't be doing that," he said.

Pepper's expression froze somewhere between agog and aghast. "What do you mean?"

"Doctor"—Josh was past being polite—"I don't have to tell you crap. But since you ask, I'm not sure you have a clue what you're doing. If your medical skills are as good as your communication skills, you suck!"

"She's my patient! This is a nasty, aggressive cancer. It metastasizes exceedingly rapidly. Time is of the essence! You can't just—"

"No, Josh shouted, "*You* can't. That's not just another case in the room back there. That's my daughter. Got it? *Mine*. So I make the decisions. Not you. Me."

But for a knock on the conference room door, Josh might have slugged him. A nurse poked her head in. She looked first at Josh, then the doctor. "Everything okay?"

"Fine," Josh croaked. No wonder the nurse had come running. He must have been shouting to high heaven.

"No problem," said Pepper.

The nurse left. Pepper slumped in his chair. After a minute, he said, "I shouldn't have yelled. I apologize. Sometimes I forget that when a kid is sick, the parents are patients, too." He pushed his glasses to the top of his head, and sighed. "How's your wife doing with all this?"

"She's dead. She doesn't feel a thing. Two years ago. Breast cancer."

"Oh Christ." It emerged as a single word. "I'm so sorry for . . . everything. I didn't know you had a history."

"Of defeat."

"I have faith we can make this one turn out differently."

Josh remembered how it had been with Sharon—the constant worry, the clinging even to the faintest hope, and the endless rounds of chemo followed by sickness and suffering. And finally death. Since then, faith was something he'd done without. Facts were what counted, answers what he needed. "I need to make a phone call," he said.

"Of course. Have the nurse find me when you're done."

Pepper was barely out of the room before Josh was on the phone to Allison. "This guy's screwed up," he said, pacing. "I don't think he knows what he's doing."

"His reputation is one of the best in the business."

"Then I'd hate to see the worst. We haven't done any tests but he's pushing me to admit Katie today."

"If she's sick, the clock *is* ticking."

"Her soccer camp starts Saturday."

"Let's cross one bridge at a time. Have them do an MRI and bone scan. They're relatively fast, painless and I predict it'll tell us that whatever's in the leg hasn't spread. Follow that up with a core needle biopsy. It's going to hurt some but she won't have to be admitted and it'll tell us if it's cancer and what kind. They'll have the results in a few days. We'll figure out soccer camp from there."

"Will do." Josh hung up, called the nurse and sat at the conference table. Pepper arrived a minute later.

"You have a remarkable daughter. She's very mature for her age, very grounded."

"She hasn't had much of a chance to be a kid." Seated, Josh felt like he was begging. He stood so the two men looked eye-to-eye. "Pepper, here's the deal. Do an MRI, a bone scan and a needle biopsy. If there's no cancer or if it hasn't spread, she goes to camp. If there is cancer, I'll bring her directly here at the end of camp."

"No," Pepper said. "She goes to camp only if she's clear."

Josh decided to let the matter drop. With any luck, it wouldn't be an issue. He paced in the waiting room while Katie, dressed in a hospital gown adorned with the children's hospital mascot giraffe, was pushed off for her MRI in a wheelchair. He caught his next glimpse of her through an open door ninety minutes later as she rolled by on a gurney, covered to her neck by a green sheet. A tube ran from a plastic bag suspended over the gurney to a needle in her left arm. A nurse walked alongside.

Josh sprinted into the hallway and caught up. The gurney kept moving. Josh kept pace. He took Katie's hand. "Hey, sweetheart. How's it going?"

"Fine. The hardest thing was staying still. But they gave me headphones so I could listen to music."

Josh caught the nurse's eye and nodded to the bag. "What's that?"

"Technetium ninety-nine. It's a tracer that accumulates in damaged bone so it shows up on the gamma camera scan."

"It's radioactive," Katie volunteered from the gurney.

"It is," the nurse confirmed. "Perfectly harmless. Half life of about four minutes. Got to keep moving."

Josh dropped back as the gurney picked up steam.

He insisted on being present during the needle biopsy. Katie lay on the gurney, only her face exposed. A nurse pulled back the green sheet, swabbed the leg with Betadine and secured it with a Velcro strap. Josh took Katie's hand. An orthopedic surgeon appeared, selected a syringe from a tray, palpated the area just below Katie's knee, and gently inserted the needle. Josh winced. Katie looked the other way. The surgeon removed the needle a few seconds later.

"That's it?" Josh said hopefully.

"That's lidocaine. We'll let it freeze this knee and be in and out in a flash." The surgeon began to hum "Frosty the Snowman."

He reached for another needle, this one much larger than the first. "Fourteen gauge should do it," he mused. He slid the needle into the flesh just below Katie's knee.

Katie cried out, "Dad, you're hurting me!"

Josh realized he had Katie's hand in a death grip.

The surgeon withdrew the needle. Josh heard a click. The surgeon plunged the needle in again.

....

CHAPTER TEN

"Pfizer man's here."

Allison marked her place in the *Atlas of Dermatology*. Coretha stood in her door. "Skip the Viagra samples but get as much of the Lipitor as you can."

"You told him last time you'd eat lunch with him."

Allison groaned. Drug company sales people made a practice of providing lunch to busy physicians and their office staffs just to get a few moments to talk with them about the latest wonder drug and to leave samples. In many offices, it was a tradition—the Pfizer man on Mondays, the Merck woman on Wednesdays and so on. The Winston Medical Clinic had few pharma callers and Allison couldn't have cared less about the ones who did show up. But samples allowed her to provide medicines to her many patients who could not afford them. Lunch with the drug rep came with the territory.

At the moment, however, she couldn't even think about eating. She'd almost vomited when she removed the sock of fifty-eight-year-old Wanda Faggart, her first patient Monday morning. The putrid smell of the black, oozing, gangrenous fourth toe on her right foot still clung to her nostrils. On top of that, the call from Josh in Columbus had left her stomach churning.

"Apologize to him for me. And don't forget to get the Lipitor." Allison returned to the medical text and found a section dealing with what she had observed in Faggart: a large necrotic ulcer with overlying exudate and surrounding erythema, edema, and eschar formation.

But what had caused the death of the tissue? She turned to her computer and searched her medical sites for causes. There were plenty, from vasculitis to streptococcal infections to a dozen different syndromes and phenomena. But occurrences were extremely rare. In all her prior practice, she'd never seen a single case where the cause wasn't immediately apparent. Now, within days, she'd seen three cases of tissue death in otherwise healthy people. Scruggs's nipple ring involved a piercing. He had done it himself. Streptococcal bacteria on the instrument was the presumed cause. In the case of Faggart's toe and the woman with the infected ear—Audrey Pringle, according to the file she'd retrieved—dirty instruments could not be blamed. Still, she couldn't shake the feeling that the incidents were related. But how?

She remembered another patient, the woman with the tongue piercing. She buzzed Coretha. "Bring me the file of that that woman whose boyfriend beat her up last week. Sugar something."

"Candi. Candi Cloninger."

"Right. The one with the black hole on the x-rays."

Allison reread her notes. Cloninger had shown swelling and blood near the tongue piercing. Allison had attributed it to the beating. Maybe it was something else. An early stage of what she was seeing in her other patients? She withdrew an x-ray of Cloninger's skull with the black void in the middle as if there were no bone in the way. "What's the word from the company about checking the machine?" she asked.

"They can't get a tech here until Wednesday."

"Wednesday? We need to know before then."

"Is there a way we could do our own test?"

Allison thought about it. "Can't hurt, I guess."

"Start with a fresh box of film in case there was something wrong with the last one."

A new box was lying on the counter. Allison opened it and took three views of Coretha's wrist and hand.

The x-rays showed just a touch of arthritis in Coretha's fingers—and a very unexpected dark black ring about the diameter of a nickel that cut into Coretha's wrist in two of the films. The area inside and immediately around the ring was almost as dark. The ring wasn't visible on the third.

"That's weird." Coretha rubbed her wrist. "What the heck is going on?"

"Something's wrong somewhere, that's for sure," Allison agreed. She reviewed the variables—machine, film, Coretha—and concluded she could rule out Coretha because the black ring wasn't always there.

In terms of the machine, she couldn't think of a problem that would produce two unexpected and very different anomalies—a tennis ball-sized void in Cloninger's mouth and the ring-like void in Coretha's wrist.

Coretha anticipated her next thought. "I'll call our film supplier. Maybe someone else has reported problems."

"Good idea. And let's hope no one comes in with a broken leg."

Coretha laughed. "At least until Wednesday."

Still brooding at the end of the day over the unexplained occurrences of tissue death, Allison packed the stack of medical journals she had set aside for the evening—even though she knew they likely would go no further than the pile on her bedside table—and went home.

She knew something was amiss as soon as she cracked the front door. Invariably, Hippocrates sauntered up the greet her. Not today. She checked his usual napping places—under the bed, in the towel bin, on top of her winter boots in the closet—and found no sign of her beloved cat.

"Hippocrates!" she called. She waited for the sharp cry of acknowledgement that always came. Silence.

She tried to reconstruct the morning. Was it possible she mistakenly left the cat outside when she'd gone to work? She slid open her patio door and called into the evening. Quiet, except for the muted engines of a passenger jet throttling back overhead and the whoosh of tires on a nearby road.

Panic swelled within her as she imagined the worst. Hippocrates was her truest companion—unquestioningly loyal, unconditionally loving, consistently comforting. Plenty of research showed that pets could enhance their owners' mental health and sense of well-being but she believed Hippocrates actually had the power to heal. Strange, she knew full well, that a doctor would believe such a thing about her cat. But she had evidence. Just as she had rescued the malnourished black and white shelter kitten during the meltdown stage of her marriage, Hippocrates had rescued her.

Now, the only friend she could count on was missing. Worse, it was her fault.

Her search of nearby roads turned up no sign of the cat. She felt sick. An innocent life had been entrusted to her and she had fallen short. She returned to her condo and cried. When she was done, she took a deep breath, curled up on the couch with a throw and resolved to wait up for him. She couldn't think of anything else to do.

To pass the time, she tried to think about the other mystery of the day—the cases of unexplained tissue death among her patients. At least that mystery offered her leads to pursue. She dialed the clinic. Coretha wouldn't be there until the morning but Allison wanted her to get the message first thing. "Find Audrey Pringle, Ricky Scruggs, Candi Cloninger and Wanda Faggart. Get them to come to the clinic. I need to give them another look."

She sank bank into the cushions, readjusted the throw and resumed torturing herself.

....

CHAPTER ELEVEN

The night brought Josh no peace.

He thrashed in bed, his mind caroming crazily and unproductively between trying to recall details of the day's meeting with Dr. Pepper and reviewing things Katie needed for camp. At 1 a.m., he gave up on sleep and opened Sharon's closet, still full of her clothes.

Her scent enveloped him, as if Sharon herself had breezed into the room. He hugged her robe, burying his face in its soft folds. For a moment, she was with him, not just the aromas of her shampoos, lotions and perfumes.

He found a pain pill in the pocket. How like her! Wanting to be present for every possible moment with their daughter, Sharon had resisted taking them because they knocked her out. But in the end, the agony had been overwhelming. With Josh and Katie at her bedside, she'd slid imperceptibly from sleep to eternity aided by a powerful morphine drip.

Josh rummaged around the closet until he found Sharon's sewing basket. He settled at the kitchen table, threaded a needle with considerable difficulty and set out attaching name tags to every stitch of clothing, towel and sheet Katie had laid out to pack.

When he was done with the nametags, he double-checked her non-clothing items against a list Camp Kanawha had provided: Bug spray. Tennis racquet. Flashlight. Water bottle. Sunscreen.

He had added a few items of his own. Disposable camera. Journal. Stamps. *Things so that I can know what it's like for you even though we're apart,* he thought.

He fell into a fitful sleep but was beset by a recurring nightmare in which it was past deadline and the *Winston News* printing press would not start.

He was grateful for Tuesday, a day closer to answers about Katie.

He looked in on his daughter at 7a.m., still asleep amidst a zoo-full of stuffed animals, each at one time indispensable, all now observers from her bookcase except for the favored koala that sat on her pillow; glittering soccer trophies, each one taller and more elaborate than the next, crowding for space on a section of her dresser with tubes of lip gloss and mascara (had he been right to allow it?); a wall of soccer team pictures and posters of boy bands. John Steinbeck's *Travels With Charley* lay open by her bed. On her bedside table sat the team picture of the fifth-grade Black Ravens with the "13-0" sign held by Katie. The team had insisted she hold it. Even the other parents knew she was the best player. And the best kid, too, at least by his thinking. Katie could score all the goals in a 5-0 shutout and she'd credit her team. But if the opponent scored, Katie usually took the blame for allowing the goal. A gorgeous woman stood in the back row of the photo. Sharon. The team mom. Gibbs bent over and woke his daughter with a kiss and a whisper.

She sat up and rubbed the sleep from her eyes. "Only four more days, Dad! I'm soooo excited about camp!"

After microwaving a packet of oatmeal and toasting a bagel for her, he sent her off to school.

A familiar feeling washed over him—a hollow, empty, pit-of-the-stomach feeling, a true heartache—and after a moment he identified it. He felt homesick. No parents. No wife. No soul mate. One child and she would soon be gone. Maybe just to camp, but it was the beginning. In recent years the focus of his life had been fulfilling his promise to Sharon that he would take care of their daughter. Now she was going away and he was the one who was homesick. Or perhaps, it was more than that, he acknowledged to himself. Perhaps the feeling was fear, fear that he would be left alone once again.

He did his best to pull himself out his funk. The *Winston News* needed to print its next edition whatever his mental state. The masthead boasted that the paper had been publishing since 1896 and it would not do to break the string. And he needed to get busy selling for the Old Fashioned River Days special edition which would be distributed at the festival's opening ceremonies and which carried so many ads it often determined whether the newspaper made or lost money for the entire year. The *News* literally couldn't afford to fall short there, not with the prospective new buyers in the midst of due diligence checking every dollar of revenue and dime of expense. If it was usually the difference between profit and loss, this year the section was the difference between selling for a reasonable amount and being forced to unload the *News* at a fire-sale price.

It hit him that Katie's diagnosis could change everything. If she did face a year of treatment and rehabilitation, then not being a one-armed paperhanger at the weekly newspaper was a very good thing. On the other hand, a move would mean changing Katie's doctors mid-treatment. And what about health insurance? His head spun.

Josh found his voice mail light blinking and a note from a carrier and a misprinted copy of the *News* pinned to his desk chair when he arrived at the office.

Mr. Gibbs, this is what they give me to deliver to my customers. Can you talk with someone about it? This is just terrible to have to deliver this type of paper to my customers. I been with the News *for the last ten years off and on and this is the worst I seen.*

Josh sighed. Checking voice mail could wait. Too soon to hear from Pepper and any other calls were almost guaranteed to mean another distraction. He assumed the misprint problem wasn't widespread and he had until Thursday to smooth the feathers of the carrier before the next edition. Sales for the River Days special section, on the other hand, could not wait.

He started with his most likely prospects—the businesses that had advertised in the section the previous year. The bank which held the mortgage on the newspaper building renewed for page three. The Recovery Metals plant reserved its usual full-page ad. A metal recycling facility and foundry, the plant bought plenty of classified employment advertising in the *Winston News* but since it sold nothing directly to the public, this was the only display ad it ran all year, its purpose simply to generate goodwill by showing support for a very popular local event. The car dealerships quickly fell into place, as did the furniture store. The Cotter Funeral Home, a regular, tried to pull out on the grounds that a funeral wasn't an impulse buy but Gibbs reminded owner Mark Cotter that the River Days issue was a keepsake in many households, sure to be close at hand year-round.

He ran into unexpected resistance from Woody Conroy, this year's Chamber of Commerce head whose River City Appliance store had taken the back cover—the most expensive piece of real estate in the section because of its high visibility—for as long as anyone could remember. "Okay," Conroy said when he finally relented. "But this ad really needs to pay off for us."

"It worked last time. I bought a refrigerator from you."

At the end of the day Tuesday, Josh dealt with the nagging voice mail light. It was Allison, asking for an update on Katie. He'd call her tomorrow when, hopefully, there would be news to pass on.

....

CHAPTER TWELVE

"The Chair recognizes the member from Illinois."

One of the country's best-known congressmen rose on the half-empty floor of the U.S. House of Representatives. Nearby, a representative from California scrolled through the *Sporting News* on an iPad concealed within a copy of *Congressional Quarterly*. A knot of members huddled near the Speaker's chair erupted in guffaws at the conclusion of a colleague's joke. The Illinois representative propped a poster of a half-dozen mug shots on an easel and launched into speech lauding outstanding federal employees, undeterred that no one was listening.

Congressman Harry Dorn yawned. His Illinois colleague really wasn't *that* bad a guy. Too bad his political career was about to be cut short, and by scandal at that.

Dorn pushed away from his desk—a real conversation piece since it contained a bullet hole from 1954 when Puerto Rican nationalists opened fire from the balcony and injured five members—and made his way to his party's cloakroom, the hallway-like area just off the floor housing easy chairs, a row of dark wood phone booths, portraits of partisan heroes, political cartoons lampooning the opposition and a snack bar, recently outfitted with two flat screen televisions. The two House cloakrooms were the political parties' clubhouses, havens during official sessions where members like Dorn could suck down a cigarette, take a phone call or engineer a deal away from public view.

Dorn grabbed one of the cloakroom's official yellow phone message pads. He filled in the Illinois representative's name. He checked the boxes labeled 'Returned Your Call' and 'Please Call Back' and wrote down a phone number he had seen in one of DC's alternative newspapers.

A recess followed the Illinois congressman's speech. Dorn crowded on to an elevator with his colleagues who were were set upon by a gaggle of reporters as soon as they stepped off at the basement floor. Dorn let the yellow phone message fall from his hand, confident that when the crowd moved on, some enterprising reporter would find it. The number would be called and the Illinois congressman would be linked to the phone number of a gay escort service.

It didn't matter whether the congressman had ever patronized the service. In fact, Dorn assumed he hadn't. But the note would raise the question. Actual indiscretions might surface and if not, gossip would take over. It would not play well in the congressman's conservative downstate district.

Personally, Dorn was not specifically opposed to gays. He understood there were a number of them closeted among his colleagues, even on his side of the aisle. But the representative had crossed him one too many times, most recently voting against Dorn's energy bill which he had previously promised to support. Outing was the price. Of course, his well-honed leak technique ensured that no one would have any way of connecting the assassination to Harry Dorn.

Four hours later Dorn was boarding a Cessna Citation V for a trip back to the district. His phone rang just as he reached the top of the gangway. He couldn't believe his ears.

"No black people?" he exploded into the phone. "What the hell do you mean there won't be any black people?" He put his hand over the mouthpiece and handed the phone to Clendenin. "Fix it."

Dorn selected one of the plush leather seats and stretched out. He could afford to. Of the eight seats on this particular plane, only three were occupied this Tuesday night—by himself, by Clendenin, now across the aisle, and further to the rear, by another aide. The curtain between the cabin and the cockpit slid open and the co-pilot emerged. "Drink, sir?"

"Scotch." Dorn nodded to Clendenin who was still on the phone. "One for him, too." Dorn looked at Joel Richey, the aide in the back. "Nothing for him."

His cabin mates couldn't be more different, Dorn thought. Peering at maps and screens of polling data through horned-rimmed glasses while working his calculator and Blackberry, Dan Clendenin *looked* like the reigning genius of American political strategists. Snoring, with his hair uncombed, his tie askew and his mouth open, Joel Richey looked like what he was—a deadweight slacker who owed his position to his father's campaign contributions, an irritating daily reminder that money came with strings and could lead to problems—like a TV commercial with no blacks in the crowd shots.

Strategists. Gurus. Aides. Advisers. He could barely keep track of them all. He'd always had a fair-size office staff, dozens of different people if he thought back over the years, bright-eyed young people who came to Washington looking for glamour and believing that they could make a difference. A few stayed—those like Richey who couldn't get better jobs anywhere else—but most left much wiser a few years later, turning over so quickly he remembered a few of them only as "the blonde" or "the black guy" or "the sissy" or whatever fit. Add a senatorial campaign, with new hires like Clendenin, a high-powered itinerant political guru who only joined campaigns he thought could win, and other consultants for every conceivable thing from wardrobe to political issues, and the personnel lineup became a parade of faces.

The co-pilot delivered the drinks and disappeared into the cockpit. The plane tore down the runway and lifted into the sky moments later.

Through wispy clouds Dorn picked out the bright spike of the Washington Monument, the pale lunar glow of the Capitol, the Rayburn office building, the White House.

He got a clear view of Dulles and, beyond that, snaking red arteries of tail lights—the cars like corpuscles being pumped out from the city's heart each evening before being sucked back to its chambers beginning before dawn. A half moon hovered over the right wing, illuminating the folds of the Blue Ridge.

He identified Interstate 66 and Interstate 270. West Virginians could thank two of his colleagues for them—United States senators who understood that the highways would serve as neural pathways connecting their mountainous, nearly impassable state to the outside world. One had grown northwest toward Fairmont, Morgantown and Wheeling (where one of the senators lived) and the other had branched west and south toward Beckley and Charleston and Huntington (where the other senator lived), not coincidentally passing White Sulphur Springs and the Greenbrier resort, home of the government's Cold War emergency capital. Those highways, Dorn devoutly believed, represented *true* public service, the kind of service he would deliver when he succeeded one of the senators, who was retiring.

The roads, he had to acknowledge, had come at a price. They had slashed through the mountains and bled the state of people—whole communities which seeped from the hollows and flowed out the hillbilly highways to the factories and cubicles in far-away cities. Over the past few decades, the population of the state had actually declined. But the highways also nourished new development—vacation homes, wood chip mills and ski resorts crucial to further growth. And, it could be argued, the roads brought an infusion of federal spending that spawned many new government jobs for the state. And incumbent congressmen could now drive home from Washington in hours instead of days, facilitating their repeated reelection and, therefore, their seniority on important committees. He was an example.

Dorn was grateful he no longer had to make the drive very often. He was well into in his eighth term in the U.S. House and he had done it plenty of times in the early years. But as easy as the interstates made things, why drive when courtesy of some corporation or lobbying group, he could be at Chuck Yeager Airport in Charleston two hours after leaving his House office building and at his retreat on the river an hour after that?

Or, if traffic was particularly light, Dorn reflected as he sat on his front porch watching the river the next morning, in forty-five minutes.

He called his retreat Possum Island.

The actual Possum Island was a spit of land that broke the surface of the Ohio River about fifty miles south of Winston. Dorn had spent his favorite times there as a boy, poling a log and plywood raft across a shallow channel that separated the island from the West Virginia side, catching crawfish that hid in the detritus that collected on the downstream shore, climbing the tall beech trees that grew in the island's center, watching the endless procession of river traffic—barges mostly, heaped with symmetrical hills of coal. Much of what he knew about the river came from observing the island—how it could be a mile long and a quarter mile wide with flat muddy banks extending even further into the riverbed in the fall after a dry summer; how it could shrink to the size of a football field in the late spring when the melting snow in the mountains and the ice in the Monongahela and

Alleghany tributaries flooded the river basin; how, inevitably, the island grew longer every year—no matter what the season—as the grains of rich topsoil eroded from upstream farms caught and collected on the island's north end.

He had adopted the Possum Island name for his splendid compound because the location overlooked the island proper and because of what the retreat recalled for him. It was his refuge and his touchstone to real life, life outside the Beltway, a place to think.

It seemed like the perfect place to spend a few days working out the details of his campaign's first television commercials—commercials that would immediately thrust him into the position of front-runner. Unfortunately, there was an array of problems. Not surprisingly, Richey was in the middle of them.

Conceptually, things were perfect. The plant itself, everyone had agreed, was exactly the right backdrop, a strong visual connection to Dorn's major campaign theme of economic liberty. That, after all, was where it had all started. As a young representative, Dorn had called in some of the few favors he was owed and arranged passage of a local bill that allowed Recovery Metals to shortcut several onerous and unnecessary environmental regulations and build a facility near Winston. Jobs had been created. The facility and the town of Winston had prospered. Along with recruiting a three hundred-job defense facility for another county in his district, the legislation was one of Dorn's proudest achievements as a public servant.

Soon, lawyers discovered Dorn's bill permitted a number of facilities in every state to take a self-policing approach to many regulations. Savings on environmental control equipment and improved profits soon followed. Right behind them were political contributions, access to corporate jets, and luxurious vacations for Representative and Mrs. Dorn. Encouraged, he had begun to give speeches on the topics of individual and economic liberty—ideas more powerful than any fanatical religious or totalitarian movements, he liked to remind his audiences.

His timing had been good. The public, fed up with an over-governed, politically correct economy, had responded to his demands for lower corporate taxes and a rollback in government. And too much government was a problem worldwide. Others had taken up the call. The Liberty Agenda, as the movement he championed had become known, was gaining international traction. The plant was the perfect symbol of all that.

Not only that, his aides had learned that by happy circumstance the next week represented the tenth anniversary of the plant's ground-breaking. Given that he was responsible for its existence and that it was about to be the lynchpin of his effort to achieve higher office, Dorn did not find it at all surprising when his consultants reported that the good folks at the plant had been happy to integrate their celebration with the congressman's effort—quickly agreeing to erect a stage in front of the facility's least unattractive side and to shut the entire operation for an hour the following Monday so every worker on the day shift could leave to attend as happy, dedicated workers, the whole tableau a picture of progress.

The news media had already risen to the bait. CNN was dangling the possibility of live coverage in exchange for an exclusive interview with the congressman following the event.

But, as always, there was the unexpected. Folding chairs, flags, red, white and blue bunting—even long tables to display his campaign literature—all had been reserved for the upcoming River Days celebration. Replacements had to be trucked in from Charleston and Cincinnati.

While ultimately accommodating, management had been unusually greedy during discussions about how long and how prominently the company logo would be displayed during the campaign commercial. Vince Bludhorn, the plant attorney, had insisted on at least one-eighth of the screen for a minimum total of six seconds during the thirty-second spot. The campaign's ad agency, which had scrambled a top-flight production crew on short notice, agreed in principle but insisted on final creative control. Dorn had been forced to end the discussion in a way that satisfied no one—telling the agency that he, not the agency, had creative control and telling the folks at the plant, as he had learned to do so artfully on the Hill, that he was personally committed to their point of view and that he would do his very best but could make no promises.

Now, the problem was that there weren't enough blacks employed at the plant, at least on the day shift, to reflect the new ideal of a racially diverse America. Women were adequately represented and so were Hispanics. But not the blacks.

Most of his aides, he believed, were competent. Manipulative, backstabbing, self-promoting, certainly. But competent. He couldn't say the same for Richey who had once mistakenly handed him a copy of a press release about his speech instead of a copy of the speech itself, leading Dorn to give a talk in which he ended a stirring sentence by saying, "Congressman Harry Dorn declared today," in effect quoting himself. The fact that Richey's chief interest was using his business card to impress the district's women had never been an issue before. Now, all the aide's shortcomings were becoming glaring liabilities.

The sound of Clendenin's heels on the wooden front porch interrupted Dorn's thoughts.

"The crowd problem's handled," he said. "The plant's promoting a black guy and a black woman from the night shift to the day shift. When the camera shoots the crowd from over your shoulder, they'll be front and center."

"What about the big crowd shots?" Dorn asked.

"We're busing in the whole congregation of the Tabernacle Church of the Cross in Charleston."

What's in it for them?"

"New church bus."

"You're amazing."

"I'll take that as a compliment."

Dorn stared at a bend in the river. The wind had picked up, creating little wavelets that made the Ohio look like it was flowing upstream, against its natural current. "We need to dump Richey. He's bad news."

Chapter Thirteen

Allison opened the sliding glass door. The fog of the previous evening had thickened into a heavy mist that wet the patio bricks outside her condo. She could smell the river. She waited. Still no Hippocrates.

She had been unable to sleep for the second straight night. She was worried about Katie and disappointed not to have heard from Josh after the trip to Columbus. She had had no luck finding her x-ray patients. And there was still no sign of her missing cat. It was as if they had all been transported to some other world, a place maddeningly beyond her reach.

She arrived at the clinic just as Coretha was accepting a package from an overnight delivery service. "Good news," she announced. "Replacement x-ray film. The supplier's looking at the old stuff to see if it caused the problem. You're early, even for you."

"Any call-backs?"

"Only Wanda Faggart, the lady with the toe. She's coming in later this morning. Pringle's moved. No forwarding address. Cloninger listed a post office box for her address. She doesn't have a land line, at least in her name. None of 'em are on Facebook."

"Cloninger probably hangs with that abuser, Darryl, whoever he is."

"Ricky Scruggs lives out in Blood Run. I left a message on his phone. I haven't heard back but I also sent registered letters to everyone except Pringle. They should get them today."

"If they're around to receive them. Let me know as soon as you reach anyone else. Keep the afternoon clear." Allison poured herself coffee. "Any word from Josh Gibbs?"

"Nothing from him either."

Josh had arrived at the newspaper knowing he had to finish as much of the week's edition as possible, given the uncertainties ahead. The chance to escape the torture of imagining every outcome for Katie had been a pleasant prospect, a much-needed distraction from worry.

But it was still work. He had ripped through the filings from the community stringers, each of whom earned ten dollars weekly for sending in reports from their hamlets—births, hospitalizations, even news of out-of-town visitors (weddings and deaths got separate treatment)—and hurriedly updated the Little League standings. He had dashed off an innocuous editorial urging readers to support the local farmer's market and reluctantly selected a photo of the police department's new rifle range for the front page. It wasn't much of a news picture but Chief Holt was extremely proud of the facility and had been badgering Josh for coverage for days.

He had been about to finish page design when the phone interrupted. He was hoping for a call from Dr. Pepper with the results of Katie's tests. But he had specified that the doctor call his cell phone, which he had kept at the ready 24/7 since leaving Columbus. This wasn't that call and he didn't need an interruption. But he could see on the caller ID that it was Allison.

"I was going to call you," he said, before she could even ask the question. "No word yet. It's frustrating."

Allison could feel his tension through the phone. "How's Katie?"

"Scared. But better than I am. How are you?"

"Frustrated," Allison admitted. She was increasingly despondent about her cat but she decided against mentioning it. Hippocrates was the only family she had but he was trivial compared to what Josh was facing. Instead, she told him about the cases of unexplained tissue death and her difficulty reconnecting with any of her patients except Wanda Faggart who had come in that morning. And while it was still possible she might learn something from the lab work on Faggart's blood and tissue samples, her second exam of the woman had so far only added to the puzzle. Faggart had recalled no cuts or other trauma to her toe that would have provided an entry for infection.

The one possible lead Faggart had provided was a stretch, at best, Allison told Josh. Newly employed at a commercial cleaning service, Faggart had previously worked at the Sternwheeler Hotel with a waitress named Candi or Candy who fit Allison's description of Candi Cloninger. She hadn't known the woman's last name and she didn't know if the woman wore a tongue stud since they were prohibited for on-duty Sternwheeler staffers, along with all facial piercings. But Allison told Josh it had gotten her thinking: perhaps her tissue death patients had been in contact with each other.

"What about interviewing the others?" Josh asked.

"Pringle's a dead end. Left a voice mail for Ricky Scruggs."

Josh thought back to his reporting techniques. "Why don't you just drive out and see them? Nothing like just showing up."

"Well, Scruggs's address is the only one we have."

"It'd be a start."

Allison found the idea appealing. The tissue death mystery was gnawing at her—in the same obsessive way, she realized ruefully, that uncompleted tasks, even a puzzle, had gnawed at her father. More than once the man had declined to join his wife and daughter for Sunday dinner because he could not bring himself to abandon the crossword. Just like Horace Wright, Allison had to have answers before she could move on.

There was another upside to the trip. Josh needed a distraction. "Maybe you should come with me," Allison suggested.

"I've got bigger things to worry about."

"You've done all you can for Katie for now. Sometimes it's good to get your mind off things."

Josh considered the idea. With another hour of hard work, he'd be caught up. The prospect of gut-grinding waiting for Pepper's call with nothing important to do was not attractive. "All bets are off if Pepper calls."

"Fine. If he doesn't, be at my place at 2:00."

Chapter Fourteen

Josh let the Ohio Valley Medical Supply van pull away from the curb and took its parking spot in front of the clinic. He was disappointed to see three patients in the waiting room. Mom and a kid who'd been bit by a snake. Fifteen minutes, he estimated. Old man in a John Deere hat with a nasty gash on his arm, forty-five minutes, depending on the number of stitches. A young woman with crutches and an icepack on her ankle. That might mean X-rays. He figured at least ninety minutes for everyone.

Two hours and two *Field & Streams* later, Allison entered the room in jeans and a ponytail tied with a red ribbon—a particularly welcome sight, Josh concluded, after one had been looking at nothing but photos of deer and cutthroat trout.

He assumed they would take his Volvo but she had other ideas. "We'll need four-wheel drive and good ground clearance," she pointed out. "Besides, I want to drive."

He climbed into her blue Jeep Wagoneer unable to remember the last time he had been a passenger.

"They checked the x-ray machine today," Allison said. "I know it's not what you want to hear but it's working fine. We haven't heard back about the film."

"Those x-rays won't matter once Pepper calls." He thought of the phrase Sharon had ultimately found so comforting: It will be what it will be.

Heavy mist turned to rain as they headed east, away from the river. Winston's old homes, quaint downtown and new subdivisions gave way to a dirt-streaked house trailer behind a huge satellite dish in a scraggly cornfield, an ancient half-painted farmhouse with plastic sheeting in the window and a blue couch on the porch, a collapsed chicken coop overgrown with weeds, a pile of rusting farm implements.

They were all reminders of something Josh had long observed:

the further you moved away from the river, the harder life seemed to get.

Near the rivers were great stretches of flat land ideal for farming, a business, a housing development, a town. The state's cities—Charleston, Huntington, Parkersburg, Fairmont—had developed there. But the mountains buckled quickly from the river plains and developable land elsewhere was scarce. A swatch along a big river tributary might support several dozen farms, some churches, a few stores—a community with a name frequently containing the words "Branch, Fork, Run, Lick." Further upstream, along the rocky creeks and narrow streams, a parcel of five or ten acres might be found, enough for a hard-working man to support a family through farming, a few animals and the occasional odd job—enough if he and the family had no higher aspirations. But there was no question: when wide rivers turned to creeks and streams, the land got narrower, backyards got more vertical, the going got rougher.

And, it had to be acknowledged, the people and the customs often got stranger. Mountains meant isolation, with education and change sometimes less prevalent than marriage between blood relatives. Vestiges of Elizabethan English, snake handling, and people with abnormal chromosomes could be found in the deep hollows. Josh himself had encountered inbred, pinched-faced, hawk-nosed women and children with skin so translucent, locals unremarkably referred to them as "the blue people." In covering the trial of two men accused of the murder of their mother, he had learned about the mountain cult that practiced crucifixion.

Josh shifted his attention to Allison. The rain was still light and she drove easily, left hand on the steering wheel, right hand toying with her hair ribbon. He happened to fix upon the position of her driver's seat and was again struck by her long legs.

They slowed for a six-man state highway crew filling potholes from the previous winter's freezes.

"Three guys to do the work, one to lean on the shovel, one to drink the coffee and one to watch," Allison muttered as the smell of hot tar infused the Wagoneer. "All getting overtime."

The rain began to fall harder. The Wagoneer's windshield wipers worked to keep up.

Twelve miles later, they turned onto a narrow gravel road that ran parallel to a churning stream red with mud, swollen by the rain. Steep hills loomed around them, deepening the gloom. Allison switched on the Wagoneer's lights. "We're almost there," she said.

Josh bounced hard in his seat as they lurched from one water-filled pothole to the next, the back end of the big vehicle clawing for traction in the mud. Playing the brake and the accelerator perfectly, Allison handled the challenge like a veteran off-road driver. Josh thanked his lucky stars they hadn't taken his Volvo.

By the time they crossed a rickety metal bridge, water had risen to within a few inches of the top of the bank and only three or four feet below the grated surface of the bridge. A half-mile down the road, they came across a scattering of tired, frame houses on small plots of land. Allison slowed the Wagoneer near a sign that read "Blood Run. Unincorporated."

"Which place is his?" Josh asked.

"Don't know. But chances are they're all Scruggs one way or another."

Allison assessed which house was most likely to contain people who would help them. She had developed the skill during her medical school residency at Detroit City Hospital when one of her assignments had been tracking communicable diseases. That meant going into neighborhoods where cooperation with authorities was not always highly valued. She found she was more inclined to be welcomed, or at least tolerated, in homes with some external sign of hope—flowers in a window box, toys in a yard, a vegetable garden out back.

A single-story house, with a tin roof and walls clad in faded brown shingles caught her eye. A ringer washer sat on its sagging front porch, along with the one bright object in the whole rainy, dreary landscape—a child's tricycle with multi-colored tassels hanging from the handlebars. She noticed a wisp of smoke curling from a large weathered shed that sat behind the house on the edge of the creek.

"Might as well start here." Allison parked the Wagoneer, pulled on her poncho and started down a muddy driveway that ran between a few scraggly rows of corn and a barbwire-fenced pasture occupied by a single anorexic cow. As she walked she became aware of a sweet, cloying smell that permeated the air despite the hard rain. Like sour apples cooking, she thought.

Allison had already knocked on the front door and was attempting to peer through a rusting screen on the clouded front window when Josh caught up with her. "No one here," she declared. She stepped off the porch and headed around back. Josh followed.

"Smells like someone's cooking applesauce," Allison said.

The rain had become a downpour. Allison pulled her poncho over her head and sprinted to the shed, taking shelter beneath a section of the rusted tin roof that overlapped one side. She heard noises. She peered through a gap in the planking.

There, illuminated by a single light bulb, she saw a young man holding a fly fishing rod bent double. As the quivering rod twisted and turned and the man reeled frantically, it looked for the entire world like the man was in the fish-fight of his life.

Josh pulled up beside her. "I'm not believing this," she whispered, not moving her eye from the gap in the planks. The momentum of the fight shifted. The reel sang as yards of line spooled out. Then she caught sight of the fisherman's prey. A large brown rat. With what appeared to be a strip of leather clenched in its jaws, it scampered across the floor of the shed, flipping and twisting like a rainbow trout on a fly as the fisherman fought for control and maneuvered to keep the line from tangling. She abandoned her peephole only after the rat darted behind a stack of empty plastic milk jugs, the lure still in its mouth.

In the next second two events occurred so closely together that even as everything turned into slow motion and she watched the earth coming up to meet her she could not tell which came first—the roar of a shotgun or the tremendous force that struck her between her shoulder blades and slammed her into the soggy ground.

She knew she was not dead when she detected again the sweet and sour smell of cooking apples, now mixed with the sharp edge of spent gunpowder. Wet spread across her shirt and jeans and she waited for the pain. She tried to move and couldn't. Something heavy was holding her down, a feeling she'd known before but couldn't immediately place.

She became aware of muddy black boots just inches from her face. Her eyes followed the boots up a pair of jeans and a flannel shirt and into the face of the man she had seen with the fly rod.

The weight lifted from her back and she realized that Josh had been lying on top of her. He pulled her to her feet. "You okay?" he asked.

"I think so," she said, performing a quick assessment of every part of her body.

The fisherman spoke. "You dang fools almost got yourselves kilt. This is private property. Who are you and what in hell are you doin' here?"

Allison scraped mud from her poncho and jeans. "We're looking for Ricky Scruggs. I'm his doctor. We didn't know we were trespassing. You had no reason to shoot at us."

"I didn't shoot at you. You musta hit my trip wire. Rigged up to a little ol' four-ten over there in the woods. Just birdshot but it'll remind you to keep your distance. You're lucky your fella pushed you out of the way. Who did you say you are?"

Josh stepped forward. "I'm Josh Gibbs. This is Doctor Wright. She's Mr. Scruggs's doctor and she needs to talk with him. I assure you we're not revenuers."

The man spit. "You don't look the part," he agreed. He turned to Allison. "Why do you need to talk to Ricky? Is he sick?"

"He came to see me. I'm following up."

"Ricky's my brother but I couldn't tell you where he's at now. Goes wherever the jobs take him. Sometimes we don't see him for weeks."

Allison pulled a card from her back pocket card and gave it to the man. "If he shows up or if you hear from him, please ask him to call me."

"Mr. Scruggs, I have to ask you one more thing," Josh said. "Back in the shed, you had a fly rod—"

"Rat fishing," he interrupted. "Trout won't bite in muddy water. Days like this, you tie yourself a piece of jerky on the end of a line—deer holds up best—and you go out to the shed or the barn or wherever there's rats and pretty damn soon you're rat fishing. Once them things get ahold of that meat, they fight like the devil."

The adrenalin released by the shotgun blast dissipated by the time Allison arrived back at the Wagoneer. She realized she was exhausted, not to mention soaked, muddy and chilled.

"How did you know to push me down?" she asked as she and Josh stripped off their wet ponchos and toweled off with one of the blankets she kept in the back seat.

"I knew it was moonshine from the smell. I happened to spot the trip wire just as you were about to trigger it. How about if I drive home?"

"Thank you," she said. "I'm kind of beat."

The mud-red, rain-swollen water of the creek had risen over its banks and lapped at the grated surface of the rusty bridge as Josh piloted the Jeep through the narrow hollow of Blood Run.

Allison grabbed a fresh blanket from the back, pulled it around herself and snuggled into the seat. Not having to drive was welcome but it felt strange. She was unable to remember the last time she had been a passenger.

....

CHAPTER FIFTEEN

"Care to come to my place for a glass of wine?"

"I could sure use one." Josh looked at his watch. "Yeah, thanks. Katie's at a pool party until nine." He parked Allison's car behind his Volvo in front of the clinic and handed her the keys. "I'll run by the house, change into something dry and head over."

Allison slid the key into her front door lock. Did she hear mewing or was it wishful thinking? Her heart pounded. She hip-checked the door.

She felt the cat swish through her ankles as she reached for the light switch.

"Hippocrat. . ." The word died in her throat. Her ex-husband lounged in her easy chair chewing a fat cigar. Her stomach dropped.

"Good evening, Allison," Vince Bludhorn said smoothly.

"How'd you get in? What do you want?" He'd knocked her off balance for a moment but now she was angry.

"Is that any way to treat the rescuer of your beloved cat? Hippocrates would be in the gas chamber by now if it weren't for me." Bludhorn inspected his stogie. "You really are an irresponsible person, Allison. Someone found him wandering in traffic and took him to the pound. He was on Death Row."

Bludhorn hoisted the cat by the scruff of the neck. "Fortunately, they found his microchip and notified his rightful owner. We enjoyed getting reacquainted, didn't we, big boy?" Hippocrates hissed and bolted.

Allison felt rage transforming her—face contorting, her blood pressure reaching the roof. "He belongs to me," she said tightly.

"That's not how his microchip reads. It would be an interesting legal question—"

"Get out!" She was shaking.

"As you wish." Bludhorn lifted himself from the chair. "It's not in your nature to be caring, Allison. We both know you only think of yourself. But at least *attempt* to be responsible. Act like an adult. Lock your door. And don't leave your pet out. I hear people sacrifice 'em at Halloween, especially black cats like Hip."

The screen door closed behind her ex-husband. Allison scooped up Hippocrates and collapsed onto the couch, her emotions ricocheting between hate, self-doubt, relief and fear. Had she really been so careless as to leave Hippocrates out when she went to work? Is it possible she had left her front door unlocked? She'd never be able to forgive herself if anything happened to Hippocrates. Maybe she was what Vince said. Selfish. Irresponsible. A bad cat mom.

The alternative explanation was just as distressing. Vince had kidnapped her cat and had broken back in to return him. Why?

That was no mystery. So he could demonstrate in some twisted way that she was still dependent on him. So he could show her that he still had access to her whenever he wanted, that despite their divorce, he was still in control. So he could make her feel terrible about herself.

And it had worked. Here she was questioning her competency and her very security. If she'd been careless with Hip, she hated herself for that. If Vince was responsible, she hated herself for once again being sucked into playing his game, for letting him continue to push her buttons. The sound of Josh's car in the driveway didn't end her self-torture.

Josh took in the details of Allison's living room—a couch with a floral print, a glass-topped wicker coffee table, a stack of DVDs and a large TV that could be hidden when the armoire was closed, a series of pastels depicting river scenes. "Nice place," he called. He focused on the book shelves. The books a person read revealed so much that Josh felt that looking at someone's book shelves was almost as voyeuristic as peeping though the keyhole of their bedroom door. Allison's reading, he decided, was remarkable for the areas in which she concentrated—medical texts, not surprisingly, a large collection of paperback bodice-rippers featuring rugged men rescuing/seducing/ ravaging passionate women, and several shelves housing what had to be every self-help, esteem-building book ever written, including, improbably, *Self Esteem For Dummies*.

"Red or white?" Allison yelled from the kitchen.

Josh's cell phone rang. His stomach dropped. Fear closed in, an on-rushing train that could not be avoided. He knew the verdict even before the doctor said, "It's cancer. I'm sorry."

Josh felt the blood drain from his head. Everything in his experience as a skeptical journalist and a burned widower had told him to expect this. He had tried to prepare himself but, in the background, still part of the picture, there had always been hope. Now, the worst had happened. Prayers had not mattered. Once again. "Are you sure?" he asked.

"One hundred percent. The very good news is that we caught it early and it's treatable. The scans show that it hasn't spread."

Suddenly, he was exhausted. He felt as if he'd been cast into the Ohio and was being swept downriver by forces beyond his control like just another piece of driftwood. Resistance was futile. It will be what it will be. He sagged onto the couch. "What's next?"

"A surgical biopsy so we'll know if we have a chance to save the leg. If there's no chance, we amputate and we're done. She'll be cured. Cancer-free. If there is a chance, she'll get her first round of chemotherapy."

"When?"

"A week from Wednesday. I want our top pediatric surgeon handling this."

"How about after soccer camp?"

"No."

"The only reason we diagnosed this now is Katie happened to need a physical. We could have gone weeks before finding it. What's the worst that could happen?"

"Her leg could break and complicate the treatment. In kids, these things normally present when the limb breaks because the bone has been weakened by the disease."

"Then you know how to deal with it."

"We've already had this discussion. The answer is no."

Josh turned to Allison as soon as he hung up. He felt scared and alone—he and his daughter versus The Rest of The World. "It's just what you said it would be. But I still don't know about that guy. He's willing to put treatment off a week so he can have the doctor he wants but not long enough so Katie can go to camp. Her heart's set on this. And if, God forbid, she should lose her leg, this will be her last chance to play."

Allison settled beside him. She couldn't imagine Josh's burden. She'd had enough trouble making good decisions for her own life, much less someone else's. "There's something to be said for having the right doctor and for acting quickly," she offered.

"Medically, what's another week? She's thirteen years old. She's going to have one helluva rough time. I don't want to risk her life but I do want Katie to have this chance to go to camp."

Allison nodded.

"I can't make this decision alone. Allison, if she were your daughter, what would you do?"

"I believe in my heart that this is going to work out fine for Katie. And I believe in what Dr. Pepper advises. Maybe there is a way to work in both. Isn't there a short session and a long session? Have you thought about sending her to camp for just the first ten days?"

CHAPTER SIXTEEN

Since the trip to Columbus Josh had dodged Katie's questions—and avoided reality—by explaining that no one would know anything until they got the results of all the tests. Only when he collapsed into bed Wednesday night could he focus on how to tell his daughter she had cancer.

Experience, he realized sadly, made it harder, not easier. Cancer had killed Katie's mother, his wife. His past hopes and prayers for defeating it had never been answered. The doctor's assurances of "I think we got it this time" had never been met. Nothing had ever worked out. It had never been okay.

By the time he fell into a fitful sleep, he hadn't thought of a way to say it that would lessen Katie's fear.

He struggled the next day at the office. Usually, he thought long and hard about which stories to place where, striving to find a balance between the important and the interesting, the long and the short, between "good" news and "bad." Today, he found it impossible to care.

Writing headlines—a task he was quite good at and usually enjoyed—proved to be impossible. Each time he would start to read a story, his mind would wander and he would have to start over. At noon, Maude Furbee, the newspaper's bookkeeper, office manager and enforcer of deadlines since before Josh had thought about the profession, informed him that production could wait no longer. She ejected him from his seat in front of his computer and wrote the last headline herself—"Hoarse Play"—above a story about the upcoming River Days Hollerin' Contest.

"Okay?"

"Great," he said. "That does it."

He was first in the pick-up line at 3:15 p.m. Katie threw her backpack in the backseat, slammed the door and instantly apologized. He regretted the times he had scolded her for that.

Katie kissed his cheek and buckled herself in. "Did you bring my flute? It's the last lesson before camp."

"Not today. We need to talk."

He picked the spot beside the river—picnic tables, a few benches and an asphalt path along the bank—that had become Sharon's and his refuge in the hard months. They had cried there, cursed there, prayed there. They'd found solace in the slow movement of the water, comfort in the river's permanence. It would outlast them all.

More than once, Sharon had raised the subject of her looming mortality and given thanks her husband was a kind, loving man, fiercely protective, who would cocoon their daughter against cruelty and nastiness. She had it backwards, Josh thought. Sharon was the strong one. Even as cancer and chemo ravaged her once strong and glowing body, even as she was broken, she was the strong one. It was she who comforted him.

He and Katie sat on a picnic table bench watching the muddy water. For a moment it seemed that time had looped back on itself. Josh took a breath. "The doctor says your leg has a bone disease. It's something they can treat."

"How?"

"It depends. Maybe surgery. Maybe just medicine."

"Like chemo?"

He felt a shock. He had not been able to plunge the knife, had not said the word "cancer." But she already knew. His stammers merely confirmed it.

Katie sprang from the table and stalked down the path by the riverbank. Josh hurried to catch up.

She whirled to face him "*Cancer*?" she shouted. "I have *cancer*?" She picked up a stick and helicoptered it over Josh's right shoulder. "No. I can't. No way." Her expressions mirrored her thoughts: anger, bewilderment, defiance, denial.

She ran. Josh chased her briefly but she pulled away.

In time, he returned to the picnic table. A line from a hymn by Isaac Watts played in his head. "Time like an ever-rolling stream bears all her sons away . . ." *Wives, too*, Gibbs thought sadly. *And daughters.* Alone, he allowed himself to cry.

He waited for her a long time and then, suspecting she might have run there, he drove home. He found the house locked, the lights off, the mail unretrieved. He called Katie's name. He checked downstairs, then up. He felt a flutter of fear and then an idea came to him. Yes. Of course.

It was dark when he pulled off a dirt road about four miles from town and parked the Volvo by a cast iron fence on a high bluff overlooking the river. A full moon had risen over the Ohio hills, its reflection painting a wide, shimmering path of white light on the dark water. Josh opened a latch on the fence and walked quietly among an army of gravestones and their long shadows cast by the moonlight.

Katie sat with her knees to her chest, her back propped against a simple granite marker. He sat beside her, careful to respect the wilted, brown flowers he had left last week. And the previous week. And every week since Sharon had been laid to rest. Zinnias, when the season allowed. Her favorite kind.

He locked his arms around his daughter and pulled her close. Her head rested on his shoulder and he inhaled the familiar scent of her. They sat without speaking until Katie asked softly, "Daddy, how did I get it?"

It was a question that had yet to occur to him. Why would a thirteen-year-old get bone cancer? Why would a thirty-four-year-old woman get breast cancer, for that matter? Did anyone really know? That made it more of a question for God than for scientists or doctors.

"I don't know," he answered.

"Am I going to die?"

He chuckled. "Eventually. But not from this. You're going to be fine, I promise." He flinched. He knew it was coming even as he said it.

"You promised about Mom."

"Your mother was very . . . unlucky." He was immediately disappointed in himself. Unlucky was the word Sharon's oncologist had used. Unlucky! That was a term for cards. Dominoes. Roulette. Josh still resented the doctor for saying it. He still resented God for letting it happen.

"If I got unlucky, I'd get to see Mom. Would I be buried here?"

He stroked his daughter's ponytail. "You know what? Your mother is the reason you are going to be fine. You have an angel who's looking over you."

The moon bathed the graveyard in light as they made their way back to the car. He spent the ride home praying: *Don't let us be unlucky again. Don't let us go zero for two. Don't let me break my promise to Sharon.*

Katie stuck her bad leg out from underneath the covers when he tucked her into bed.

She stared at it. She flexed her quadriceps, her calf muscle, wiggled her toes. "Daddy," she said as her eyes filled with tears, "I'm scared."

At one time he might have said, "I promise you'll be fine." But Katie deserved better than that. Instead, he wrapped his arms around his sobbing daughter, cradled her head against his breaking heart and made a vow he knew he could keep. "I'll take care of you," he said.

In time, her sobs quieted. "Can I still go to soccer camp?"

Pepper's order echoed in his head. Screw him, Josh thought. Pepper had the same problem as Sharon's doctors. They saw the illness, not the patient. Sharon was a cancerous breast to them, not a person. So it was the cancerous breast they had treated, not the wife, the mother, the woman. Even when there was no hope, they had gone about the business of treating the cancer while prolonging, even exacerbating Sharon's suffering. Her last three weeks were a delirious, vomiting hell. Wouldn't she have traded them for a quicker, easier end? Or for one more good week at the beginning? Screw the witch doctors!

"Please, Daddy. Can I go? I'll do the dishes for a month. You'll never have to remind me to clean my room or get off the phone or . . ."

"A regular Cinderella," he laughed. "Go ahead. Have a blast."

Katie threw her arms around her father's neck. "I love you, Daddy."

He remembered the wise counsel he'd received from Allison. "But just for the first session. You're going to the hospital as soon as you get back."

"I understand."

He waited until he was sure Katie was asleep then crept quietly to his room and collapsed on his bed. He prayed he was doing the right thing.

CHAPTER SEVENTEEN

Friday evening Josh and Katie shared a pizza and packed the last of her things for camp. Then she chatted on the computer with—he hoped and trusted—her known friends and played her flute. At 10 p.m. she called from her bedroom and said she was ready to say goodnight.

He found her on the bed holding the framed color photo of The Black Ravens. "The best team ever," she said. "Fifth grade. I remember what I was thinking when they took this picture."

"What?"

"I do not have a worry in the world."

A moment passed before she said, "Thanks for letting me go to camp, Dad." She ran her hand down her leg. "I'm going to be okay. And next year, I'm gonna be all-state."

Just after 8 a.m. Saturday the last sleeping bags were loaded, the last soccer balls stowed, the last goodbyes said. The bus for Camp Kanawha ground into gear, belched a smelly, black cloud of diesel exhaust and pulled away—the campers inside already transported to their new world. Parents stopped waving and drifted back to their cars, except for Josh who stood unmoving until the bus was out of sight.

He closed his eyes and did his best to summon the memory of Katie—beaming face pressed against the bus window, baseball cap on backwards, mouthing the words "thank you." The vision appeared and he savored it and filed it away, along with the others he had started so consciously preserving.

"You made the right decision."

Josh turned around. It was Allison. He wiped his eyes. "She looked so happy."

"I'll say."

"Thanks for coming. You didn't have to give her your cell number."

"Just in case. She'll be fine, I'm sure." She looked him up and down with a diagnostic eye. He was care-worn, haggard, exhausted. Katie's cancer was already taking a toll. "You had breakfast?"

"No."

"Come. I'm buying."

Between them, Josh figured he and Allison knew half the people in the Winston Diner. He nodded to Mark Cotter, the funeral home owner. Spotting a t-shirt that read "Remember Wounded Knee," he moved to where he could be seen by pressman Jimmy Mayes and signed "hi." Dismissing a slight worry that their joint appearance on a Saturday morning might cause talk, Allison stopped to speak with the mayor who sipped coffee at the counter before joining Josh in a booth that overlooked Main Street.

Josh savored two eggs over easy, link sausage and a biscuit. That he hadn't cooked it and wouldn't need to do the dishes made the meal particularly delicious. When Allison finished her stack of blueberry pancakes and ordered another rasher of bacon, he said, "How's breakfast?"

She flashed a coquettish smile and flipped her hair. "Are you horrified?"

"No," he said before catching himself. "I like a woman who eats." He felt himself flush. *Are we flirting?* "I mean, it's just . . . where do you put it?"

"Genes," Allison said. "My mom—tall, five-nine at least—ate like a horse. One hundred twenty pounds all her life." She took a bite of pancakes. "She died in 1983. I was eleven."

Josh reeled.

"Yeah," she said. "I know."

An insistent buzz emanated from beneath the table. Allison signaled for the check, picked up her cell phone and scrolled through a text message from Coretha. Rick Scruggs was at the clinic. She showed it to Josh.

"So," he observed. "One of the body jewelry people finally shows up."

CHAPTER EIGHTEEN

Body jewelry people. As she hurried to the clinic from breakfast Saturday morning, Allison considered the tag Josh had invented for her tissue death patients.

She reviewed the known commonalities among Pringle, Scruggs, Cloninger and Faggart. All were white, although she could think of no race-related disease that could cause the symptoms she was seeing. All lived in the same area, meaning there was a chance their paths could have crossed—a notion supported by Faggart's recollection of working with someone named Candi or Candy at the Sternwheeler. Indeed, the Sternwheeler was popular enough that it could be a place where all four lives had intersected.

But she didn't know that all her patients wore "body" jewelry—except in the sense that *all* jewelry was body jewelry. Sure, Scruggs sported a nipple ring and Cloninger a tongue stud. But as far as she could see Pringle wore only what was considered more conventional jewelry—a necklace, the earrings—although why earrings were conventional and nipple rings weren't, Allison couldn't say. As far as Faggart's jewelry use, she hadn't noticed.

So Josh's tag of "body jewelry people" was a headline that didn't quite fit. "Jewelry people" certainly applied to at least three. But where did that get you? The term fit close to one hundred percent of women and, if you counted wedding rings and fancy watches, a majority of men.

Her own suspicions had focused not on the jewelry but on the hole—Scruggs's kitchen-table nipple job, Pringle's pierced ears, a hypothetical, unremembered cut on Faggart's toe, Cloninger's pierced tongue. All breaches of the skin, even old ones like Pringle's ear piercings, could be welcoming homes for a variety of opportunistic bugs.

One of the bugs was Methicillin-resistant Staphylococcus aureus, known commonly as MRSA. She blamed herself for not considering it sooner.

If it was MRSA, she and her patients were in for a battle. MRSA could cause the creeping destruction of tissue like she had observed, even pneumonia and death. Not for nothing had it been referred to in the popular press as a "flesh-eating superbug."

The problem was that over the years, MRSA had become resistant to antibiotics that once destroyed it—including the antibiotics she had prescribed for her patients. If MRSA were involved, they would not be getting better.

She knew MRSA was being seen more and more in hospitals. A sick patient, susceptible to infection because of a compromised immune system, would touch something on which the pathogen resided—a telephone, a nurse call button, a TV remote or another person. Others in the hospital would touch the infected patient. The superbug would take hold.

One of her medical journals had recently detailed increased infection levels among groups with lots of skin-to-skin contact like team athletes, military recruits, and prisoners. And MRSA was spreading so fast in the general population that a new term—Community Associated (CA)-MRSA—had been developed to describe it. Perhaps her patients *had* been in contact.

MRSA's preferred medium was organic matter—flesh and blood. But the superbug could survive on non-organic surfaces for as long as three days. If people could get MRSA by touching hospital equipment that had the bacteria on it, Allison reasoned, they could get it from kitchen equipment at a hotel. Or, to Josh's point, from jewelry. A problem with the jewelry and a MRSA theory weren't inconsistent.

Or perhaps her patients had garden-variety staph infections, not MRSA.

Or maybe there was a different problem—allergic reactions to cheap metal, for instance, although the odds of so many people suddenly having the same uncommon allergy had to be small. Or perhaps the infection and tissue death cases were entirely unrelated, had no connection at all.

If jewelry was the tissue death culprit, she hoped she was dealing with allergies or simple staph. MRSA was nasty. And with thousands of people descending on the town for the festival, an epidemic could overwhelm her. Either way, she concluded as she arrived at the clinic, she couldn't rule out Josh's jewelry idea. Lab tests would be needed.

For years, the Winston Medical clinic didn't open Saturdays. Allison's father had restricted his weekend practice to emergencies and to those whose work schedule simply wouldn't permit another appointment. For Horace Wright, Saturday was for personal pursuits—golf, fishing or hunting, depending on the season. Having never been invited along and therefore having developed no such interests, his daughter had opened the clinic Saturdays, starting at 8:30 a.m. Not that she wanted to work all weekend, or even thought it was a good thing. But when someone needed treatment on a weekend, Allison didn't have anything that took priority.

Coretha dabbed a drop of syrup from Allison's blouse and handed her a lab coat.

"Coretha, do you remember if Wanda Faggart wore jewelry?" Allison asked.

"I'm guessing 'yes.' What woman doesn't?"

"Don't guess," Allison snapped, immediately scolding herself for failing to suppress the impatience she'd despised in her father, a man who made no apology for prizing intellectual discipline over people's feelings. She tried to make amends. "Look, I don't remember, either. In any case, bring her back in. I want to write her a new script."

Allison buttoned the lab coat and entered the examination room where Ricky Scruggs waited. "Thanks for coming," she said.

"Had to." He peeled off his shirt. "It's acting up again."

Allison pulled on gloves, carefully removed the dressing Scruggs had improvised. She probed the badly inflamed nipple with her fingers. Scruggs yelped as the pressure of her fingers expressed pus from the wound. She saved a sample and drew blood. The whole process took fifteen minutes.

"Where's the ring?"

Scruggs hopped off the table, reached into his jeans pocket, extracted the ring and dropped it with a clink into a stainless steel pan Allison held.

"I'm guessing you wore it again after you left here," Allison said.

"Until yesterday."

She decided there was no point in reminding Scruggs that he'd disobeyed doctor's orders. "I'd like to test it," she said.

"Why?"

"To see if it's causing your problems." She rubbed the ring with a swab and put the swab and the ring in separate sterile lab containers.

There was a knock on the door. Coretha stuck her head in. "I have that information you wanted," she said. Allison excused herself and stepped into the hallway.

"Faggart says she wears the normal stuff—necklaces, bracelets, a wedding ring," Coretha reported. "Plus, get this, she used to wear a toe ring her grandchildren gave her."

"Which toe?"

"I knew you'd ask. Fourth toe on the right foot. Maybe it was too tight and cut off circulation."

"Could be. Or it may have had staph on it. Or it could be unrelated. The best we can say now is that all the patients did indeed wear jewelry. But like you say, who doesn't? It's not much of a connection. Have her bring it when she comes."

"Too late," Coretha said. "She sold it when she began having toe problems."

Allison frowned.

"There is some good news," Coretha said hopefully. "The hotel got back to me. Candi Cloninger did work as a waitress until a couple of weeks ago. But the only address they have is the same P.O. box we have for her."

Allison didn't think it was good news at all. The implications of a MRSA infection at the Sternwheeler were frightening. Hundreds of people might have been exposed—might still be being exposed—particularly if the bug was inhabiting the food-handling area. The miracle was that she'd seen only four cases. But that could be because most of the people at the hotel were just passing through. Any infections wouldn't become apparent until they had returned home. She'd need to get the Sternwheeler to contact employees and recent guests. If management proved reluctant, which was possible, she'd have to appeal to the notoriously understaffed state department of public health.

On the other hand, there wasn't enough evidence to ring the alarm bell just yet. Any alarm, even a false one, could put the place out of business. She needed more to go on. The MRSA determination needed to be made as soon as possible.

Allison made herself a note to have Coretha ask the hotel if they had had an employee named Audrey Pringle. She collected her thoughts and returned to the examination room. She checked Scruggs's glands—they weren't swollen—and stuck a thermometer under his tongue.

"Ever been to the Sternwheeler?" she asked.

Her stomach jumped when Scruggs nodded that he had.

The thermometer beeped. Scruggs had a slightly elevated temperature of 100.5 degrees.

"Recently?"

"You asking me out for a drink?"

"I have three other patients with infections like yours. Two of them work or used to work at the Sternwheeler. When were you last there?"

Scruggs looked at the ceiling. "Two years, at least."

Relief mixed with concern. The hotel still should be checked for MRSA; Cloninger had worked there. But because Scruggs obviously had not acquired his infection there, she was back to square one. Perhaps her patients had indeed crossed paths—but somewhere else.

Aware she was likely violating patient privacy regulations, she asked Scruggs if he knew Faggart, Pringle, or Cloninger.

He didn't.

Allison considered another tack and settled on Josh's suggestion that jewelry tied her tissue death patients together. Unlikely as the theory was, it was true that Pringle wore earrings and had infected ear lobes, Cloninger had presented with bleeding and inflammation around her tongue stud and Faggart had lost the toe where she had worn a ring. "How did you acquire your nipple ring?" she asked Scruggs.

"What's that got to do with anything?"

"Maybe nothing but there's always a chance it's the problem. I'd like to get back to the source and everyone they've sold to."

"*You'd* like to get to the source? I paid two hundred dollars to that asshole!"

"Who?"

"Dude at the tattoo parlor—Spike—makes the pieces himself and sells 'em out of his car. Cheaper than the stuff they sell inside but just as good. Supposedly."

"Lil' Bob's Body Art?" Everyone—likely including her patients—knew the place.

"That's it."

She finished cutting away the dead skin from Scruggs's areola, stitched things back together in a way that would result in a minimum of scarring and gave Scruggs a more potent version of Bactroban that was thought to still be effective on MRSA. Just in case. She told him the lab would pick up his tests Monday, that they would take several days to process and that she'd call with the results.

"When do I get the ring back?"

"When we determine it's safe."

Allison called Josh at the paper as soon as Scruggs left.

"What are you doing tonight? I need to go to Lil' Bob's. I don't want to go alone."

"Getting a tattoo?"

"Hardly." She explained her MRSA infection theory.

Josh weighed an evening home alone against another adventure with Allison and said, "I'll be there."

Allison's last patient was Carl McGraw, a regional officer with the department of fish and game who had been snagged by a fishhook. Allison extracted the hook, gave McGraw a tetanus shot and applied a bandage—no stitches required and no charge. Allison was happy to accept McGraw's thanks, but the truth was, hassling with the state reimbursement program was more trouble than it was worth.

As soon as the clinic closed, Allison slipped out of her khaki skirt and lab coat and into a snug pair of faded jeans and an Old Fashioned River Days t-shirt from three years back. She tossed Josh her keys when he arrived. "You drive."

The car still held the heat of the afternoon. Josh was reminded that summer was only days away.

It was dusk when they arrived at the yellow-painted cinderblock building with the rusted tin roof. Neon signs—declaiming "Tattoos" in purple letters, "Piercings" in green, "Open" in red—glared from small windows that flanked the front door. Josh navigated slowly through the lot and parked. A rush of cigarette smoke and stale air washed over them as they entered. On one side of the room, a heavily tattooed man in leathers and a woman in black jeans and a black tank top slumped reading motorcycle magazines in vinyl chairs that bled stuffing from long gashes. On the other side of the room, the largest human Josh had ever seen stood behind a counter punching numbers into a calculator. His head was shaved smooth. He wore an open black leather vest with no shirt underneath and appeared to be tattooed from his neck to at least his waist. Josh could identify on the man's massive left bicep an amazingly detailed depiction of Marines raising the U.S. flag on Iwo Jima.

Allison strolled over to a series of racks on which hung framed poster-sized sheets of paper. Each sheet contained more than a dozen tattoos, arranged by theme, size, color and complexity. She leafed casually through the pages of flash art, pausing occasionally to examine a particular sheet in detail, as if she were considering swatches of $100-a-square yard fabric in her favorite upholstery shop.

"If you don't see something you like, we can pretty much do whatever you want freehand," the man behind the counter offered.

"Just looking," Allison smiled. "We're more interested in piercing."

"We can handle that." The man walked from behind the counter. "Hi. I'm Lil' Bob."

"I thought you might be, "Allison said.

Lil' Bob turned to Josh. "What were you thinking of?"

It wasn't a question Josh had ever considered. Flustered, he said, "Oh, the latest thing."

Lil' Bob's eyes sparkled. "That would be your Prince Albert."

"Prince Albert?"

"Trade talk for pubic area. A pelvic piercing." He turned to Allison.

"Perhaps something less . . . adventurous," she said. Josh nodded dumbly, his mind still spinning from the notion of Prince Albert. Allison didn't look the slightest bit uncomfortable, which he attributed to the fact that she'd probably seen everything during her medical training.

"I see your jewelry is certified," Allison said. "Do people ever supply their own?"

"Sometimes. Maybe they want a custom design. Or they use their own metal—maybe from their first Harley—for sentimental reasons. You can get body jewelry made anywhere, including Tiffany's."

"Or your parking lot?" Josh asked.

Lil' Bob sighed. "We used to run Spike off but now we don't bother. Truth is, his stuff's not terrible and people will do what they do. He out there yet?"

"Didn't see him," Josh said.

"It's early. He's probably sleeping off his hangover."

New patrons arrived as Josh waited and Allison shopped the array of rings in the parlor offered for sale. Allison purchased a very plain fourteen karat gold ring. Josh couldn't fault the design, but since Scruggs had not purchased his ring from Lil' Bob, he was unsure of her intent.

Lil' Bob offered to handle the piercing himself on the spot, noting that his parlor passed regular health department inspections and boasted separate rooms for "intimate" and "non-intimate" piercing. "State law says there has to be a witness in the room when I pierce private parts." Lil' Bob gestured to Josh. "I guess that'll be him?" Josh felt his face flame bright red.

"I'm having it done later."

"Suit yourself."

They left the parlor. "This is our baseline to test against what we get from our traveling salesman," Allison said. "And there he is."

Night had fallen. A streetlight with a single harsh bulb illuminated the dusty gravel parking lot where half a dozen cars now sat in no fixed order, like farm cats sprawled around a barnyard. Three black Harley soft-tails lazed near the front door.

They crunched across the gravel to a green Subaru wagon, its trunk open to reveal a velvet-covered board displaying gold and silver jewelry. A young man with short black hair, wire-rimmed glasses, a close-cropped mustache and goatee got out. Josh couldn't keep his eyes off the two silver spikes that protruded from his lower lip and the tiny silver barbell stuck though his left eyebrow. Allison noticed he was wearing gloves.

"See anything you like?" It sounded like he was talking with a mouth full of oatmeal.

"You have some very nice things," Allison replied, eyeing his wares.

"Thanks. Make 'em myself. I can beat the price on the stuff you find inside."

Josh estimated there were more than one hundred pieces here, from rings to earrings, plus studs, spikes, bars and dangling things. He fingered a few pieces. "Sell many tongue studs?"

"A ton."

"Recently?"

"Sure."

"How about toe rings?"

"Not in a long time. A bit passé once old chicks started wearing 'em."

"Where do you get your metal?" Josh tried to make the question sound as innocuous as possible.

"Metal dealers. Pawn shops. People bring me jewelry they're tired of." He eyed Josh warily. "It's not like we're melting down grandma's stolen silver service."

"We're not cops," Josh assured him.

Allison inspected a bar and gold chain. "Do you keep a customer data base?"

Spike looked at her like she was crazy.

"In case I wanted to check references," she added hastily.

Spike stuck out his lip. "Dude, check it out. I'm my *own* reference."

"Ever had any complaints about your work?" Josh asked.

"Heck, no."

"I heard some guy bought a nipple ring here and it made him sick," Allison said.

"Sounds like one of those Internet rumors."

"I notice you're wearing gloves. Something wrong with your hands?"

"What's with the questions? If you don't want to buy anything . . ."

"No, no, it's fine." Allison pointed to a simple ring from the velvet-covered board. "I'll take this one. This one, too."

"One hundred fifty." Spike slid the rings into a tiny cloth bag. "For the two. Cash only."

"Make it a hundred," Josh countered.

"Dude, I got a mom and a grandma to support. One twenty-five. Best I can do."

Josh produced the cash.

Back at the Jeep, Allison stashed the bag with the jewelry in a stainless steel pan she had placed in the cargo area. She took a can of aerosol Steri-Foam from her black physician's bag and dispensed a dollop into Josh's palm.

Josh rubbed the disinfectant into his hands. "You think Spike's gloves are hiding an infection?"

"Good chance. I'm going to try to get him to follow us back to the clinic. Or at least let me examine him here." She grabbed her bag and was making her way toward the Subaru when a pickup skidded to a stop beside Spike's car. Music blared from the pickup's window. Even at his distance Josh could feel the thump of the bass. Ricky Scruggs jumped out, sprinted to the Subaru and rapped on the driver's side window. Spike got out and slammed the door.

"Wait," Josh said. "Scruggs may help convince Spike he's got a problem." Allison stopped in her tracks.

Scruggs pulled up his tank top to reveal his still-bandaged nipple. Spike shook his head and shrugged. Allison and Josh couldn't pick up what was being said over the music.

The discussion ended with Spike reaching for his wallet. He withdrew some bills and handed them to Scruggs who counted them, climbed into his pickup and left.

"C'mon." Allison said. They were halfway to Spike when he spotted them, slammed the trunk and jumped in the Subaru. "Sorry. Closed." He gunned the engine and spun out of the lot.

Allison jerked Josh back to the Wagoneer. "Let's go. He needs to know the situation."

Spike's tail lights winked a quarter mile ahead of them by the time they hit the highway. Allison drove hard to keep the Subaru in sight as Spike sped toward the surrounding hills. Fog had settled into the hollows. The Wagoneer's automatic wipers activated, smearing the reflection of red tail lights across the windshield like badly applied lipstick.

The rear of a huge dump truck—its bed covered by a flapping tarp—appeared ahead in the gloom. The Subaru zipped around it. By the time Allison caught up, the dump truck had entered the hills. They hugged the bumper of the behemoth through a series of sheer-sided switchbacks. Allison passed at the first opportunity and hit the gas.

The fog disappeared as quickly as it had come. Josh searched for the tail lights.

"Lost him," Allison said. "But I got his tag numbers." She performed a perfect three-point turn and piloted them back to town as if they'd been out for a relaxing drive.

The moon edged over the hilltop, bathing the hollows in milky glow. Shadows leaped and capered. Josh's thoughts turned to his daughter. He envisioned a beam projected from his eyes to the moon, bouncing off and finding Katie, uniting them.

Compared to what Katie was facing, this amateur sleuthing seemed rather pointless, almost juvenile. On the other hand, he realized that he'd just spent several hours not wallowing in worry about Katie. In fact, there were times he'd even enjoyed himself. It was like investigative reporting without the scrutiny. He could ask questions, develop theories, research information—in short, be a reporter—without the risk of publishing a story. If this was what he needed to keep himself on his feet and moving forward, he'd play along.

....

CHAPTER NINETEEN

Sunday Josh focused on his torment. Not in a theological or cosmic justice sense, but in the scientific, the practical.

People got lung cancer because they smoked. People suffered heart attacks because they ate poorly and didn't exercise. Sharon had breast cancer and so had her mother. There was a genetic connection. What had caused Katie's cancer? Why had it happened?

As a journalist, unanswered questions bothered him. Beyond that, not even his experience with Sharon had totally abused him of the conviction that if he knew enough about a problem, he could solve it.

In this case, he knew the Who (Katie). He knew the What (Has osteogenic sarcoma). He knew the When (Now). He knew the Where (Tibia). What he didn't know was the Why? Genetic? Environmental? Or just bad luck?

It was the question Katie herself had asked first.

Unshaved and still in his pajamas, he made coffee and settled in front of his computer. He typed the words "osteogenic sarcoma" into his search engine and got hundreds of results. He started at the top with the entries from Google Health and Wikipedia. They gave him the basics, most of which he'd already heard from Pepper. On page two of the search results, he found sites with detailed information about chemotherapy treatments—Cisplatin, Carboplatin, Cyclophosphamide, Doxorubicin, high-dose Methotrexate with Leucovorin and Ifosfamide. He made notes so he could research each drug more completely later. Websites for cancer treatment centers started popping up on page three.

Fatigue and frustration forced him to quit at 5 p.m. He had come across a few intriguing facts and had found a couple of articles worth printing but most were so elementary as to be useless or so technical as to be incomprehensible to anyone without a medical degree. He wished there was an on-call expert who'd take time to listen to his questions and answer in plain English. Someone who was not Pepper.

His phone rang. "I've been collecting some articles about osteogenic sarcoma," Allison said. "Also, some general information on caring for a sick child. I thought they might be helpful. I can drop them by, if you'd like."

Josh was speechless for a moment. "I've been doing the same. I need answers."

"I'll be right over."

He shaved and had the house looking presentable by the time she arrived.

He met her at the door. Allison handed him a stack of manila folders, each labeled with a different color tab.

He thumbed through the folders. They contained pieces from the *Journal of the American Medical Association*, a study from the *New England Journal of Medicine* and monographs from the National Cancer Institute's website. They were divided into categories: causes, symptoms, treatments and so on.

"Some of them are a little dense but I think you'll get through them," Allison said. "There's one on caring for a sick child. I wasn't sure if you'd had much experience with that."

"This is amazing."

"Some of this might need explaining."

It was a moment before Josh realized he was being asked for an invitation. "Please," he said. "Come in."

They settled at the kitchen table. Josh opened the folder labeled "Causes" and began to flip through some of the articles. Allison had drawn stars in the upper right hand corner of the first page of each article to indicate its relevance. Josh saw she'd also highlighted key passages and made concise, legible notes in the margins. He was stunned.

"Quid pro quo," she said. "For helping me."

"Can you stay?" he asked. "Give me the headlines if I make dinner?"

Then added, "That is, if you're not busy."

"We do need to eat."

"It's the least I can do."

Josh uncorked a simple red wine, poured two glasses and handed one to Allison. "*A votre santé*. To your health."

Allison clinked his glass. "To Katie's health."

Their eyes met as they sipped.

Josh put a pot of water on to boil and removed a quart of spaghetti sauce from the freezer.

Allison turned to her research. "Where do you want to start?"

"Causes. We already know symptoms. And what Pepper and you've already told me about treatment pretty much matches what I found on the Internet."

Allison opened the folder with the red tab. "There's been a lot of speculation, some research but not much hard information when it comes to causes. There's some relationship to injury and some have hypothesized that repeated injuries to a certain area—like a leg bone— might lead to increased and rapid production of bony tissue and that might lead to malignancy."

Josh put the spaghetti sauce on to heat and started assembling the makings of a salad. "Could soccer injuries have something to do with it?"

"Possibly. But most experts feel an injury simply brings the cancer to the person's attention and there's no causal relationship. That makes sense to me since we'd see a lot more cases if injury were to blame." Allison picked up a monograph. "Genetics may have something to do with it." Allison realized Sharon had just entered the conversation.

Josh turned the heat down on the sauce and put the pasta into the pot of boiling water.

"There's no breast cancer connection. If a child has a genetic abnormality that causes a problem like Paget's disease or dysplasia, they're more likely to develop osteogenic sarcoma." Allison picked up a printout. "Radiation exposure can be a cause but obviously not in Katie's case."

Allison refilled their glasses and set the table. "Smells delicious. I know Sharon was a great cook. I didn't know you were, too."

"Sharon was a very good cook *and* a very good cooking teacher. She couldn't have me poisoning our daughter."

Josh smiled. He wasn't accustomed to talking about Sharon to anyone but Katie. That Allison was a doctor made it easier, but it was more than that. She listened and, unlike so many MDs, she didn't hide behind her training.

"Garlic on your French bread?" he asked.

Allison blushed.

For no reason, she scolded herself. Josh was her best friend's husband—before Sharon's death and since. Period. Still, it was easy to see what had drawn her friend to him.

Josh was attractive. His journalistic interest in aiding the downtrodden was admirable and mirrored her focus as a physician. He had maintained his sense of humor in the face of tragedy. His devotion to his wife and daughter was complete. He was what he seemed to be.

How different from her ex-husband! Vince was good-looking but that's where the similarity ended. There were actually two Vinces, she had learned too late. The loyal, connected, ambitious corporate lawyer and the other—the controlling, narcissistic physical and emotional abuser whose humor came always at another's expense.

How different Josh was—even from her father. For all of his good qualities, Allison had come to regard her father, too, as a bully. His bullying was intellectual, not physical. He did not discuss things with his wife, he debated them. And whether through logic—usually—or just by arguing louder, he always won. And having won, he would start again, belittling her for failing to prevail.

When Allison's mother died, Horace Wright's focus turned to his daughter. Allison had felt like she was an actress in a nightly drama, a play whose curtain closed with Allison in tears and with another reason to feel insecure and unconfident.

The argument that led to the breaking point had come when she was seventeen. "Damn," she said, unaware of herself. The memory always left her angry.

"Garlic on your French bread?" Josh repeated.

Allison returned to the present. "Only if you have it, too."

She located two cloth napkins in a hutch. She brought two candles from the dining room and searched the drawers for a match. In one, she saw a blue hairbrush with blonde silken strands of hair still clinging from the black bristles. Sharon's, she knew. Josh was nowhere near recovered from the loss of his wife. It was so unfair. Death had targeted the perfect couple instead of the deeply flawed. She closed the drawer without a word.

Allison lit the candles. Josh placed the salad bowl on the table and dished out the spaghetti. He withdrew a chair for Allison and seated himself. "Sharon had radiation treatments. You don't think that could have affected Katie, do you?"

"Not unless she was in the room with her for those treatments."

"It couldn't transfer over, then . . . ?"

"No. In fact, most childhood sarcomas arise spontaneously. They've investigated links to diet, injury, growth rates, all sorts of things. No one has been able to make a connection. I know you want an explanation but the fact is, finding the cause of Katie's cancer isn't going to cure her. There could be a million reasons for it—or none. Just . . . be there for her. She's a fighter and she's going to be okay. There's more steel in her than you realize."

She gave his hand a squeeze. "Trust me," she said, and hoped to God he could.

....

Chapter Twenty

Pedro Cardenas's fly to center—a real can of corn, Holt griped—ended the Cincinnati Reds' chances and the chief's hopes with them. He snapped off the radio and lay on his bed in the darkness. It was

1 a.m. He wouldn't—did not even try—to sleep. Soon, his cell phone would ring and Viggy would tell him what he already knew—with the Reds' latest loss, his credit limit was maxed. No more bets until he was current. He knew from past history that the bookie would require immediate payment of half the $10,000 that Holt owed.

How was he to recover his losses if he wasn't allowed to bet? He certainly couldn't generate that kind of cash with his lousy police chief's salary. He'd have to find it somewhere else.

He sat up, felt for his wire-rimmed glasses on his nightstand and shuffled to the living room/kitchenette of his tired two-room apartment. A week's worth of sports pages open to the box scores marked the passage of time like soil layers on an archeological dig. Styrofoam boxes containing the remnants of takeout meals—provided gratis by the Winston Diner—spilled out of a plastic trash can. Two empty microwave dinner trays—tonight's meal—sat on the yellow Formica counter. The stuff was loaded with sodium and bad for his high blood pressure. But who had time to cook?

It occurred to him that the tableau was a like crime scene, his detritus evidence. No, he decided, the empty plastic and Styrofoam containers were more like visual accusations, recriminations from a life with a no-count job, a life as empty as a microwave tray and as disposable as a take-out food box. The worst part was, he knew the accusations were accurate.

Holt hit the remote and his 52-inch flat screen, the one luxury he had allowed himself, came alive with ESPN News. He poured himself a shot of bourbon, tossed it back and measured out another. He caught a glimpse of himself in a small mirror on his refrigerator. The mirror had been a goody-bag item at the state law enforcement convention. It had a magnet on the back and a frame that read, "World's Toughest Cop."

If only that were true. The man looking back at him might as well have been Old Cheese Face. Old and tired. Alcohol-bloated and out of shape. Defeated. A far cry from what had been expected of one of Winston High's all-time great baseball pitchers.

Ironically, looking back, baseball was where his fall had begun. As a senior, he'd beaned a kid. Hit him hard enough on the left cheek that the kid's eyeball had popped from its socket. The eye could not be saved.

He was amazed the kid never held a grudge. But his own guilt was so great he could barely bring himself to speak when the former rivals passed on the street.

Ultimately, the incident had cost Holt the ability to throw his fastball—his best pitch—without fear. He was never good again. He gave up playing the game. But he did not give up on himself. Not then.

Like most Winston kids, Holt grew up hunting. An ability to focus so completely that everything faded but the plate had made him a great pitcher. The same qualities made him a great marksman. He joined the Marines with hopes of making Special Forces.

But a heart murmur—which even now he wasn't sure ever existed—had derailed his plans. He'd returned to Winston and joined the force. He already knew where the high school kids hung out to drink beer. He quickly learned a few other lessons of small-town policing. Like that if he arrested every Winstonian who broke a law, the jail couldn't hold them. And that the people who complained most about speeding were the speeders. After fifteen years, he'd been named the top cop.

Holt downed the second shot of bourbon and poured another.

Top cop, indeed. But not top paid. The fact is, he'd gotten a lot more respect as a ballplayer.

Occasionally, he fantasized about a major crime occurring in Winston, something he could really sink his teeth into, something that would showcase his skills. Maybe then, law enforcement would truly be appreciated. Maybe then, he'd have something to show for his life. Maybe he'd made a mistake in not going after Old Cheese Face. It was strange enough . . .

Holt's cell phone rang. Viggy. The third shot of bourbon disappeared down his throat. He knew it was pointless to ask for an extension. There was only one alternative and that was to ask for yet another "advance" from the place where he moonlighted. It was awkward—he had no respect for the security goons he had to work with—but he at least he could be thankful that these days they seemed to need a lot more of his hours than usual. He would be free and clear with Viggy—able to get back on the winning track again—but in the hole to the employer for, now, $28,000. It would take a lucky streak or a lot of moonlighting to pay that back. But you had to do what you had to do.

He looked in the World's Toughest Cop mirror. Old Cheese Face stared back.

CHAPTER TWENTY-ONE

"Ladies and gentlemen, I give you a true friend of liberty. I give you the man without whom our jobs would not exist . . ."

Senate hopeful and presidential prospect Harry Dorn—as CNN was calling him now, not the congressman from West Virginia—poised offstage like a runner waiting for the starting gun.

"I give you our own congressman, the next senator from West Virginia, Harry Dorn!"

A crowd of several hundred workers from the plant and a busload of faithful from a church in Charleston rose from ranks of folding chairs stretching from the outdoor stage to the edge of the woods. Dorn waited as always for the applause to swell. It didn't. That's gratitude for you, Dorn thought. Didn't these folks realize they owed their livelihood to him? He waved and bounded energetically to the lectern anyway, almost bowling over the man who had introduced him.

"Thank you, ladies and gentlemen. Thank you, my good friend Vince Bludhorn. Now don't sue me for almost knocking you down!"

The plant lawyer mimed a guffaw. Dorn peered at the unresponsive crowd and was unsettled. Most of the people assembled here looked as if they'd rather be anywhere else. Others appeared to be napping. Were, in fact, napping. Perhaps it had been unwise to shoot tape for the campaign's knockout commercial on a Monday morning, a cloudy, dreary one at that. A man in a black turtleneck and headset at the foot of the stage motioned for him to keep going.

Dorn launched into his standard speech, starting with a preamble which his staff always tailored to the specific location and occasion. He thanked the plant managers by name for inviting him. He saluted people in the audience including newspaper editor Josh Gibbs, "a distinguished representative of the fourth estate." He invoked his local roots, mentioning the loyal service of Police Chief J. P. Holt who delivered a snappy salute from the side of the stage. He told workers how much he appreciated them taking time off work to see him and attempted another joke—"I'm sure you'd rather be back at the furnaces." Nothing. Crickets. Dorn's unease grew.

He stumbled over his signature line—"This plant is a tax-paying, product-producing, job-providing example of what happens when the principles of economic liberty combine with the power of American industry." Instead of "tax-paying" he'd said "taxing." Even botched, the line elicited cheers from plant executives in the front rows. But the reaction from those behind them was indifferent. His closing line, "This plant and the proud people who work here are the heart and soul of my campaign," fell flat.

The folding chairs were empty five minutes after the speech ended. Discouraged, Dorn endured fifteen minutes worth of grip-and-grin photo-ops and made his way to the video production trailer.

The man in the black turtleneck gave him a thumbs-up from an editing console. A dozen TV screens flickered overhead.

"You've got to be kidding," Dorn said. "That was terrible. No energy."

"It was fine. We got everything we need. I've already made a rough cut. We'll pump up the applause level and add music and voice over later but here—take a look."

All the screens switched to Dorn smiling at the lectern. Overhead, a scattering of white, puffy clouds drifted across a gorgeous blue sky. Behind the stage, a row of American flags snapped smartly in the breeze. Behind that, the massive main building of the plant dominated the landscape, the company logo the only adornment on its gray steel walls.

Dorn heard his voice. "This plant is a product-producing, job-providing example of what happens when the principles of economic liberty combine with the power the American industry." Magically, his mistake had been eliminated.

The camera cut to the crowd—attractive people, happy people, apparently pleased to be associated with the plant and with Dorn's campaign. Even the Charleston people, carefully positioned to represent just the right amount of racial diversity in the shots, looked happy.

Dorn heard his voice again. "This plant and the proud people who work here are the heart and soul of my campaign." Thunderous applause and cheers followed as the screen faded to black.

Dorn smiled. It was just like he had imagined in his dream.

CHAPTER TWENTY-TWO

Allison had been on hold with the state department of public health for nine minutes, fuming as the timer on her office telephone ticked off more seconds. To heighten her irritation, an instrumental version of "Close to You" by The Carpenters was repeating for the third time—a threat to the public health if there ever was one.

Too often the practice of medicine had to do with small-minded, turf-guarding bureaucrats instead of making people well or preventing illness in the first place. This was an example.

She'd decided to notify state health officials first thing Monday about her MRSA concerns and to request expedited lab reports on Pringle, Scruggs and the jewelry samples. She had arrived at the clinic before dawn to finish an article on advanced care directives for the fall issue of *Mountaineer Medicine,* the quarterly publication of the West

Virginia Medical Society, but the Internet had been down and she still wasn't done by the time she heard Coretha start the coffee pot.

She had been about to call when Coretha reminded her that state offices didn't open for another thirty minutes and that she had promised to deal with backlogged insurance claims. The next thing she knew, it was 11 a.m. She dialed the regional office of the state health department which served Winston and surrounding counties but got an answering service. In the interest of avoiding panic, she kept her message vague.

After a lunch courtesy of Schering-Plough, the early afternoon had brought the usual array of medical issues—from the removal of Bobby Joe Jimpson's stitches to the renewal of Betty Shinn's high blood pressure prescription. At 1:45 p.m. she'd dialed the regional public health director again. When she'd pried from the answering service that he was in the Caribbean for the week, she swore loudly and uncharacteristically. Coretha had come running. "Get me the main public health office in Charleston," she had raged.

That had been all of—what? She looked at the timer on the telephone. Twelve minutes and fourteen seconds ago. At the office all day and she hadn't been able to alert public health and was listening to the Carpenters for the umpteenth time. She rolled her eyes.

"Chill out," Coretha said. "You're wound up tight as a tick."

Allison covered the mouthpiece. "Sorry. Bad day. Nothing but bureaucratic BS."

"The rep from Schering was easy on the eyes."

"Listening to the contraindications of the latest incontinence drug over corned beef sandwiches was certainly romantic."

Coretha pressed, "You've been spending a lot of time with Josh Gibbs."

The combination of Coretha's prying and the beginning of another cycle of "Close To You" pushed Allison over the edge. "Coretha, I would like to make clear that I am not interested in *any* entangling relationships. I do not need a partner to be a complete person."

"He has a nice butt."

"Coretha!" Allison blushed and turned away from her assistant. She had to admit, she'd observed the same thing. And it was true her physical needs hadn't entirely disappeared. But a romp in the hay just for the fun of it wasn't in the cards. Winston was a small town. Everybody knew her. The details of any local liaison—even a date that merely got carried away—would be known quickly. Of course, she had plenty of opportunities out of town—if plenty meant the annual three-day convention of the state medical society where she was propositioned at least three times per reception by men with fish-white circles on their ring fingers who invariably began the conversation by recalling their friendship with her late father.

She slammed down the receiver. "Twenty-five minutes on hold is long enough. Damn budget cuts. If the state would rather ignore a problem than answer the phone, the hell with 'em."

....

CHAPTER TWENTY-THREE

Maude Furbee dumped the mail on the conference table. "Don't forget, Congressman Dorn is due here at three."

Josh looked up from his computer screen. The day was turning into a series of ambushes—just what he didn't need. He had planned to devote time to sales for the River Days special edition. Deadline was approaching, as he was regularly reminded by the Main Street banner promoting the nightly pageants which portrayed Winston's founding (loosely interpreted) by George Washington, and General Andrew Lewis's 1774 victory over the great Shawnee chief Cornstalk, which the banner touted as "the bloodiest battle ever fought between the Indians and white settlers."

But that was before he'd learned that he'd need to cover Harry Dorn's speech in connection the plant's tenth anniversary celebration. On top of that, he'd received a call from the congressman's deputy saying that Dorn wanted to come by the newspaper office that afternoon and pay his respects.

It was little more than a media-stroking campaign visit, Josh knew, but of course he agreed. With Dorn widely considered to be a top senatorial contender, an hour spent on a Q &A for the *Winston News* certainly could be worthwhile. And by providing any resulting story to the Associated Press, he might even get some publicity for his little newspaper.

Plus, he had to admit, he felt flattered. The editor of *any* weekly would.

He turned to the mail. Furbee had sorted it into piles: bills, which he would not even open until the weekend; checks to be deposited that day; letters to the editor; and junk, often national press releases.

A postcard featuring the University of Georgia bulldog mascot sat apart from the rest. The caption read *Kickin' Ass and Takin' Names.* Josh flipped it over and smiled. "Saw this and thought of you," it read. "When you coming back to the fight?" It was signed by one of his former Atlanta colleagues.

He was about to give Furbee the checks when he came across a manila envelope with a hand-written label and no return address. He tore off the end and shook it over his desk. A shower of one hundred dollar bills floated out, along with a standard *Winston News* contract for advertising in the River Days special section. The customer's signature was illegible. Where the ad copy was supposed to be written, he saw the notation "TK," newspaper shorthand for "to come," meaning the ad itself would be provided later. He scanned for the name of the person who had sold the ad and saw his own. The top of the contract listed the name of the customer. He handed the paper to Furbee. "Who the heck are the Friends of Chief Cornstalk?"

Furbee studied it for a moment. "Probably a promotion for the pageant or an Indian rights group trying to place a protest ad."

Josh scooped up the bills and counted. Two grand. The price of a full-page. "That's all we need to reserve their space. Maybe we should start getting payment up front from *all* of our customers."

"Good luck with that," Furbee scoffed.

Josh handed the cash to Furbee and returned to his computer. Whoever the Friends of Chief Cornstalk were, he didn't have time for them at the moment.

Dorn and aides arrived at the *Winston News* building just after 3 p.m. The obligatory tour of the newspaper, conducted by Furbee, usually took only fifteen minutes. But every staffer had wanted a photo of themselves with the candidate and even though it tied up the newspaper's only photographer on an important news day, Josh didn't mind because the delay had allowed him to shoehorn in a few more sales calls. So it was 4 p.m. when Dorn finally reached Josh's office.

Josh directed the congressman to one of the armchairs that circled his coffee table and settled into a seat across from him. Dan Clendenin, Dorn's chief political aide, sat to the congressman's right, pushed back to the periphery—not physically part of the conversation but available should the congressman need clarification. Joel Richey, Dorn's senior office staffer, sat at the conference table cooing into a cell phone until Dorn silenced him with a glare.

Josh pressed the "Record" button on a digital recorder and began with an open-ended question that allowed Dorn to talk about why he was running, which was essentially a version of his standard Liberty Agenda speech. Josh took notes in order to appear interested although, as a weekly newspaper editor, his own political focus and that of his readers was more on whether the state was giving the county its fair share of road money or whether voters would approve a bond issue to build a new middle school than it was on the philosophies of the Liberty Agenda. That was stuff for the *New York Times* and his old paper in Atlanta, material he might use if he gave part of the interview to the Associated Press.

He was preparing to inquire about Dorn's future presidential ambitions, when another question popped into his head.

"Congressman Dorn, what would the Liberty Agenda mean for healthcare?"

"Healthcare should be a private matter between an individual and his or her physicians, period," Dorn said. "The responsibility for providing healthcare in this country must be removed from the back of corporate America. Do we ask American business to provide your housing? We do not. Do we ask American business to provide your food? We do not. But we do ask American business to pick up the tab for your healthcare. Where is the logic in that? When did healthcare become a right, say, over food and housing? All that ought be asked is that business pay a fair day's wage for a fair day's work and give the American people the liberty to do with their pay what they wish."

"How will that help high healthcare costs?"

"It will be like everything else in our great country—a market economy. If not enough people will pay $50,000 for a heart bypass, believe me, the heart doctors will find a way to make it affordable. The free enterprise system will produce the best in healthcare. But not everyone will be entitled to it. I may want a Cadillac, but I may only be able to afford a Ford. I may want a house on a golf course but I may only be able to afford an apartment. I may want a brand name drug but I may only be able to afford a generic."

Clendenin scooted his chair forward and whispered in the congressman's ear.

"Plus, tort reform," Dorn added. "A lot of these excessive healthcare costs come from ridiculous liability verdicts. Millions of dollars in pain and suffering because a waitress spilled coffee on your leg. Gotta stop."

Josh's body language must have betrayed him. "Mr. Gibbs, is healthcare a particular concern of yours?" Clendenin asked.

"You might say that," Josh shot back bitterly. And having felt invited, he gave Dorn the broad strokes—Sharon's death and Katie's cancer.

Dorn clenched his jaw. His eyes managed to convey compassion, anger and determination at the same time. "Dammit," he said in a way that suggested this was the strongest epithet he ever used. "That's just terrible." He patted Josh on the knee. "My heart's with you."

Josh understood why Dorn had been reelected so many times. The man had done nothing yet he felt oddly comforted in his presence.

Clendenin signaled that it was time to wrap it up. The men said their goodbyes. Josh watched the entourage make its way to Dorn's SUV before he returned to work. A minute later he answered a knock.

Richey stepped inside and handed Josh the congressman's card. "The congressman wants you to call him if there's anything he can do to help," he said.

Josh thanked the aide. A kind gesture, he thought. But none of his problems had political solutions. He was back at his desk only for a moment when Furbee interrupted. "Composing needs a photo for an inside early page. Pronto."

He found a photo of a pageant actor dressed as George Washington talking on a cell phone during a break in rehearsals. Josh typed the caption, "Answering His Country's Call."

"Perfect!" Furbee pronounced.

Josh decided to forego sales and stick with content. He turned his attention to the Dorn interview. Lucky timing. The story could pass for news and its question and answer format made it a quick edit.

He finished the transcript and remembered the mail. He resumed sorting through the stack, this time looking specifically for something else—a postcard addressed to him in his own handwriting.

He knew it was crazy. Katie'd been gone from home—what?—a little more than forty-eight hours? Even if she'd mailed one of the pre-addressed postcards as soon as she'd arrived at camp, it could not have been picked up and delivered to him so soon. He tried not to be disappointed when he found nothing.

....

CHAPTER TWENTY-FOUR

Allison's heart dropped. Her ex's BMW squatted in front of the Java Joynt. She tucked the Wagoneer in behind a parked truck. A minute later Vince Bludhorn backed out of coffee shop, a trademarked 'Counselor' in each hand. His outfit—heavy shoes, khaki pants and an olive field vest—explained the unusual hour. Bird-hunting was best at dawn.

Bludhorn set the steaming paper cups on the trunk which Allison knew contained his shotguns. He opened the door, retrieved the coffee and settled in. The BMW roared away. She counted to one hundred and stepped out of the Wagoneer.

Allison joined the order line at the Java Joynt, catching her reflection in a full-length, Victorian-era mirror that stood near the counter. She saw she was scowling. No surprise. Even Hippocrates had given her wide berth on his way to the food dish while she tromped around the house getting ready.

She had reasons. Her buddies at the state police headquarters in Charleston, whom she had gotten to know after an injured driver was brought in without i.d., hadn't gotten back to her about tracking Spike through his license plate. None of her other jewelry patients had surfaced. Coretha had learned late Monday that the state health director and the assistant director were traveling to a Hong Kong conference on flu pandemics.

She unclipped her tortoise shell barrette and shook her light blonde hair until it touched her shoulders. Closer to the mirror, she fluffed her bangs and examined her turquoise eyes. Just a few crow's feet. From Vince, undoubtedly. She looked at her profile. Suddenly, she felt too exposed. She tugged down on her black skirt and forced a smile that had faded by the time she left the coffee shop.

The task waiting for her at the clinic—fighting with insurance companies over reimbursements—did nothing to improve her mood. She had not gone into healthcare to return calls from clerks with absolutely no medical training who presumed to question whether a drug or a procedure she had prescribed was really medically necessary. Or to explain that, yes, her charges for a particular treatment were indeed "reasonable and customary" for the region, particularly given that she was the region's only full-time doctor. Or to deal with what were the insurance companies' obvious errors—like the very file she was looking at now regarding Katie's scheduled surgery.

The intercom buzzed.

"Another case," Coretha said. "In the examination room."

Spike's jaw dropped so far the jewelry in his lower lip almost disappeared when she walked in. He was wearing yellow rubber dish gloves. "You were at Lil' Bob's! You're a doctor? The sign said *Horace Wright*."

Allison could not believe her good fortune. "Horace was my father. But, yes, I'm a physician. Dr. Allison Wright. Hands getting worse? Let me see."

"My fingers aren't working right."

Spike's swollen fingers oozed blood and pus. She wasn't sure she could save them.

She examined his facial piercings. No signs of inflammation, so if the problem was body jewelry, it wasn't all body jewelry.

She looked into Spike's eyes and saw a scared kid instead of a cocky entrepreneur. "What's happening to me?" he croaked.

"That's what I want to find out. We tried to warn you, but you took off. Some of your customers are also ill, like Mr. Scruggs."

"So he claims. But that's bull!"

"You have an infection and so does he. Possibly, it's MRSA. I'd like to test the possibility it's from metal you've been working with."

Allison took blood samples. She gave Spike a prescription for clindamycin and the MRSA-effective salve, a proactive step since it would take at least forty-eight hours for test cultures to grow and reveal if MRSA was the culprit. She explained that if the lab confirmed MRSA, he might have to be hospitalized. Vancomycin, a powerful antibiotic known as the treatment of last resort, could only be administered intravenously.

Spike stared at his fingers. "From the metal? Damn that sonofabitch!"

"Who?"

"Darryl. I'm gonna kill that cockroach!" Spike stood as if he were ready to go after Darryl that minute. Allison guided him back to the examination table. "I don't know about killing him but we're definitely going to want to find him right away—as well as anyone you sold jewelry to."

"I don't exactly keep credit card receipts."

"What about Darryl? What's his last name?"

"Dunn."

"Where's he live?"

"Out Betheltown Road."

At lunch, Allison left a message with Furbee for Josh who was meeting with an advertiser. Then she dialed the number Spike had given her for Darryl.

A woman answered.

"Darryl Dunn, please. This is Doctor Wright in Winston."

"He's on a run."

"When will he be back?"

"Later today. Don't never know exactly. He's a trucker."

"Does he have a cell phone number you could give me?"

"He'd beat the crap out of me if I gave that out."

"Please. This is important."

"Okay. But you didn't get it from me."

Allison dialed Dunn's cell phone and got voice mail. She left a message saying she needed to speak with him about metal he may have sold and asked if he was experiencing any medical problems.

The afternoon brought a deluge of patients but no more progress. Every half hour meant another call to Darryl Dunn but always with the same result.

Josh returned her call just as the clinic closed at 5 p.m. Allison told him about Spike showing up in the clinic and how he had named Darryl Dunn as his source. "Dunn won't call me back," she concluded. "He lives out toward Betheltown. If I don't hear from him soon, I'm going out there tonight."

"It's safer if Darryl comes to you. Plus, you could examine him."

Allison decided Josh had a point. "Maybe he'd return a call from you," she suggested.

"Why would he?"

"You could use the old Woodward and Bernstein technique, 'Talk to me or I'll put your name in the paper.'"

His pain reawakened. Decades after their work, everyone still knew of the famous Watergate reporters from the *Washington Post*. Their names were part of the vernacular, their techniques familiar to journalists and non-journalists alike. The continuing recognition, Josh believed, was a well-deserved reward for notable public service.

But it also had never failed to be a bitter reminder of what could have been, what *would* have been in Atlanta.Were it not for his failure.

Rumors of suburban cops shaking down Atlanta prostitutes and stealing drugs from dealers had reached the newsroom. A six-month investigation by Josh's team yielded a blockbuster series with pictures that ran across the top of the front page for three straight days.

The experience was the highlight of his professional life. The interviews, the stakeouts, the thrill of the story hitting the streets, the competition forced to chase tail, the grand jury, accolades from his colleagues, the prizes—first local, then state—those were things that reporters lived for. Everyone was confident the series was a lock for the Pulitzer Prize.

Until an alternative weekly followed up with one of the prostitutes who casually disclosed that one of the newspaper reporters had paid her. The article implied that the payment was for information or sex, or possibly, for both. Josh was sick when the story came out because the reporter had been him.

This was not checkbook journalism, he explained to his bosses. And he had never paid for sex. But the woman had asked for payment after the interview. She was desperate for money. Josh believed her when she said she had a baby to care for. And, he reasoned, she was accustomed to being paid for her time. So he had given her $300.

Josh's bosses suspended him for a month and demoted him from the investigative staff to general assignment. He had made a serious professional mistake, they decided, although not one deserving of dismissal.

But the damage had been done. The Atlanta media morphed the

story from one about extortionist cops into one about the prostitute and the reporter. Although no one ever disputed the accuracy of the newspaper's series, the revelations about Josh's payment tarnished the story. The following April, the Pulitzer was awarded to an entry with less baggage, denying Josh and his cohorts journalism's highest honor.

His colleagues were understanding. Some would have done the same thing. But within a year, Josh had resigned and moved with Sharon to West Virginia and exile. He regarded himself a pitcher who gives up the winning run in the seventh game of the World Series and walks away from the game.

He pushed the 'stop' button midway through the whole terrible re-play and set his feelings aside. No, he realized, not the 'stop' button, the 'pause' button. For such nightmares could not be so easily ended.

"I'm not sure . . ." he said. "I've been happy to help until now but I'm not seeing this as a story. The threat isn't exactly one I can back up."

"A MRSA epidemic caused by contaminated jewelry isn't a story?"

"Well, *that* would probably be a story," Josh conceded. "But you have what? Three or four cases? And no confirmation?"

"Maybe five," Allison said. She explained that a woman who said she was pregnant had called the clinic for advice on a stomach rash. Coretha had recommended an oatmeal bath but wished later she'd asked her to come in.

"Not much to go on," Josh said.

"Please. I have to talk with Darryl. And this *could* be a story some-day. MRSA is serious stuff."

Josh, too, got Dunn's voice mail. He identified himself, told him he was working on a story about jewelry being sold locally and that his name and the name of his suppliers might appear in an article unless he could explain some things. At Allison's request, he gave Dunn a deadline of 8 p.m.

Chapter Twenty-Five

Allison slapped her cell phone shut. "No service."

A mile later, Josh eased the Volvo onto the exit ramp. The towering signs of an Exxon and a Petro-Go station loomed like two electric palm trees over an island of illumination—the service stations, a Waffle House with its bright yellow sign, an EZ-Mart convenience store awash in fluorescence, a Days Inn and a Marriott Courtyard, their facades bathed in floodlights like multi-story billboards.

"Petro-Go," Allison said. "They'll have lots of phones."

A dozen tractor-trailer rigs idled in formation in an asphalt lot on the truck side of the Petro-Go Auto and Truck Plaza. On the car side, a battery of twelve gasoline pumps stood empty beneath a white aluminum overhang. In between sat the Travel Store, a large single-story, brown-roofed building with glass windows much of the way around. Josh pulled into a spot near the front.

Josh followed Allison inside. "Need some help?"

"I think I can handle this part myself." She smiled and headed toward a door marked *Heifers*.

Josh surveyed the brightly lit interior as he waited—to the left, telephone cubicles and a neon sign pointing the way to showers; in the back, a good-size restaurant with a bank of three televisions mounted above the grill, one tuned to the Country Music Channel, one to ESPN and one to The Weather Channel; up front, a store featuring an astounding range of items from belt buckles and cowboy hats to satellite radios, American flag towels and perfume. Josh wasn't surprised to find country music amply represented among the racks of CDs, including compilation CDs bearing the label 'Not Available in Stores.' He *was* surprised that the collection had a decent selection of the kind of music Katie listened to.

At a booth a few feet away, a younger man with a shaved head punched keys on an iPad. He wore a black t-shirt, black jeans and a gold earring. His cell phone sat within arms reach on the Formica table so it took him only a second to answer when it trilled. "You find a load?" he asked. A new generation of trucker, Josh reflected. Blackberrys instead of CBs. Hip-hop instead of Merle Haggard.

The smell of pot roast permeated the restaurant, reminding Josh of how long it had been since he had eaten. His hunger dissipated quickly as he remembered Sunday pot roast dinners in the old days with Sharon and Katie. Nothing had been allowed to interfere, not school work, not the ball game, not the *Winston News*. Nothing, he thought bitterly, except death.

Allison's voice knocked him from his reverie. "Still going to voice mail at Dunn's but my state police buddies came through. Dunn's got brown hair, brown eyes and isn't an organ donor. Plus, I got a better handle on his address. All Spike gave me was some vague directions."

Josh nodded—unenthusiastically, it seemed to Allison. "I appreciate you coming with me," she said. "Dunn wasn't going to call and with him on the road during the day, this is the best time to find him." She approached the trucker with the iPad. "I wonder if I might borrow your machine?"

"For you?" he winked. "Anything." Allison smiled, but Josh didn't like the way he said it. The trucker handed the tablet to Allison who searched the address on Google Earth. In seconds, a satellite photo materialized of what Josh took to be Winston, from the familiar bend in the river. Allison zoomed in on a grove of trees outside of town.

"Can't tell much from this." Allison switched to Mapquest and repeated the process. A map appeared with a red star in the middle. She sketched a copy by hand on a napkin.

Sunset pink washed the wedge of sky between the steep hilltops. Deep in the hollows, where the road ran, night had already fallen. Allison studied her map under the Wagoneer's dome light. Josh squinted into the gloom. A shotgun-peppered road sign appeared in the headlights.

"Betheltown," Allison read. "Take a right."

Josh turned onto a gravel road which tracked a rocky creek. "I've never been to Betheltown," he said.

"No reason since it doesn't exist anymore. It never was much—a gas station, a grocery store, a few houses. Everyone had to move out when the plant bought the land. People still live on the road leading to the old place."

Josh rolled down the window. The chirping of tree frogs and the high buzz of cicadas flooded the car.

The road narrowed, the walls of the hollow growing steeper and the lights of civilization less frequent—a bare yellow bulb on the porch of a shack halfway up the hillside, the gray glow of a black and white television from a trailer shoe-horned onto a flat spot beside the creek.

Jaw-jarring potholes jounced Allison out of her seat. She cinched her seatbelt tighter. "Should be just ahead," she said.

The hollow widened into a compound illuminated by a pair of blue-tinted security lamps on utility poles. A brown and white mobile home with a green awning and plywood porch on the left; in the middle, a Jim Walter prefab home; on the right, an open-front double-bay garage, more properly a lean-to, constructed of trimmed cedar logs and corrugated aluminum. A utility light burned inside one bay where an engine hung from a hoist and a rusted steel drum overflowed with used oil filters. The other bay held what Josh recognized as a restored yellow '85 Corvette and a candy apple red Ford pickup supported by monster tires. Two tractors and a backhoe rested in patches of overgrown grass in the front yard. A state-of-the-art bass boat and two personal watercrafts lolled proudly on trailers.

Allison pointed to a mailbox.

"Dunn," Josh read. He parked in the shadows.

Allison reached for her doctor's bag. "Let's hope Darryl understands we're here to help."

Josh's heart skipped. He'd been so intent on finding Dunn that he hadn't contemplated what might happen when Allison confronted him.

Light bounced through the woods, the beams of another car traveling the same way they had. "This may be him," Josh said.

The car turned into the compound. The headlights blinked off. A figure emerged and knocked on the door of the prefab.

"Whoever it is doesn't live here," Allison observed.

When another attempt produced no response, the figure shouldered the door open and barged in. A series of thuds came from inside, followed by a prolonged crash.

"There goes the dishware," Allison whispered. She could sense Josh's skepticism. "Believe me, I know the sound of crashing place settings."

The door of the prefab opened. Light fell across the car that had parked in the compound—a green Subaru. "Spike," Allison said.

The Subaru's trunk opened and slammed shut. Spike headed for the garage. Allison reached for the car door.

Josh stopped her again. "He's got a gun."

"I think it's a bat."

What followed was ten minutes of mayhem that held Josh and Allison riveted by the violent choreography playing out on the stage of the two-bay garage.

The bat flew from Spike's bandaged fingers when he took aim at the Corvette so he stomped through the fiberglass hood and trunk in a dozen jagged places. For good measure, he karate-kicked in each of the Corvette's windows.

He abandoned the car for an acetylene torch in the adjoining bay. Allison held her breath. Spike ignited the torch from the pilot light of a nearby gas water heater, adjusted the valve controlling flame with his teeth and went to work on the candy-apple pickup, starting with the chrome pipes. The light of the torch reflected in the safety goggles made Spike look even more other-worldly, Josh thought. A different description occurred to Allison: demon-possessed.

With the Corvette and Ford trashed, Spike bee-lined for the bass boat. But something else caught his attention—a small metal safe stationed under a work bench. He used his legs to shove it off the shelf and onto a tool cart which he wheeled out to his Subaru. After a struggle, he loaded the safe into the car and drove off.

Josh and Allison watched in slack-jawed silence.

"We need to make sure he didn't kill someone," Josh said.

"Wait." Allison commanded. She outfitted them both with sterile hospital gloves.

Josh pushed the front door open with his foot. "Anyone home?" he yelled.

"Mr. Dunn?" Allison yelled. No response.

Josh reached into the hallway and turned on the light.

The place was a shambles. Spike had flipped over furniture and pulled clothes from closets. The remnants of a 72-inch TV, a stereo and a computer lay in shards in the living room. A snowfall of papers blanketed the den.

The kitchen was even worse. The pantry and cabinets had been stripped. The floor was ankle-deep in crockery shards and dented cans of food.

Allison became aware of an unmistakable smell and spotted its source. She realized what she had first taken for the random scrawling of a child was a barely legible note written on the counter in human feces. *"Darryl,"* it read. *"Don't shit in your own bed!"*

She held her breath as she approached the bedroom. Spike wouldn't have hung around trashing the garage if he'd killed someone in the house, she reasoned, still . . . she was relieved to find nothing except more damage. She checked the rest of the house with the same result.

"The answering machine has been played back," Josh yelled from the living room. "Dunn obviously got our messages."

Allison found a small box containing a tongue stud in the bedroom. She almost laughed. Tongue stud. Darryl. Trucker. Abusive boyfriend. How could she have missed the connection?

"Candi Cloninger lives here," she called. "She's Dunn's girlfriend."

Josh joined her in the bedroom. "I don't want to be here when they show up. This is matter for the police."

Chapter Twenty-Six

Josh awoke Wednesday morning and pulled his fur trapper outfit from the closet. The coonskin cap still fit, as did the buckskin shirt. A year ago, Katie had claimed that the leggings made him look like an aging punk rocker in Spandex. This year, they seemed even tighter. But he seldom wore anything that didn't acutely embarrass his teenager one way or another and decided the leggings would do.

Shortly before noon, he set off in costume for Old Fashioned River Days pageant rehearsal where, in addition to practicing for his role, he knew he'd find the chief of Winston's police, J. P. Holt.

Most weeks of the year, a grown man dressed like Davey Crockett driving a Volvo down the streets of Winston would have attracted attention. But as he neared the pageant site at Riverfront Park, Josh passed a British redcoat on Harrison Street, a riverboat gambler at Fifth and Main and what seemed like several divisions of Civil War soldiers (Union and Rebel) lined up out the door of the Java Joynt. He recognized most of them as employees at the plant.

By the time Josh parked at the Sternwheeler, the grand home of a turn-of-the century bank president which had been converted to an inn, the trickle of costumed characters on their way to or from rehearsal for their respective segments of the Old Fashioned River Days pageant had swelled into an historically confused flood. Revolutionary War soldiers mingled with paddle wheel boat captains. Indians chatted up dance hall girls. Josh counted at least three versions of George Washington—General George Washington (as in Crossing the Delaware); President George Washington (as in Gilbert Stuart), and the young, entrepreneurial surveyor George Washington, the George Washington who actually had the most to do with the history of Winston.

He climbed the stairs to the pageant stage and scanned for Holt, searching without success until it dawned on him that he shouldn't be looking for a police uniform or for the camouflage jacket and Cincinnati Red's cap that the chief wore during his frequent visits to the shooting range. No, he remembered, Holt was a fur trapper, just like himself. In seconds, he had zeroed in on him. With his buck teeth and round, brown eyes made even bigger by his steel-frame glasses, Josh thought Holt looked like a fat beaver, especially wearing his furry cap.

Josh scrambled from the stage and pushed through the growing throng—townspeople involved, he deduced from their costumes, in the skit depicting the bloody battle between the Indian confederacy led by Chief Cornstalk and the colonists led by General Andrew Lewis. The skit was a long-time favorite for two reasons—its depiction of carnage (140 colonials killed, 300 Indians) and because its finale included a stirring tribute to America's Manifest Destiny capped by a medley of "America, The Beautiful" and the National Anthem by the Winston High School Band.

He waved to Woody Conroy who played the role of General Lewis. Several of his deaf press operators from the *News* were made up in war paint. He signed a greeting to them. He always found it ironic that the pageant warriors did not include Jimmy Mayes, an actual Indian. Despite grousing from pageant officials, Mayes had consistently declined to participate and spent the festival period racking up overtime covering for colleagues who had pageant duty.

He spotted Furbee, reprising her role as pioneer wife abducted by Indians, holding hands with boyfriend Charles Angerson, whose job in finance at the plant made him the ideal choice to portray the founder of Winston's first bank.

The bullhorn-toting pageant director took the stage accompanied by fife and drum music that began to surge from the stage's speakers. Josh found Chief Holt among the crowd.

The chief was delighted to see him. "Hey, thanks for getting the shooting range picture in. I owe you."

Josh took him by the elbow. "Big news," he said. "Let's go where we can talk."

Holt looked at his watch. He'd been called in unexpectedly to moonlight and was due at the job soon. He hoped the big news didn't take long to hear about and that it didn't require anything of him.

They settled at one of the park's weather-beaten picnic tables away from the flow of rehearsal traffic. In their buckskin clothes and fur-covered caps, Josh thought they could have passed for two eighteenth century trappers swapping stories or working out a trade. "JP—" he began.

A cell phone chirped from Holt's pocket. Holt squirmed to retrieve it, squeezed a button to stop the noise and looked at the screen.

Josh ignored the interruption. The chief's obsession with baseball scores was well known. "JP," Josh repeated, "There's a problem you have to look into." He started with Allison's patients and her worries about sources of infection.

"Jesus, what women will do for fashion," Holt cut in.

"The nipple ring was on a guy."

Holt was appalled. He had heard of such things, but in Winston? "Doesn't sound like anybody from here."

Josh recounted their dealings with Spike at Lil' Bob's, and how Spike had led them to Darryl Dunn, the apparent source of the metal in Spike's jewelry.

Holt was skeptical as Josh recounted Spike's rampage at Darryl's home off Betheltown Road. He hadn't received any reports mentioning anything like that and said so.

"I doubt Darryl's eager to involve the police in his activities," Josh replied.

Holt needed to wrap this up. "We'll look into it but unless Darryl complains about his stuff getting trashed, or someone complains they were defrauded by Spike, I'm hard-pressed to see this as a crime. I've seen upset wives do a lot worse."

"How about shutting Spike down?"

"On what basis?" It was the question he always asked the preachers who wanted to close the carnival's Green Door.

Josh thought about it. The chief was right. So far, Allison only suspected Spike's jewelry was the problem. Until the lab tests came back, there was no proof. "Well, at least check him out. Maybe he doesn't have a business license . . ."

Holt started a slow burn. A business license infraction! The editor was becoming worse than the preachers! "Josh, we have tens of thousands of tourists getting ready to invade this town—not to mention vendors, all sorts of traffic and let's not forget a damn 10k run and Congressman Dorn. I've got the same undersized department I do every other week of the year when Winston is a nice little place of mostly peaceable people."

"It's a matter of public health." Josh watched sweat pop out on the chief's forehead, matting strands of fur to his red face.

"You got what? Four or five cases? Maybe?" He pointed to an ice cream vendor who'd shown up to take advantage of the rehearsal crowd. "There's more people gonna get sick from that ice cream than will ever get sick because of some nipple ring."

Holt had to get going. He swung his arm around to encompass the entire Old Fashioned River Days tableau—the stage in the riverfront park, the dozens of milling actors, the rental tables soon to be piled with merchandise (much of it off-size or outdated) from downtown stores on sale at "old-fashioned prices," the quaint alley where potters and painters would display their wares for the juried art fair, the sidewalks where concessionaires would be setting up lemonade, ice cream and hot dog stands. The fringe on the sleeve of his buckskin jacket trailed like streamers. Josh thought he looked like an early settler surveying the western horizon

"We'll check into this Darryl situation, but you need to relax," Holt said. "I'm no reporter but I do know something about facts and you have damn few of them."

"You know me better than that."

"You've been wrong before."

Josh felt his ears burn. There was nothing to say.

Josh walked back to the stage and spotted Coretha Hall talking with a woman in a white peasant blouse and puffy sleeves—Allison in costume as an 1812 War-era tavern wench. His eyes roamed across her bare shoulders and lingered on her neckline.

Perhaps it was the accumulation of things—the flirting at the diner, the sexual tension of the tattoo parlor, and now this—but he felt desire for the first time in years, green shoots of renewal springing up in a long-barren field. The feeling surprised him, pleased him. And made him uneasy.

He realized he'd been staring. He was thankful that Allison didn't seem to have noticed. He filled her in on his meeting with the chief.

"What about Spike and his jewelry?"

"He says there's nothing to do. And if you get right down to it, there really isn't much to go on."

Josh could sense Allison's disappointment. "I could check at the Winston Jewelers on the way back to the office and see if they've heard of any problems," he offered. "At least they'd be on alert."

"Thanks. MediScan should have the first lab results back tomorrow. That should tell us a lot. And maybe the chief will turn up something that will help us find Cloninger and Dunn."

CHAPTER TWENTY-SEVEN

Following rehearsal, Josh arrived at the office focused on content for the all-important River Days section. The day-by-day schedule of events would take up the bulk of the space. The photos of the River Days Queen and her court would chew up some more and he had a file full of other possibilities—a profile of the pageant director, a map showing the location of the street vendors, a list of the merchants who had contributed to make the festival possible.

The difficult part would be freshening the annual piece that recounted Winston's history from its initial surveying by George Washington to the settlers' battle with Chief Cornstalk to the riverboat era to modern times. History hadn't changed. His challenge was to find a story behind the story, to reveal a facet of Winston's past that previously had been hidden.

The Friends of Chief Cornstalk ad, while its content was unknown, reminded him that there was a perspective on Chief Cornstalk and the Indian battles that was very different from the version taught to school children and celebrated in the River Days historical pageant.

In the early 1740s, George Washington surveyed the Ohio River valley and, as was the custom, claimed a portion of the vast acreage as a fee. Frontiersman and white settlers who followed were dismayed to find that the land was the home of a number of Indian tribes, notably the Shawnee. In the 1760s, war parties, led by the young tribal chieftain Cornstalk, attacked the white settlements. Washington and the other landowners responded by raising a militia to fend off the attacks and protect the value of their land.

By the 1770s Cornstalk had become chief of all Shawnee and head of a confederacy of northern Indian tribes including the Cayugas, Delawares, Mingoes, Shawnees and Wyandottes.

On October 10, 1774, less than two years before the beginning of the American Revolution, Cornstalk's band of twelve hundred braves prepared to attack a white settlement near the confluence of the Ohio and Kanawha Rivers near Winston. The colonial militia responded with an equal number of fighters. Contemporary accounts paint a picture of ferocious fighting. One hundred forty colonials and more than twice that number of Cornstalk's men, outgunned by the white man's muskets, died in the bloodiest Indian battle in American colonial history. Cornstalk and the survivors retreated to the far side of the Ohio River. So ended Indian hegemony in the east.

For the white settlers, the victory was another step in the westward march of Manifest Destiny, further confirmation of divine favor and of Christian superiority over the heathen.

There were even those who made the direct connection between the success of the local militia against Cornstalk and George Washington's realization that such a militia might be transformed from merely protecting the interests of land owners, such as himself, to the task of winning independence from the British. It was, after all, only twenty months until July 4, 1776. So went the story celebrated in the River Days pageant.

From the Native American point of view, Josh understood, the battle represented racism, land stealing, and slaughter, no different from that practiced by any oppressive outside power. It was not for nothing that the intruders were called colonials. The ugly story of Washington's land and Cornstalk's battle could certainly be seen as the triumph of colonialism in its most vicious form, with the beloved Father of the Country merely a thief with an army, not the hero of liberty, democracy and freedom.

But it took some care to delve into that in the pages of the consciously upbeat River Days special section. Imagine trying to explain presenting differing points of view—not to mention the whole notion of Native American political correctness—to his very traditional advertisers.

Josh was still wrestling with his approach when Allison called to suggest that they grab a late lunch at the diner. Josh hesitated for a half-second but he hadn't eaten all day. Hunger triumphed over orderly copy flow.

He was just leaving when Furbee brought him a one-page fax. Due diligence on the Paddlewheel Project was being accelerated. No reason given. The fax was from Bella Partners.

He could feel Furbee waiting for an explanation but he said nothing. The Paddlewheel Project was the code word he and the Pennsylvania-based chain had given to the proposed purchase of the *News*. Bella Partners was lined up to provide the financing. He'd kept the planned sale secret from everyone, Furbee included. Now, for an unstated reason, progress on the deal was speeding up. He felt a twinge—seller's remorse—that he hadn't expected.

He stuck the fax in his pocket and, feeling guilty for not being forthright with the loyal Furbee, headed out the door.

Outside, he phoned his contact at the acquiring company but reached only a secretary with a message: Bella was offering him a $250,000 premium if the sale could close within the week. He had no notion of why. The whole idea was mind-blowing, not just the cash. So many details still needed to be taken care of, starting with informing his staff. He'd have to drop everything else and work around the clock.

Even then, closing in a week might not be doable.

He was still distracted when he arrived at the diner. Allison waited in a booth. She had already ordered him iced tea and a salad.

"I thought we should take stock of where we are, figure out what's next."

Josh tossed his salad with vinaigrette dressing. "Go ahead."

"Spike needs continued treatment but he's gone missing. We know Candi Cloninger gave up her tongue stud because we found it at Dunn's house. But she still may need treatment and she's skipped, too."

"Probably along with her boyfriend."

"I hate just relying on the chief. He's overwhelmed. Isn't there something else we can do?"

"Maybe, but that needs to wait a while. I have to figure out what's going on with . . ." He caught himself. "I got the River Days section, then Katie comes home."

Allison touched his hand. "I'm up to my neck in alligators, too. But nothing like that. That reminds me." She shuffled through her purse. "I hate to add to your 'to do' list but there's some issue with your insurance company about Katie's case. Expect a call from them."

She handed a note to Josh. "I'm sure it's a misunderstanding. Happens all the time."

Josh sighed. Now he needed to speak with the insurance company *and* the newspaper's prospective buyers once he got back to the office.

Furbee handed him a message as he walked in. He recognized the number as the Columbus hospital but not the name—Mrs. Dunlap.

Despite repeated exposure to life's unpredictability, Josh still worried about things that hadn't happened yet. He imagined that Pepper had learned he was disobeying doctor's orders by allowing Katie to go to camp. His heart pounded as he punched the hospital key on his speed dial.

Mrs. Dunlap got right to the point. "We need a credit card before we can accept your daughter."

He was relieved that Mrs. Dunlap was in finance, not healthcare.

"How much?" he asked.

"It should be able to handle a twenty-five thousand dollar charge. MasterCard, Discover, American Express or Visa."

"You mean a twenty-five hundred."

"Twenty-five thousand," Mrs. Dunlap snipped.

"But I've got insurance." He could hear her keyboard clicking. Josh tried to keep his cool.

"You've got insurance for amputation and chemotherapy. If you want leg-saving procedures, that's on you. Twenty-five thousand won't cover the difference but it'll get us started. The good news is, you still get the negotiated rate. And you won't need to spend it if they can't save the leg. MasterCard, Discover, American Express or Visa?"

Josh couldn't believe what he was hearing. "This is outrageous!" he protested. "It's pure greed!"

Josh heard more keyboard clicking. "Mr. Gibbs, it's not like we haven't been generous with you. Your wife's treatment alone cost more than one hundred thousand dollars."

"How was this decided?" Josh demanded.

"All I know is what it says here."

Josh was finding it hard to breathe. "Then Mrs. Dunlap," he managed, "You don't know shit."

He heard her gasp just before his hand piece hit the cradle. He dialed Dr. Pepper. Amazingly, the doctor answered.

"There's been a screw-up," Josh said, trying to be calm. "They have Katie down for an amputation."

"I was getting ready to call you. Your health insurance company says they'll pay for everything—medications, outpatient, rehab—but only if you elect amputation followed by chemo. Surgery, two-terms of chemo and reconstruction of the limb all would involve a very prolonged hospital stay and won't be covered."

Josh stood up from his chair. He felt the blood rise up his neck. "On what damn basis?" he yelled into the phone.

"Their position isn't unreasonable. There are no guarantees that chemo and bone grafts will work. Without amputation, the chance of the cancer returning will always exist. If things don't go well, you could be looking at chasing this thing around for years. It isn't that the insurance company is right and you're wrong. There are no guarantees, only odds."

"What are the odds of success with a chemo and bone graft, something that would save her leg?"

"Eighty percent, at least for the short-term. Long-term, it's hard to tell."

Josh swallowed hard. "Twenty percent failure?"

"The wrong decision could kill her. Amputation is a sure cure. And the cost difference for you is enormous. Chemo followed by a series of bone grafts is something few people could pay for on their own. Any hospital that would undertake the procedure on the underinsured would require the money up-front first."

Josh didn't even try to restrain himself. "I want one of those insurance company assholes to come down here and look my daughter in the eye and tell her they want to cut off her leg—because their CEO has decided their shareholders need a better return."

"We could appeal," Pepper said. "But I wouldn't expect—"

"Put away your hacksaw, Pepper. My daughter's keeping her leg even if I have to pay for it myself."

He was still reeling when Furbee dropped off a postcard with the address in his own hand-writing.

"Dear Dad," it read. "Having fun. Camp is cool. Please send a care package. Love, Katie." A smiley face and a P.S. followed. "Scored three goals."

He closed his eyes and imagined he had been there to see them, as he had so often before—Katie using a burst of speed to dart through the defense and a head fake to freeze the goalie; Katie employing her height and spring to rise above the defenders and head in a game-winner; Katie taking aim at the top right corner and unleashing a rocket from forty feet out with that incredibly powerful leg. That leg that the insurance company wanted to dispose of, along with their liability.

He became aware of how much he missed his daughter, how much she was the focus of his life. He felt lost without her.

He looked at his watch. Katie and the other campers would be back in their lodge for "quiet time" before afternoon electives. She had a cell phone for emergencies but, in general, campers were prohibited from using them. Impulsively, he picked up the phone and dialed the camp's main number. He was switched to the lodge. A counselor located his daughter.

"Hi, Dad. What's up?"

His spirits lifted immediately. "Hi, sweetheart. I just wanted to hear your voice. How are you?"

"Great. Did you get my postcard?"

"I did. Congratulations on the three goals."

"Thanks. Could you make sure there are some energy bars in my next care package? My friend Pam ate half the ones I brought with me. Hide them. They don't like parents sending food."

Josh smiled. "Will do. How's your leg?'

"About the same. Maybe a little sore."

Alarm crept into his gut. "It's worse?"

"Not really worse. I can play fine."

She said she had selected pottery as her elective and that the tennis racquet he had insisted she bring had indeed come in handy—when her lodge mates had used it to capture a mouse.

Josh was slightly bothered that she sounded so excited about that evening's big Sadie Hawkins Day dance and not at all surprised to hear that her account at the camp store needed replenishing.

He felt let down when Katie said she had to leave for pottery but overall, Josh felt relieved. His daughter sounded good.

He was just hanging up when Furbee returned with the rest of the mail.

"Maude," he said. "I can't envision her with one leg."

"Katie's strong," she said gently. "She got through the death of her mother. She'll get through this."

Katie *was* a remarkable girl. Perhaps his worries were not so much for Katie herself, but for how others would react to her. Would they regard her with pity? Would they look at her in a wheelchair or with shiny permanent crutches and assume she was mentally handicapped, too? Would someone want her as his wife? Would someone other than her father fully love her?

"She loves soccer with a passion. She's phenomenal, Maude, a level above everybody out there. Sharon always brought her birth certificates to games because her coach would have to prove Katie wasn't older than the other kids. Soccer saved her after Sharon died. She lives for it. They can't take that away from her. Whatever I have to do, she'll keep that leg."

"That's the spirit." She picked up a business card from the corner of his desk. "Hmm . . . I wonder if there's anything Congressman Dorn could do?"

Josh recalled Dorn's vague offer to be of help. Why hadn't he jumped on it immediately?

His reluctance started with the credo that is hard-wired into every self-respecting newspaper editor: never accept a favor from someone you might have to write about because it will cause your editorial objectivity to be questioned.

Dorn's offer could be viewed as an attempt to curry favor with a newspaper editor whose editorial endorsement the congressman was seeking. If Josh accepted it and it became known, readers would perceive him as beholden to the congressman. Anything the *Winston News* ever wrote about Dorn would be viewed skeptically.

But this was his daughter they were talking about. Her life. He could make the argument that Dorn's offer was simply service to a constituent, something the congressman might have done for any citizen of West Virginia.

This was a case of a bureaucratic, uncaring agency being forced to do the right thing—placing the needs of the patient before those of the stockholders. Should Katie be denied the congressman's intervention simply because she had the bad luck to have a newspaper editor for a father? This wasn't favor-seeking, it was justice.

In his mind's eye, he watched Katie scoring her three goals. He'd already sacrificed his integrity in the minds of some people. If additional questions about his commitment to ethical journalism were the price of saving Katie's leg, then so be it. He was a short-timer in Winston anyway.

"I'll think about that," he said. He took the card from Furbee and put it in his pocket.

....

CHAPTER TWENTY-EIGHT

Stars still twinkled in the royal blue blanket of the western sky as Allison left her condo. Streetlights dimmed and snapped off in succession as she drove to the clinic calculating the timeline for the umpteenth time.

MediScan had made their regular pickup Monday morning. Given her instructions to make it a rush job, she presumed the lab had placed her first round of swabs in a growth medium Monday night. Forty-eight hours to grow a staph culture meant results by Wednesday night and, she hoped, full reports in the clinic drop box this morning. She was not disappointed.

She flicked on the fluorescent lights, plopped into the chair at Coretha's desk and opened the padded white envelope. It held a sealed, sterile baggie with Scruggs's nipple ring, similar bags with the test jewelry from Spike and from Lil' Bob and five file folders—one each with test results for Faggart, Scruggs, Scruggs's nipple ring, and each of the two sets of test jewelry.

Faggart's file was on top. Allison picked it up as if it were a basket hiding a cobra.

The words sprang from the top of the page, spelling out her worst fear: *Methicillin-resistant Staphylococcus Aureus*. MRSA. It *was* the flesh-eating superbug which had consumed most of Wanda Faggart's toe. Her worst-case outcome.

Her first obligation was notifying her patients. All would require further treatment. She was in touch with Faggart and Scruggs but she suspected Spike would be difficult to find following his rampage at Darryl's. Thankfully, she'd suspected MRSA early and had started him on therapy. Pringle and Cloninger had had no good treatment and she had no idea where they were. She'd need to redouble her efforts to find them.

Next was alerting the state and county health departments. Physicians and healthcare facilities statewide would have to be instructed to watch for MRSA outbreaks. Each case would have to be catalogued and its origin identified so the source of the infection could be eliminated. It was a monumental task.

She'd also have to ask for extra help for Winston—more medicine, more lab kits and, at least during the festival, more physicians. She had no doubt MRSA had already infected some people with whom her patients had had close contact, including some who had bought jewelry from Spike. A portion would already be noticing a rash. All would need to be tested and treated. There was no time to waste. MRSA infections could spread exponentially.

She opened Scruggs's folder. Her plans went out the window. MRSA was not mentioned. Instead, her initial diagnosis had been correct. Scruggs was infected with a routine, highly treatable strain of staphylococcus. The report on Scruggs's nipple ring said it was positive for the same strain of bacteria infecting its owner. Allison was sure there had to be a mistake.

The reports on the samples of jewelry from Lil' Bob and Spike deepened the mystery. None tested positive for any form of harmful bacteria, not ordinary staph, not MRSA. The test jewelry was disease-free.

Allison was baffled. If the lab was correct, all of her theories were wrong. She left a note for Coretha to call Faggart in for MRSA treatment and moved to her office where she considered the results again.

She started by listing the unexplained tissue death cases: Pringle. Scruggs. Cloninger. Faggart. Spike. Although Spike's tissue tests wouldn't be back for another day, she was confident that he suffered from an infection along with the others. What she didn't know was whether infection or tissue death had come first.

The fact that two patients worked at the Sternwheeler had initially led her to suspect patient proximity as a factor—her patients had been in contact and developed a common infection somehow. But now that theory was shot. Scruggs hadn't been to the Sternwheeler in years. Moreover, he didn't have the same kind of infection as Faggart. That meant no bug had passed between them.

In addition to having infections, all her tissue death patients wore jewelry in the area of the infection and tissue death. That had led to her second theory—that her patients had been infected through jewelry that had been contaminated with bacteria and that the surrounding tissue had died as a result. But that theory had taken a hit when the jewelry samples she bought from Spike and Lil' Bob proved to be bacteria-free.

Nothing made sense. Was it possible that the lab was mistaken? She called MediScan as soon as the place opened. After a few botched transfers, she reached the pathologist who had analyzed the samples.

"I don't understand how this could be," she said. "I've had zero cases of tissue death in four years of practicing here and suddenly I have four or five in a few days. These lab results tell me they're unrelated but there's got to be a ground zero for all this."

"Can't be. One of the infections is a MRSA strain we see in hospitals. The other is garden-variety staph. That's assuming the swabs you sent me were good. We have to work with what we get."

Allison reviewed the procedures she'd followed in collecting the samples. She'd been careful. She was positive there'd been no lapses.

"Darn!" she muttered.

"Why darn? Be *happy* you're only looking at one MRSA case and not an epidemic."

"I suppose so," Allison said. "But what *am* I looking at?"

"Two different infections not caused by bacteria on jewelry."

"But there was staph on the nipple ring from Scruggs."

"It came from the wound to the ring, not the other way around."

"So no possible connection between all these cases?"

"Anything's possible but I'd put my money on coincidence."

Allison thanked him and hung up. Maybe there really was no connection between her cases. Maybe it was simply that Faggart had a cut on her toe she hadn't known about, had somehow come into contact with MRSA and had become infected. And maybe her first theory about Scruggs was correct. He'd gotten a staph infection from a botched piercing.

But that didn't explain Pringle or Cloninger. She really needed to find them and have them tested. And she'd learn more Friday when MediScan delivered the results of Spike's lab work. In the meantime, she was bamboozled, frustrated and back to square one.

The intercom buzzed at 10 a.m.

"What?" Allison barked.

"The x-ray film company's on the phone," Coretha reported. "They say their film's fine. No one else has reported any problems. They're pointing back to the machine or, possibly, a mistake we made."

"But we had the machine checked out."

"That's what I told them but that's what they say. I thought you might want to talk with them."

"No time," she told Coretha. She'd had plenty of experience with the various parties responsible for her Internet service all pointing the finger at each other whenever the service went down. It was *always* the other guy's fault. Discussions were futile. Besides, since the initial anomalies, x-rays had been coming out fine for days.

"Sorry for interrupting," Coretha said, clearly hurt.

Allison hadn't meant to come off so brusquely. Impatience had gotten the better of her again. "Sorry," she said. "I'll talk to them." Perhaps, she thought, she'd get at least one answer today that made sense. She grabbed the faulty x-rays from a shelf and picked up the phone.

Ten seconds into the conversation she realized that the company rep was telling her, albeit gently, that the film was fine and that she and Coretha were likely to blame.

"What do you mean, double-exposed?" she demanded.

"Each of the sheets of film we looked at was exposed twice before it was developed," the rep explained. "One exposure caused the ring-shaped voids that appear on some sheets and the big void in the middle of the other. The second captured your patients just as it should have."

"Double exposure means a problem with the machine."

"No, because not all the wrist x-rays were messed up. More likely operator error. Don't feel bad. It happens."

Allison hung up, dissatisfied. It wasn't like Coretha or her to make such mistakes. Besides, if she or Coretha had mistakenly used each film twice, the exposures would show two sets of patients.

The films, she concluded, had to have been exposed to two different sources—the x-ray machine and something else.

She slid the test x-rays she'd done on Coretha into her light box. She stared at the ring-shaped void and the surrounding area which looked to have less directly exposed. It reminded her of something.

She retrieved the baggie containing Scruggs's nipple ring from the MediScan package and compared the ring to the void on the films. They were the same size. She stacked the x-rays on top of each other. The ring was in precisely the same place on the two flawed films. On the film where the ring hadn't appeared, the spot matched up to a part of the x-ray that included no bone. So the ring *could* have been there, the dark circle simply had nothing to contrast against. She recalled that Scruggs had removed his nipple ring and placed it on the counter during his first visit. Had he actually put it on a box of unexposed x-ray film?

She picked up an x-ray of Cloninger's skull which was normal except for the tennis ball-sized void in the middle of her skull where bone should have showed up. The center of the void lined up with the position of Cloninger's tongue stud.

Could Scruggs's nipple ring and Cloninger's tongue stud be the second sources of radiation exposure? And if so, how? And why?

CHAPTER TWENTY-NINE

She was sure there had to be another explanation. The idea that the jewelry itself was giving off radiation was as improbable as it was frightening. She reminded herself that she had a theory and very little evidence. Nothing had been proven to be radioactive. She could hear her father saying, "A-s-s-u-m-e. When you assume something, it makes an *ass* out of *you* and of *me*." She placed the jewelry from Scruggs, Spike and Lil' Bob in her father's old lead drug safe as a precaution and turned to her medical books to see if radiation exposure fit the symptoms she was seeing in her patients.

In cases of topical exposure, she learned radiation initially produced the effects she had observed—skin burns, redness, blistering, inflammation, infections, open sores and tissue death. One entry quoted John Hersey's *Hiroshima* about the burns, " . . . yellow at first, then red and swollen, with the skin sloughed off, and finally, in the evening, suppurated [to discharge or form pus] and smelly." The description was right on target. It was as if the writer had been looking over her shoulder.

Vomiting and diarrhea usually followed a short time later—symptoms Cloninger had said were plaguing her boyfriend, Darryl Dunn.

If the exposure were long enough or the radiation intense enough, victims could expect hair loss, dehydration, disorientation and fever. And finally, as their stomachs and intestinal tracts ulcerated and sloughed off, death.

Treatment options, she read, were limited. For external exposure, decontamination was called for. To reduce damage to internal organs in cases of limited exposure, physicians could administer ferric hexacyanoferrate, known as Prussian Blue, to hasten the elimination of radiation from the body, or non-radioactive iodine to block absorption of radioactivity by the organs. Allison still had a small supply of both which the government had issued years earlier to physicians and other first-responders who'd have to handle the fallout from a terrorist nuclear attack.

For cases of severe exposure, there was no treatment. The best the medical texts could recommend was hospice care.

The crucial factor was how much exposure a person had and how quickly he or she was treated.

She reviewed her cases. She didn't know much about Pringle but Scruggs's symptoms fit radiation poisoning. Tissue death had come first in his case, followed by infection.

Coretha had learned that one of Faggart's janitorial clients was an extended care facility, suggesting the typical healthcare connection for the MRSA infection in her toe. But what if Faggart had suffered a radiation injury first and her MRSA was merely an opportunistic infection that arose after radiation had already started to kill tissue? Radiation poisoning in her case could not be ruled out.

Cloninger's visible symptoms fit, too, although they seemed to be in an early stage.

But still, she didn't know enough. The best that could be said was that radiation exposure was possible in each case. Further tests were needed.

She told Coretha how she was using her lunch hour and drove to the home of Darryl Dunn. Except for the yellow police tape which fluttered in the afternoon breeze, the place appeared as she had last seen it. If Chief Holt had done any more than a preliminary investigation of Dunn, it wasn't apparent. She took in the havoc Spike had wreaked in the garage—she hadn't been able to appreciate it fully at night. Shards of metal, plastic and fiberglass littered the floor. She picked up a piece of the Corvette's distinctive taillight and a piece of metal etched with overlapping circles.

She stepped into the house. She saw that the papers strewn about the den were pages ripped from what appeared to be a diary. She gathered the pages along with a file of bills of lading, receipts for the loads Dunn had picked up. She hoped they contained a clue to his and Cloninger's whereabouts.

She found what she had come for in the drawer in the bedroom: Cloninger's tongue stud. She picked it up with forceps and wrapped it in a lead apron that she used to shield pregnant women during x-rays.

Back at the clinic, she placed the stud on a sheet of unexposed x-ray film still in its light-proof jacket. She retrieved the test jewelry pieces from the drug safe and added the pieces to the film. She waited a minute, then ran the film through the developer. The outline of Spike's jewelry, Scruggs's nipple ring and Candi Cloninger's tongue stud showed up clearly. The rest of the film, including the area where she had placed Lil' Bob's jewelry, remained unexposed.

There was no longer any question in her mind: the jewelry belonging to Spike, Scruggs and Cloninger was radioactive. She had no doubt Faggart's toe ring and Pringle's earrings were, too.

But how had the jewelry become radioactive? Nuclear power plants produced trace amounts of precious metals but she knew of no nuclear plants in West Virginia. (Who needed nuclear power when there was all that coal?) She didn't know of any nearby government nuclear facility like the Oak Ridge Laboratory in Tennessee or the Savannah River Plant in South Carolina, although it wouldn't be unheard of for the government to have a secret installation in West Virginia. She remembered that the Greenbrier Hotel had housed an underground capitol where the President and Congress were to retreat in case of Armageddon. Its existence had been successfully kept from the public for decades.

She searched her computer. The nearest nuclear power plants were on Lake Erie in northern Ohio. None had experienced serious incidents or leakages. A uranium processing plant in Fernald, Ohio had dangerously polluted the surrounding area for almost forty years beginning in the 1950s, but Fernald was hundreds of miles away and, supposedly, the site had been decontaminated. She read that super-accurate measuring devices used in coal mining contained radioactive material. That was a possibility, although Winston was a ways from coal-mining country.

She Googled "radioactive contamination." Much of the first page was devoted to links to articles about the 2011 earthquake and reactor meltdowns in Fukushima, Japan. The top listing on the second page led to a Norwegian government site, which noted, "The Chernobyl accident in 1986 resulted in substantial radioactive fallout in parts of Norway. Radioactivity is still being transferred from the soil to plants and animals. The concentrations of cesium-137 are measured in meat and milk to ensure that food is safe."

She refined the search to "radioactive contamination injuries." The first listing took her to Gideon & Ceizlak, P.A. "Think you've been injured by radiation?" the firm's website asked. "Click here to talk to a lawyer ready to fight for you!"

She noticed that a number of headers referenced something called "Goiania." She clicked on one, a 1988 report from the International Atomic Agency in Vienna.

"In 1987, scavengers dismantled a radiotherapy machine at an abandoned clinic in Goiania, Brazil. Children spread cesium-137 over their bodies so that they glowed and sparkled. Two hundred forty-four people were contaminated, fifty-four seriously enough to be hospitalized. Four died, their bodies overwhelmed by pneumonia, blood poisoning and hemorrhaging."

The scientific journal article called the Brazil incident "a nuclear disaster second only to Chernobyl."

Of course, that was before Fukushima. Still, Allison was amazed. She had never heard of it.

She was comforted that all three events had happened outside the United States, until she came upon an August 1, 2007 article in the *New York Times*.

The article reported that radioisotopes were lost by commercial users in United States *an average of once every day* "through theft, accidents or poor paperwork." The article, by researchers at Kings College London, called for the banning of the form of cesium used in blood sterilizers and cancer therapy machines. "Just a few drops of contaminated water on the mouth are enough to cause radiation poisoning," the article noted.

MARK ETHRIDGE

A February 2008 report from the Nuclear Regulator Commission revealing the precise number of radioactive sources lost, stolen or abandoned in the United States: 4,363 over the prior decade. More than one a day.

Allison pushed back from her desk. With so many possible sources of radioactive contamination she had no idea where to start.

....

CHAPTER THIRTY

Josh felt a tap on his shoulder. Furbee made a telephone with her thumb and pinkie finger and mouthed, "Allison." Josh signaled Jimmy Mayes to start the press. It was 3 p.m. Thursday. Right on time. He followed Furbee from the pressroom and picked up a wall phone in the hallway.

"Spike's jewelry is radioactive. We have to tell Chief Holt." Allison sounded rattled.

"Slow down."

Allison took a breath and started over, adding details of the MediScan findings, her return trip to Dunn's and her tests on the jewelry.

Josh listened patiently. The notion of radioactive jewelry fell into the category of what had been known during his heyday in Atlanta as The Two-Minute Mile Rule.

The Two-Minute Mile Rule had been named for an apocryphal news story reporting that a human had run a mile in less than two minutes—almost twice as fast as the world record. The rule held that if something seemed too fantastic to be true, it probably *wasn't* true. Tough editors invoked the rule to head off time-wasting reporting forays and prevent embarrassing mistakes at the expense of the newspaper's credibility. A loss of credibility was the ultimate newspaper sin, he knew too well.

Radioactive jewelry sounded about as believable as a report of a mile being run in two minutes. Still, he couldn't think of an alternate explanation for what Allison was describing. She was a scientist—analytical, cool, careful, objective, never prone to speculation or hyperbole. He wanted to know more.

"I'm due in Columbus this evening to see about getting some relief on Katie's hospital expenses," he said. "Maybe we can get together after that." He told her about the conversation with Mrs. Dunlap and his intention to pursue all options including Pepper's suggestion that they talk with the hospital about moderating the bills.

Allison felt terrible. She wondered if Josh had any idea of the expenses he was facing. The immediate cost of Katie's treatment was likely to exceed one hundred thousand dollars. And the bills would keep coming for a long time.She didn't say so but she felt his trip was likely to be futile. Providers weren't known for taking voluntary pay cuts. And the insurance company, not the hospital, was behind the no-pay ruling. On top of everything else, Josh could be looking at financial ruin.

Why was it that so many bad things had happened—were *still* happening—to such a good man? It wasn't fair.

"Maybe I can help," she said. "Advise you about what to pursue, what to ask for. There are research budgets to tap, grants to apply for. We can start with the Sparrow Foundation. I'm going with you."

Chapter Thirty-One

"Josh and I are making a quick trip to Columbus," she told Coretha.

"You have a date!" Coretha said, pressing her palms together and raising her eyes to the sky. "Thank you, Jesus!"

Allison hoped her attraction to Josh wasn't becoming obvious. "It's not a date. But thank Jesus, anyway."

She found Josh waiting in the Volvo.

Main and River Streets were clogged with teams of workers unloading tents and pipe and drape for vendor booths. It took several minutes to circumvent the congestion.

Just a few days until hell breaks loose, Allison thought. Everyone else in town might love it, but River Days was not a time of year to which she—or her father, for that matter—had ever looked forward. On top of its normal business, the Winston Medical Clinic could count on a ten-day deluge of tourists with cut feet, upset stomachs, severe sunburns, sometimes even heart attacks and, of course, out-of-town insurance plans.

Now was when she should be making sure supplies were adequate and getting paperwork up-to-date, not trying to find money for Katie's operation or playing public health investigator. One of her father's mantras popped into her head: *A little precaution before a crisis is preferable to a lot of fixing up afterwards*—his way of avoiding the cliché, *An ounce of prevention is worth a pound of cure.* In this case, she rationalized, the ounce of prevention was ensuring Josh didn't go broke from medical expenses and finding the source of the radioactive jewelry. She found her phone and left a message for Chief Holt.

The hospital's vice president of external affairs was running late. Josh and Allison were offered coffee and ushered to seating near the administrative offices. Josh recognized it as the same waiting area he wandered into during his first visit with Katie. He was fascinated that Allison handled the wait the same way he had—by reading the hospital memos, these not on a desk but on a bulletin board.

Allison was halfway through one on Medicaid reimbursements when a notice about an inventory of blood sterilizers caught her eye. She recalled the incident in Brazil and the caution the Kings College researchers had issued about blood sterilizers—refrigerator-sized machines used to kill diseases in donated blood. Underneath that memo was one about the shipping and transport of radioactive materials.

If you were looking for a source of radioactive contamination, Allison was reminded, you couldn't ignore healthcare.

She voiced her thinking to Josh, starting with a primer. Radioactive isotopes, she explained, were used in literally millions of treatments and diagnostic procedures in most medical facilities in the United States and worldwide. The most common isotope was technetium, a diagnostic tracer that is injected or swallowed and which allows physicians using x-rays, MRIs and CT scans to get clear pictures of soft tissues and organs.

"Could something like that could affect the public?" Josh asked.

"Most of these radiopharmaceuticals decay within the patient. Technetium's half-life is just six hours."

Radioisotopes played an important role in treating diseases as well as diagnosing them, Allison said. Cobalt-60 was used in external beam radiotherapy machines. She knew Josh didn't need reminding that Sharon had received intensive radiation during her breast cancer treatments.

"I know a guy who got radioactive seeds for prostate cancer," Josh pointed out. "He was told to avoid children and pregnant women."

"Probably he was told to avoid close contact with them," Allison suggested. "That's a rare caution and very conservative. But no question, some of the stuff can be deadly if it's mishandled."

"What are the chances of that happening?"

"Unlikely. But it's worth checking out sometime."

The meeting with the hospital's vice president of external affairs and Dr. Pepper went as Allison expected. Everyone blamed the insurance company. Josh's appeal for a reduced rate was listened to politely but she heard clearly that such requests were rarely granted, particularly to someone with the resources to own a business. Allison's impression was that the man was an unthinking bureaucrat, not someone inclined to go out of his way to help them. But she said nothing. She didn't want to discourage Josh.

She was, however, happy for the opportunity to meet Pepper. She gave him a printout of clinical trials for which Katie might qualify and was encouraged when he did not make her feel like she was infringing. She raised the possibility of appealing to the Sarcoma Foundation and to the Sparrow Foundation for assistance. Before they left, Allison obtained the name of the hospital's radiation safety officer, explaining that she wanted to consult on issues that came up at her clinic from time to time.

They returned to the Volvo. Josh was buckling up when Allison asked, "Any reason you need to get back right away?"

Josh shrugged. "Nothing except work."

"I was thinking we could touch base with the radiation safety officer now. Maybe get a few questions answered. At least narrow the possibilities. That way, we don't have to make another trip, especially with River Days starting."

"Sure."

Allison rummaged through her physicians bag, pulled out an old, inactive pager and tossed it to him. "Clip this to your belt. Congratulations. You're a doctor."

Josh smiled. He opened the glove box and removed a nylon strap and a laminated pass from a long-ago soccer tournament. "Just the thing." He slipped the strap over his head and dropped the pass in his front shirt pocket, gambling that no one would check his ID. If they did, he'd simply laugh and say that he'd picked up the wrong lanyard.

"Good, but add this." Allison unclipped an engraved plastic nametag—*Horace Wright, M.D. Winston Medical Clinic*—from the lining of her bag. "It reminds me that whatever else he was, Horace was a pretty fair country doctor." She handed it to Josh.

Allison put on her white coat, checking her reflection in the passenger window to ensure that her own nametag from The Winston Medical Clinic showed prominently.

Seconds later they hurried through a cloud of tobacco smoke rising from the knot of smokers huddled by the main hospital's front door. Josh held his breath—partly to avoid the smoke, partly to ward off the hospital's hated antiseptic smell that engulfed them when the automatic doors slid open.

Given the hour, Josh was surprised at the level of activity. Orderlies and attendants in green scrubs and quiet athletic shoes streamed purposefully across the marble and carpet floor, reminding him of the travelers headed to their gates at Hartsfield. Clusters of visitors carrying flowers and stuffed bears herded toward a massive bank of elevators, a scattering of bobbing helium balloons marking their progress. Two men with stethoscopes protruding from their jacket pockets walked along oblivious to anything except their own animated conversation. In a small sitting area, visitors chatted with bath-robed patients in wheelchairs. Josh noticed some of the patients were hooked to IVs.

It never ceased to amaze Josh how easy it was to avoid security at hospitals. He'd first seen it as a reporter where he'd learned that by walking around like he owned the place, he could pretty much get to wherever he wanted. During Sharon's illness, during the endless hours of waiting for this test and that treatment and, ultimately, for the end to come, he and Katie had found themselves able to roam the halls without challenge.

But this was different. This time, not only would people need to assume he was a doctor or an otherwise authorized person, he would also have to impersonate one. He wondered if doing so was a crime.

He was relieved when the guard with whom he had grown familiar wasn't on duty. With Allison trailing, he veered confidently into a long corridor, took a left down a hallway and pushed through doors marked "Cancer Center."

Allison had been thinking about whether her plan involved a punishable violation of the rules of medical ethics or whether it was merely dishonest. She decided on the latter.

She approached the Cancer Center reception desk. "I'm Dr. Wright from The Winston Medical Clinic." She waved at Josh who lingered behind. "My colleague and I have an appointment with the RSO."

The receptionist consulted a clipboard. "The radiation safety officer is gone for the day."

"We had an appointment," Allison said firmly.

Josh stepped forward. "Dr. Pepper set it up," he volunteered, hoping detail would add to their credibility. "Peter Pepper. Pediatric oncology. I'll call him." He unclicked a cell phone from his belt and started punching keys as if Pepper's number was top-of-mind.

"I hope this isn't some bureaucratic screw-up," Allison said. "Pepper's got a temper."

"Maybe I could find you someone else," the receptionist said quickly.

Josh looked at Allison and shrugged. Allison nodded. Josh snapped his phone shut.

The receptionist punched a pager number into the phone. "You guys married?" she asked as they waited. Josh saw she was staring at his nametag.

"A year, Tuesday," Allison replied

"Congratulations."

"You don't look like a Horace," said the receptionist.

"Neither did the Roman poet," Josh said. "'Dum loquimor, fugerit invida aetas.'"

The receptionist looked at him like he was crazy.

"Even as we speak, the summer flees unseen."

The Radiation Safety Assistant who answered the receptionist's page wore jeans, a blue polo shirt and black shoes with rubber soles that squeaked as he led Allison and Josh down a series of corridors. Black, thick-framed glasses accented his spiky blond hair. A phone hung from his belt, right next to a dosimeter the size of a credit card. Allison was sure he couldn't be more than a year or two out of college.

The assistant ushered them into a small office marked with a maroon tri-foil on a yellow background, the international symbol of radiation. "How'd you end up in this field?" Allison asked.

"I liked pharmacology and, dude, this stuff is like that, only cutting edge. You say you were supposed to be set up with the RSO?"

"We talked to Pepper and Dr. Havranek in radiology, both," Josh answered, impulsively deciding to mention Sharon's radiologist.

Allison said, "Our clinic is looking at ways of handling radiopharmaceuticals and sealed sources of radioactivity."

White lie number two, Allison thought, but so far nothing punishable—at least by earthly authorities like the medical board.

"Nothing really to look at in Havranek's area," the assistant said. "The radiology guys use liquid stuff delivered daily by an outside vendor. It decays to nothing in a few hours so they just toss it or incinerate it. The other stuff is here, in the cobalt room."

The assistant approached a blue door with a metal keypad built into a stainless steel doorknob, similar to the kind Josh had seen airline workers use to access jetways. "What's the date? The thirteenth?" He punched 0-6-1-3 into the keypad and opened the door.

Josh and Allison followed the assistant into a small, L-shaped room where a two-foot-square safe sat on a waist-high Formica counter behind a wall of stacked lead bricks. A gooseneck lamp hung over the safe along with a clear shield of thick glass.

"There's cobalt in here?" Allison asked.

"Not anymore. The place was originally designed for cobalt radiation protection years ago and the name stuck." He thudded his hand into the wall. "Lined in lead." The assistant took a set of keys that hung above the safe and opened it. He withdrew a gray cylinder about five inches high and five inches across, carefully unscrewed the top and, keeping the cylinder behind the lead brick wall, tilted it toward Allison and Josh. "Cesium-137. Nasty chemical. Deadly for decades before it decays and poisonous even in its non-radioactive state."

The contents reminded Josh of a quiver of tiny black darts—several dozen as best he could tell.

"Used mostly for gynecological cancers in this form," Allison noted.

"Correct. But probably the biggest use of cesium-137 is in the machines that sterilize blood. Every decent-sized hospital in the United States has a blood irradiator."

Josh found a notepad emblazoned with the Viagra logo in his lab coat pocket and made notes. Allison was about to fire off the first of a dozen questions she had when the assistant closed the canister, returned it to the safe and said, "We've been in here long enough."

"I thought the room was extra safe," Josh said when they returned to the assistant's office. "Lead lining and all that."

"The lead walls protect people in the hospital. But the biggest danger is to the people in the cobalt room. The canister is lead. And the safe is lead. And there's a lead brick shield so you can open the safe and the canister. But you definitely get some radiation. Not enough to hurt *you*. But *I* work here every day. I have a limit." He patted the radiation dosimeter on his belt.

Allison noticed several devices she assumed to be hand-held Geiger counters perched on the cabinets. "Have you ever had an accident here, any kind of accidental release of radiation?"

"Not in my two years and not that I've heard of."

"How do the cesium implants get to the hospital and what happens to them when they're removed?" she asked.

"The manufacturer ships them here by UPS or Airborne in those canisters. FedEx won't do it. They get used and reused and then they're shipped back. Lots of record-keeping." He motioned toward a row of file cabinets. "In fact, that's ninety percent of my job. The state radiation protection division tracks the whereabouts of all nuclear sources used in medicine and once in a great while, we get audited."

"What about the nuclear material in sterilizers, radiotherapy machines, etcetera?"

"It's fully shielded and contained, but the problem for us comes when the machines need to be replaced. The feds require that they be disposed of at an approved site because the cesium is still deadly. But there is no approved site for most states, including any in the east, like Ohio. And since they shut down the last burial site in South Carolina, there's not even a place to dispose of mid-level radioactive waste like contaminated gloves and instruments."

"So what happens to it?"

"We have five sterilizers alone waiting for the federal government to tell us what to do with them. That decision is years, maybe decades away. And believe me, storage is expensive. They're heavy. They take space. They need to be inventoried and the paperwork was pretty random at some of these backwoods clinics that our medical center has been buying. There's been a lot of catch-up."

Allison felt a flush rise up her neck. In the same way that mothers warn their children about ending up in the hospital and being discovered with unclean underwear, her father had demanded she not end her clinic day before her paperwork was complete, lest she die and be labeled a sloppy physician. The assistant's comment reminded her that someone inspecting her clinic now might well describe aspects of her paperwork as "random."

"A blood sterilizer is one of the pieces of equipment we've been thinking about," Allison said. "Maybe we could look at one of the old ones?"

The attendant escorted Josh and Allison to a service elevator and punched the button for the basement. When they emerged, he led them past an iron dumpster brimming with scrap—metal piping, ducts, cartons of dented stainless steel trays and pans—to a large caged area filled with heavy machinery, office equipment and medical devices. Allison recognized X-ray machines, centrifuges, medical file cabinets, and computer printers among the massive inventory. The printers were newer than what she worked with every day.

"This is where we store old equipment," the assistant said. "Most of it gets recycled. But not the sterilizers and the radiotherapy machines. They just sit there."

Allison followed the attendant's finger to three devices that looked like blue and cream refrigerators. She noticed their red emergency cut-off buttons, a hand-written sign on one that alerted users to lengthen the standard irradiation time every sixty days due to the cesium source's decay, the small logo of the manufacturer, the skull and crossbones of the radiation warning sign, the green shield and a stylized rings and sphere logo of the hospital's Department of Nuclear Medicine. To her, the shield, spheres and rings looked like a representation of the rudimentary observations of the ancients. To the marketers, she supposed, the logo suggested something cosmic, eternal, scientific—the solar system, or perhaps an atom, in keeping with the department's focus.

Allison asked about the status of the federal government's hoped-for, high-level waste repository in Nevada. (Stalled.) Josh asked about the price of blood sterilizers (About $200,000 for a Nordion Raycell.)

They thanked the Radiation Safety Assistant for pinch-hitting for the RSO and headed for home.

"I do okay?" Josh asked as they drove.

"You'd make a terrific physician."

"I meant in the meeting about Katie."

"You did fine. Hopefully, they'll feel some pressure to cut you a break."

"They ain't seen nothing yet."

....

CHAPTER THIRTY-TWO

Having the extra telephone line installed in the study of his George-town house, Harry Dorn often reflected, was one of the smartest po-litical moves he had ever made. He seldom spoke on it and he rarely picked up when it rang, instead letting the answering machine kick in. But the phone allowed him to create the illusion of providing special access for key supporters because he could hand them a card with a number and say, truthfully, "This rings in my den. Call anytime." His wife had christened it the "nut line."

The only downside had been when the number had somehow gotten out on the Internet. He'd been deluged by all manner of crank calls—an amazing number of them obscene—and it really *had* been the nut line until he'd had the number changed. When the phone's ringing woke him from a deep, dreamless sleep Friday morning and the clock radio at his bedside told him it was 2:30 a.m., his immediate thought was that the same problem was happening again.

"I'll unplug it," he mumbled to the unmoving lump beside him, his wife.

He stumbled to the den, silently cursing technology and hoping he'd be able to get back to sleep. He hadn't had much recently and, if the last few days were any indication, there wouldn't be much opportunity for it down the road.

It had been a whirlwind of a week, nonstop since before dawn on Monday when his window-tinted, gasified coal-powered Suburban—a reminder of his commitment to *personal*, as opposed to governmental, environmental responsibility—had rolled away from the peace of his beloved retreat at Possum Island and crawled through the fog along the river all the way up to Winston. He'd given a thousand speeches and the one at the plant that morning had gotten the job done.

But he'd felt enormous stress as well as exhilaration. Who wouldn't? The cameras staring at him from every angle were unblinking reminders that he was defining himself for the crucial first television commercial of his campaign for the U.S. Senate. He regarded it as ridiculous yet unquestionable that his prospects to be the leader of the free world hung on this performance.

The speech had been followed by an easy meeting with the local newspaper which had been followed by what—even in the massive Suburban—had been a brutal ride behind gear-grinding coal trucks on winding, two-lane roads up to Fairmont. There, at the annual convention of the West Virginia Medical Society, he had been presented with an award for his years of public service which, he well knew, had come to the attention of the state's doctors after he supported tort reform legislation limiting payouts for "pain and suffering" lawsuits to $250,000. Of course, the pressing need for tort reform had come to *his* attention only after the society quietly arranged for his campaign to receive $1,000 from each of one hundred of the state's doctors, creating a deliciously symmetrical total of $100,000. It had taken him some mental gymnastics to figure out how tort reform was compatible with the Liberty Agenda, which supported individual rights over government restrictions but he had done it and he believed it. The Liberty Agenda supported not just individual rights but individual *responsibilities.* "We will not let society's freeloaders use pain and suffering awards to suckle at the breasts of medical caregivers," he had told the cheering physicians.

Following the speech, Dorn had made good on a promise to spend the night at the home of a long-time supporter in Marion County. The guest room mattress had been lumpy. The supporter's wife's snoring had resonated through the house like a chainsaw. Still jacked from two speeches, he had slept little and envied Richey who had stayed at the convention hotel in a comfortable room, presumably with a mini bar and, likely, with a young woman in a miniskirt. How Richey found them so *consistently* was a marvel. Were they getting younger or was he just getting older?

They had arrived back in DC before 10 a.m. Tuesday so Dorn could participate in an important appropriations committee hearing. He was well-known as a congressman who respected his legislative duties. As always, he made a particular effort to look engaged when the Associated Press photographer was taking pictures of the panel. Her photos, after all, were the ones that would go to papers nationwide.

Today, he was able to dominate the frame because the seat next to him, usually occupied by the member from Illinois, was empty—the member instead forced to hold a press conference denying he had patronized a gay escort service.

Following the hearing he had rushed out Interstate 66 to the headquarters of the National Rifle Association for a reception honoring its retiring president. After a late but pleasant dinner with a lobbyist at one of his favorite Georgetown restaurants, he had discussed campaign strategy with several of his aides until 1 a.m., sleeping on the couch in the den so as not to disturb his wife and awakening at dawn Wednesday with a crick in his neck.

Thanks to the ad agency's creative types and his campaign media advisers, the footage from the plant had been condensed into a thirty-second TV spot ready for his approval Wednesday morning. Technically, the spot was designed to build support for The Liberty Agenda, not for his campaign. Indeed, he hadn't even formally declared. But everyone understood The Liberty Agenda and the Dorn for Senate movement were one and the same. He had been more than a little nervous when his aides put the disc in the machine in his office and the commercial began to play.

He needn't have been. The people at the agency were worth every penny. The plant and the American flags and the blue skies and the cheering workers were the very images of prosperity and liberty. In a mere thirty seconds they had fully captured his vision. When the words "Trust The People" came up on the screen, he was moved to tears.

The ad had been scheduled in test markets during prime-time Wednesday night, but just as his savvy aide had predicted, the ad itself—or more properly, the *news* that there would be an ad—became a story on all the major networks by dinner time Wednesday. The media had recognized the commercial for exactly what it was—"the first shot across the bow," a commentator intoned, "and it was fired by the hottest star on the political scene, Congressman Harry Dorn."

The airing of the ad itself had added even more energy to the day's biggest news story. The Liberty Agenda's web address had been shown during the last five seconds of the spot and within two hours the site's server had crashed, overwhelmed by users trying to download the Internet version of the ad or make contributions. Dorn's staff found their voice mail boxes full and the phones ringing off the hook. The callers were united with one message: Harry Dorn for senator. Fully half mentioned the presidency. Just as Dorn and his aide had hoped, the ad aired in its entirety on most of the 11 p.m. television news shows as anchors sought to explain the phenomenon.

Dorn had spent Wednesday night with his press aides carefully negotiating his Thursday appearances on all the networks' morning news shows as well as Fox News, MSNBC and CNN during the rest of the day. Keeping all the networks happy while simultaneously negotiating for the prized interview time slots was a delicate balance, and the negotiations were not completed until midnight. The CBS limousine had arrived to pick up Dorn at his Georgetown home four hours later.

He had gone to bed Thursday night with a stack of telephone messages unreturned. One pile was from his party's biggest donors. Others were from the captains of the American business establishment. More than a few indicated a desire to be involved. Most mentioned checks. On top of that, the Chairman of the Joint Chiefs of Staff had called and was looking to put together a golf threesome including himself, Dorn and the chairman of Carbon Forward.

Dorn's mind raced. Donors. Political appointees. The Liberty Agenda. The plant, symbol of it all. Despite his exhaustion, it had seemed like hours before he fell into a shallow, dreamless sleep.

Only to be awaked by the ringing of the phone in his den a few minutes later.

Dorn reached the phone just as the answering machine clicked on. He was about to unplug the line but he was stopped short by the caller's frantic voice which came through the tinny speaker. "This is Josh Gibbs."

Who the hell is Josh Gibbs? Dorn racked his brain before the voice—which was going on about a daughter, cancer and health insurance—finally told him. "Once again, this is Josh Gibbs. The publisher of the *Winston News*. The guy with the daughter. Please call me."

Dorn replayed the message, this time scribbling Gibbs' number on a scratch pad lifted from the Willard Hotel. He'd pass it along to Richey in the morning.

....

CHAPTER THIRTY-THREE

Josh watched the sky lighten outside his kitchen window—the beginning, he could tell, of one of those fresh, clear June days in the Ohio Valley, early enough in the summer that the river still cooled things, before the heat of July drew up its moisture and spread it across the land like a blanket.

Pen in hand, he sat at his kitchen table, a half-full *Winston News* mug resting near his left hand, his cell within quick reach of his right.

The scent of coffee permeated the air. He heard the daily newspaper from Charleston plop on his doorstop. Uncharacteristically, he ignored it, returning instead to the stack of lavender note paper on which he had just written *All You Need Is Trust and a Little Pixie Dust!* He folded it, put it in a small envelope and tossed it into a pile with a half dozen others.

Parents, especially single parents, were mothers and fathers before they were anything else, he believed. He had promised his dead wife and himself he would do everything in his power to make up for the fact that his daughter's mother was gone. So Friday morning Josh focused on Katie, asking himself the one question he always asked when it came to caring for his daughter: What would Sharon do?

What would Sharon have done for a daughter coming home from soccer camp to face chemotherapy and surgery for osteogenic sarcoma? Bake cookies, for sure. And make something to cheer her up in the hospital, something that would show she was loved and that would make her smile, not just on the first day but every day. So he arose before dawn to write a series of notes, one for his lovely daughter to open each day. They were messages of love and hope, phrases like *Fingers Crossed* and the one promise he knew he could keep: *I'll Always Take Care of You.* And, *All You Need Is Trust and a Little Pixie Dust,* Katie's favorite line from *Peter Pan.*

It was just after 7 a.m. when the sun finally poked over the eastern hills, bathing the kitchen in light. Josh placed the notes in a straw basket. He found a scrap of ribbon in Sharon's sewing kit and labored for twenty minutes before he was able to tie an acceptable bow on the handle. He stepped back and concluded that it had all the marks of something put together by a man. But Sharon would have approved.

He packed his leggings, coonskin cap, buckskin jacket and set out for a half-day's work at *The Winston News,* followed by an afternoon rehearsal for the pageant.

His cell phone rang as he arrived at his desk. He recognized Washington DC's 202 area code from the caller ID and answered in the manner he'd adopted in Atlanta, "Gibbs here."

"Joel Richey. Representative Dorn asked me to get back with you regarding your daughter."

Josh felt reassured. At least someone was listening. He explained his problem with the insurance company and the hospital's reluctance to modify its charges. "So what they're saying is, 'We need to make more money and the price is your daughter's leg.' It's not fair," Josh concluded. "I think there ought to be a law."

"That's something to think about, although the Liberty Agenda frowns on government interference in private enterprise."

At least the aide was polite about it, Josh thought. "Katie can't wait for legislation anyway. Perhaps the congressman could perform a constituent service and make some phone calls to the hospital and the insurance company. I'm sure everyone would prefer to avoid a clamor in the news media over this case, something that might lead to calls for reform."

"I'll inquire," Richey said coolly.

Well, Josh thought, it's the best I can do for now.

He hung up second-guessing the propriety of his implied threat to have the newspaper lobby for insurance reform. Using the power of the press to advance a personal objective, particularly a family matter, was way over the line. Journalistic ethics was a slippery slope and, in suggesting he might publish a story if Dorn didn't deliver a favor, he'd begun the slide.

He became aware of a faraway shrieking—an alarm, he realized. He hurried to the lobby to find the transom over the *News*'s front door shattered and the receptionist screaming. Furbee was right behind. Alerted by a brilliant strobe, Jimmy Mayes and the non-hearing pressmen burst in a few seconds later on high alert, like linebackers looking for the ballcarrier.

Furbee punched in the code to quiet the alarm. The receptionist fell silent with it.

"What the hell was that?" Josh asked. For the benefit of Mayes and the non-hearing he asked the same question using sign language, leaving out "the hell" part for brevity.

The receptionist pointed to a rock the size of a baseball and a rolled-up copy of the *Winston News* in a mosaic of glass. Mayes picked them up and carried them to Josh.

"Want me to call the insurance company?" Furbee asked.

"What about Chief Holt?" said the receptionist, now more angry than shaken. "I don't care if he is overworked, I could have been hurt."

"First, let's get the glass cleaned up," Josh said.

Someone had already pulled a broom from the utility closet.

Josh handed the rock to Furbee and turned his attention to the newspaper. It was the current week's edition, wrapped around something heavy, cold and wet and cinched with two thick rubber bands. He removed the bands. The newspaper unrolled. A dead catfish smacked to the floor. It had already begun to smell.

"What the heck!" he exclaimed.

"Maybe it's someone payin' a bill," Furbee offered.

Josh laughed. When he passed along the line in sign language, the pressmen did, too. Everyone remembered—or if they didn't actually remember had heard the story of—the local farmer who'd tried to pay his classified advertising bill with a hog that he'd offered to the newspaper, butchered or alive.

"If they wanted to call us a fish wrapper, it would have been a lot easier just to send a letter," Josh joked.

But in truth, he was troubled by what had happened. It wasn't unusual for a newspaper to provoke strong sentiments. All you had to do is look at the Letters to The Editor column in any decent daily to see that. It wasn't even that rare for a newspaper to be called a fish wrapper, a birdcage liner, and even worse. What was unusual was for an aggrieved reader or advertiser to express himself in such a dramatic fashion.

And it was particularly uncommon at a small weekly newspaper like the *Winston News*, where coverage was more likely to focus on church news, obituaries and the featured speaker at the Rotary than on controversy and scandal.

Josh told Furbee to call the glass company for a replacement window, signaling an end to the impromptu meeting. Josh took the newspaper and unfolded it on the lobby coffee table. The back pages were still wet. Furbee and Mayes sidled up beside him.

"Any note?" she asked.

Josh paged through the edition without finding one. He scanned the paper for items that might have upset someone. The front page featured stories about uneventful meetings of the Winston school board and the city council, and an interesting photo of Hattie Duvall's '68 Buick Roadmaster halfway through the front window of Bill Booth's Barbershop on Main Street, an incident that had occurred when eighty-eight-year-old Miss Hattie hit the gas instead of the brake. Miss Hattie was uninjured, there were no customers in the barbershop at the time and Booth had gone to lunch. So the headline Josh had written above the photo was a natural. "Close Shave." Josh still liked it. The inside pages contained a routine array of ads and the usual selection of high school sports news, obituaries, garden club notes and the like. Nothing popped out.

"No clue," he said. "Normal news week."

"People do strange things," Furbee said. She pointed to the floor where the fish still stared at the ceiling with one cloudy eye. "What do we do with that thing?"

Mayes pointed to red lesions behind the gills. "Looks nasty," he signed.

Josh blanketed the fish with a fresh newspaper and hefted it. "Eight-pounder, easy." He handed the package to Furbee. "Put it in the lunchroom freezer for now. I'll tell Chief Holt. He'll complain but, truth is, he'd be disappointed if a crime in Winston went unreported—even it *is* just vandalism."

Josh returned to his office, brooding. Maybe it wasn't just vandalism. Wasn't there a mob expression about sleeping with the fishes? Maybe he had overlooked something. In terms of stories, it was always the stuff you never expected that bit you on the butt. Then again, offended readers generally could be counted on to tell you what had offended them.

Amidst the usual assortments of checks, bills, press releases and bulk mail advertising, Josh came across a postcard that sent him soaring.

Hi, Dad-

I LOVE all my friends here!!! They are SOOOOOO nice!!! Can I come next year?

See you soon!!!! Love, Katie.

Then, plummeting back to earth.

P.S. I met a boy.

So it begins, Josh thought.

....

CHAPTER THIRTY-FOUR

Allison had left her first message for Chief Holt as she and Josh drove to Columbus Thursday evening. She'd left another message at 6 a.m. Friday.

It was now almost noon and she was increasingly edgy, worried about her patients. The pregnant woman with the stomach rash—Mia McQuigg—had returned earlier in the day because oatmeal baths had not alleviated her symptoms. Allison learned McQuigg had worn belly button jewelry, although she hadn't bought it from Spike. Allison had immediately given her a dose of Prussian Blue and arranged for her to be admitted to a hospital in Charleston. Pringle and Cloninger hadn't been found. Cloninger's boyfriend, Dunn, probably was also suffering.

Beyond that, the source and degree of spread of the contamination had to be identified. Who did Spike sell to? Spike got his metal from Dunn, so who else did Dunn sell to? Where did Dunn get the metal in the first place? Who else got metal from that source? Most importantly, how did the metal get radioactive?

Based on what she'd seen—and she'd been taken aback by the hospital's casual security regarding radioactive materials; the easy code on the door, the keys above the safe, the fact that nothing seemed in place to prevent a terrorist from stealing a shipment of cesium from UPS—healthcare was a possible source. But only that. Nothing supported the idea of an escape of radioactive materials from it or any hospital, much less a connection to body jewelry. Plus, there were other potential sources like mining, construction and government that needed to be considered.

But it was frightening to think of the contamination out there no matter where it came from. The threat to public health was potentially enormous. Alerting Chief Holt couldn't wait. She dialed the department again.

Chief Holt was having a good day. Finally, there was something he and his men could sink their teeth into. Not traffic control for 10k runs, not business license violations, not petty vandalism like a catfish through the newspaper's window. Finally, there was a crime to solve, something that would enable them to be, well, cops. Because both part-time patrolmen were still mopping up at the scene, he was alone in the office when the phone rang. He considered letting the call go to voice mail but decided he'd have to deal with the issue eventually and picked up on the sixth ring. He was incredulous when Allison told him about the radioactive jewelry. "Anybody killed?" he barked.

"No, but—"

"Good, because I'm pretty busy. We found your pal Darryl Dunn dead in his house this morning." Saying it made Holt feel important. This was big news and he was in the middle of it.

Allison couldn't believe it. She had just been there. "What happened?"

"Beaten and shot in the head. He looked like hell." Holt said it like it was the kind of thing he encountered every day.

She tried to imagine the scene. "Suspects?"

"Well, the obvious one is the guy you saw smash Dunn's stuff. We found a baseball bat out there that has his name on it, literally." Holt reached for the incident report. "Spike Lee. Clarence Lee, officially.

We have an APB out for him in six states."

Allison couldn't believe what she was hearing. "Was the girlfriend there, Candi?"

"Cloninger. No. We didn't see her. But I don't think she did it. This was more violent than you usually find with a woman. Dunn must've put up a helluva fight. His hands were pulps. And he must have lost a lot of blood—he was real emaciated, if you know what I mean." Holt hadn't encountered that many dead bodies in his years on the force. Except for Old Cheese Face, Dunn's corpse was the grossest.

Holt's radio squawked. The patrolmen were reporting in. "Gotta go," he said. "Hang on to that jewelry. But right now, I got bigger fish to fry."

Allison hung up reeling. Darryl Dunn would not be answering any questions about who, in addition to Spike, had purchased his metal or where it had originated. Her search for the source of the radioactive metal literally had just come to a dead end.

Then she remembered the records she had taken from his home. Dunn could no longer provide information himself but perhaps the records could. She wondered if the same information she'd intended to use to track down Dunn and Cloninger contained clues to the metal's origins.

She retrieved what she had assumed was Dunn's diary but found it wasn't. After puzzling over the entries, she deduced it was his trucking log book which recorded the pickup and delivery runs he'd made for the past two years. Date. Departure time. Departure location. Beginning odometer mileage. Ending odometer mileage. Arrival time. Estimated fuel used.

She was able to match the log book with bills of lading which documented the contents of the loads and the name of the businesses where Dunn made the pickups. An auto salvage yard was a regular customer where the records showed Dunn picked up junked cars. Other customers included a demolition firm, a mining supply company and two commercial construction companies in Charleston. Those loads were all unhelpfully listed as "waste."

She noted that the hospital in Columbus appeared a half dozen times in Dunn's log. The pickups were recorded as "scrap." Nothing suggested the pickups contained radioactive material but she noticed several of the bills of lading were stamped with the rings and spheres logo of the hospital's Department of Nuclear Medicine.

She went to her computer and emailed the hospital's vice president whom she had met during the visit with Josh. She asked if the hospital had experienced any accidental radiation releases or couldn't account for any radioactive material.

She found contact information for KZ Demolition, H&S Construction, Mountaineer Mining Supply, and the AA Auto Salvage yard. She emailed each similar questions, starting with whether they handled radioactive materials. She was searching for information about three other businesses where Dunn had made pickups when Coretha buzzed.

"Time for rehearsal."

CHAPTER THIRTY-FIVE

Harry Dorn lunged with his five-iron and another new Titleist squirted into deep woods at the Tournament Players Club at Avenal. Dorn swore. He hated golf. It was boring. Pointless. A waste of good real estate. He played only when it was unavoidable.

Today was one of those occasions and if it were possible, his game was even worse than terrible. He had played four holes and picked up on three. On the single hole he had completed, he had taken an eight. The hole had been a 123-yard par three. He had hooked, sliced, dubbed and whiffed. Whiffed! Twice! Even the five-iron, the one club he could sometimes hit, felt alien in his hands. It was as if he were playing a game he'd never played before. Worse, a game at which he was both physically and mentally crippled.

Dorn dropped another ball in the fairway and concentrated on keeping his head down. It was a battle. Sleepless since the interruption of Gibbs' message, he had learned from the morning's *Washington Post* the disturbing news that he had a rival, the popular lieutenant governor, a former football hero. Not that he expected to waltz to the nomination without challenge but he had expected to have weeks, maybe even months of unopposed advantage in shaking the money tree before credible rivals emerged. Now, the fight had already begun.

Dorn swung and another new ball emblazoned with the plant's logo—he had a locker full of them—arced into the Maryland woods.

"Let 'em go," his partner advised. "Once golf balls have had a taste of freedom, they're no good anymore."

Dorn smiled. When the invitation is from a member of the Joint Chiefs—a golf-mad, four-star Air Force general whose driver was fashioned of metal from a dismantled Soviet missile warhead—and when the other member of the threesome is the chairman of Carbon Forward, you play golf, or at least go through the motions.

Lunch mercifully intervened four holes later. With Dorn running perilously low on Titleists and patience, they adjourned to the club's mahogany-paneled grill and ordered Reuben sandwiches and draft beers.

The general untied his golf spikes, stretched, and leaned back in his chair. "You suck at golf. I hope you're a better senator."

Dorn was tempted to respond that it would be difficult not to be. But he had not been a ten-year member of the Foreign Affairs Committee for nothing and he knew the general well. He read the unchanging expression on his leathered face, the knitted forehead accentuated by his silver crew cut, the unblinking, steely eyes, and understood the man wasn't joking. He also knew the general to be a man of precision in everything from his approach shots to his language. *I hope you're a better senator.* The general was presuming his election.

"There's a lot to like about the Liberty Agenda," added the carbon man. Tall, tanned, always gracious in public and with perfect white hair, the chairman gave the impression of a man totally at ease with himself and his business. Even the slogan on his golf shirt—"The Building Block of Life"—was designed, Dorn realized, to make the oil, gas and coal industry sound like an earth-friendly, green organization. In reality, Dorn knew Carbon Forward played hardball and the chairman was an all-star.

"The Liberty Agenda's more powerful than any fanatical religious or totalitarian movement," Dorn added.

"I like the way you're taking on the tree-huggers. If they think the atmosphere's heating up now, just wait until we resume atmospheric nuclear testing," the general laughed. "Just kidding. These new generation neutron nukes are clean as a whistle."

The general waited until the waitress who was delivering their sandwiches departed. "Harry, you've been good for us on Foreign Affairs. Over at the Pentagon, we think your Liberty Agenda is good for freedom, business, the military, everything this country stands for. Tens of thousands of companies employing millions of people do business with the military. They'd all like to see the Liberty Agenda flourish."

"That's good to hear," Dorn said.

The general took a bite of his sandwich. "The military doesn't take sides. We *do* support American ideals. If we put out the word that you'll support us, many executives from those thousands of companies will find a way to give to your campaign and their wives will, too."

"Nothing improper about that, right?" Dorn asked.

"Perfectly legal. For the most part."

Dorn swallowed hard. "For the most part?"

"Well, I'm sure the contributions get reimbursed at some companies. The company submits an invoice for some defense work. Invoice gets paid. Money in the form of a bonus grossed up to account for taxes goes to the executives who contributed. Illegal as hell. We know it works that way sometimes but what are you going to do? In the defense budget, it's small money." The general turned to the carbon man. "What about you, Charlie? Your guys ready to throw in?"

The chairman chuckled. "We still have some decidin' to do." He drained his draft and turned to Dorn. "We've known each other a long time so I'm sure I know the answer. Any skeletons in the closet? Booze? Pills? Girlfriends? Queer relatives or things of that sort?"

Dorn's stomach dropped like he was in a free-falling elevator. Not that he hadn't anticipated probing into his personal life. He just hadn't anticipated it so soon. "No," he joked. "Never had that much fun."

"That's too damned bad!" the chairman roared. "Maybe we just oughta take up a collection to get you laid!"

Dorn laughed weakly. "When do you make your decision?"

"We're meeting next week. With the general's endorsement and the relationship we've had over the years, I'd say it's yours to blow."

Dorn swallowed again. "How much might be involved?"

The general and the chairman looked at each other. The general shrugged. "Ten million, maybe."

"That's the direct money," the chairman added quickly. "Throw in soft money to the party, money to fund the supposedly unaffiliated outside groups—like the Swift Boat people—maybe close to twenty, thirty million. Almost Obama money, at least for a Senate seat."

Dorn did some quick math: There would be little need for additional fund-raising.

Dorn noticed movement outside the grillroom window. Joel Richey. "Pardon me for a moment," he smiled to the general. "I'll be right back."

Dorn found Richey by the putting green, bouncing up and down on his toes like a beered-up Redksins fan waiting for his turn at the urinal. Dressed in a wrinkled black suit, scuffed brown shoes and one of his decades-old ties, Richey looked like he belonged at the Salvation Army instead of a country club. Dorn was embarrassed to be seen with him.

"We gotta talk," Richey said as soon as Dorn got within hearing distance.

"We don't *gotta* do anything."

Richey plunged ahead. "The plant people called. They want to talk to you right away."

"They know how to reach me."

"They want you to call on a secure line."

Dorn saw the general standing by the tenth tee, waving at him with his driver. "We're up," the general yelled.

"I'll be right there," Dorn mouthed so as not to disturb golfers on the practice green. He pulled out his cell phone and started walking away. He turned back to Richey. "Joel, learn how to dress."

CHAPTER THIRTY-SIX

Josh struggled into his buckskins as if he'd never worn them. He got his pants halfway on before he collapsed into his desk chair. He was almost ready to screw the whole thing. Who'd miss another trapper? The festival was frivolous and stupid.

Two weeks earlier, the financial success of the River Days section and getting Katie off to camp had seemed like the most important things in the world. Now, he couldn't care less.

His daughter had cancer, insurance wouldn't pay the bill and the system didn't care. The newspaper's suddenly-in-a-hurry buyers still hadn't returned his phone calls. *Something* about the newspaper had provoked *someone* to vandalism. Fallout like that might happen in Atlanta, not Winston. And Katie had a boyfriend. A boyfriend!

He was depressed, dejected, and done trying to do good for the world. The effort was pointless. It presumed that you had some control over things. If that were the case, Sharon wouldn't be dead and Katie wouldn't be sick. Even with that understanding, he'd always tried to do right. But it was time to quit trying. Look where it led.

He sat there for another ten minutes.

A chestnut mare carrying funeral home owner Mark Cotter costumed as surveyor George Washington pranced in the street. Woody Conroy, the appliance store owner in full uniform as pageant hero General Andrew Lewis, shared a cigarette and a laugh with Shawnee

Chief Cornstalk, his soon-to-be vanquished foe played by barber Bill Booth. "I got a news flash for you," Booth yelled when he saw Josh. "Cornstalk's going to win this year." Josh gave him a weak thumbs-up and kept walking.

Out of force of habit, Josh checked the weather as he stood in a line of costumed characters waiting to be approved by the pageant's several wardrobe mistresses. The weather could determine whether a particular year's festival failed or succeeded. This year, it was starting out perfectly. The summer had not yet turned hot and the air was filled with the smell of growth and fresh-turned soil. The sky was deep blue. The humidity had magically lifted.

In years past, that would have been enough to make him ecstatic.

Josh felt a hand slide down the small of his back and inside the waistband of his leggings. He whirled around to find Hattie Duvall with a measuring tape clenched between her teeth. "Nothing to let out," she said, looking at him disapprovingly. "Drop a few pounds or it's the last year for those leggings."

He felt himself blush. "Maybe you oughta make 'em out of Spandex."

She slapped his butt and sent him on his way. He found himself on a collision course with Allison. His heart went to his throat. Her blonde hair fell from beneath a simple white cap and fanned out across the tops of her bare shoulders, drawing Josh's gaze to her cleavage revealed by the scooped white ruffled blouse which she wore over a long black muslin skirt. He felt enamored, and not for the first time.

She spotted him. "There you are," she said. "You heard about Darryl Dunn."

"Yeah. Holt thinks Spike did it."

"I know, but I don't think so. He could barely hold that baseball bat. And Dunn was shot. How could Spike have gotten his finger on a trigger with his hands messed up? There could be any number of people who had a problem with ol' Darryl. Maybe Candi killed him. Dunn knew from our phone calls we were on his trail about the metal. Maybe his supplier killed Dunn to keep him quiet."

"That's a pretty big leap," Josh cautioned. "I'm thinking Candi. Cherchez la femme." He shrugged. "I guess we'll never know."

Allison was starting to feel frustrated. She took his hands and forced him to look at her. "Josh, I'm really worried. We don't have an idea where this stuff is coming from and how much is out there. We need to go public. We have to warn people. You told Dunn you were going to do a story. Now's the time."

"I'm not so sure."

Allison was incredulous. "We're just going to let it drop?"

"Let's go where we can talk."

"I haven't been through wardrobe approval."

"It's got *my* approval." Feeling like a schoolboy who'd just passed a love note, he held his breath, hoping for some expression of mutual attraction.

"I'll be right back," she said. She patted him on the shoulder and smiled.

It was, he decided, the condescending smile of the head cheerleader asked to the prom by the class geek. He felt like a fool. Obviously, he'd misread things.

They moved to a bench by the river when she returned—the same bench on which he and Sharon used to sit and where he had talked to Katie about her leg.

Josh explained his reasoning. "No question Darryl's murder is a huge deal, but we don't have a story nailed down yet that connects him to dealing in radioactive metal."

"We have Spike."

"One source isn't enough," said the newspaperman. "Plus, the timing's bad. It's two weeks until we print a regular issue again." He wished now that he'd invested in a good website for the *News* instead of agreeing to Bella Partners' request to hold off until the new owners took over.

"You could put it in the River Days special section. We'd be *saving* Winston. It's what a newspaper is *for*."

"Saving Winston? We don't know where the metal's coming from.

We don't even know that there's more out there. Besides, saving Winston has never been on my agenda. I'm not in the business of crusading anymore."

Allison had spent a hard week on the trail of radioactive contamination and a Friday short on her passion—patients—but long on her nemesis—administrivia. She'd done much of it with Josh and she'd become worried about the threat they'd uncovered together. "That's selfish," she shot back.

"Selfish?" Stinging from rejection, Josh felt the blood rush to his face. "*Selfish?* That's something coming from a woman who doesn't have to worry about anybody but herself. You make this big deal about caring for the public—Detroit, Appalachia, wherever 'the public' needs help. You care for patients but do you know what it's like to actually care for a person?"

He regretted lashing out as soon as the words left his mouth. "I'm sorry," he stammered. "I know you want to do the right thing. I do, too. But Katie's facing the fight of her life and I have to be there for her twenty-four/seven. She's . . . all I've got. I failed Sharon. I will not fail Katie, too."

"You're not the only one who grieved when Sharon died. She was my best friend," Allison reminded him. She had come to feel that she and Josh were better together than they were alone—not only in doing what was best for Katie but also investigating the cases of tissue death. Now, he had abandoned her. "Are you sure you're not worried about failing yourself?" she challenged.

"What do you mean by that?"

"I suppose the surest way to never screw up a big story again is to never do another big story."

"That's unfair!"

Preparations had reached fever pitch. A lamb, a goat, and some chickens roamed part of the riverfront park that had been staked out for a petting zoo. Nearby, workers erected a small stage that would be used for The Little Miss River Queen pageant, gymnastic and square dance club exhibitions and demonstrations of household products. On the other side of the street, two water colorists argued over a prime location that provided a place to display work and a picturesque scene for the artist to capture as crowds meandered past. The food vendors, Allison knew, would be the next arrivals, peddling everything from candy apples and cotton candy to shish kabobs and other fare whose connection to the Ohio River, West Virginia, George Washington or anything else being celebrated was remote at best.

She swept her hand over the scene. "We're talking about protecting *them*. You have an obligation to do the story."

"I have an obligation to Katie," Josh said firmly. " . . . To Sharon."

"Sharon's not here anymore. They are."

Allison understood completely his devotion to Katie. She felt badly about calling him selfish. And maybe it had been unfair to bring up Atlanta, even though she was sure what happened there contributed to his reluctance.

But he was also wrong about her. Admittedly, she had a hard time trusting, given everything that had happened. But the fact is, she *did* know what it was like to care for someone. Her doggedness was proof she *did* care for people. She cared for Candi, Wanda, Ricky, Spike and her other patients. She had cared for Sharon. She cared for Katie, especially. She'd always keep that promise to her best friend.

Allison looked at him with an expression between sadness and regret. She leaned over and kissed him tenderly on the cheek, leaving Josh weak-kneed and speechless, his cheek still burning where she had kissed him and his thoughts so jumbled that all he could do was watch her disappear into the crowd.

His eyes caught Vince Bludhorn observing from a distance.

Chapter Thirty-Seven

The bass bellow of a steam whistle rolled through Winston, lingered, and repeated as Allison arrived back at her office. She hurried to an alcove at the end of the second-floor hall that afforded a sightline to the Ohio River. She was joined by Coretha just as the bow of the stately paddle wheel steamer *Cincinnati Queen* slipped into view.

"The *Queen* had a minstrel show back when your daddy was alive. I really looked forward to that."

"Why on earth?"

"It was the only time I could count on seeing another black person in Winston." Coretha turned. "I've had enough for the week. I'm leaving."

"I'm going to be here a while. Lock me in."

A stage-whisper sigh followed from Coretha.

Allison paid no attention. She had already re-immersed herself in Dunn's trucking logs. The records didn't show where he'd delivered the loads but they did show where he had picked them up and how many miles he had driven. During rehearsal she realized she could use fifth grade math to determine where the loads had gone.

She checked a bill of lading from the hospital and found the matching date in Dunn's log book. Dunn had made the hospital pickup and then logged one hundred sixty-six miles to the delivery. The other hospital pickup logs showed the identical distance.

She studied the pickup logs from the auto salvage yard and from Mountaineer Mining Supply and found that the delivery distances for those loads also were identical for each trip—ninety-two miles and thirty-five miles respectively.

She switched on her computer and pulled up MapQuest. She found Columbus and zoomed in to street level. She adjusted the map so the hospital's main building was dead in the middle. She zoomed out, creating a map with 200-mile radius, the hospital at the center. She clicked her mouse and her printer hummed into action.

She retrieved the green plastic compass she'd purchased on her way home from rehearsal. After spreading the compass to a tad over one hundred sixty miles on the map's distance scale, she drew a circle with the hospital at the center.

She repeated the process for AA Auto Salvage and Mountaineer Mining Supply, using the mileage Dunn had driven from each location as the radius of each of the circles.

The circles came close to intersecting near the Ohio-West Virginia border. Allison studied the routes between Dunn's pickup locations and the area where the circles almost overlapped. Adjusting her calculations for bends in the highways, she drew a circle on the map where the routes and distances came closest together—an area the size of a dime, in the hills just outside of Winston.

She noted the coordinates. The drop-off point for Dunn's loads had to be within a few miles, assuming he'd kept accurate logs. She grabbed her IPhone, plotted a route to the coordinates and was surprised to see that she could travel most of the way on paved roads. In a few minutes, she was on the way in her Jeep.

Allison had often heard people describe the Recovery Metals facility in ways they could relate to. Instead of saying a building was five hundred thousand square feet, it was, "bigger than ten football fields."

But as she stood beside her car and looked over the massive aluminum-sided structure at the heart of the operation, Allison realized even those everyday comparisons failed to convey the plant's scale.

Except for a brick-faced area in the front that contained the executive offices, there were no windows in the eight-story building. Ten-foot diameter pipes topped by valves so huge they required two men to open ran in pairs along two sides of the structure, supplying fuel to the giant furnaces central to the facility's mission.

A three hundred-foot smokestack towered over the scene. Visible from every point in town even at night with its two hypnotically blinking red lights, the smokestack was an icon for people in Winston. Particularly during Old Fashioned River Days, it appeared on tee shirts, lapel buttons and porch flags of many families who worked there.

Allison punched the Columbus hospital's address into her phone and asked for the shortest route. One hundred sixty-miles, the device instantly told her. She did the same for AA Auto Supply and Mountaineer Mining. Ninety miles and thirty-five miles. She smiled. She'd hit the final calculation on the nose. No question about it, the plant was Dunn's drop-off place.

She parked and walked to the entrance. A burly guard in a police-like uniform met her at the door.

"Do you have a pass?" he asked.

"I'm just here to ask personnel about a truck driver who delivered here." Allison smiled. "I'm a physician."

"I don't care if you're the Pope. You need a pass."

Allison reddened. "How do I get one?"

The guard handed her the director of personnel's business card. Submit a request in writing, he told her. "They'll get back to you."

Sure, she thought.

She went to the Recovery Metals website when she got back home. It made no mention of the plant handling radioactive material. The federal government's Nuclear Regulatory Commission site confirmed what the radiation safety officer in Columbus had told her. There was no facility that handled high-level nuclear waste from most of the United States. The county landfill in Barnwell, South Carolina once processed low-level material but was closed except to three states. She was at another dead end.

She emailed the plant's personnel director asking for an appointment to talk about Darryl Dunn. Perhaps there was something in his record that would shed some light on his activities and she reasoned that since Dunn was dead, she wouldn't get an argument about violating his privacy.

Before bed, she curled up with Hippocrates and a glass of wine and examined her motives and feelings. She hadn't planned to kiss Josh at the rehearsal, although, looking back, maybe it had been bound to happen. She couldn't help noticing the way he looked at her sometimes. It pleased her to be desired, pleased her especially that she was desired by *him*.

The truth, she had to admit, was that the kiss happened because her feelings for Josh were growing. More than she'd realized. More than she wanted. And that made her care even more.

But he was *so* vulnerable. Was that the basis for his feelings—for *her* feelings—or was it something else?

And even if her feelings were real, what then? Did she even want a meaningful relationship? Relationships meant compromises and she liked being able to make all the decisions.

Beyond that, was she *capable* of a successful, meaningful relationship? So far, there was no evidence of that. She didn't want to lead him on and end up compounding his hurt.

And what about Sharon?

She was dying to talk to him but that would have to wait until morning.

CHAPTER THIRTY-EIGHT

Friday night Josh dreamed he and Allison were having dinner at a restaurant while being waited on by his late wife Sharon. Patrons at other tables struggled to manage silverware with stubs for hands. A parade of one-legged people hobbled by outside, some lurching on crude prostheses, some on crutches, some hopping on single legs.

He awoke in a sweat and completely confused. He was elated, almost giddy, over the kiss from Allison. He'd found it exciting to be kissed by a woman again and Allison was very appealing. More than that, she was smart. He could tell she cared for Katie. And she viewed the world the same way he did.

But he hadn't been prepared for the fact that his attraction was becoming more than physical. He was feeling guilty because of his devotion to Sharon. He wondered if it was even fair for him to be in any serious relationship when he knew in his heart it could never be the same. He'd started the flirting but now he felt like a dog chasing a car. Chasing Allison was irresistible but what would he ever do if he caught her?

Beyond that, he was disappointed in himself. Even though he felt he had journalistic justification not to print anything in the festival section about radioactive jewelry, he knew that in Atlanta, he would have written a story and the desk would have gone with it and the chips would have fallen where they might. Fallout wouldn't have been an issue.

But things were different in Winston. Winston was *his* town and his actions could put his advertisers—*his* guileless friends and neighbors—in economic jeopardy. He envisioned pageants playing to empty seats; brave locals knotted on a nearly deserted Main Street instead of meandering throngs of free-spending tourists. He thought of Woody Conroy, one of his biggest customers, whose store was already struggling against the big box stores and of the Hansons who kept Clayton's Barbeque solvent only by putting every family member to work and by operating a mobile barbecue wagon which showed up at the plant at meal times. All because of an alarm based on pretty scant evidence. People would be angry. And rightfully so.

And angry with him and, by extension, the *Winston News*. And that would be the case even if his and Allison's concerns were justified. What if there was no real threat? What if they were wrong? It happened. How would he explain the imperfections of reporting to a bankrupt Clayton Hanson?

Sale? He'd be lucky if he could give the paper away.

Still, his decision not to publish wasn't sitting well. Winston was Katie's home, Allison's home. Thousands of people were about to arrive. Already, he'd felt like he'd failed them. He ached to call Allison but couldn't decide what to say and abandoned the idea for fear of making a fool of himself.

He got out of bed and went to his computer. Maybe he couldn't do a newspaper story but that wasn't the only way to warn Winston. There *was* something he could do.

It didn't take him long to come up with a one-pager he was happy with. "Jewelry Alert!" the 72-point headline on the flyer screamed. The 18-point body copy urged residents and vendors to purchase jewelry only from trusted sources and to seek medical help if jewelry they had purchased was causing a reaction.

It was 3 a.m. when he arrived at the *Winston News*, the lobby illuminated only by the glow of the soft drink machine. The new transom window was sparkly clean. He ran off two hundred copies of the flyer on the high-speed machine in the mail room, swiped strapping tape and a staple gun from circulation and left as quickly as he had come.

He finished just before dawn and drove to the high bluff. A mile upstream, the Ohio River floated gently through a wide curve, split obligingly for a narrow, wooded island and reunited in a great, wide flood. He had picked this spot for Sharon's grave as much for himself as for her. He found it impossible to be here without being reminded of the cycle of life, the feeling of being part of something larger, a connection to immortality, whether it was the stunning sunsets over the river bend in winter, the unmistakable feeling that generations of humans from the dawn of time had watched this same sun set from this same place and maybe also buried their loved ones there.

That feeling of connectedness, of continuity made it easier for Josh to preserve his relationship with Sharon. In the same way that a tree falling in the forest makes a sound because someone is there to hear it and that a painting becomes art only when someone views it, he believed that relationships existed because of what people held in their heads. What is perceived is what exists. Death would not end their relationship—as long as he didn't let it.

So every week he left flowers here and talked with Sharon. He always knew what she would say. He could hear her words, see her lips pursed in disapproval, feel her smile. She was still here for him and so he had come again. He had no flowers this morning, only a question.

Head bent, Josh looked at the simple headstone and asked it: *Sharon, what do I do?*

And then it came to him. She had already given him the answer years ago, in their talk at the bench by the river.

Josh said he would always be true but Sharon stopped him, stretching a bony finger on a withered arm to hush his lips.

"Don't bury your heart with my body," she said. "Don't forsake the living for the dead and stay married to a ghost."

He lifted her hand and kissed it. Her veins traced blue highways on her parchment skin. "You are all I ever wanted and all I will ever need."

Sharon stiffened. "We have a daughter. I need you—she needs you—to face life as a strong man open to new opportunity. You can't wall yourself off from the world. It's unfair to you and it's unfair to Katie." She withdrew her hand. Josh was surprised at her anger. "You're a great dad. Katie worships you. But you can't be a mother and father both."

"Katie has a mother."

"For now."

"No, goddammit!" Josh howled.

Sharon slid her hand down to his and locked fingers. "You'll have to let me go. Life's for the living . . . and love. But you have to be there."

Josh's mind switched to an image from Sharon's funeral—Katie in the front pew, a phalanx of her schoolmates and teammates filling row after row behind her, a children's army of support. Kids and funerals, Josh mused. Maybe God's way of telling us that life goes on.

He looked at Sharon's gravestone. "I don't want to lose you," he whispered. He selected a perfectly preserved zinnia from one of his old bouquets and folded it into his shirt pocket, next to his heart.

The leaves of the nearby elms rustled. Josh felt a gentle breeze sweep across the bluff—Sharon reassuring him that she had heard him. She understood and was here—would always be here—for him, no matter what.

CHAPTER THIRTY-NINE

JEWELRY ALERT! The words practically sprang off the flyer.

Allison slammed the Wagoneer into park and dashed across the intersection.

She couldn't believe her eyes. Posters had blossomed all over town—on trees, utility polls, even in the window of the Java Joynt. Josh must have been up all night running them off and plastering them everywhere before dawn Saturday morning.

She was thrilled. The poster was perfect. Its warning to avoid buying jewelry from unknown sources and to seek treatment for unexplained skin rashes, infections or intestinal upsets was exactly right.

But the posters were more than a warning about jewelry, Allison knew. They were an apology to her, an incredible commitment, worth so much more than words.

CHAPTER FORTY

Furbee delivered bad news when Josh arrived at the office Saturday morning, deadline day for the River Days section: the Friends of Chief Cornstalk ad still hadn't shown up.

"Maybe we can buy more time," Josh said. "I could have some pizza brought in."

"You're missing the point." Furbee pointed to the parking lot where a half dozen cars and her own low-riding Lincoln waited. "That ad's the only thing standing between the production crew and the rest of their weekend. We have to finish pre-press today if we want to get this delivered before the festival kick-off Wednesday. Make the deadline or forget about sending any of the advertisers a bill.

"There's a solution for the Cornstalk ad," Furbee pressed. "I've talked to some of the staff. We'd like to put a full-page ad in the section—something where people could contribute money to help pay for saving Katie's leg. I'd like to help myself."

Until then, Josh thought he had done a good job putting up a brave front—largely for Katie. He had learned when she was a toddler, as every parent learns, that if he laughed when she fell off the swing, she would laugh and that if he showed he was afraid, she would cry. So he had tried to be brave.

But with Katie absent, he found bravery difficult. Her being away now was too much like her being gone permanently. It was a constant reminder of a joyless future, a preview of a nightmare. It took a moment before he could speak. "I can't tell you how much that means, but we can't use the newspaper for my personal crusade."

"It's not for you, it's for Katie. We'd be paying for it."

He was tempted. But if he were perceived by his readers as using the pages of the *Winston News* for personal gain, the newspaper's credibility would be compromised. It would be his newspaper promoting his family cause, not that it hadn't been done regularly by the most famous of publishers from William Randolph Hearst to Rupert Murdoch. No, the only way he could use the newspaper to raise the money for Katie's operation was to sell it, provided that was still an option. He felt terrible keeping the secret from Furbee. Her life was the *Winston News*.

"Sorry," Josh said. "Use a regular house ad to sub for Cornstalk."

"Please," Furbee pleaded. "I want to do *something*. You're the best boss a person could ever have. And you've kept me on when some people would have turned me out to pasture. We all know how much you love Katie. We want to do something to help her, to help *you*."

Josh felt her need. You had to feel like you were doing *something*. His phone interrupted. It was Allison.

"Thanks for doing the flyers."

"It was the right thing to do."

"Yeah, it was. Josh, another thing. I apologize for being a little forward yesterday."

Josh's heart sank. Was she sorry she'd done it? "It's . . . fine."

"Good. Clinic closes at noon. How about we grab lunch at the diner and I'll fill you in on my research?"

"Best offer I've had all day."

Josh could see the posters piled outside the newspaper's front door when he got to the empty lobby. There were dozens, maybe hundreds, tattered, torn at the staple holes, trailing remnants of strapping tape and pieces of twine. A gust of wind plastered a half-dozen against the glass door. It took ten minutes to scoop up all of them. Allison was already seated when he walked in and dropped the posters on the table in the diner.

"These were stacked outside the newspaper's front door."

She groaned. "They'll all be gone before the festival even gets underway. No one will get the warning."

"No worries. I printed up three hundred extra on neon green paper just in case. We'll put them up the day the festival starts."

Owner Pete Kokenes arrived to take their order. Allison folded her menu. "That's crazy. I thought the posters would be appreciated."

"Well, I can tell you they're not appreciated here," Kokenes volunteered. "One showed up in my window. I'd have torn it down myself if someone hadn't gotten to it first. We don't need that kind of crap, not this time of year."

"Pete, *I* put it there," Josh said. "We have a public health problem. We're trying to warn people."

"Right. And they won't come. Keep it up and you're gonna kill attendance at River Days. That's one-quarter of my annual profit."

"I can't figure out why whoever tore down the posters took them to the newspaper," Josh said as they waited for their orders.

"Because you made them," said Allison.

"Yeah, but who would know that? The newspaper's name wasn't on them. The only people who know we've been investigating the jewelry are the cops, your patients, Darryl Dunn and whoever they might have told. Spike's on the run. We can't find Candi and Darryl's dead."

"The real problem is we still don't know where Dunn got his metal and how much of it is out there," Allison said. "There's got to be some other way we can find out about Dunn's metal dealing." She told Josh about the chilly reception she's received after tracking Dunn's pickups and deliveries to the plant. "Do you think they're hiding something?"

"Nah," Josh said. "Security types are usually cop wannabees who didn't make the grade. They get off on power. Besides, it makes sense that Dunn would deliver scrap to the plant. That's what they do. Half the town owes their paycheck to that place."

Josh saw Allison's disappointment. He put down his fork. "We could go to the paper after lunch and make some phone calls. I used to play poker with the plant's PR guy. Maybe he knows Dunn."

"I walk with the woman who runs information technology."

Furbee met them at the door with news of an attempted ad cancellation in the River Days section.

"Because of the posters?" Allison asked.

Furbee shrugged. "No reason given. People get upset. You won't believe this, but someone actually threw a fish wrapped in a copy of the paper through our transom yesterday."

"Fish-wrapper. Clever. Any explanation?"

"No," Josh said. "That's the weird thing." He showed her the catfish in the freezer.

"That things got problems," Allison said. "Look at those lesions behind the gills."

"I should probably toss it."

"I'll take it. I know a guy at state fish and game who'll want to see it."

Josh called his old poker buddy. He hadn't seen Jerry Baker in years—his seat in the Thursday night games had passed to someone else when Sharon got sick. Baker answered on the third ring.

"Jerry! Josh Gibbs. Long time, no see. You still drawing to those inside straights?"

He waited for a snappy comeback, Baker's trademark. Instead he heard, "Hello, Josh. I didn't expect to hear from you." Baker sounded a bit formal, Josh thought.

"Hey, Jer, I'm hoping to get back in the game someday—win back some of that money you bluffed out of me—but I'm calling because I'm hoping you can help me out."

Silence.

Josh plunged ahead. "Jerry, did you know that guy who got killed the other day? Darryl Dunn? Trucker who maybe delivered to your place."

"I'm sorry, Josh, I can't talk to you."

"Why?"

"Because they—look, I just can't okay?"

"Jerry, consider me a journalist asking the PR man. The guy may have been involved with some contaminated metal."

"I have nothing to say. Not now."

"How about I email you a few questions in case anything changes."

"It's a free country."

"Jer, what's going on? You know you can trust me." He tried a light touch. "I promise I'm not bluffing."

Silence.

"Okay, Jer. Hey, great talking to you. I'm emailing the questions now. And I'll give you a call when I can come to the game." Josh hung up. He turned to Allison, surprised and troubled by Baker's response. "Stonewalled."

"Let's try the in-person approach."

They took the Jeep and Allison was relieved to see Sara Cline's BMW in her driveway when they arrived. Josh hung back as she rang the bell. No one answered. She pressed against a window, straining to see inside. Josh saw the rustle of curtains in an upstairs window. Allison knocked. And knocked again. They left after five minutes when no one came.

"Someone was upstairs," Josh said. "Why would anyone be bothered that we're asking about Dunn?"

"Maybe the problem's not Dunn," Allison said. "Maybe it's me."

"How so?"

"Think about it," Allison said. "Does anyone who works for Vince Bludhorn want to be seen cooperating with his crazy ex-wife?"

"Like he's going to fire them or something?"

"You don't know Vince."

There was pain in her voice, and something else.

"I'm serious. You have no idea what he's capable of. Last week he broke into my house, took Hippocrates for a day, then broke back in and put him back."

"Why?"

"To prove that he can still get to me. To show he's still in control."

Josh raised an eyebrow. "That sounds—"

"Paranoid?" Allison asked. "Maybe so." Over time, she'd come to understand that it was easy to blame her ex for all her problems, including ones that were not his fault. "But as I said, you don't know him like I do. Whatever the case, I'm out of ideas on what to do next."

CHAPTER FORTY-ONE

Dorn could almost hear the chop of the Potomac slapping against the hull of his beloved *Liberty*. Just *thinking* of the twenty-four foot sport fisherman soothed him. Docked at a marina in Lorton, the bobbing boat was his refuge an easy drive from the Capitol. A birthday gift from a coal industry lobbyist, the *Liberty* was Possum Island without the plane trip.

Sitting by his office window in the Rayburn building, he felt the summer sun warming his back. With any luck, he'd be pulling out of his slip at the marina by mid-afternoon Saturday. Shortly after that, he'd be at the fishing hole.

"Harry!" Dan Clendenin's voice snapped Dorn out of his reverie. The sun had been blazing all day and the room heated beyond the capacity of the building's air conditioning. Dorn removed his coat and surveyed the three casually dressed people—two men and a woman—who sat at a table in front of him. Former television journalists, each recognizable, they were now expense items on the Dorn campaign committee's financials. A brilliant move by Clendenin, Dorn thought, to have real media types advising the presumptive new senator on how to deal with the national media. Today, Dorn knew, they would be impersonating the actual journalists who would be grilling the candidate on the Sunday political talk shows—appearances Clendenin had easily arranged once the Dorn campaign ad hit the airwaves and a Harry Dorn interview suddenly became the week's number one media "get." Next question," Clendenin was saying. "Policy-related, if possible."

Dorn put the *Liberty* and Possum Island out of his mind. The importance of Sunday appearances was always magnified by the fact that they usually produced news for two days—on Sunday when they were aired and then again in the Monday morning papers and on television news shows because there was usually little else to report.

Across the room, a phone in a drawer of Dorn's oak desk warbled. It went to voice mail while he fielded a question about whether, as president, he would categorically rule out the use of nuclear weapons by the United States. "Certainly, we would never want to—and never expect to use—such weapons," he said. "But to rule out their use categorically would mean that we should never have developed them and I do not believe that to be the case. In addition to their importance as a deterrent, their development has created thousands of jobs and led to important technological breakthroughs over the years."

Clendenin applauded. "Well done!"

The phone warbled again. Dorn rose to answer it.

"Sit down," Clendenin commanded. "You can call them back. Next question. Hardball!"

The phone went silent just as the woman reporter's voice boomed, "Congressman, have you always been faithful to your wife?"

Dorn twitched but recovered quickly as the phone resumed ringing. "Of course," he smiled. "Excuse me."

He walked to his desk and extracted a ringing silver cell phone from the drawer. He listed for a few seconds, mumbled something and hung up.

Clendenin told the journalists they were free to go. Dorn retreated to his inner sanctum and dialed the secure phone. Clendenin and Richey were waiting when he emerged a minute later. "Bludhorn at the plant," he said.

"What'd *he* want?" Clendenin asked.

Dorn rolled his eyes. "Help, as usual. Some problem that the local paper's digging into. I cut him off. I can't be diddling with every single fine or regulation violation or whatever other mess they've gotten themselves into this time. Besides, it's nothing. Just the *Winston News*."

"I doubt they'd be calling you if it was 'nothing,'" Clendenin said. "And if it's anything, once word gets out, even if it *is* only the *Winston News*, the national press will be like sharks in a feeding frenzy. Every slip-up the plant has ever made will be dragged under the microscope and they'll go from there to the money trail. They'll dig up every dollar you or your campaign ever got from any executive, committee, or business associated with the plant. If you don't believe me"—he gestured to the empty table, where the retired journalists had been—"ask them."

Clendenin reminded Dorn of a doctor confidently predicting the course of a disease.

Clendenin continued, "If the worst happens, we can adopt the Will Rogers strategy: If a mob's after you, stop running and start leading it."

Dorn was appalled. "Turn against the plant?"

"You're not the first politician who's had to run from someone they were in bed with. Perhaps the plant has outlived its usefulness. If anything comes up, you declare yourself shocked—*shocked*—at the plant's problems, this betrayal of public trust," Clendenin continued. "You pledge to return every cent associated with the plant that's ever come your way. Hell, you could even call for hearings."

"Would we have to go that far?"

"If we can prevent a story, none of this is an issue."

"We've got some leverage over the editor," Richey reminded Dorn. "He called a couple of days ago on a health insurance problem he's having. I told him that the Liberty Agenda doesn't support government interference in private enterprise. But there's always room for an exception. And you already have an appearance in Winston for the River Days kickoff."

"Do nothing for now," Dorn decided. "Ideally, there's no story. But if a story does get out, Bludhorn's on his own."

....

CHAPTER FORTY-TWO

Chief Holt squealed into the newspaper's parking lot just as Allison was climbing into the Wagoneer. Good timing, he thought. The doctor and the editor were making his life difficult. It needed to stop. He rolled down his window and halted her with a hand. "Cool your jets, Dr. Quinn, medicine woman."

Holt got out of the patrol car. The chief's day had started badly with a reminder from Viggy that he was overdue again. Then, he'd been told to prevent unauthorized people from talking to plant personnel. For whatever reason, the contact was a problem for his employers and that made it a problem for Holt. Another one. One he didn't need. The call had interrupted practice at the range. Holt was still his wearing camouflage jacket.

Josh had emerged from the newspaper building. "What's this about?" he asked.

"You know exactly what," Holt snapped. "We've got Old Fashioned River Days. We've got a murder. Then you come along with the warning signs, the snooping at the plant, all this uproar about radioactive jewelry. Like we have nothing else to do."

"Chief, it's not just about jewelry," Allison argued. "We could be looking at a health emergency. We need to protect the public."

"Which should be your job," Josh injected.

"Screw you." It was all Holt could do to keep himself from decking the editor.

Allison took a deep breath. They needed cooperation, not confrontation. "Chief," she said calmly, "I know you're maxed out with River Days. But exposure to radioactivity can be deadly. People have already been hurt."

"Wackos with nipple rings," Holt snorted. "Instead of worrying about radioactivity, how about helping us find that Spike character. Now there's a real killer."

"He didn't do it," Allison said firmly. "He couldn't even hold a bat when we saw him, much less pull a trigger."

"It was him or another one of Dunn's drug customers. The guy was a meth dealer. We found all the equipment." Holt was certain of his facts. He personally had found the meth cooker.

Allison didn't see how that could be. She hadn't seen any signs of drug use by Spike or evidence of sales by Dunn on either visit. With her experience in Detroit, she knew what to look for. But perhaps she had overlooked something. "Even if Dunn was a meth dealer, that doesn't change the fact that he was selling radioactive metal," Allison said. "We don't know how he got it but we do know he made pickups at places that handle radioactive material and that he delivered many of his loads to the plant."

"They're stonewalling us for information," Josh added. "That always makes me suspicious."

"Get over it. They're just private. I know. I moonlight up there from time to time." Holt saw a look pass between Josh and Allison and realized he'd made a mistake.

Josh was incredulous. "Seems to me your moonlighting is serving two masters—the town and the plant. That's a conflict of interest."

Holt was incensed. His work was private. He never let the plant take priority over his work for the taxpayers. Not only that, the question was patently unfair. If anyone ever compared the hours he worked versus what he was paid, he wouldn't be getting the minimum wage. "My loyalty's to Winston but if Winston wants a chief who doesn't need a second job just to pay the bills, then it needs to raise the pay, pure and simple. You know what I get paid to be the police chief? Forty-two grand. I need the money." Anyway, he was thinking about giving it up. He needed the money but the plant people were becoming increasingly demanding.

"Plenty of families live on that."

I could, too, if the Reds could hold a lead, Holt thought.

"Have you heard anything about problems while you've been working at the plant?" Allison asked.

Holt shook his head. If there had been any, no one had told him. "I keep people out. That's all I do."

"You're a law enforcement officer," Josh protested. "You *have* to be aware of things."

Allison wasn't so sure. She had great confidence in her ability to read people. As she watched Holt rub the lenses of his glasses with his shirt, as if cleaning them would somehow bring the picture into focus, she was inclined to think he was telling the truth.

Seeing Josh ready for another assault, she stepped in. "Chief, ask your bosses at the plant if there have been any radioactivity problems. You decide what to do from there."

Allison's question about problems had made Holt curious enough that he had already decided to make some inquiries—but discretely, not in the direct manner Allison had in mind. Meanwhile, he needed them to back off. "I'll ask around but you should cool it. They've never taken kindly to people who stick their noses into their business—whether it's unions or federal regulators. Or for that matter, the local doctor or the local newspaper editor. Watch yourself."

Allison nodded. Holt looked at Josh who nodded, too. Holt felt satisfied that the message had gotten across, that he had done his job. Best case, he could report that he had succeeded in calling off the dogs. At minimum, he had bought some time. He returned to his car and drove off.

"All bark, no bite," Josh said. "Empty threats from a lackey."

Allison believed Holt. She thought she'd seen fear in the police chief.

Josh looked at his watch. "It's late. Let's meet at my place tomorrow morning and figure out where to go from here."

Josh's phone rang just as Allison's tail lights faded from sight. Katie's cell phone. To be used at camp only in emergencies. His heart skipped. "Hi, sweetheart. Everything okay?"

The shrieks and laughter of teenage girls reassured him even before Katie spoke.

"Hi, Dad. I'm fine. I had to use my cell because someone's on the lodge phone. I have to talk fast because my battery is low and I didn't bring my charger. Can I stay for the second part? I'm having a really great time."

Josh heard a girl shout in the background. "Let Katie stay!"

He had anticipated such a last-minute appeal.

"Please, Dad. All my friends are staying."

There was no way. Just today he'd received a letter from Dr. Pepper about the pre-admission procedure for Katie. He wanted her there early Tuesday for the pre-operative work-ups. His hand-written postscript—"Time is of the essence!"—had been underlined.

"I'm sorry, Katie, but you know the situation."

"Puhleeze," she pleaded.

"You can go for both sessions next year."

Katie would have none of it. "I don't see how a few more days matter. Besides, my leg feels fine."

Josh held firm. "Sorry. Doctor's orders."

"That's so mean!"

He swallowed hard and changed the subject. "Tell me some news."

"I got camper of the week."

"That's wonderful," he said brightly. "I'm very proud of you."

"I gotta go now. Campfire is in fifteen minutes. I guess I'll see you Monday." She made no effort to disguise her disappointment. Katie's tone reminded Josh that for all her virtues, Katie was quite capable of being a sullen teenager.

Josh felt terrible. No parent ever liked to disappoint their child and Katie had already endured a lifetime's worth of disappointment. He told her he loved her and hung up. It was a while before he could stand.

He was about to lock the newspaper's front door when he became aware of the rhythmic sound of the copying machine coming from the business office.

Inside, he saw a table full of clean glass jars and Furbee hunched over a machine that was spewing out copy after copy of a poster. The big type at the top of the poster read, "We Can Save Her Leg!" Underneath was a photograph of his daughter.

....

CHAPTER FORTY-THREE

Dorn steeled himself as his cab arrived at Vivace, one of his regular Georgetown haunts since he was first elected to Congress. He hopped out, opened the door for his wife Sally and whisked her into the busy restaurant.

Heads swivelled to track him. He sighed. Advice and requests for autographs were sure to follow.

There was a time not so long ago, Dorn recalled wistfully, when truce was observed in Washington, D.C. starting at quitting time on Fridays. When senators and congressmen called a temporary halt to the political wars and launched no broadsides, fired off no statements, initiated no ideological offensives. When even the most dedicated lobbyist refrained from the usual well-financed incursions to claim territory in the heart and mind, and golf became simply about putting the ball in the hole and winning the card game afterward.

When—except for the pro-forma Sunday morning political talk shows and shooting footage of the President at church—even the media disarmed, content to subsist until Monday on stories about buses plunging into ravines in South America or ferry disasters in the Indian subcontinent.

Back then, Dorn could fish Saturday afternoon, then go to dinner in Georgetown with his wife and have a drink, or maybe several, plan for the week ahead and never be asked for his position on an issue or even be recognized.

All this had ended with the advent of twenty-four hour cable news and the Internet.

Now, he couldn't go anywhere without people yelling at him— usually just, "Hey, Harry" for some reason—or asking him to stop and pose with them for pictures. Only a few days ago, he had been amused to encounter a time-saving alternative—a sidewalk entrepreneur charging tourists $10 to be photographed with a life-size stand-up of him that came from God-knew-where.

He was relieved to see his favorite maitre d' sweep quickly toward him. The maitre d' dramatically kissed Mrs. Dorn's hand and hugged the congressman like a long-lost friend.

"The balcony this evening?"

Dorn was tempted. Not only was a balcony table a spot to see in, it was a spot to *be seen* in, a wonderful venue for a politician intent on staying in the public eye. But not on Saturday night with no truce in place. "Perhaps the Red Room . . . if it's available?"

The maitre d' bowed grandly. "Of course. Follow me." He led the Dorns past walls with custom reliefs and Italian tiles down a hall past another dining room and into an alcove with a baroque red wallpaper, red oak floors and a single table. "*Godere*," he said, exiting with another sweeping bow.

Dorn pulled out a chair for his wife of thirty-eight years and seated himself.

Washington society regarded their long marriage as quaint, their weekend dinner tradition as charming. In fact, Dorn knew—and he knew that his wife knew—these days theirs was largely a marriage of convenient mutual admiration where sex had ceased being a matter of importance. She enjoyed the perks and the status. He enjoyed the political benefit of appearing to be an unquestionably devoted husband. They both valued the social convenience.

Dorn ordered a Manhattan for Sally and a double scotch on the rocks with a twist for himself and tried to focus his attention fully on his wife.

He had learned that much in his marriage could be forgiven, even frequent absences and suspicions of infidelity, if he devoted his complete attention to Sally even for just a few hours a week. That was particularly true if he divulged enough Capitol Hill truth and gossip during their leisurely dinners to allow Sally herself to feel like an insider with information she could in turn selectively share.

And making someone feel special, that they were the only other person in the room, was something he was good at. Continuous eye contact and the appearance of complete attention was a trick Dorn had mastered and applied not only to to his political life but also to his relationship with Sally.

Their drinks arrived. Dorn began by reviewing the pork for West Virginia that he'd buried in the current version of an omnibus spending bill—including, he proudly pointed out, a $150,000 grant for Sally's pet cause, the West Virginia Association of Animal Shelters.

Soft buzzing interrupted his discourse. Dorn withdrew his phone and silenced the annoyance. Two buzzes let him know the caller had left a message Dorn squinted at the incoming number. *Vince Bludhorn, the pest!* With growing irritation, he slid the phone into his pocket.

His blood pressure soared when it buzzed with a text message as the waiter took their orders. Bludhorn again. *Call ASAP!*

Dorn was steaming.

"Turn the thing off, dear," Sally said sweetly. "The world will go on."

Dorn tried to smile. "I apologize, dear, but I need to take care of this. I promise there will be no more interruptions." He ignored the turning of heads and slipped out to the sidewalk.

Bludhorn answered on the first ring. Dorn wasted no time on pleasantries. "Vince, forget it."

"Hold it, Harry," the lawyer barked. "Hear me out. We've got a problem down here—"

"And you need me to call someone, blah, blah, blah."

"Listen to me!" Bludhorn shouted. He paused. Dorn could hear him breathing. "This is not going to go away that easily. The newspaper editor's poking around, apparently prompted by my ex-wife, Little Miss Do-Good Doctor, the bitch! God, she's trouble!"

"And you can't handle your problem yourselves?"

"We have some leverage and we're using every bit of it. But we need someone to talk to the editor, at least buy us time."

Dorn had to cut the cord. "I can't help," he said firmly. "What would I say to stop a story anyway?"

"Tell him it's national security. Tell him the government requests his cooperation. Offer him Secretary of State."

"Vince, you need to switch to decaf."

"Harry, do I need to remind you that you wouldn't be where you are without us?"

"I appreciate all you've done but if you've got your ass in a crack over something that's going to reflect badly on me and the Liberty Agenda, I'll be returning everything you ever sent me. With interest." Dorn ended the call. He was feeling much better. Independence was good.

Seconds later, his phone buzzed with a text from Bludhorn. He opened the attached photo: himself and a young girl. Both naked.

He felt ill. He'd relegated this particular worry to the back of his mind, but now it was here. When he'd started in politics, side action was acceptable—as long as it was outside your area code. And Joel Richey—no doubt diverting a few for his own purposes—had proven adept at procuring anonymous and accommodating young women who made sure Dorn was never lonely on the road unless he wanted to be. But months earlier, Dorn had made a solemn vow he would stop because if you aspire to be President of the United States, the country itself was your area code.

He examined the photo. Even in the tiny screen, he was easily identifiable. He remembered the girl. The occasion had been memorably delicious because the girl had arrived with a young friend—a friend, he only now ruefully realized—who must have snapped their photo with her cell phone.

But how would the plant know about these women?

He speed-dialed Bludhorn. "How'd you get this?"

Bludhorn chucked. "Harry, where do you think the girls came from? Surely you don't believe Joel found them on his own."

Dorn slumped. He looked to see if anyone was in earshot. "I'm not the first politician running for president who's chased a few skirts. Clinton, Kennedy, FDR. Hell, even Eisenhower. Any more, who cares?"

"About fifteen-year-olds, they care."

Dorn leaned into the wall to steady himself. Fifteen? He'd never even thought to ask. How stupid he'd been! "Tough to prove," he croaked.

"Is it?"

Dorn found his focus hijacked by a whirl of mental pictures; a headline reading *Dorn Had Sex with 15-Year-Olds;* an image of his Sally and their children; an image of himself wearing prison orange. *So close* he'd been to freeing himself of the plant. Now, they had him by the balls.

He felt a tap on his shoulder. He turned to see two women, one holding a camera. "Congressman," one said, "could we have our picture taken with you?"

"Hold on," he told Bludhorn. With incredible effort, he morphed into Congressman Dorn, the political up-and-comer. Welcoming. Friendly. Trustworthy. The woman with the camera persuaded a passerby to snap several photographs.

Dorn raised the phone. Took a breath. Asked, "What do you want me to do?"

Chapter Forty-Four

Pleading the need to catch up on his reading, Dorn holed up in his study when Sally left early for church. When he was sure she would not be returning for some forgotten item, he latched the door, unlocked the bottom drawer of his office desk, removed the false bottom and withdrew a worn hardback copy of *War and Peace.* He removed the contents concealed in its hollowed-out pages, walked swiftly to a nearby apartment building and ditched the book in a dumpster.

The contents—mementos, trophies from the past—needed to be completely and immediately destroyed. Destruction would be liberating, representing the end of the person he had sometimes been. Filled with determination, he lit the dual burners on the Thermador gas grill on his patio, distributed the girls' underwear over the surface, closed the cover and pledged he would be worthy of his office.

Now, to the tougher issue—defusing the threat from the newspaper editor, Gibbs. It had kept him up all night. He could try the sledgehammer approach—"stay out of this, the government is aware and knows best"—but he'd found that usually only raised journalistic antennae. Beyond that, the only leverage he had was what amounted to bribes—perhaps the offer of a well-paying media relations position in the campaign or, as Richey had suggested, intervening with the insurance company on behalf of the editor's daughter. If he wanted to go that route, he'd have to manufacture a subtle approach—nothing as obvious as "stop your investigation and I'll help your daughter."

Either approach required him to acknowledge being aware of the plant's problem. For the briefest moment, the thought crossed his mind that he should resign his seat, abandon his campaign for the Senate and end the scrutiny. But even that wouldn't get him out of the jam he was in. If Bludhorn ever leaked word about the girls, his life would be over, whether he was a candidate for the top office in the land, a member of the U.S. House, or just a citizen.

He'd start with the subtle approach, he decided. He monitored the clock anxiously until 10 a.m. and dialed Gibbs.

"Good morning, Mr. Editor! This is Harry Dorn."

Josh sat up straight in bed. It *sounded* like Dorn. Still, a Sunday morning prank wasn't beyond the imagination of his buddies from the Atlanta newspaper days. "Right," he answered neutrally.

"Congressman Harry Dorn. I hope I haven't interrupted your morning. I called because I'm coming to town for River Days. I'd like to see you."

Josh still thought his leg might be being pulled. "Sure," he said.

"Great. Tell me how things are with your daughter?"

It really *was* Dorn. Hope flickered. Josh quickly suppressed it, lest the gods consider it blasphemous. "Thank you for asking," he said carefully. "We start treatment Tuesday."

"Joel Richey said you could use some assistance. I don't think he fully understood the issue. Let's talk about that when we get together."

Josh dared to speak the words. "Are you saying you might be able to help?"

"We'll see. When are you available?"

"Anytime. I have no deadlines except for getting Katie to the hospital. The River Days section prints tomorrow. We don't publish news pages for a couple of weeks."

"Two weeks? There's no paper for two weeks?"

"No."

Dorn couldn't believe his good fortune. No paper. No story. No problem. The plant had the time it needed. He hadn't needed to mention the words radiation *or* investigation. He wouldn't be required to pull any strings with an insurance company. He actually no longer needed to meet with the editor. But since he'd brought it up, backing out now would be awkward. "I'm coming to town this evening," he said. "How about I swing by the office tomorrow morning, say around nine?"

"Perfect," Josh said. "Let me tell you again how grateful I am . . . I mean, that you'd even consider helping."

Dorn hung up and congratulated himself on his luck. Sally returned home from church a few minutes later and, as she had for years, helped him pack for his trip.

....

CHAPTER FORTY-FIVE

Dead flowers in the window boxes. Cobwebs in the corners of the overhanging porch. Shrubbery in need of trimming. Nice place but suffering from the prolonged bachelorhood of its occupant, Allison decided. She picked the Sunday paper from Josh's front stoop and rang the doorbell.

The smell of oatmeal cookies wafted out when Josh opened the door, comforting aromatherapy on a cool, gray day. Maybe she'd been wrong to convict him of domestic neglect. "Smells delicious," she said.

"For Katie. I thought I'd be done by the time you got here. Hopefully, this next batch will work and we can figure out where to go from here."

Allison chiseled a cookie from the sheet and bit into it. It was as thin as a quarter and almost as hard. Her father would have called the cookie a "misadventure"—his word for a botched medical procedure. She had a different term for Josh's kitchen performance: malpractice.

Josh began mixing another batch. Only when he spooned a silver dollar-sized portion on to the cookie sheet and began flattening the mound with a spatula, did she react. "Don't flatten them. Do it like this." She grabbed a tablespoon and dropped a dollop of the mixture onto the cookie sheet, leaving it rough and mounded. "See if that doesn't make a difference."

Josh poured coffee and they adjourned to a table in an alcove of the kitchen.

"I got some hopeful news this morning." Josh told Allison about the call from Dorn and the meeting scheduled for the next day.

"We should tell him about the radioactivity," Allison interrupted.

"Chief Holt can't or won't help. The state guys are away. Tomorrow's the perfect opportunity to get the feds involved."

"Good thinking," Josh said. "Our meeting's at the newspaper office at 9 a.m. You should come."

Allison's beeper and the stove timer sounded simultaneously. Josh pulled the cookies from the oven. Perfect. Allison checked her page.

"Not a number I recognize," she said. She punched the numbers into her phone.

A frown crossed her face. "You're kidding." She made notes in the margin of the newspaper.

Josh tried to read them but they were in the illegible scrawl that physicians used for prescriptions. "Where is it now?" she asked. "What's their time frame? You'll need to get tested right away. Don't wait."

She hung up. "This is getting stranger all the time. The fish that crashed through your transom was hot. Radioactive."

"You're kidding!"

"That was Carl McGraw. He took the fish to the state fish and game offices this morning. The radiation detectors they got after 9-11 went crazy. They're keeping it in a biohazard box until they can figure out whether it's a matter for the Health Department, Natural Resources, the Nuclear Regulatory Commission or the EPA."

Josh was reeling. He tried to reconstruct his encounters with the catfish.

"Allison, I touched that fish. So did Maude. Others too, maybe. There's gotta be antidotes, treatments."

Treatments. The nightmare had looped and was beginning again. First, a medical catastrophe for his wife. Next, his daughter. Now, the agents of sickness and death had their sights on him.

Allison was bombarded with a thousand thoughts. The radiation contamination issue had suddenly assumed huge new dimensions. Using her emergency room training, she performed a sort of mental triage to help her take stock. The most immediate issue was a panicked Josh Gibbs.

"Everyone who was exposed to it will need to get tested but odds are there's nothing to worry about," she said. In fact, she was anything but confident. She had no idea how radioactive the fish was. That made all the difference in terms of degree of exposure.

Josh wasn't fooled. "But we don't know for sure."

"Right. We don't know."

"A radioactive fish," Josh said, still disbelieving.

"There's more," Allison said. She consulted her notes. Nothing in her training had prepared her to deliver this kind of news.

"They found a rolled-up letter in the fish's mouth. It was mostly illegible but they could identify a few letters and one complete word—CURSE. Carl says the state crime lab is working to decipher the rest of it but their theory is someone was trying to harm you."

Josh was incredulous. "I don't have any enemies."

"You've made *somebody* unhappy."

"I don't buy it. If they were after me, there are better ways to—"

"I agree. But if you're right, we have an even bigger problem. If someone didn't contaminate that fish to hurt the newspaper or you, then it got contaminated on its own. And if that's the case, we're not just dealing with contaminated jewelry. Radioactive material may be wherever that fish lived, maybe even in the water supply." The notion was mind-boggling.

Josh's head spun. Either he was a target or the contamination was far more widespread than they had imagined. "I want to see that note," he said. "Get your guy to fax over a copy."

CHAPTER FORTY-SIX

Dorn felt liberated Sunday afternoon as he boarded Carbon Forward's Cessna Citation Five for the trip to West Virginia.

"Big day tomorrow," Clendenin noted. "Decision day for the carbon boys."

An hour later a hand pushed aside the curtain separating the cockpit from the passenger compartment. The co-pilot twisted around to face them. "I'll make a low pass over Winston before we approach Charleston. The weather's not great but it's still quite a sight."

Dorn gave a thumbs-up. The jet descended from a clear blue sky into a thick layer of gray clouds. Rain appeared on the windows. Dorn sensed the plane was dropping but visibility was zero and he couldn't tell. Just as he was getting nervous, the plane dropped below the clouds and leveled off—still comfortably above the ground but low enough so that he could see houses, fields, streams and roads.

The first thing Dorn noticed was the RVs. Short of when the WVU Mountaineers were headed to an undefeated season and Morgantown became a parking lot on six fall Saturdays, he'd never seen so many land yachts at one time. And the community itself seemed to have doubled in size geographically, principally because of the midway that extended all the way through Winston and ended in a carnival, already up and going, long neon tubes brightening the afternoon gloom.

"Wow!" Dorn breathed.

"Woodstock!" the pilot yelled over the engine roar. He hit the throttle. The jet gained altitude and banked toward Charleston, providing Dorn a magnificent view of the river, the fold in the ridges, and, in the distance, the blinking red lights on the towering smokestack of the plant.

The limousine carrying the candidate and his aide pulled into the Sternwheeler Hotel in Winston after 9 p.m. Dorn would have much preferred to stay at Possum Island and come to town in his SUV in the morning. But the organizers had worried about traffic and timing. He had just enough time to unpack before Clendenin knocked and entered with an ice bucket and a thick black briefcase that Dorn knew contained a bottle of Old Forrester Kentucky bourbon.

Clendenin made drinks. Dorn switched on the 10 p.m. television news from Charleston. The third story included footage shot in Winston that afternoon of tourists arriving for the kickoff of River Days. Dorn heard the anchor mention that Senate frontrunner and local hero

Harry Dorn would be speaking at ceremonies Tuesday. He raised the volume. "Listen to this," he shouted.

Clendenin rushed in just as footage of Dorn speaking appeared on the screen. "It's the speech from the commercial," Dorn said in amazement.

"Getting great coverage. We never paid to run that ad outside of Washington. Now it's on the local TV news and it's gone viral on YouTube."

Dorn chugged his bourbon and immediately made himself another.

When the news was over, Clendenin left for his room. Dorn removed his trousers and stretched out on the bed. The exhilaration of making a fresh, clean start was fading. The bourbon and the hotel room were resurrecting memories that were better left buried. He scrolled through his catalogue of encounters, each tagged with a scent, a sensation or another cue that triggered the replay. He was quickly aroused.

He got up and poured a third drink to knock him out until morning. Tapping came from his hotel room door. "Clendenin?" he asked.

No answer. Light knocking again. Dorn peered through the peephole. His knees weakened. He eased the door open until the safety chain pulled tight. He peered through the crack.

A sweet young face smiled back at him. "I thought you might like some company."

Dorn intended to be strong. "Who sent you?"

The girl looked hurt. "No one."

Dorn desperately wanted to believe her. He looked again—heavy eye makeup, low-cut blouse. In the worst case, he reasoned, he could contend he thought she was at least eighteen. Longing melted logic and his resolve. Ardor defeated intellect.

This time would truly be the last, he promised himself. This was not failure—just a farewell to a former acquaintance, like an alcoholic having one last drink before swearing off liquor forever.

He unlatched the door.

CHAPTER FORTY-SEVEN

"You're making it difficult this morning."

Allison's bed partner responded with a guttural grumble and snuggled closer.

"I'd love nothing more than to stay in bed with you, Hippocrates, but I've got a huge day ahead." She slipped from the covers so as not to disturb the snoozing cat.

She selected a pantsuit for the meeting with Josh and Dorn. Inspecting herself in the mirror, she concluded she'd need to put aside her distaste for shopping and acquire something less dowdy for the River Days ball even though she was attending as a single.

She said goodbye to Hippocrates, set the alarm, locked the door and walked to her car through a light drizzle. A padded manila envelope sat on the passenger seat. She stopped, looked around for whoever had left this for her.

Spotting no one, she slid into the car and picked it up. The package contained a disc—perhaps, she thought, one of the DVDs drug and medical equipment company sales reps desperately tried to get her to watch.

She turned the package over. The mailing and return addresses were blank. The only identifying feature was her name. She tore the envelope open. No letter or press release, just a DVD. She read its hand-written label and her body turned to ice.

Chapter Forty-Eight

Josh checked the parking lot for the tenth time. Still no sign of Allison. It was unlike her to be late. Dorn was due at any minute. He punched her number on his speed dial and got voice mail—again. He slammed the phone shut in frustration. He was about to jump out of his skin.

He was coming off a sleepless Sunday night, his mind ping-ponging between wondering who was out to get him and all the things that would be decided in the next forty-eight hours, starting with his daughter's leg. Much hinged on this meeting with Dorn.

Consuming two 'Counselors' at the Java Joynt while lingering on a mistaken hunch that he'd encounter Vince Bludhorn had stretched his nerves even tighter.

Then he'd arrived at his office to find a note pinned to the back of his office chair and his voice mail button blinking like crazy. The note was from a production supervisor: the regular ink delivery had been mysteriously cancelled. The weekly press run had left the *News* almost out. The voice mails were from advertisers withdrawing their ads from the River Days section—first a car dealer, then the drug store, then the bank.

Customers canceling ads was hardly an unknown phenomenon. A product might not arrive at the store on time and an ad would need to be pulled. Cash flow problems sometimes intervened, although it was usually the publisher who decided to pull the ad since, unlike a car or a television set, the ad could not be repossessed.

But only the bank vice president mentioned a reason. "We're not going to support tabloid trash investigations."

He was about to phone the advertisers when Dorn's SUV wheeled into the visitor spot at the *News*.

Dorn killed the engine. The scent of the girl rose fleetingly from somewhere and he was swept by arousal, then shame. But that was behind him. So was his relationship with the plant. But it wouldn't be the messy, perilous divorce that Clendenin had suggested. Instead, it would be gradual, like an office affair that cools without recriminations when novelty wears off and practicality sinks in.

The easy exit was possible because, thankfully, the *News* would not publish for two weeks. He hadn't even needed to use his leverage to keep the paper from publishing whatever it was pursuing regarding the plant, although it would be ideal if Bludhorn believed his efforts had actually led to the news blackout. For that reason, he would help the editor with his daughter. It figured to be a quick meeting. He cracked the car door, popped open his umbrella and stepped into the rain.

Allison still hadn't shown up by the time Dorn settled into a chair in Josh's office. The congressman didn't waste time. "How's your little girl?"

"Scared, I imagine. I know I am. She's home from camp this afternoon and then it's off to the hospital tomorrow."

"Well, let me remove one of your worries. I came by to tell you I'm going to contact your insurance company first thing when I get back to Washington. And they'll listen. Makes a nice impression when they get a call from Capitol Hill. No one wants questions from government regulators."

Josh shook Dorn's hand. "This is wonderful! This means everything." A guilty twinge tempered his elation. "I hate asking for a special favor."

"Nonsense. Constituent service."

Josh swallowed any unease. "On those terms, agreed." He would never have accepted Dorn's favor on his own behalf, but for Katie there were no lines he would not cross.

"Glad we can help. Joel Richey will get back to you on the details." Dorn stood and extended his hand. "Sorry to run but I know you have a lot ahead of you. If there's nothing else—" Dorn felt he had made a mistake as soon as the words left his mouth.

"As a matter of fact, there *is* something else."

"I only have a minute," Dorn backpedaled.

"A couple of weeks ago, a local physician started seeing people suffering radiation injuries from body jewelry. Nipple rings, that sort of thing. We traced the jewelry to a roadside dealer and from there to a truck driver who was supplying the metal. Before we could find him, he was murdered."

Dorn's stomach sank. He had a bad feeling about where this was headed. He adopted an expression that he used for congressional hearings that said "attentive" but revealed no bias.

"There's more. A few days ago someone threw a catfish through our office window. It, too, turned out to be radioactive."

Alarms sounded in Dorn's head. He felt immediately that the murdered truck driver was related to Bludhorn's "problem" although nothing had been said to indicate that. "Who's aware of this?" he asked cautiously.

"The local police. And several state agencies are aware of parts of it. But Chief Holt's overwhelmed and the key state people are away. We put up posters to warn people about the jewelry but a lot got torn down. We have more posters but, Congressman, we need federal help. We have tens of thousands of people coming to town."

Dorn relaxed a little. Contaminated jewelry and a murder, bad as they were, didn't rise to the level of congressional attention, especially with the local authorities already involved. The newspaper editor hadn't even mentioned the plant. His biggest problem might be how to satisfy the editor that he was making a difference while actually doing nothing.

"Radioactive catfish," Dorn said. "Sounds like what happened with one of the tabloids. Had Anthrax mailed to it. Same nut sent some to members of the House."

Josh remembered the incident well. The anthrax had killed a photographer. The newspaper building had to be abandoned for five years.

"The posters were a fine idea," Dorn commended. "It sounds like the appropriate local authorities are aware of the killing and jewelry. I don't know what alphabet agency this falls under but I'll look into it as soon as I'm back in the office. Meanwhile, I think you can relax."

"Maybe we could—"

Dorn patted Josh on the back. "You've done all you can. Allow the authorities to do their jobs. See to what's important to you. Take care of your little girl. Leave the rest to me."

Back in his car, Dorn debated whether to call Bludhorn. The situation had become unnerving. On the one hand, he really needed to know the facts to prepare himself in the event that he'd have some explaining to do. On the other hand, he might learn more than he wanted. There was a lot to be said for deniability.

Curiosity got the better of him. He called Vince and asked his questions carefully.

"This problem, was there anything dangerous involved?"

"Depends on your definition," Bludhorn said cooly. "Crossing the street's dangerous." Dorn took that as confirmation.

"Did it involve a death?"

"Harry, there are going to be regrettable accidents, even fatalities, in any industrial situation."

Dorn's stomach sank. "Did you know about this when I was down there?"

"It was *handled* at that time."

Dorn hung up. He felt ill. These plant people were crazy. Clendenin was right. He needed to break the bonds as fast as he could.

CHAPTER FORTY-NINE

When his attempts to reach Allison failed, Josh drove to her condo. The Wagoneer was parked in its usual spot. He rang the doorbell and knocked. No one answered. He trooped around back, scaled a plank fence and dropped onto the rain-slicked patio. The door was unlocked. Hippocrates scooted out as Josh stepped in.

He found himself in Allison's bedroom. Her bed was unmade. A beige bra lay strewn on the floor. A silky nightgown pooled on the seat of a chair. Josh took a deep breath. The place smelled feminine, intimate. The only light came from a television which flickered silently in the corner with the image of a naked woman. Allison.

He watched transfixed. Even for a jaded newsman, the images were shocking, well beyond commercial pornography. The DVD loop began to repeat. He could not tear himself away. Josh stepped closer. He studied Allison's face. Was she aware she was being recorded? He was stunned by what he saw and horrified by his fascination with it. What kind of sick bastard got pleasure from humiliating someone like Allison he would never know. He felt his rage building. Feeling like a participant in Allison's violation, he grabbed the remote, snapped off the video and turned on the overhead light.

His heart stopped. Allison stood in the doorway. Gone was the poised, confident physician. She looked half dead. He'd seen the look before—in disaster survivors and on the faces of people after the bombing at the Atlanta Olympic Games. He rushed to her and drew her tightly to him.

Allison pushed away. "Get away from me," she said woodenly.

Josh took a step forward. "Are you okay—?"

She lashed out at him with both arms. Josh grabbed her wrists and pinned them to her sides. She fought to get free but Josh held on until Allison stopped struggling and melted into heaving sobs.

He held her until the sobs became sniffles. He led her to the edge of the bed, sat beside her. She would have to speak first.

"I never thought . . ." She shook her head. "I'm going to have to leave town. My life is shot."

Allison slammed a pillow to the floor. She'd worked so hard to gain the respect of her patients, to regain her own self-respect. Now, she'd been crushed. She dissolved back into tears.

Josh wanted to make her feel better but he couldn't think of the right thing to say.

The phone broke the silence. Allison didn't move. She let the call go to the answering machine. "It's Carl. We've restored almost the whole note. I've emailed you a scan."

She could sense Josh's anxiety. They both believed the note in the fish had been aimed at him. The DVD's arrival helped her appreciate his need to know who was targeting him and why. "Check my email," she said. "I'm signed on."

Josh went to her computer. He found the email and opened the attachment. "W-Y-N-E- something-U-E-C-H-S-I-K-A- apostrophe—S. Followed by the word CURSE," he read. "We knew about 'Curse.' There's also a signature. 'One of the Remaining.'"

He studied the smudged letters. Something about the note looked familiar but he couldn't place it. "What starts with W-Y-N-E?"

He went to dictionary.com and typed the letters. No results.

"The apostrophe means it possessive. Maybe it's a person," Allison suggested. She could feel her own natural curiosity pulling her back from the brink.

Josh Googled WYNE. "WYNE is a radio station in Erie, Pennsylvania. And there's a stripper named Brandy Wyne."

"See what you get if you type in all the letters we have and guess at the one we're missing. Start with A and keep going until we get a match. There are only twenty-six possibilities."

Josh studied the letters. "It almost has to be a consonant." Seconds later, he reported, "The word is Wynepuechsika. It means maize plant. It's the Indian name for Chief Cornstalk."

"'Cornstalk's Curse.' Signed 'One of the Remaining,'" Allison said. "What the heck does that mean?"

Josh Googled "Cornstalk's Curse." The site of the West Virginia Historical Society came up first. "It says Chief Cornstalk issued a curse before he died and supposedly a lot of local disasters have resulted—coal mine accidents, bridge collapses, that kind of thing."

"Might as well blame him for the Marshall football team plane crash, as long as they're at it."

Josh scrolled further. "Actually, they do. Here's the curse itself. '*May the curse of the Great Spirit rest upon this land. May it be blighted by*

Nature. May it even be blighted in its hopes. May the strength of its peoples be paralyzed by the stain of our blood."

"That's one upset chief. But what's the curse have to do with a radioactive catfish? And why direct it to you?"

"Interesting." Josh looked again at the scan of the note. "Bradley Hand," he said.

"What?"

"The fish note is typeset. A font called Bradley Hand. You don't see it often except in newspapers."

....

CHAPTER FIFTY

Josh and Allison drove to the *News*, the baggage of the DVD riding uncomfortably in the front seat with them.

Josh could not erase the images from his mind. He ached to know more. But he would not take away the only vestige of control Allison still had and bring it up. As much as his reportorial instincts and natural curiosity protested, that right would have to remain with her.

Allison was despondent. In a stroke, the DVD had stripped her of her painstakingly constructed armor and violated her very essence. She felt broken, befouled. But more than that, she felt ashamed. How could Josh not think the worst of her after what he had seen?

Why had she left the DVD running? Was it to punish herself? To prove that she was dirty and weak? Had she hoped Josh would see it and flee from her life forever and prove once again that she was unworthy of affection and esteem, undeserving of companionship and love?

The awkwardness grew with each mile. The flip-flip of the windshield wipers fell into the same rhythm as her pounding heart. Finally, she could take it no longer. "Pull over," she said. Josh did.

She took a deep breath. Then, slowly, haltingly, almost beseechingly, she began. "What you saw—"

"You don't have to explain."

She took another deep, almost fluttering breath, and resumed. "What you saw is something I can't defend. But it happened. It's part of me."

"But how? I mean—"

"Vince was a control freak. I couldn't go anywhere without his permission. He'd check the odometer to make sure I hadn't driven while he was at work. He set up spy cameras in every room to monitor me."

Josh was staggered. What he had seen on the DVD were the actions of a sex slave. Bludhorn was the leather-hooded master. Josh felt his rage building. Bludhorn—damn him!

"So the things on the DVD . . . you were forced?"

Allison sighed. "Some people would say so but it's more complicated. I permitted it to happen. I didn't have to."

"Why'd you marry him in the first place?"

"There was a time when I was rebellious, to put it mildly. I hated my father. I hated myself and did all the things that reinforced my low self-esteem. Vince was the captain of the football team. I got pregnant. Abortion wasn't an option. He gave up a scholarship and we got married at 18."

"But the child?" Josh couldn't conceal his shock.

"I miscarried at four months. Vince and I tried to make a go of it, but things went downhill fast. He resented me. He believed that I'd trapped him, that I'd cheated him out of his dreams. I suppose his way of responding was to try to control me completely, even if that meant beating me. Once, I ended up with his boot on my neck and his shotgun jammed to my temple."

"You should have left immediately," Josh said firmly.

"Again, it's complicated. He was always sorry. And my self-respect was such that I believed I deserved it, that it wouldn't have happened if I hadn't done things to make him angry. But I could never do enough and I did anything, no mater how degrading. It got so bad I came to believe suicide was a way out."

Josh swallowed hard. "You tried?"

"No, I called the suicide hotline."

"They talked you out of it."

"No, they put me on hold. But that was enough. I decided a world where the suicide hot line puts people on hold is a world more screwed up than I am."

"So the DVD—"

"Is his way of still controlling me."

"Wouldn't he leave a note?"

"No need. I got the message."

"But why this? Why now?"

"Just to show he can," Allison said glumly.

Josh wasn't so sure. "Maybe you're right that the DVD is only about you and Vince. But that doesn't explain the posters. And the fish. And I've had cancelled ads. I think we've stirred up some kind of hornets' nest. I'd say the DVD is about you backing off."

"No question we've upset a lot of people. But what links it all together? Who are the hornets?"

Josh had no answer. He stared out of the window. Perhaps the right thing to do was to follow Dorn's advice and let everyone do their jobs. "Do you have any doubt Vince would go public?" he asked.

"None."

"Allison, you've done everything anyone could expect of you, trying to track down the victims, notifying the local police, the state agencies, the feds. I won't let that bully ruin your life. I'm taking it from here."

An image of herself as a patient undergoing surgery came into Allison's head. Naked, vulnerable, body and soul, past and present, stripped and laid open for the world to see. At the mercy of someone else.

No, not just at the mercy of someone else. At the mercy of Vince Bludhorn, her psychopathic ex. That was the scariest notion—worse than public exposure and humiliation. She hadn't fought all these years just so Vince could put his boot on her neck again. "No," she swore. "I'm not quitting."

Allison and Josh went directly to the pressroom where the crew was readying for the River Days special section run. Josh waved the foreman over. He showed him the printout of the Cornstalk Curse note. "Who set this type?" he signed.

The foreman motioned Josh and Allison to a terminal which controlled the newspaper's high resolution typesetting machines. He scrolled backwards through the log of output jobs, stopping to open each file that contained too few kilobytes to be a full advertisement or a story. The first two were headlines that had been set separately from the stories they went with. The third file was the one they were looking for—the electronic original of the Cornstalk note. The log identified its creator as Jimmy Mayes.

Josh and Allison followed the foreman to the lockers where the pressmen exchanged their street clothes for work coveralls. Inside Mayes's, Josh found a copy of the catfish note, a dream catcher, books on Native American history, and a file labeled 'Friends of Cornstalk.' The file containing several pages of handwriting and a sketch of an advertising layout.

"Where's Jimmy?" he asked.

"He didn't show up today."

"Do you know where he lives?"

"Betheltown," the foreman signed. Josh translated.

"But nobody lives there," Allison said. "It's been a ghost town for decades."

....

CHAPTER FIFTY-ONE

"We've been assuming the fish was an attack on me," Josh said as they hurried to Allison's car. "But it wasn't. It was a warning from a friend. How did that curse go again?"

Allison consulted a printout. "The curse of the Great Spirit will spread across this land, blighting it by nature."

"Jimmy was trying to tell the newspaper something bad was spreading, blighting nature, harming fish. Cornstalk's Curse is being fulfilled again." In that sense, Josh realized, the radioactive catfish *was* like the anthrax incidents. In both cases, the intention wasn't an assault, it was an alert. The difference was, Jimmy Mayes wasn't trying to hurt someone to make his point.

Josh realized he'd been guilty of giving short shrift to the pressman, failing to get to know him, perhaps even stereotyping him. Mayes wasn't simply a hearing-impaired Indian who kept to himself, Josh understood. He was a man who honored his home, his family and his traditions. Even though his job was running the press, Josh realized Jimmy Mayes was a journalist—a crusader, very much like Josh had once been himself.

"How would he know the fish was radioactive?" Allison wondered.

"Probably didn't. But it sure as heck wasn't healthy, with all those lesions."

"Why throw it through the transom?"

Josh smiled. "Inside newspaper joke. Big stories that come to a newspaper unsolicited are said to come in 'over the transom.'"

"Why not just tell the newspaper directly? Why write a note and identify yourself as 'One of the Remaining'?"

Josh shrugged. "We'll ask him right after we find out where he got that fish."

The rain fell harder as Josh turned on to Betheltown Road, retracing the route they'd traveled several nights before. The Wagoneer bucked like a bronco as Josh swerved to avoid one water-filled pothole only to splash into the next. Yellow police tape snapped in the wind as they passed Darryl Dunn's.

A mile beyond Dunn's, a muddy, two-rut driveway led to a rust-streaked mobile home wedged into a crevice by a creek. A steel barricade crossed Betheltown Road a quarter-mile later. Josh parked just short of the rusted sign that still pointed to the abandoned community. "We'll walk in," he said. "It can't be more than a mile. Watch your step.

The place is crawling with snakes."

Allison pulled on a parka to protect against the increasing drizzle and tightened the laces of her hiking boots. Josh was amazed at how nature had reclaimed the road beyond the barricade. Delicate wildflowers flourished among the pieces of crumbling asphalt. Years of leaves hid curves and dips. The roadbed vanished in places.

They had walked for ten minutes when silver flashes of a lake gleamed through the woods and rain. "This looks familiar," Allison said.

The details of the day remained burned in her memory—her father's pickup laboring into the hills; her jacket sliding across the battered truck bed as the faded green Dodge swayed through the switchbacks, fresh air spilling into the cab blended with the sounds of the straining engine and the low hum of cicadas.

They had turned at a county road sign and had rumbled across a rickety steel single-lane bridge. After another mile, a flagman had waved them to the side of the road where they parked behind a line of cars.

All Winston had showed up as if the event were a picnic, entertainment.

But the solemn parade of Betheltown's houses creaking down the mountain on flatbed trucks followed by station wagons sagging with suitcases, furniture and forlorn families was the saddest thing Allison had ever seen.

The little black dog with the white belly who struggled to keep up with the caravan was the most heartbreaking of all.

A rivulet of cold rain sliding down her neck snapped Allison back from her reverie. Josh was already tromping toward the lake. Allison picked her way behind.

She caught glimpses through the trees of what remained of the place: row houses that had been too fragile to move, their porches collapsed, their rusted tin roofs peeled back to the sun-bleached framing; a bare plank wood building with a giant Coca-Cola bottle cap logo faded on the side; a rusted Esso sign; a pine tree shooting through the crumbled asphalt of a street.

"An entire community," she said when she caught up to Josh by the lake. "Houses. A little store. Even a church. On the map one day, gone the next."

"Betheltown was part of the land bought by the plant, right?"

"Claimed under eminent domain by the government and given to the plant," she corrected. "The people had no choice. They were uprooted and cast aside. Families who'd lived in this hollow for generations had six months to accept their settlement and move out."

Josh led Allison toward the bridge to the abandoned town. A sheet of rain swept across the lake signaling a new intensity to the storm. A hut emerged from the gloom. "We'll wait it out here," he said.

The hut smelled of a forest in summer—the rich, heavy odor of moss and dark soil, the sweet scent of new growth and decaying leaves. The snare drum rapping of rain on the tin roof cut them off from the outside world.

Allison peeled off her poncho, shook off the water, spread it on the floor and sat down, her legs stretched out before her, back propped against a wall.

Josh looked at her long legs, tight jeans, blonde hair pulled into a pony tail, her simple white t-shirt stretched just to the side and up, revealing her navel. He sat beside her. Her left hand rested on her thigh. He rested his hand on top of hers. He was delighted when she made no effort to move it. He waited for a full minute before he slid his arm from her hand and slipped it around her waist. The touch of her skin sent a bolt of pleasure through him.

Josh tightened his hold on her waist. Heart thudding in his chest, he abandoned all pretense, pulled Allison close and kissed her on the mouth.

She pulled away. "I'm sorry. I'm just not ready to go there." She put her hand on his. "If it were anyone, it would be someone like you."

Josh's faced burned with heat. "I'm confused," he said. "When you kissed me at rehearsal, I thought you were encouraging me. Heck, you *were* encouraging me."

Allison blushed. Josh was right and she knew it. She hadn't intended to send mixed signals but she had. In fact, she realized she'd been a tease.

Looking back, it was almost inevitable that she'd come across that way. Josh was attractive. He was kind. He was a great partner. She cherished his company. She'd learned a lot about Josh Gibbs over the last week and discovered some things about herself as well. She was *better* in his presence. She knew without a doubt that there was a connection between them. Despite her best efforts, her feelings had pierced the tough armor she'd developed and Josh had picked up on them. Still . . .

She had no confidence in her ability to have a healthy relationship with *any* man. She'd idolized her father only to realize later that her hero worship had been grounded in her desperate attempts to win his affection. Her marriage to Vince was a combination of acting out against her father coupled with her continuing need to please. How could she be right about Josh when she'd been so wrong in the past?

And larger questions, questions that lay down the road but that nevertheless demanded to be answered before she would permit herself to acknowledge her feelings. Was she ready to be a wife again? Was she ready to be a mom? Would she a better parent than her father?

She had sent mixed signals because that's what she felt—a growing love for Josh against fear of another failure, a fear that meant she had to reinforce her emotional armor and hold him at arm's length.

Josh's phone rang. He answered in a tone transformed from frustrated to warm and loving. "Hi, sweetheart!"

Allison could guess Katie's end of the conversation from his questions—"How bad? When did it start?" She was moved by his determination to reassure her: "Don't worry. Things will be fine. I'll be there to meet you when you get off the bus."

When Josh told his daughter, "Of course. You'll always be beautiful," Allison wept. At that moment, she understood that Josh Gibbs was solid ground on which she could stand.

Josh had been right about her and she knew it. Altruism, not love, defined her life. And love had a power that altruism did not. Josh's love for his daughter was a fuel infinitely more powerful than her impersonal concern for public welfare. Even after the pain of his wife's death, Josh hadn't stopped loving. In the face of tragedy, he was willing to risk it, to be hurt again. That was, she realized, the difference between them. After Vince, she had so little love left to risk, least of all for herself, that in attempting to build bulwarks against the savagery of the world, she'd inadvertently sealed herself inside a prison of her own making. Love was such a big part of Josh that he was willing to give it to others without regard to the consequences. He had survived the past. That was his triumph and her failing. Fortunately, it could be rectified—at least this small part of it—easily enough.

There was only one hurdle.

She didn't catch Josh's last few words but as he hung up she turned to him. "What about Sharon?"

Josh's head had been far away, with his daughter.

"Josh, did you hear me? What about Sharon?"

Josh's focus returned to Allison. He used her own words. "Sharon's not here anymore. We are."

"But do you think she'd understand?"

"I wouldn't have kissed you if I didn't believe she understands. Sharon wants what's best for Katie and for me."

Allison knew Josh meant her. She loved Josh. She loved his daughter. She was willing to devote herself to their happiness.

In an instant, he had wiped away all her self-doubt. That the best man she had ever known could care so deeply for her gave her a confidence and belief in herself that she had never felt before. The past failings had been her father's and Vince Bludhorn's. They had not been about her. That Josh loved her meant the world.

"Please, kiss me," she said.

"Are you sure it's okay?"

"Try it."

Josh kissed Allison lightly on the lips. He couldn't believe their softness. He took her into his arms and kissed her again.

How different, Allison thought, from Vince's brutish, animal-like slobberings, clumsy preludes that inevitably left her feeling like an object. Josh's kisses communicated tenderness, comfort, love. She felt like she was being kissed for the first time.

When they parted, Josh asked, "Was that over the line?"

"I don't know. Later, we'll have to try again."

The downpour eased. They left the hut and spotted a one-story frame house nearly hidden in the trees. Josh noticed a red cedar picnic table in the carport, along with a half-full bag of Kingsford charcoal, a can of lighter fluid and a grill. "Someone lives here," he said.

And then, a voice from behind him, "That would be Blanche Lee."

Josh whipped around. Not five paces away was a woman he judged to be at least eighty dressed in a camouflage raincoat and holding a rifle. She was barefoot. "And you are?" she asked.

"Josh Gibbs."

The woman swung the gun from Josh to Allison who immediately raised her hands into the air.

"You from the plant?"

Allison shook her head 'no.' "I'm Dr. Allison Wright from Winston Medical Clinic. This is Mr. Gibbs from the newspaper."

Blanche lowered the rifle. "Hell, don't just stand there. Get out of the rain."

They followed the woman into the house. The kitchen smelled of Ajax. Josh spotted a *Winston News* coffee mug—the product of a recent circulation promotion drive—in the draining rack by the sink.

"How long have you lived here, Mrs. Lee?" he asked.

"All my life."

"Wasn't everyone supposed to leave when the plant came in?"

"Not all of us did. My momma's buried in Betheltown. So's my daddy. And two brothers and a sister. And two kids. Hard to be torn out of a family place especially if you have no reason to leave."

"But you've lived all this time with no utilities, no police, no power, no phone, no water."

"Never had nothing but an outhouse anyway. Propane runs the

stove and the lights. No one's gonna mess with me. I may be eighty-five but I can still shoot."

"What about water?" Josh asked

"We share a well."

"Who's we?"

"Me, Spike, all of us do."

Allison and Josh exchanged a look. "Spike?"

"My grandson."

"Sells jewelry?" Allison asked.

"Makes it and sells it. Come to think of it, maybe you could take a look at him. You said you're a doctor, right? His hands are a mess and he's been throwing up constant two straight days."

Spike lay on a bed in a small room covered by a white sheet. What remained of his hair clung to his head in clumps. Black eyes burned from his hollow skull. The piercings in his lip and eyebrow had turned into gaping holes. He was wasting rapidly. If she hadn't known better, Allison would have said that he was suffering from full-blown AIDS.

"How you doing?" she asked gently.

"Bad," he croaked.

She pulled the sheet away. Spike's body had shriveled to a fraction of its former self. His flesh oozed. Bones poked through the burned flesh of his hands. Spike was the sickest person she had ever seen. Death was inevitable and approaching quickly. No treatment could save him.

Allison replaced the sheet. She touched Spike's shoulder "I'll try to make you more comfortable."

"I'm sorry," she told Blanche back in the kitchen. "Radiation poisoning. There's nothing I can do. It's too far gone."

"I told him nothing good could come of stealing," she wailed. "I told him not to break into that safe."

"The safe he took from Dunn's," Josh remembered.

"He said Darryl owed him. He got his metal from Darryl so he was sure something valuable was in there—gold or silver. He worked on it all night before he finally broke in. But he said all he got was dust and a piece of metal that glowed bright blue. He liked that. But then he started getting sick."

Just like the Brazil children who died after painting their bodies with glowing blue matter from a radiotherapy machine, Allison thought. She took a deep breath. "The blue stuff was cesium. Do you know where it is?"

"Day before yesterday, he threw it in the lake."

Allison's stomach dropped. "You need to see a doctor right away. The material is radioactive. It could be in the well water. Everyone in Betheltown needs to leave immediately. How many people are still here?"

"Twenty-three remaining."

"The Remaining," Josh whispered.

Blanche nodded.

"Do you know Jimmy Mayes?" he asked.

"Lives right up the road."

"Let's go," Josh said to Allison.

"No point," Blanche said. "Haven't seen him in days."

....

CHAPTER FIFTY-TWO

Allison's mind raced.

This was cascading into something far worse than anything she had imagined. What had started with isolated cases among body jewelry aficionados—she still hadn't found them all—had led to Spike, the jewelry manufacturer. Between his jewelry sales and the stolen cesium polluting the lake used by the Remaining, who knew how many people Spike might have exposed?

Spike had led them to his metal supplier, Darryl Dunn. Surely Spike wasn't Dunn's only customer. Who else did Dunn sell radioactive metal to?

And where did Dunn's metal come from?

At each stage, the circle of endangered people grew larger and larger. Already, more people had been injured than had been at Three Mile Island. Was Winston's water supply threatened? To what degree had she and Josh been exposed?

A comparison to Fukushima might end up being more apt, Allison thought grimly. A slew of federal agencies would need to be involved—from Homeland Security to Public Health to the Centers for Disease Control. There was no time to spare. She pulled out her cell phone, thinking she could get Coretha to make calls for her, but there was no service. She resumed her march to the car, blazing a shortcut trail through the thick woods.

She stepped on a fallen tree trunk. It disintegrated into rot, plunging her boot into a slithering nest of baby copperheads. She screamed and bolted fifteen yards. A few feet later, a branch hissed and insolently slithered away. Snakes. The place was infested with them.

"At least we know where Jimmy caught his fish," Josh said when they arrived back at the car.

Allison was about to agree when she thought of something. "Didn't Spike's mom say he dumped the cesium in the lake day before yesterday?"

"Yes."

"That's the same day the fish showed up at the newspaper."

"Right."

"Those lesions weren't brand new and that thing was already starting to decay."

"So?" Josh was having trouble seeing where Allison was going.

"The fish was a few days old. It had to have been caught before Spike dumped the cesium. If the fish came from the lake, that means the lake was radioactive even before Spike did his thing. There would have to be a prior source of contamination."

Josh looked at his watch. The special section was now on the press. The short-session bus with Katie wouldn't be arriving from camp for several hours. "We could poke around some more."

Allison removed two lead protective aprons from the cargo area.

She handed one to Josh and put the other one on herself. She retrieved a shoebox-sized device from the back seat and switched it on. It clicked irregularly. "Normal background radiation," she pronounced.

"Geiger counter? Where'd you get that?"

"Let's just say it's on loan from the radiation safety department at the hospital. I thought it might come in handy. You can hide a lot under a lab coat."

They headed back to the lake as another squall swept through.

They had traveled a quarter-mile when they came across a fire hose snaking down the hill. Allison traced it to its end where a torrent of foul-looking sludge pulsed into a rain-swollen gully, raced down the slope, and billowed like a building storm cloud as it poured into the Betheltown lake. Allison saw that the lake was rising. Radioactive soup lapped at the top of the banks like coffee in an over-filled cup.

Josh switched on the Geiger counter. Static hit like a hailstorm. "Red zone," Josh read on the dial. Panic rose in him. He knew nothing about radioactivity. He wondered if there was a way to protect himself, if he should try to run, if it would even matter.

He looked to Allison for guidance but she was already tracking the hose up the hill where the woods ended in a clearing. Josh followed. If a medical professional was willing to take the risk, he decided he could, too.

The hose crossed a dirt road and over a dirt berm which was topped by a cyclone fence. Allison scrambled up the muddy bank. Josh was right behind.

In front of them, hundreds of carbon arc lights buzzed like giant one-legged-mosquitoes, creating diffuse balls of yellow light suspended in the rain and gloom above a parking lot. Beyond that lay the Recovery Metals plant—a giant gray box sprouting pipes, valves, and a towering smokestack, surrounded by a hundred desolate acres where pile after pile of scrap awaited weighing and sorting before reprocessing.

"It looks just like that photo the Martian Lander spacecraft took of itself," Josh said. "A human creation plopped in a landscape devoid of life."

Allison thought about the analogy as she took in the scene. Forklifts moved like dodge 'em cars while electromagnetic cranes scanned piles of scrap for ferrous metals. Hard-hatted workers swarmed over the property like ants on a playground candy bar. Some wore HazMat coveralls. Smokers on break huddled on a loading dock. A line of loaded dump trucks, tractor trailers and tankers idled outside the industrial gate while a guard checked their plates against a clipboard and motioned them through one by one. Empty trucks exited through another gate. A ten-foot cyclone fence topped by razor wire surrounded the entire enterprise.

They moved closer. Odor and clamor overwhelmed them: hot tar, burning rubber and ozone from an electrical fire; the loud, deep rumble of the diesel engines on huge trucks, the grunting and grinding of a fleet of bulldozers, the jarring clang of metal on metal and, above all, the roar from the furnace and the smokestack.

Paint peeled from the walls of the main plant building. Flaming hot gases sparkling with bits of still-burning ash shot from the top of the massive smoke stack which, Allison noticed for the first time, was stained with long columns of rust. The tiny things hitting her skin, she realized, were not gnats but flecks of ash which fell in a light, never-ending gray snow.

A tug pulled a railroad hopper car brimming with scrap into the incinerator building, giving her a glimpse of the glow and flicker of one furnace and an army of mask-wearing, coverall-clad workers, soot coating their faces with grime so dark they could have been mistaken for coal miners. "Like something out of Dante," Allison yelled. Proximity had transformed the high-tech Martian Lander into a crude, filthy, industrial colossus.

She traced the fire hose to a large lagoon of electric green liquid bordered by an eight-foot red clay dam. "They're siphoning," she noted. She walked the perimeter, searching for a way through the fence.

Josh stopped her. "Electrified," he said, pointing to a thin wire at the top "This place is buttoned up tighter than Fort Knox."

Allison spotted a small corrugated aluminum building by the perimeter road. "Maybe time to leave," she said.

"I don't think anyone's home."

Allison pointed to tire tracks in the mud. "But someone's been here recently."

Josh hurried fifty yards to the hut, snuck around a corner to a window and eased up to look inside. A desk. A phone. A logbook. A couple of magazines. An easy chair. A reading light. A radio. And hanging on the wall, a raincoat with something stenciled on the back. It took a moment before Josh realized it spelled *Winston Police*. He sprinted back to Allison. "Chief Holt's security shed. This is where he hangs out when he's not on plant patrol."

Allison looked at the tire tracks. "Why would he be moonlighting on a Monday afternoon?"

A car moved slowly toward them along the perimeter road. "Beat it!" Allison commanded. She hustled down the berm and into a grove of trees. Josh was right behind.

A sweet smell flooded their nostrils when they permitted themselves to breathe. Allison recognized it as the cloying odor of deteriorating flesh.

They followed their noses deeper into the woods, the smell becoming more putrid with each step. The pinched, twisted face of a dead possum appeared in a pile next to half-eaten carcass of a deer crawling with maggots. The flattened bodies of a couple dozen rabbits floating in a yellow custard of decay. Josh felt his gorge rise.

Next to the rabbits, a pile of geese, some already just bones and fathers, other apparently freshly dead. On top of the geese, the stinking remnants of a fox.

"Geurnica," Allison whispered.

She switched on the Geiger counter. The machine erupted. "The animals are radioactive." She backed away from the pile. Her hands shook.

Allison was more scared than she had ever been in her life, more scared than she had ever been with Vince. Vince was a threat only to her. This was a threat to her, to Josh, to Katie and to everyone else in

Winston. Beyond that, she knew the kind of evil Vince could bring. This evil was entirely unfamiliar.

They tried to put things together back at the car. "Even if the plant is allowed to handle radioactivity, which I don't think it is, this kind of thing can't be normal," Josh said. "No way those workers should be exposed."

"This is bigger than us, Josh," Allison answered. "We have to get someone's attention. If contaminated jewelry, a dead metal dealer, high radioactive levels at the plant and a mountain of dead animals aren't enough to divert everyone from River Days, I don't know what is."

CHAPTER FIFTY-THREE

"You need to do a story."

"We're not ready," Josh said as they drove back to town. "Still too many holes."

"Like what?"

"Like how do we know the Geiger counter works? Maybe the hospital had it on that shelf because it was broken. Or maybe the plant's allowed to do this."

Allison looked unconvinced.

"And we don't know for sure where the hot fish came from," Josh continued. "All we got is Spike's word that Dunn is the bad guy. We're really no farther along that we were."

Allison threw up her hands in frustration.

Josh felt badly about being so negative. "But I still have posters," he added.

Allison wasn't mollified. She was worried about the threat to public health. Josh was in the best position to warn people quickly. He had seen the same evidence she had. She simply couldn't fathom his reluctance to go public.

"You're a journalist, for god's sake! This calls for a full-blown story, not some anonymous posters! I'll help with the research. Maybe other recycling facilities have had radiation problems."

"We can't afford a mistake."

Allison boiled over. "You need to get over Atlanta," she snarled.

Josh felt like he'd been kicked in the gut. "It's not about Atlanta," he protested. "Everything is working against us. We still have no confirmation and we don't publish for two weeks."

"What about the River Days section?"

"Already on the press." He looked at his watch. "Anyway, I have three hours until Katie gets home. I'm going to be out of commission for days."

Allison understood the roadblocks but she still believed Josh was afraid—though not without good reason. A story about radioactive contamination was sure to invite intense scrutiny. People with reasons to hide the truth would attempt to knock it down by discrediting the writer. The unpleasant past would be dredged up, including the old comparisons with Janet Cooke, the *Washington Post* reporter whose Pulitzer was withdrawn after it was discovered she had invented things. Josh would be forced to relive the nightmare.

But that didn't outweigh the demand that they alert the town. Lives were at stake. Josh would have to make peace with the past sometime and there would not be an occasion more important than this. She would do whatever she needed to help him.

She touched him on the shoulder. "Everyone knows what happened in Atlanta, even in Winston. The only person who hasn't forgiven you is you. Josh, this isn't just about telling people not to buy nipple rings from strangers. This is about a potential nuclear catastrophe and we're at ground zero. We've got thousands of people coming to town and you've got the best way to warn them. I need you—we need you—to be a journalist again."

Allison was just like Katie in some ways, Josh thought. The night they had returned from the devastating visit to Columbus, Katie had stopped him with a question as he tucked her into bed: "You know those kids we saw in the waiting room at the hospital?"

He recalled the room of children—boys and girls and with translucent skin and emaciated frames, with head scarves, bald heads, and missing limbs giving the lie to the bright colors and cheerful cartoon animal décor of the waiting room. He remembered his feelings at the time: How can this be right? How is this part of any plan?

"Yes, I remember."

"I feel *so* sorry for them," Katie had said.

I feel so sorry for them! Even in the darkest times, Katie's concern had not been for not herself, it was for others. Just like Allison.

Josh realized that Allison was right. He had screwed up. He'd given up the decisive World Series homerun. But the problem wasn't that he'd never been put back in the lineup. The problem was that he'd never asked for the ball.

They hurried to the newspaper and into the pressroom where the pages of the River Days section flew through the rollers. He searched frantically until he finally made eye contact with the foreman. "Stop the presses," he signed.

Chapter Fifty-Four

Furbee met them as they left the pressroom.

"Bad news," she reported. "We're getting sued."

"By whom?" Josh was stunned. The *Winston News* had never been sued in more than one hundred years of publishing. "What for?"

"Dunno. We haven't been served yet."

Josh was about to back-burner the problem—people occasionally threatened to sue but never followed-through—until Furbee added, "Charles told me it's going to happen. It's all the buzz at the plant."

Josh looked at Allison. Their eyes met. Furbee's boyfriend, Charles Angerson, worked in finance. He was the friendly plant insider they'd been looking for. "I should have thought of him earlier," Josh said.

He turned to Furbee. "He says the plant's suing us?"

"I figured you'd want the details so I had him come in. He's waiting in your office. I promised we'd protect him. He's afraid for his job." Josh nodded. Granting confidentiality to sources was normally the price for obtaining inside information.

They joined Angerson around the coffee table.

"You gotta protect me," he said. "Talk about a conflict! I've been in knots. The plant is talking about suing you guys."

Angerson took a sheet of paper from his briefcase. He handed it to Josh. It was from the office of the legal department at Recovery Metals.

Josh read it and said, "A memo from Bludhorn to all plant supervisors. It reminds them that unauthorized contact with the media is a firing offense. It says the reminder is being issued because erroneous information about the plant is being circulated by 'muckrakers.' Now, that's a term you don't see much anymore. It says the plant will sue any media that publishes information about it that has not been authorized. Interesting interpretation of the First Amendment. It doesn't specifically mention me or the *News.*"

Angerson interrupted. "But they told us in a special meeting they meant the *News.* Bludhorn made a big speech about how important the plant is to the local economy, that our jobs are at stake, how we need to circle the wagons and keep plant business at the plant. He said anybody doing business with the *News* needed to stop."

Josh was floored. That explained customers backing out of their ad contracts. And the cancelled ink delivery. And probably the posters. They'd obviously stumbled upon something bigger than they had ever imagined and the forces arrayed against them were bigger and more powerful, too.

"We've found the hornets nest," Allison said.

"And the hornets have lawyers," Josh added.

Furbee leaned forward. "Charles, do you know what they're so concerned about?"

Angerson looked stricken. "Promise this is confidential, for background only. You have to confirm it yourselves."

"Promise," Josh said.

"One of our truckers brought in some stuff that contained high-level radioactivity. It got through the radiation detectors because it was encased in lead. But as soon as the lead melted in the furnace, the stuff went everywhere. Eight tons of metal got contaminated. One of the buildings is still hot in places. It was a mess."

"Whoa!" Furbee exclaimed. "Anyone hurt?"

Angerson sighed. "I hear they're seeing some problems. Burns. Hair loss. Maybe a dozen cases so far. There's a rumor one guy died. I understand it's going to get worse. But they've set up a clinic on site so they can deal with the problem there."

Josh scribbled notes. "If it was an accident, why are they so uptight about it?" he asked. "Why not just say what happened?"

"Too great a chance they'd have to stop operating for a couple of weeks. They had me do some calculations. It'd cost millions. They deactivated the detectors to keep them from alerting, so we're still up and running."

Josh was shocked. Not only was the plant behind the radioactive contamination, it had undertaken a massive and continuing cover-up.

Allison started a new mental tally of the victims: Darryl and the manufacturers like Spike who bought his metal; her patients and anyone else who'd bought contaminated jewelry, all the Remaining in Bethel-town; the whole work force at the plant. "Where's the contaminated metal?" she asked, fearful that she already knew.

"They're holding it in a lagoon. But I hear they've found a buyer—in Asia, I think—because they're draining it."

"Why would they pollute their own property?" Josh wondered.

"Well, the lagoon overflowed when they first dumped the metal in there. The radioactive water just dissipated into the woods. The engineers think the same thing will happen when they empty the whole thing. They say what isn't absorbed will flow into a lake and be contained. No one lives down there anyway."

Allison and Josh exchanged a glance. A clap of thunder shook the building. "Of course, I don't think they figured on all this rain," Angerson added.

Allison felt sick. In addition to not considering the rain, the engineers' thinking was flawed because of two things they didn't know. First, somebody—the Remaining—did live there. Second, the Betheltown lake was already dangerously radioactive because of the cesium Spike stole from Dunn.

If the flood of contaminated lagoon water overwhelmed the lake, cesium would race down the steep hills toward the Ohio River and the intakes for Winston's water supply. The town was facing an environmental catastrophe, a nuclear nightmare, a true public health disaster. Winston would become another Chernobyl or Fukushima, uninhabitable for years. The last scene of the pageant would finally be written.

Images of her patients paraded before her. How strange that the town could die—Winston nothing but a fading memory like Chief Cornstalk or Betheltown.

Perhaps the forlorn trail of refugees she had seen at Betheltown had been a preview. Perhaps—as a girl—she had been allowed to see her future.

Angerson left. Furbee paced. Josh wrote, taking care only to use information from Angerson that he had confirmed independently.

Allison seated herself at Furbee's computer and went to the website for the Environmental Protection Agency to determine if there was precedent for Angerson's story. She quickly came across an unsettling report.

There have been at least twenty-six recorded accidental meltings of radioactive material in the United States . . . One such case happened in Texas in 1996 when a Cobalt-60 source was stolen from a storage facility and sold as scrap metal. Workers and customers of the scrap yard and law enforcement officers who conducted investigations at the scrap yard were exposed to the source and may have received dangerous levels of radiation.

Why was this just now coming to light? She typed "Texas" and "Cobalt-60" into the search engine and scrolled through three pages of listings of stories about University of Texas Longhorn running back Marquis Cobalt before finding another promising item. The summary read:

In 1983, a Picker 3000 radiotherapy machine once owned by a Texas hospital ended up in a Juarez junkyard where its Cobalt-60 was recycled into six hundred tons of contaminated steel. Radioactive table legs and rebar made their way to twenty-three states, Canada and Mexico where one hundred nine houses built with radioactive steel had to be demolished.

She clicked on the next item and scrolled down the item from the website of WKYC-TV in Cleveland reporting a 2004 incident where cesium-137 ended up in a Canton, Ohio steel plant, apparently delivered as part of a shipment of scrap metal.

Allison relayed the information to Josh.

"Make sure I have room for a big headline," he told Furbee. "Seventy-two points at least. How's the ink supply?"

"We blew some on that false start this morning but there's enough for half the run."

"Print as many as you can."

"Any response from the plant to the questions I emailed Jerry Baker?"

"Not even a 'No comment.'"

He finished writing. The story simply reported the provable facts: the victims of radioactive jewelry who had come to the attention of Dr. Wright, at least one of whom was not expected to survive; the murder of Darryl Dunn the metal dealer; Geiger counter readings that showed the much higher than normal radiation levels at the plant and deadly radiation levels off-site, including in the lake at Betheltown; the radiation injuries at the plant; the draining of the lagoon.

A companion piece warned readers not to buy jewelry from unknown sources and to avoid the local water. Another sidebar incorporated the information Allison had uncovered about past incidents of contamination at metal recycling plants.

The stories would, Josh fully understood, be the death knell of River Days even before it began, and would mark the end of the *Winston News* because there would be no advertisers and there likely would be no sale—certainly not at the new wildly inflated price Bella Partners was now offering.

That would mean the end of his life in Winston. Even if the town managed to avoid disaster, the Winston years would be bundled up and buried. He and Katie would start over somewhere else. He would lose Sharon again. And Allison.

He took a long, bracing breath and told Furbee. "Okay. Let 'er rip."

He wanted to make the night special for his daughter.

Before he moved Katie's bed into the living room so she wouldn't have to climb stairs. Before she started six months of chemo. While she still had both legs.

Normal for one last night. Or at least as normal as it ever gets for a thirty-something father raising a teenage daughter by himself.

He had not felt such focus since the days immediately before Sharon died when his priorities were obvious and uncomplicated and he knew without a doubt what was required of him.

In an hour or so Katie would step off the bus with the rest of the ten-day campers and he would take her in his arms and he would hear all about camp—and, God forbid, maybe this boy—and they would have a nice, cozy dinner.

And then he would drive her to the hospital and entrust her to Dr. Pepper. He could stop worrying whether sending her to camp had been the right thing to do and they could finally get on with it, stop waiting and worrying and start fighting.

At home, Josh set the plate of cookies—the ones Allison had helped wth, not his own, coin-thin hockey pucks—and the straw basket with the ribbon on the dining room table where Katie would be sure to see them first and began preparing Katie's homecoming meal: lasagna, a family specialty and Katie's favorite.

Sharon was waiting for him in the kitchen. In the pantry, where he kept the pasta, he spotted two cans of beets which he knew neither he nor Katie would ever have bought. Sharon held these once, he thought. As he followed the recipe Sharon had written on the now-stained three-by-five note card, he saw her sitting at her small kitchen desk, glasses pushed to the top of her head, holding the hair back from her face. The glasses were still in his dresser drawer.

He stirred the tomato sauce with a spoon from a Sears set they had bought as newlyweds and placed it in a spoon rest decorated with an illustration of a couple kissing that they had received as a wedding present. He saw the picture of Sharon in her wedding gown and his heart swelled, just as it had then.

He looked to the refrigerator where her picture still hung—Sharon toward the end, bald head hidden under a pink bandana, face thin but smile as wide and radiant as ever. And then he heard her voice. "Katie needs a mom."

Josh stared at the picture. Sharon smiled back.

The timer dinged. Josh returned to the stove, grabbed two hot pads and withdrew the glass pan from the oven. Minutes later he was on his way to the bus station.

On impulse, he detoured to a section of River Street where vendors were displaying their wares. He bought a huge bouquet of daisies for ten dollars and walked to the bus depot.

He passed several costumed acquaintances and was sure they were shunning him even though, he conceded to himself, it was possible they were merely hunkered down against the steady rain. He hurried past a drug store before he realized there had been a mason jar with Katie's photo—Furbee's doing—on the counter. He backtracked and peeked in the window. The jar was empty. Someone had defaced Katie's picture with a mustache. Anger rose in him like bile.

The sound of grinding gears and the roar of a diesel engine pulled him from darkness to light and sent his heart soaring. Screw them and their pettiness, he thought. Katie was home.

By the time the bus from Camp Kanawha pulled into view, Josh was smiling from ear to ear despite the fact his daughter was suffering from bone cancer, his business was going down in flames and his town was facing the threat of nuclear disaster.

Knots of chatting mothers surrounded him beneath an overhang as the bus eased to a stop. Fathers, loners for the most part, ended cell phone conversations, set aside their newspapers and drifted in from a parking lot filled by a fleet of minivans adorned with expressions of devotion to the game. Tiny soccer balls topping radio antennas. Magnetic soccer balls clinging to the fuel filler door. Bumper stickers declaring that Soccer Players Kick Grass.

A blast of compressed air escaped with a whoosh as the bus's hydraulic doors swung open. The driver emerged, opened the cargo area underneath, and began dragging out suitcases, sleeping bags, duffel bags and footlockers and piling them beside the bus. Parents began sorting through the pile for their camper's belongings. A minute later, the first of the girls tumbled off dragging a net holding three soccer balls. Then another girl. And another. And another. A whole line of girls. A few paused to pose for final photos with new friends before drifting away with their parents.

Josh eyed each girl who came down the stairs. No Katie. As the flow of girls slowed to a trickle, Josh began to fret. He stood on his tiptoes. There were a few more girls inside and he watched with growing anxiety as they stepped off one by one. Katie was not among them.

Josh stepped around the luggage and the knot of campers and bounded on to the bus. He paced down the aisle heart pounding hoping to find his daughter still asleep in her seat. The seats were empty. Bathroom, he told himself as fear metastasized into panic. He rapped on the lavatory door, shouted, "Katie!" He pulled the latch and threw the door open. Empty.

"Forget something, mister?" Josh turned to see the bus driver standing in the aisle.

"My daughter," he said. "She was supposed to be on this bus."

"I loaded forty-seven and I dropped off forty-seven," the driver said defensively.

"Stay here," Josh commanded. He squeezed by the driver and sprinted to the parking lot where the last of the minivans was pulling away. Still clutching the daisies, Josh ran up and pounded on the driver's side door. A mother lowered the window. Josh recognized one of his daughter's teammates in the backseat.

"Where's Katie?" he shouted.

"She wasn't on the bus," the girl answered.

"Why not?" he almost shouted.

The girl recoiled. In his dripping coonskin cap, Josh realized he looked like a madman.

The minivan pulled away, leaving Josh bewildered and alone in the street.

....

CHAPTER FIFTY-FIVE

Josh sprinted back to the bus and pounded desperately on the door until it eased open. He bulled past the startled driver and, as if he could have overlooked a five-foot, ten-inch, thirteen-year-old the first time around, re-searched the bus. No Katie.

He whipped out his phone and dialed Katie. Voice mail. "Gimme the camp's phone number!" he demanded of the driver.

The man handed him the passenger manifest with a number at the top. Josh dialed with speed-blurred fingers.

"This is Josh Gibbs in Winston," he told the camp director. "I'm on the camp bus. My daughter Katie was supposed to be on it. She wasn't."

"You're sure she's not part of the long session? Sometimes there a mix-up, both parents aren't on the same page."

"She was supposed to be on the bus," Josh said sternly.

The director cleared his throat. "One thought does occur. Is it possible that your daughter may have needed a little space, given what she's facing?"

In years of reporting, Josh had learned to rule out nothing, to assume even the most bizarre scenarios might be possible. The thought had even crossed his mind that Katie had simply disobeyed instructions and stayed at camp. But he had dismissed it. Teens could be unpredictable but Katie generally wasn't.

And Katie running away didn't add up. She may have needed time to herself when he'd broken the news to her about the cancer, but Katie wasn't the type to flee—she faced challenges head-on. "There has to be another explanation," he insisted. "You search every inch of that camp." The camp director promised to call with any new information. Josh stumbled off the bus.

"Good luck, mister," the driver said. The bus shifted into gear and pulled away, leaving Josh on the sidewalk. His head was swirling. The drumbeat of the rain made it impossible for him to think.

He dialed Allison and got a fast busy. He dialed again with the same result. The third time he pounded the numbers even harder, as if sheer force could bring about a connection. Fast busy again.

An icon on his cell phone screen alerted Josh to a voice mail left by an Ohio area code number. He got through the third time and retrieved the message—from Pepper reminding him to observe Katie's pre-admission procedure, including nothing to eat after midnight. It ended with "It's important that there be no more delay."

Josh was beside himself. He dialed Allison again and got another fast busy. "Damn phones!" he swore. Like a reliever picking a runner off second base, he wound up and whirled to deliver a fastball into the brick wall of the bus station.

He balked at the last second. He took a deep breath. He turned the phone off, waited with waning patience for what seemed like an eternity as it rebooted, then redialed. Fast busy. Temples pounding, he tried again. This time, the call went through. But instead of the emergency dispatcher, Josh heard a confusing babble of competing conversations, one of which seemed to be about which Winston restaurant was most likely to have an open table for dinner that evening. He wanted to cry.

The problem, Josh realized, was not with his phone. The cellular transmission towers had simply been overwhelmed by the volume of traffic from the thousands in town for River Days. *Everyone* had phones, even Katie. He recalled the cell phone argument with his thirteen-year-old daughter. *Not until you're driving,* he'd ruled initially. *It's for safety,* she contended. Thank goodness he had relented. If only he could reach her now! He dialed three times before he got voice mail again. He followed up with a text. No response. Perhaps her battery had finally died.

Josh hurried back to the car, frustrated by the festival crowds leisurely crossing the street and blocking his path. He did a quick U-turn and headed for the office and a landline.

Cocktail hour had arrived and stayed. Despite the rain, a surprising number of early arrivals roamed the town, many wearing red commemorative River Days rain ponchos (ten dollars) and carrying commemorative Old Fashioned River Days mugs of beer (eight dollars). Vehicle traffic, slowed even more than usual by the weather, had reached gridlock. Josh choked the steering wheel and his blood pressure spiked. When a wheelchair van stopped to unload a group of geriatrics from the Hillcrest Manor Retirement Home, trapping the Volvo between a tour bus and a horse and buggy, he could take it no longer. He leaned on his horn for a full five seconds before leaning out the window and screaming, "Move! I need to find my daughter!"

"Relax, Davey Crockett! Have a beer," the man in the buggy shouted back. General laugher. Then from a woman, "If you'll pay her college tuition, you can have mine!" More laughter.

By the time he reached the office Josh was half-fearing he might drop from a stroke. Trailed by Furbee and a half-dozen staffers, he raced into his office and dialed Allison. He put the call on speaker and raised his hand for silence. "Katie's missing," he said so everyone could hear. "She wasn't on the bus. The camp director thinks she might have run away. I don't believe it. That's just not like her. Allison, those strings you have with the state police? Now's the time to pull them."

"Congressman Dorn could scramble the FBI," Furbee suggested, snatching up a phone book. "He's at the Sternwheeler." She read the hotel's number.

Josh dialed and was immediately placed on hold. He paced, stretching the phone cord to its limit—two steps one way and two steps back. Finally, a clerk answered. Josh blurted his name and position with the newspaper and demanded to speak with Congressman Dorn.

Josh heard clicking and the distant sound of a player piano.

"I'm sorry, sir. His phone is on 'Do Not Disturb.' Would you like to leave a message?'

"This is an emergency. I need to talk to him now."

"I'm sorry but when it's on D-N-D, I can't get through."

"THEN SEND SOMEONE TO HIS DAMN ROOM!" Josh mouthed "Sorry," to Furbee. He sucked in a calming breath and tried again with the clerk. "I understand you're overwhelmed with everyone checking in. But I need the congressman now. Can you at least give me his room number? I'll come down and see him myself."

Josh listened, his frustration building to outright fury. "Right," he snarled. "You don't give out that information." He slammed the handset into the cradle.

His hands were shaking. No, not just his hands. His whole body shook with rage-fueled palsy. Never could he remember being so angry. Even his long-time employees eyed him silently and warily, unspeaking as though fearing that breaking the silence might trigger another outburst of the boss's wrath.

Only Allison's fortuitous arrival a moment later snapped him out of it. Drained of anger, Josh felt unsteady on his feet, as though his legs had turned to rubber.

"Any troopers in the area are deployed for River Days. But the dispatcher told me they can't really do anything until someone's been missing twenty-hour hours anyway," Allison said.

"Dorn's our best hope," Josh said. "Let's go."

Chapter Fifty-Six

Allison extracted a blue-domed light from the glove box and stuck it on the dash of the Wagoneer. "Strictly for emergencies," she said. The Jeep exited the *News*'s parking lot in a rooster tail of gravel and burning rubber.

Josh checked his cell phone display every few seconds as though willing it to ring. Alerted by the emergency flasher, sedans, campers and station wagons veered obligingly to either side ahead of them, the parting of a red sea of brake lights. Josh caught glimpses of the people inside, adults up front, children in back, faces pressed against the window, straining to see. He scanned each face as if one might be that of his daughter. He envied the parents, their children safe, seatbelted just feet away.

He closed his eyes and tried to conjure Katie. He visualized her in places he knew—on the soccer field, at the park, in her room, in Winston. She was *somewhere*.

Outside town, traffic slowed to stop and go. Josh pounded the dash. "Of all the days. . . ."

"Hold on." Allison shifted to four-wheel drive and revved the Wagoneer up the curb and into Riverfront Park. Blue light flashing, they tore past startled tourists, detoured deftly around the pageant stage, and turned onto a midway lined by souvenir trailers on one side and food booths on the other.

Josh felt the back of the Wagoneer begin to slide. Working the pedals like an expert and steering into the skid, Allison straightened the vehicle just in time to avoid taking out a substantial portion of the Old Fashioned River Days art fair, including a half-dozen booths packed with handcrafted stoneware.

She bounced back onto the street not far from the hotel. They parked on the sidewalk and set off for the Sternwheeler. Josh's leg ached. He realized he'd been hammering down a non-existent brake pedal during the Wagoneer's long slide.

In keeping with the hotel's name, the Sternwheeler's lobby was made to look like a riverboat. Curtains, carpets, wallpaper and stained glass competed in an eye-popping collision of color-rich patterns. Columns outside the Paddle Wheel dining room had been painted to look like ornate, filigreed smokestacks. A portrait of the author marked the entrance to the opulent Samuel Clemens piano lounge where drinks were named for the characters in his Mark Twain novels. An order for a Becky Thatcher brought a Cosmopolitan. A painting of a very modest reclining nude—said to be the mistress of the original owner—hung above the bar. The bellhops wore mustaches, white broad-rimmed gamblers' hats and string ties.

A gaggle of tourists queued up at the reception desk waiting to speak with one of two clerks dressed as dance hall girls.

"Get in line in case we need to talk to a real person," Josh told Allison.

The house phone was a candlestick model. Josh picked up the earpiece and was connected to the hotel operator.

"Congressman Dorn's room, please."

"I'm sorry that line is busy. Would you like to leave a message?"

"No, just his room number please. I'm in the hotel."

"I'm sorry. We can't give out that information."

Josh slammed the earpiece back on the cradle so hard it drew the attention of one of the bellmen. "Careful, sir!" he admonished. "That's an antique."

Allison had advanced only a step or two nearer the reception desk. "We need to bust the line," Josh said. "Your white coat is in the car. They'd tell a doctor, wouldn't they?"

"You exaggerate my clout. We need someone they'll give the number to no question."

She saw a faded red Sunbird pull into a hotel's loading zone.

"You have cash?" she asked.

"Some. Maybe eighty dollars."

"C'mon."

Josh followed her outside. He understood when he spotted an antenna windsock and a magnetic Angelina's Pizza sign affixed to the driver's door. The young delivery woman had just gotten out. Allison asked, "How would you like to make a really big tip?"

The driver, who was shorter than Allison but of almost identical build, wore a uniform of a white tee-shirt shirt and cap displaying the Angelina's Pizza logo. She regarded them with a mixture of suspicion and possibility. "What do you have in mind?"

"Come with me," said Allison. "I'll explain."

Five minutes later, the delivery girl exited the lobby dressed in Allison's clothes. Allison followed a minute later wearing the delivery girl's jeans, t-shirt and cap. The delivery girl gave her a pizza.

Allison entered the lobby like a waiter with a tray of entrees. With no objection from the guests standing in line, she set the pizza box on the front of the desk and told the clerk, "Got a delivery but I can't read the room number. Name's Dorn."

The receptionist motioned her closer and whispered, "Room twenty-two."

Brain addled by alcohol and arousal, U.S. Congressman and Senate frontrunner Harry Dorn thought for quite some time that the banging echoing through his hotel room came from the bed's headboard, not, as he now perceived, from the door.

He cursed the efficiency of the Sternwheeler staff. It seemed just minutes since he'd ordered first, from room service, a bottle of scotch, then, seconds later, some fries and a hot fudge sundae. He'd not expected such prompt delivery. "Don't go anywhere," he told the girl beneath him. "One minute. I'll be back as good as ever." He rolled out of bed and grabbed a towel and his wallet. His towel hid his nudity but not his erection which thrust against the cloth. Those blue pills were a marvel!

On the other side of the door, a voice called out, "Congressman Dorn! Congressman Dorn!" Room Service. Prompt. He appreciated the man's eagerness if not—just now—his timing.

Dorn eased the door open to the length of the security chain. A wild-eyed man loomed inches away. Dorn moved to shut the door.

Josh stopped it with his foot. "Wait, please!" he shouted. "It's Josh Gibbs."

Dorn regarded him with a bloodshot, Cyclopsian eye.

"It's an emergency," Josh pleaded. "My daughter. Please. I need your help!"

"Tomorrow," Dorn slurred. His breath reeked of whisky.

Josh wasn't about to be put off. He needed help locating Katie and Dorn was his best chance. His threw his weight against the door.

The chain ripped from its anchor. Dorn was thrown to the carpet, leaving his towel behind. The crazy man in the coonskin cap and a pizza delivery girl landed on top of him. Dorn was naked beneath them.

"What do you think you're doing?" Dorn yelled. "Get the hell off me!"

"Somebody owes me three hundred dollars," the girl said, pulling on her jeans.

Allison untangled herself. She was aghast. The girl could not have been more than fifteen.

Josh rolled off the congressman and helped him from the floor. Part of him wanted to slug the scumbag. He shut it down. Allison could play the white knight. He was here for Katie. "Katie's disappeared, maybe kidnapped. I need help now."

Dorn retrieved the towel and tried to look as dignified as circumstances permitted. He'd been in tough spots before but nothing like this. His options, he understood, were limited.

"Mr. Gibbs, your daughter shouldn't suffer for another stupid decision, mine or yours. No stories about this or the plant and I'll expedite this with the FBI. Agreed?"

Josh swallowed hard and nodded. "Deal. Provided they actually do something."

Before they left, Allison pulled the camera belonging to the *Winston News* from her purse and snapped a photo of Dorn and the girl. "You're trash," she told him.

She took the girl with her. "Where's my three hundred dollars?" the girl wailed.

Dorn locked the door, turned the deadbolt and, hands trembling, reattached the chain to the splintered doorframe. He'd bought time, but that was all. No way was he calling the FBI. Even if a federal crime were involved the last thing he needed was a bunch of investigators in town asking questions. He felt drained. His life was over: The Carbon Forward money. Dead. The Senate. Dead. His marriage. Dead. The only thing very much alive was the possibility of prison. Unless Josh and Allison could be stopped.

Dorn hated what he had to do next but he was out of options. He opened his phone and entered the digits with numbed fingers. Bludhorn answered on the second ring. "Vince," Dorn blurted. "I need your help."

CHAPTER FIFTY-SEVEN

Josh accepted three hundred dollars from the ATM in the Sternwheeler lobby and handed it to the girl—the second time, he mused, that he had given money to a prostitute for no sexual services in return.

The girl left. Josh tried Katie. Voice mail again. He settled into a couch in the lobby, his head spinning as he tried to make sense of everything that had happened. The scene with Dorn had been deeply disturbing. Josh couldn't look at the girl without thinking that she was almost the same age as his daughter, that somewhere she had a father, a man just like him. His heart ached for them both. But then, he thought bitterly, at least the girl wasn't missing. There was no pain greater than loss.

"Do you think that it's possible Katie just ran away?" Allison plopped down beside him, still wearing her pizza delivery hat. Josh removed it. She fluffed her hair.

"Always possible. But I tend to agree with what you said earlier. She's a pretty grounded young woman."

"But kidnapping? Who would—" He stopped. He remembered the cat. "You don't think Bludhorn . . ."

It fact, her very first thought when Katie went missing was that Bludhorn was responsible, that Katie's disappearance was orchestrated by the same dark forces that had perpetrated a nuclear disaster, attempted to blackmail her with an embarrassing DVD and turned the town against them both. But she had said nothing to Josh at the time. There was no reason to panic him without evidence. "He's capable," she acknowledged. She could see Josh pale. "He did bring back Hippocrates unharmed."

"Well, we got Dorn's help," Josh noted. He had no second thoughts about suppressing a story in order to aid the recovery of his daughter. If it ever came out, people would understand. It was no different from a prisoner of war signing a false confession to save his own skin.

"I wouldn't count on Dorn," Allison said. She hated to be so discouraging. She understood the decision to kill a story in exchange for Dorn's assistance. But Josh deserved the truth. The congressman was an unprincipled, alcoholic, lying, pedophile whose only interests were sick sexual gratification and reelection. Politicians like him were why kids like Katie couldn't get decent health coverage. He was in the same class of abuser as Darryl Dunn and her ex-husband. "I don't trust him for a minute. That's why I took the photo. It's insurance in case he doesn't come through."

"So what now? I can't just sit here and do nothing."

Allison felt the same way. Katie was missing. Winston was facing a public health catastrophe. They had to turn to someone, someone who would sound the alarm. State and federal officials had been no help. "What about Chief Holt?"

"I think he's in on it. He has to be. He works for the plant. Plus, how else would he know that we were out there?"

"Same question we had before," Allison said. "Is he one of the good guys or the bad? We don't know. But he's our last, best hope."

Josh's cell phone beeped with voice mail. He seethed. He had never understood how a call went to voice mail when his phone hadn't even indicated a call coming in. He pounded in the code and held the phone to his ear. His heart leapt when he heard Katie's voice—"Daddy"—followed by a burst of static that sounded familiar but which he could not identify.

"Where are you?" he shouted to the recording. But that was the entire message. The call had been dropped or the phone had died.

"She's alive," he gasped with audible relief. He dialed Katie back. The call went to voice mail.

He tried over and over with the same result. Katie was alive. But now what? What had happened? Where was she? Just because she was okay now didn't mean she was out of danger. He was ready to try anything. "Let's find the chief," he said.

"Where do you think he is?"

"Cop shop's right around the corner. If he isn't there himself, someone will know where to find him."

CHAPTER FIFTY-EIGHT

Josh cut sharply around a cadre of Civil War soldiers ambling from the Sternwheeler bar. Allison trailed him like a halfback following blockers. They bee-lined for the police station three blocks away. The door was locked. Josh knocked, cupped his hands and squinted through the window. "I don't think anyone's home."

Allison noticed a cup from the Java Joynt on a railing. Checked boxes on the side identified it as coffee with a double-shot of espresso. It was still warm. Had Vince just been here or was she just being paranoid?

She dialed the department, heard the phone ring inside and left a message about the cesium-saturated lake at Betheltown. She needed

Holt to understand that the threat from the lagoon was far greater than the people at the plant realized. She hoped he was on their side and checking messages. She hung up. "Where would he be?"

"Riding herd on the festival."

"We haven't seen him," Allison pointed out.

"Maybe he worked the 10k this morning and went home. We should check."

The Wagoneer sat where they left it.

Allison threaded the car through the crowds to Holt's apartment building, a drab converted motel. "Blinds are drawn," she observed. "Squad car's not in the lot."

"That's his only ride," Josh said. "So he isn't here, either."

"Where's that leave us?"

Josh wished he knew. He was running out of options. He tried Katie again. No luck. It was hopeless.

"Maybe he's at the plant," Allison suggested.

Josh thought it was possible—especially given the plant's recently heightened security—but was reluctant to risk a trip. "I need to be here if something develops. Anyway, it's a long shot."

"But it's our *only* shot."

Allison took Josh's silence as assent. She steered away from the river, in the opposite direction from the flood of cars, vans and campers converging on Winston. A few minutes later, they were climbing the hills toward Holt's outpost.

Josh was glad he'd gone along. It felt better to be doing something instead of nothing.

The rain had become heavier and fog filled the valleys. A huge outcropping of bare rock loomed ahead, covered in hand-painted declarations of devotion, the Greek letters of various fraternities, the graduation years of high school classes and ten huge white block letters that cut through the gloom: "Jesus Saves." Josh wasn't a church-goer but decided a prayer for Katie couldn't hurt.

The emergency flasher and the fog combined to envelope the road in an aura of milky blue as Allison steered through the slick switchbacks, rock walls on one side, cliffs on the other. Josh thought back to the incredible scene in the hotel room. Dorn a pervert! He told Allison it was hard to believe.

"Not for me," she said. "He stayed in our home one night when I was fourteen. He tried to feel me up. My parents told me I was imagining things. Until today, I wasn't sure."

The beginnings of a trail of mistreatment, Josh thought. He was beginning to understand. "Why did you let me ask him for help?"

"I didn't want to ruin the chance he might help Katie."

Allison's attention shifted rapidly between the road and the rearview mirror. "Someone's behind us," she said. Josh swiveled for a look.

The headlights drew to within a car length. Allison slowed and edged close to the rock face. The car pulled along side. It was a BMW. Vince's. He was at the wheel. A man Allison didn't recognize was in the passenger seat. Her eyes returned to the road.

"He wants you to pull over," Josh said.

"Should I?"

Josh was torn. If Allison was right, Bludhorn knew something about Katie. Maybe this was Bludhorn returning the cat. On the other hand, he was the attorney for the plant. The plant was evil. The DVD and the kidnapping—if it was that—of Katie were not acts of reasonable, compassionate men. "Keep going. We have to find Holt."

Allison punched the gas, sending a spray of gravel down the hillside. The BMW quickly pulled back alongside. She glanced over. Bludhorn was waving frantically for her to stop. Should she trust him or should she not? Allison tried to read the eyes of her husband before she looked back to the road.

Bludhorn leaned on the horn. Allison looked again. The passenger raised a pistol. Disbelief registered in her ex-husband's eyes. She knew instantly that this was far more than even he had bargained for. Bludhorn was many things but he was not stupid when it came to his own self interest. An accident at the plant, even with a big fine, even leading to shame and bankruptcy, was one thing. A murder rap with a life sentence was something else. Not even Vince was willing to risk that. But his people were. His people were out of control.

Allison hit the brakes. Bludhorn swerved sharply to the left, deflecting the gunman's aim. The Wagoneer's side window exploded, showering them with glass. Allison shrieked. The Wagoneer's back end fishtailed dangerously. Then the Jeep straightened out with a shudder.

Josh looked behind them. The sharp turn to the left on the wet road had put the BMW into skid. Tires screeching, it careened at top speed toward the cliff. Flaring brake lights turned the fog a baleful red. The shriek of rending metal and the whipcrack of snapping trees split the air as the car swept over the edge.

Allison brought the Wagoneer to a quick stop. They got out and rushed to the cliff's edge. The BMW rested partially submerged upside-down in a shallow creek bed, engine running, steam rising from its radiator.

They watched for a minute, too stunned to speak. Gradually Allison's heart stopped pounding. "Dial star H-P for the Highway Patrol," she said.

Josh did as he was told and handed her the phone.

"It's Doctor Allison Wright," she told the dispatcher. "I'm on my way to the Recovery Metals plant. Two miles short of the entrance. Two men in a BMW just went over the cliff. One of em's my ex, Vince Bludhorn. The other one's armed and dangerous. He just shot out my car window."

They returned to the Jeep. Allison steered the Wagoneer onto the gravel road that defined the plant's perimeter. Holt's shack emerged from the gloom. A pickup truck sat out front. Josh couldn't restrain himself. He jumped out of the car and sprinted toward the shack. Allison put on the lead apron she'd brought from the clinic and followed.

Josh got to the truck and froze. Blood trickled down the running board and swirled into a puddle of rainwater. His friend and employee Jimmy Mayes lay curled up on the front seat, his life draining to the floor.

Allison rolled Mayes over. His neck had been slashed but she found a faint pulse. Allison couldn't believe he was alive. "We'll get help," she promised.

"He can't hear you," Josh pointed out. "He's deaf."

Mayes's eyes flickered open. He lifted his right hand, began signing. "Poison metal. In the lagoon," Josh translated. "They're gonna bulldoze it."

"They can't!" Allison said.

Josh got the picture. The radioactive tide would flood Betheltown lake and be on its way to the Ohio River and Winston's water supply.

Mayes signed again. "He says we don't have much time."

Allison stroked his forehead. "Who did this to you?"

"Those who defiled my ancestor. Who stole land. Who poisoned creatures," Josh translated.

Josh signed a question. "Why throw the fish? Why not go to the cops?"

Looking in Mayes' eyes was like watching two candles burn down. Allison knew he had only seconds left. His fingers twitched, signed, "Sacred. No Move."

And then the candles sputtered out. Before Allison could save him. Before Josh could even say he was sorry. If he and Allison hadn't been so hot on the trail of the plant, Jimmy Mayes might still be alive.

Josh removed a piece of paper from Mayes's pocket and unfolded it. It was a final proof of the Friends of Chief Cornstalk ad.

Allison laid Mayes's head back on the seat. "What do you think he was saying?"

"Betheltown's sacred ground. I think he was afraid that going to the cops would lead people to discover the Remaining. The people who never left when the plant came in would be forced to leave."

"Why do you think Mayes was here at the shack? Did Holt kill him?"

The idea had already occurred to Josh. If Holt had killed Mayes, there was no longer any question whether the chief was one of the good guys or the bad. He wasn't just a tool of the plant, he was a murderer. But Josh wasn't ready to convict him yet.

"I don't think so. If Holt killed Mayes, why leave him here? I think it's just as likely Jimmy was attacked—probably by one of Vince's out-of-control plant goons—and came to Holt's shack, thinking it was the closest place he could find help."

"But where's the chief?"

Terrified of what he might find, Josh eased open the shack's door and turned on the light. The place was empty. Chief Holt's police uniform hung on the back of a chair. Allison noticed the radio's glowing dial. She turned up the volume and The Cincinnati Reds post-game show filled the small room. The Reds had won. The radio was replaying the call of the walk-off homer.

The sound of ash on horsehide stirred something deep in Josh's consciousness. He dialed his voice mail and replayed Katie's message, listening this time not to the voice but for ambient noise—for clues to Katie's whereabouts. The recording was so brief that he had to listen to it four times before he was able to isolate a sharp crack at the end of the recording, followed by the static.

He played the message for Allison. "The last noise sounds like the start of a CB radio transmission," she said. "You know that funny noise when they first push the talk button? Could she be with a trucker?"

Josh played the message again. Allison was right about the static. But the only trucker he knew was dead. Who else used radios? He played the message again. CRACK!

That was it. The sound of a sharply hit baseball. Followed by static from the beginning of a CB radio transmission, like that from a police radio. "Katie was here," he concluded. "With the chief. While the ballgame was on."

They were getting close. He was equally elated and scared to death.

CHAPTER FIFTY-NINE

Josh scoured the perimeter road for any clue that might lead to Katie but even his own footprints were immediately obliterated by the downpour. "Katie!" he shouted again and again, his words dying in the pounding rain.

Allison scrambled up the berm to get a view of the lagoon. More drain hoses had been added. Radioactive water cascaded down the hill toward the rain-swollen lake. She felt so helpless. Everything—finding Katie, preventing the cesium-filled lake from overflowing—depended on their ability to find Chief Holt.

Provided Holt was on their side. If he wasn't, Katie was in the hands of a killer facing the same horrible fate as Jimmy Mayes. And even if Holt was on their side, it was game, set and match unless he could persuade the plant from draining the lagoon or at least summon more powerful authorities to stop it on their own. Saving Katie and saving Winston lay in the chief's hands. He could be their best hope or their worst nightmare. They had no idea which. She took a deep breath and tightened her lead apron.

Josh was down to hope. Sharon gone. The *News* gone. Katie gone. Only hope to hang on to. Only hope and Allison.

He refused to believe he would never see his daughter again. He arrived at the top of the berm simultaneously with the odor of diesel as the motor on a piece of heavy equipment rumbled to life. A bulldozer driven by a man in work clothes crested a hill a quarter mile away and crawled toward the lagoon.

"This is it," Allison said. "We're too late."

Chief J. P. Holt watched the bulldozer advance from the perimeter road. He was tired. Tired of being a puppet. Tired of being a slave to his addiction, to his bookie, to Bludhorn and the bullies.

It was time to just say no. No to Viggy. No to another bet, to another drink. No to the plant.

He would still owe them money—almost $50,000 by now—but he would no longer grovel for loans, no longer do things that increasingly were against his nature, against the whole idea of public service. He would reclaim the man he had once been.

The man he had been before the beaning.

Only two people knew it had not been an accident. His coach—a bully very much like Bludhorn, Holt saw now—had told him to fire a high, hard one right at the batter's chin. Payback for an earlier homer. Something for the batter to be afraid of, something that hurt.

He had said yes. He had not expected the kid's eye to pop out. He'd not even expected to hit the kid, just to brush him back. But no matter. He had said yes to the bully. It had ruined his life, ruined it far worse than the life of the kid he had blinded.

He would not say yes to bullies again.

Holt walked into the path of the bulldozer and extended his palm like a traffic cop.

Until that moment, Josh, transfixed by the dozer, hadn't even seen the man. Even then, he wasn't sure he could believe it. Allison spoke for both of them. "Good Lord!" she said. "That's the chief!"

The bulldozer driver waved Holt out of the way.

Holt recognized the driver. One of the goons. He wanted no mistake about his intentions. He widened his stance and held up both hands now. He had never expected to get in as deep as he was, but they were mistaken in thinking he did not have limits. You did what you had to do. Sometimes, drawing the line was what you had to do.

The dozer kept coming.

The greed of these people was obscene. And kidnapping the girl. Beyond belief! Now, they intended to bulldoze the lagoon. Based on what Allison Wright had said on his voice mail, that was something he just couldn't let happen. He had lived here all his life. This was his town. They'd not poison it on his watch. He stood his ground.

The bulldozer closed to within thirty feet of the lagoon.

I should have known, Holt thought. I should never have thrown the pitch. I should never have bet. He cursed his weakness. He would not be weak now. He'd called for help. He hoped it was on the way.

Allison watched in horror. "It'll stop, won't it?"

Josh stared frozen. Could it end like this, with Katie still missing? He thought his fear of death had ended with Sharon's. He thought he'd seen the worst it had to offer. There were times he had wished for it for himself because death would end the pain. But his daughter—missing. That was almost worse. Please, God, don't let it end here, he prayed.

The bulldozer picked up speed.

The dozer was on almost him. Suddenly, Holt knew. These people were responsible for Old Cheese Face. They were willing to take a child. They were willing to kill him. The dozer was not going to stop. Holt heard the grinding of gears as the driver lowered the blade.

Safety lay six feet to the left. Holt planted his foot and sprang but the wet ground gave way. His feet went out from under him and he hit the ground hard. Holt clawed desperately toward safety as the descending blade passed over his head.

Josh tried to shield Allison but neither could avoid seeing the lower half of the chief's body disappear beneath the churning treads in a mist of blood. Allison felt sick. There was no way the chief could have survived.

Holt regarded his situation with a sense of detachment. He found it interesting that he should still be alive, face down in the mud, when he existed only above the hips. He was amused that the plant would never get its $50,000. He was very curious about what would come next. He did not feel pain, he felt *aware*. Perhaps, the feeling was peace.

He unsnapped his holster and took out his gun with his right hand. He used his left to lever his torso from the mud.

The dozer sliced into the berm and backed off for another run.

It was getting harder for Holt to see. The Recovery Metals logo on the goon's uniform was out of focus. He knew he did not have long. He raised the gun.

The logo became a catcher's mitt. He knew what to do. He blotted out all else and squeezed the trigger.

The bulldozer's engine roared.

The blade rose above the cab. The driver slumped in the seat, blood spreading from a single hole in his back. The dozer climbed the bank until it was almost vertical, lurched to the left and flipped over on its back, treads churning like legs on a centipede.

Josh's heart thumped against his chest. He and Allison ran to where Holt lay. The lower half of his body looked like flattened hamburger. Allison felt for a pulse. She didn't see how he could still be alive. He was, but he didn't have long.

Josh knelt beside the chief. "Where is she?" He lifted Holt by the lapels. "Where is my daughter?"

The chief's eyes rolled back. Pink spittle bubbled from his mouth. Allison touched Josh's arm and shook her head. Josh knew Holt was gone and with him, the last link to his daughter. Or had he been mistaken about the noise? Had his overactive mind played tricks on him?

Despair overwhelmed him. The nightmare that had begun with the lost Pulitzer and continued with Sharon was not over. It had once again turned real. Mayes was dead. The chief was dead. Dorn was corrupt. Everything he had hung on to—his newspaper, his town—was about to be wiped out. Maybe he could rebuild from all that, but not without Katie. Without Katie, why would he want to?

Allison knew what he was feeling. The people at the plant were ruthless killers willing to poison the earth for eons. And all for a buck. But even that didn't matter against the fact that the trail to Katie had been lost. She loved the girl as much as she had come to love Josh. She put her arm around him and held him close.

Allison picked a pair of steel-rimmed glasses from the mud and handed them to Josh. "Chief Holt saved us. I have to believe Katie's okay."

Josh wanted desperately to believe, but he was cursed. He couldn't recall the last time his optimism had been rewarded. The chief had performed heroically at the end. But had his conversion from the dark side come soon enough?

An ambulance arrived, then a van from the West Virginia State Environmental Defense Team. The regional health director emerged from a sedan. The director was nicely tanned.

A couple of state police cars parked on the perimeter road along the woods behind the lagoon. Josh and Allison were heading over to report Katie's disappearance when something large, long and heavy dropped from the sky and landed with a thud in front of them. Josh could read the lettering on the duffel bag in the gloom: Camp Kanawha. Katie's legs dangled from a limb twenty feet above.

Josh's heart felt like it would burst with joy.

He snatched her from the trunk before she finished shinnying to the ground and gave her so many kisses he didn't even try to count. Allison wrapped her arms around them both.

When they had stopped crying, Allison took Katie and asked her some questions in private. "The chief did her no harm," she reported.

They were making their way back to the Wagoneer when a state official stopped them. "One of you Allison Wright?"

"That's me."

"We have some questions for you and Mr. Gibbs."

CHAPTER SIXTY

Sirens had given way to the hum of gasoline generators powering banks of portable lights by the time Josh and Allison finished answering the authorities' first round of questions. Allison volunteered to remain at the plant to work with the growing army of state and federal authorities, not including, Josh noted, the FBI. Holt's deputy drove Josh and Katie home in a patrol car.

It was 11 p.m. when they walked into the kitchen. Josh remembered Katie could have nothing after midnight. He warmed the lasagna. Katie wolfed down two helpings—"better than camp food," she mumbled—

and started on the plate of Allison's oatmeal cookies. She opened the first of her notes. *You are a star!*

Josh listened with delight to the stories from camp—about the games, the goals, the coaches, the electives, but mostly about the other girls, her camper friends. His heart melted when she unfolded the huge "Good Luck, Katie" poster they'd given her at the last camp fire—along with the award for best camper. He wanted to ask about the boyfriend but decided that could wait until later. There'd been enough excitement for one day.

He cautiously broached the topic of Chief Holt. Allison had explained that it would be therapeutic for Katie to talk—but only when she was ready. "Give her an opening and see," she had suggested.

It turned out Katie was eager. Josh was glad to listen. "He told me he was picking me up because the people at the plant were going to kidnap me. He said the only way he could stop the kidnapping was to get to me first. He took me to his little shack. I called you from there on my phone but it ran out of battery." She took another cookie. "He said they were going to bulldoze the pond and it would poison everyone. He said they'd already killed two people and dumped one of them in the river. He said he had to stop them. We watched from the woods until we saw the bulldozer. He told me to hide until it was safe."

"Did he tell you why they wanted to kidnap you?"

"To stop you from reporting something bad they'd done. He said I should be proud of you because you're a hero."

Josh swallowed hard. There was no escaping the fact he had put his daughter's life in danger.

After dinner, he started a load of laundry.

Wait," Katie said. She unzipped her duffel and handed her father a blue and gold lanyard. "I made this for you in arts and crafts." She reached back into the duffel, and pulled out a hand-thrown pottery mug. "We made these for our moms. I'm giving mine to Allie."

Later, he packed her bag for the hospital. Katie made sure he included plenty of books, and pictures of her mother and the 13-0 Black Ravens.

At 1 a.m. he tucked Katie into bed, kissed her and turned out the light.

Furbee was waiting when he arrived back at his office. He had one question. "Where do we stand?"

Furbee answered. "With all the starts and stops, we have enough ink to print a four-page section. That's it. And only a few thousand copies at that."

Josh didn't hesitate. "We're going with an Extra on everything that's happened. Three pages of news and one full-page ad on the back cover—from the Friends of Chief Cornstalk."

He caught Furbee's raised eyebrow. "They're prepaid," he pointed out. "Plus it fits the content."

Furbee clapped her hands. "I'll call in the crew. Press rolls at 6 a.m."

Allison arrived looking drawn and tired from all the questions but eager to get out the news.

Josh switched on his computer. Three pages of content and it was all up to him. He rewrote the contamination to encompass the developments at the plant, changing it frequently based on reports from Allison.

The story quoted Allison about the hazards of exposure to radiation and listed places victims could turn for help.

The story devoted significant attention to the life and death of Chief Holt, a hero who died doing what he was sworn to do—protect the citizens of Winston.

Josh wrote a separate story about Congressman Harry Dorn. He made sure there was room for the photo Allison had taken at the Sternwheeler.

A third story spotlighted the *Winston News*'s own Jimmy Mayes. Josh cobbled it together from what he had seen in Betheltown, what he had learned from the dying Mayes and the content of the Friends of Chief Cornstalk ad.

The ad was headlined: *The Third Betrayal of Chief Cornstalk*. An italic precede said the purpose of the ad was to alert the community to the danger from the plant, which also meant correcting the version of history portrayed in the Old Fashioned River Days historical pageant.

The story began with a recounting of Betheltown, the community on land condemned and seized for the plant but never used. Most of the five hundred inhabitants relocated but a few—who referred to themselves as the 'Remaining'—never left.

Some like Jimmy Mayes, Josh wrote, regarded the land as sacred, the resting place for the body of Chief Cornstalk. For Mayes, the plant and its actions defiled sacred ground and represented another betrayal of the great Shawnee chief.

The first betrayal, the Friends of Chief Cornstalk ad explained, was Cornstalk's death. Josh quoted from the ad:

"Following his defeat near Winston on October 10, 1774, Cornstalk and the Shawnees relocated to Ohio and agreed to end attacks on settlers on the east side of the river. In 1777, at the height of the American Revolution, Cornstalk journeyed to Fort Randolph to warn the Colonials that the British were inciting his tribe to attack but that, instead, his tribe was prepared to join the Americans. Cornstalk was seized and imprisoned. A month later he was shot twelve times, murdered along with his son. As he lay dying, he spoke a curse." Josh's story quoted it in full.

"I was the border man's friend. Many times I have saved him and his people from harm. I never warred with you, but only to protect our wigwams and lands. I refused to join your paleface enemies with the red coats. I came to the fort as your friend and you murdered me. You have murdered by my side, my young son . . . . For this, may the curse of the Great Spirit rest upon this land. May it be blighted by nature. May it even be blighted in its hopes. May the strength of its peoples be paralyzed by the stain of our blood."

The ad listed the area disasters that followed—the worst coal mine disaster in American history in Monongah, West Virginia in 1907; one hundred fifty local people killed by a tornado in 1944; the Silver Bridge disaster which sent forty-six people hurtling to their death in the Ohio

River in 1967; the 1970 crash of a chartered plane near Huntington which killed the entire Marshall University football team; the 1978 deaths of fifty-one men working on the Willow Island power station. The plant catastrophe was the most recent on the list.

Cornstalk's second betrayal, the ad said, was the disrespect accorded his body in burial. He was originally interred near the fort where he was murdered. In 1840, some of his remains were moved to the courthouse grounds. When they were unearthed again and reburied in 1954, only three teeth and fifteen bone fragments were found.

The third betrayal was the conduct, indeed the very existence, of the plant.

The story concluded by noting that the ad had been signed by the *News* pressman who identified himself as president of the Friends of Chief Cornstalk group. In the ad, the pressman noted he was changing the spelling of his last name to his family name, the name of his ancestor, Wynepueschiska. The signature read 'Jimmy Maize.'

At 6 a.m., Josh felt the Goss Community offset press rumble to life—a familiar and comforting feeling at a very unfamiliar time.

Allison dropped Josh off at his house and went home to change. She was still wearing the pizza delivery uniform.

Josh woke Katie. An hour later, they were crossing the Ohio River on their way to Columbus.

....

CHAPTER SIXTY-ONE

The attendants paused short of the automatic doors reading Pediatric Surgery. Josh leaned over the gurney and kissed his groggy daughter—thirteen times, plus one for luck. He looked at the photograph she held of the famous Black Ravens girls' soccer team, 13-0. He turned to a man wearing green scrubs, a Donald Duck surgical cap and blue clogs with yellow smiley faces on the front. "Throw everything you got at it," he told the surgeon. "We need a win." The surgeon nodded. The doors opened. Pepper, the gurney and Katie disappeared.

A nurse directed Josh to a waiting room. He was its only occupant. He leafed through two magazines. He identified each of the species in the soothing tropical fish tank. He figured more than an hour had passed and he was starting to worry. A short surgery, he reasoned, meant a good biopsy and no immediate amputation. A bad biopsy and immediate amputation was likely to take much longer. He looked at his watch. Only thirty minutes had elapsed. Journalists, he decided, were not meant for waiting rooms. They needed to be close to the action, the first to know. Josh bolted from the waiting room and established a sentry post in a plastic chair just outside the automatic doors.

At first, he sprang to his feet each time the doors opened. As the parade of orderlies, nurses, doctors and other surgical cases became endless, he numbed to the sound. Only the clatter of gurney wheels got his attention. Was it Katie? Tubes, oxygen masks and surgical caps made it difficult to tell. He developed a quicker test. They came out feet first. One leg or two?

The doors opened with no sound of a gurney. Elbow resting on his thigh, hand supporting his chin—a pose like The Thinker—Josh was calculating the number of dots per tile in the floor. He didn't look up until a pair of bright blue clog shoes with smiley faces on the front walked into his view. The surgeon, accompanied by Dr. Pepper. The verdict was in.

Josh sprang to his feet. Too fast. His knees felt wobbly. Pepper was still wearing his mask. Josh searched his eyes for a sign. Was he seeing defeat or relief? He thought he might faint.

Pepper removed his mask. "The Black Ravens," he smiled, "are still undefeated."

His joy did not prevent him from respecting the admonition of Walker Burns, his first city editor, to take nothing for granted. So only after he had seen for himself that Katie still had two legs and only after the doctors assured him that it would be hours before she awoke, he called Allison. She was ecstatic.

"I'm afraid the news isn't so good here," she reported after pumping Josh for the details about the operation. "Spike was airlifted to Charleston but it was too late. His grandmother appears to be okay, along with the rest of the Remaining, but we've already identified two dozen plant workers who received high levels of radiation exposure. Four of them won't make it to the weekend. Of course, we won't know the final number of fatalities for years."

"At least eight," Josh noted. "Jimmy Maize. Spike. Darryl. Chief Holt and the four from the plant."

"Make it nine. A body washed up on Possum Island. They think it's a guy who died in the original accident."

"What about the cleanup?"

"Teams from Homeland Security are all over the place. They've already recovered Darryl's cesium from the lake and the metal from the lagoon at Recovery Metals. The stuff's going to be loaded into these huge casks that they use for spent nuclear fuel but there's a whole other problem about where to put it after that—the same problem the healthcare business has getting rid of high-level radioactive material in the first place. They've put the plant and about ten square miles around it totally off limits until the cleanup is complete. They say it could take years."

"It's just as bad as you said it would be," Josh observed.

But beyond that, he found himself unable to react. Each of the events of the preceding two weeks—Katie's cancer, her disappearance, the murders of Jimmy Maize and the chief, the Dorn scandal, the radioactive threat, even his developing relationship with Allison—were consuming, life-changing experiences. Experiencing them all at once had left him emotionally drained, numb. He had nothing left—beyond a conviction that whatever the challenge was he would find a way to get through it.

"There is one positive development," Allison continued. "Congressman Dorn resigned. His office says he's entered a treatment center. Blames the stress of the campaign."

So many story ideas flooded into Josh's brain he couldn't keep track.

He had no doubt: he was right in the middle of the biggest story of his life. He called the newspaper after he hung up with Allison. "Furbee, how are we going to cover all this? There's enough news for a year! How can we even publish this week? I've got Katie—"

Furbee interrupted him. "Some of your old Atlanta buddies showed up to cover the story. They learned about your situation. A couple are taking vacation time to stay and more are coming later to help the *News* until you're back and things slow down." Josh was flabbergasted. "I do have one question. Do these Atlanta guys know how to make deadlines?"

Josh had to laugh. "What about ink?"

"We're floating in it. The trucking company called to apologize. Claims it was all a mix-up. And apparently they buy ink by the truck-loads in Atlanta. Your guys didn't think they'd miss a few barrels."

Josh shook his head in amazement.

"I'm just getting to the good news. Somehow, your reporter friends found out about Katie. One of them started grilling the health insurance company. Kind of reminded them that they'd look pretty bad if they didn't pay for everything, especially now that you're a hero."

Hero. Josh had never thought of himself that way. If there were any heroes they had to include people like Furbee who never quit trying. He had no doubt how the information about his insurance problems had made its way to the Atlanta reporters. He could never leave a profession that produced people like his colleagues in Atlanta and a newspaper that included people like Furbee. No matter how big the offer from the group in Pennsylvania and Bella Partners, there would be no sale of the *Winston News* for as long as he had anything to say about it.

"Another thing," Furbee said, as if she were on his wavelength. "A fax came in from Bella Partners and the Paddlewheel project is off. I'd never heard of them but Charles said Bella Partners is affiliated with Recovery Metals. What's the Paddlewheel project?"

Josh couldn't believe his ears. He had come *that close* to selling the *Winston News* to the people behind the plant, owners who would then be free of any threat of independent oversight. "Nothing," Josh replied. "Nothing at all."

....

CHAPTER SIXTY-TWO

The sky darkened and the wind whipped small cyclones of dead leaves through the gravestones in Winston Memorial Gardens.

Under a green vinyl canopy, a minister concluded a final prayer over the casket of Darryl Dunn. Allison crossed herself. Her hunch had been wrong but she was glad that she had come. Even Darryl Dunn deserved at least one mourner.

She was returning to her car when she noticed a woman in black watching from a distance. So she had been right after all. She walked up to the woman and extended her hand.

"I'm sorry for your loss," she told Candi Cloninger.

"He wasn't all bad, you know," Cloninger said. "He had his faults but they had no cause to kill him."

"Why did they, Candi?"

"To keep him quiet. He figured out they'd paid him off in poison metal. They thought he was going to talk."

"Let's get out of the weather. Coffee's on me. You can tell me how the whole thing worked."

Cloninger stirred her Java Joynt latte. "The plant had a deal with the truckers. In addition to their base pay, Darryl got a nice commission on 'undocumented' metals."

"Undocumented?"

"Stuff that's not on the manifest. Maybe it's stuff he didn't pay for. Maybe it's stuff that might not fit environmental regulations, so to speak. Darryl collected his commissions by retaining recycled platinum, gold and silver which he'd sell. Only he found out one batch was bad."

"How'd he learn that?"

"When the newspaper called. The guy left a message saying he was going to do a story about Darryl and his supplier. Of course, that was the plant. His bosses freaked out when he told them."

Allison felt terrible. In some ways that meant she had been responsible for Dunn's murder. She had badgered Josh into leaving the message in an attempt to get Dunn to respond to her calls. Instead, he'd told his bosses. She swallowed hard. "So they killed him to keep him from talking to the paper."

"It was more than that. Darryl was pretty upset when he found out he'd been paid off in bad metal. He threatened to blackmail the plant with some undocumented medical machine he'd kept as evidence to tie them into this. That was his mistake."

Allison felt a little better. She remembered finding the metal with the Columbus hospital logo amid the wreckage at Dunn's.

"Candi, you remember Darryl putting something from the machine in his safe?"

"Oh, sure. Some neat powder that glowed bright blue. But someone stole the safe. Probably when they trashed the house."

She had one more question. "Did Darryl cook meth?"

"He did a lot of things but not that. I heard they found a cooker but the killers must have planted it to throw the cops off track."

The women finished their coffee. Allison suggested they go to the clinic where she was pleased to see that Cloninger's tongue had healed and that early intervention had prevented further problems.

Josh was delighted to find Allison waiting in the driveway when he arrived back home. He found a long-forgotten bottle of red wine and poured glasses while Allison boiled pasta to go with her homemade spaghetti sauce. "Katie's going to need some live-in care when she gets out of the hospital—someone to help me cook and to get her in and out of the shower."

Allison drained the pasta into the sink. Steam billowed from the strainer. "Maybe a part-time nurse?"

Josh put his hands on her waist from behind. "I had a little higher level of care in mind. Someone more like a doctor."

Allison wondered where it would lead. Josh had mentioned help for Katie but she knew he was telling her that he was open to more. If the relationship developed that way, she'd like that. Unlike her ex, Josh was capable of love and commitment. And she had come to see that a relationship with him was not a betrayal but the ultimate fulfillment of her pledge to Sharon to take care of things.

She smiled and turned into his arms. They fit together as if they'd been made for each other. "I'd be good at that."

He held her tight. "You would indeed."

ABOUT THE AUTHOR

Mark Ethridge is a third-generation reporter and writer who directed two Pulitzer Prize-winning investigations for the *Charlotte Observer*. Ethridge is the author of *Grievances* (NewSouth Books, 2006) and wrote the screenplay for the movie adaptation, *Deadline*, starring Eric Roberts. He lives in Charlotte, North Carolina, with his wife Kay.

Learn more about *Greivances, Deadline*, and *Fallout* at www.newsouthbooks.com/ethridge.

CPSIA information can be obtained at www.ICGtesting.com
Printed in the USA
BVOW070137100212

282568BV00002B/1/P